For Billy, Jeffrey, Shawn, Jennifer,
And the next one. . . . *Love you all!*

BEAUTIFUL ENEMY

"Kiss me, Angela, kiss me as you would dream of kissing a man."

Winding slim arms about his neck, Angela, wide-eyed, stared up at him as she gave him a swift peck on his mouth. He looked amused. "Again, Angela, longer this time, please."

Taking a deep breath, she scooted closer to his chest, drawing a painful moan from the man whose lap she perched upon. Hers were the kisses of gentle raindrops when he would much rather savage her mouth with passionate ones—but all in good time. He brushed his lips against the hair of this young woman, his beautiful enemy.

Taking the tiny span of her waist into his hands on either side, Gypsy lifted her and deposited her carefully on the bed.

Her eyes were big and bright, delft blue, dilated, as she gazed up at him in wonder and some fear.

"I want to make love to you, Angela."

Good, she thought. She had his mind off her being his enemy and now she had him right where she wanted him.

Or did *he* have *her* exactly where he wanted her? . . .

TANTALIZING ROMANCE
From Zebra Books

CAPTIVE CARESS   (1923, $3.95)
by Sonya T. Pelton
Denied her freedom, despairing of rescue, the last thing on Willow's mind was desire. But before she could say no, she became her captor's prisoner of passion.

LOUISIANA LADY   (1891, $3.95)
by Myra Rowe
Left an orphan, Leander Ondine was forced to live in a house of ill-repute. She was able to maintain her virtue until the night Justine stumbled upon her by mistake. Although she knew it was wrong, all she wanted was to be his hot-blooded *Louisiana Lady*.

SEA JEWEL   (1888, $3.95)
by Penelope Neri
Hot-tempered Alaric had long planned the humiliation of his hated foe's daughter. But he never suspected she would become the mistress of his heart, his treasured, beloved *Sea Jewel*.

SEPTEMBER MOON   (1838, $3.95)
by Constance O'Banyon
Ever since she was a little girl, Cameron had dreamed of getting even with the Kingstons. But the extremely handsome Hunter Kingston caught her off guard, and all she could think of was his lips crushing hers in a feverish rapture beneath the *September Moon*.

VELVET CHAINS   (1640, $3.95)
by Constance O'Banyon
Desperate for money, beautiful Valentina Barrett worked as the veiled dancer, Jordanna. Then she fell in love with handsome, wealthy Marquis Vincente and became entangled in a web of her own making.

Twilight Temptress

Sonya T. Pelton

ZEBRA BOOKS
KENSINGTON PUBLISHING CORP.

ZEBRA BOOKS

are published by

Kensington Publishing Corp.
475 Park Avenue South
New York, NY 10016

First printing: July 1987

Printed in the United States of America

Prologue

South Carolina, 1842

Her hands were like fluttering white birds as Angelica gazed down at her newborn son nestled in the blue receiving blanket. She'd given birth to Robert Neil II only three days before.

Angelica had scarce given thought to her firstborn since the baby had arrived; besides, she'd hardly missed the lad since she'd become pregnant with Robert's son. Her unruly seven-year-old was always out in the stables with the thoroughbreds anyway, so hard to find just when one wanted him for something; even a short visit with the lad was of late difficult to obtain for Gypsy Smith was as wild as the wind.

Without warning, Angelica and her husband were about to have their first argument since the child's birth. Robert Neil Fortune entered Angelica's sun-

7

filled bedroom, his authoritative step unmistakable in the morning silence.

"How's my favorite son?"

Robert Neil boomed this, his breath reeking of brandy-laced coffee as he leaned over his wife, and then gave her a swift, clinical kiss on her moist forehead. Quickly he straightened.

Angelica stared reproachfully up at Robert Neil. "What about our other son?" she murmured.

"*Our* son, madam?" He blinked lazily, his brown eyes arrogant.

"Yes. You did marry me to provide a home for my firstborn. And I in turn gave you what you wanted." She gazed down at the handsome babe securely cradled in her arms, her heart nevertheless overflowing with new love.

"A bastard, madam."

"Neil!"

He showed her his broad back as he went to stand at the huge, curtainless window, staring out at the Ashley River. Tamarind stood on the west bank of the river some miles above Charleston. Large water oaks stood as sentinels along the banks, draped with long gray moss. But the magnolias were the most magnificent, Robert Neil thought; he'd always loved them. His startling sherry-brown eyes flashed. *Tamarind*. His own plantation. He'd never tell Angelica he had murdered his own brother to gain the inheritance. His older brother . . . he'd been nothing but a lush anyway, so what did it matter, he'd thought then as he did now.

Robert had one other relative, a younger brother

8

over at Persimmon Wood, Harrison; and then there was Harrison's lovely wife, Jana . . . they were childless so far.

Now Robert Neil had his own son! The bitch had not given him a daughter as he'd feared might happen. His lips tightened as he thought of the gypsylike boy who'd disrupted his household ever since Angelica had brought the babe here with her exactly seven years ago. Gypsy Smith, she'd named him. How Robert had come to hate that name, and the child. He would not have a bastard rule and run his Tamarind! Only Fortune blood ruled here.

Robert Neil had never accepted Gypsy Smith as his stepson, despite what the lady might think. The lad had looked no more than a gypsy beggar, with his scrawny legs and huge, dark, mahogany eyes. Staring, perusing eyes. It had been the last straw when his cronies had asked Robert Neil how he'd come by the Arab slave boy.

Angelica had no idea what blood flowed in the veins of the dark-haired sailor who'd seduced her with his handsome face and virile charm. All *she'd* known of the dashing ravisher besides his roguish name was that he'd possessed the brown-black hair and odd-colored dark eyes Gypsy Smith had inherited. His rapscallion father had been nothing but a romantic wanderer from another country. But Robert knew a lot more about Gypsy Smith than he let on. The lad's sire had been one-quarter Cherokee, the other parts foreign. So the rumor went. Then one day, Gypsy Smith had come looking for Angelica but Robert had sent the man on his way with the warning

9

of six lads prodding him with just as many weapons held at his back. Dark, heathenish looks, they had, the lad and his sire. Gypsy's brows were thick and raven-dark, his chin set and stubborn. Only the arrogant, high-bridged nose made Robert Neil pause to wonder of the lad's *other* other ancestors on his father's side. Angelica's features were delicate as a fawn's, but her hair was a rich, luxuriant sable. Her luscious body had brought her up to this station, having been nothing but a sharecropper's daughter before Robert came along to rescue her from a life fraught with drudgery. The rice fields of Carolina had prospered well, and so had Turpin, Angelica's father. He'd not had to pay a share of his crop as rent, not when Robert Neil had come along seeing his daughter swollen with child (a beautiful sight to him) and whisked away old Turpin's only child. He'd married her the very day she'd borne the black-haired snap. Turpin had died not long after that . . . never setting eyes on his daughter's wee bastard.

Now Angelica's firstborn was gone too. Robert Neil had taken care of that matter. Before he'd had the lad taken away, Robert had summoned the black voodoo woman. Melantha, the Black Flower, had chanted some words over Gypsy's head. She'd guaranteed Robert that she had cast a spell over the lad, that he'd never remember where he had come from. But Robert Neil had not caught Melantha staring at his back with intense hatred glazing her inky eyes. Robert coerced the black woman to drum it into Gypsy's head that he wasn't wanted at Tamarind.

His mother had a new son.

He wasn't loved any longer.

And so, Gypsy Smith had been taken away, far away to Africa. Now the mean-spirited Robert Neil turned to his wife, saying, "My dear, I've been trying to summon the courage to tell you this. Just this dawn your son vanished."

Part One

Windswept Angel

Love is a smoke rais'd with the fume of
  sighs;
Being purg'd, a fire sparkling in lovers'
  eyes;
Being vex'd, a sea nourish'd with lovers'
  tears.

—Romeo and Juliet

Chapter One

African Coast, 1855

Great green trees, thickly interspersed with tall ferns, loomed above the beach, dappled with jungle pinks and orchids at their feet where forest and sand met. The air itself seemed breathless, thick, waiting as the threatening sounds of bare feet pounded through the underbrush to the accompaniment of blood-chilling drumbeat in the distance. A figure of a slim woman dressed in white lawn, Paris fashion, slipped through a frond-laced opening and stood, breathing heavily, ready to be galvanized into action once again.

She was limping, too, badly.

Her heart thudded in time with the drumbeat; rivulets of perspiration trickled down her forehead into her great brown eyes. Quickly, without further thought or hesitation, she held up the hem of her ravaged skirts and ran along the beach. Deep sand sucked at her feet and slowed her progress. A sob caught in the tunnel of her throat; it was like a slow-moving nightmare!

Now she could hear the natives as they pounded closer, nearing the beach, the tall rawboned black men threshing and stabbing about in the undergrowth with seven-foot spears.

Her dark brown hair streamed back and strands of it stuck in her eyes as she ran as best she could with her ragged limp, one she'd gotten from a childhood accident, ran in her limping gait until she thought her lungs would burst.

Suddenly, right in front of her, a huge apparition burst into sight at the same time the African sun blossomed like a huge sunflower above the sea. She looked up, tottering on her weak limbs, sank to her ankles in sand, and shielded her eyes from the giant rays of sun blasting over her.

The thing, like a huge balloon, impossible though it seemed, came floating eerily toward her and began to descend.

Which way to turn. The natives were very near now. The young woman knew she was dying of exhaustion and fright. Her lungs must have burst then, that was it, because there were sharp pinpricks of pain in her chest. The apparition swooped down . . . must be an angel. . . . There must be some mistake, God. I'm not ready to die yet. Paul . . . I must see Paul again, God, I love him.

Stephanie heard the cadence of excited natives' voices. Why did they sound scared? What was that odd *whooshing* sound? Wings? The voices and wings drifted away, hazily, as in a dream, and Stephanie's body slumped to the sand, her brain bathed in golden sunbursts and kaleidoscopic pinwheels.

*　　　*　　　*

Slowly the huge, yellow balloon with a red dragon painted on its puffed belly, rose from the platform which had been ingeniously erected at the stern of the ship. The *Black Moon*, a rakish, topsail schooner, gently rode the swells as the crew watched their young, handsome captain lift off, and then the beautiful aerostat was airborne. He looked down, with a huge white grin pulling taut the olive skin of his powerfully virile face.

"Open the neck, Cap'n!" one of the crew shouted upward. With his hands on his hips, Huey nodded, watching his captain open the neck at the bottom of the balloon.

Captain Benjamin smiled, a dark, rakish face grinning over the basket of his balloon. He glanced upward, feeling the wind in his black hair, combing it back from his aquiline features. It was just him and the balloon now, a part of the air. He was feeling the same exhilaration he did while commanding his four-master. Riding the swells of the wind. There was no bumping, no noise, however, as was on the ship oftentimes. No creaking, no groaning of timbers.

As always when he took the balloon up, the captain lost his sense of earthliness and gained a feeling of being part of the infinite space, almost a part of . . . eternity.

"Man is man," he said with a chuckle, "and the time comes when one must return to earth, ah, I mean to *ship* in this case."

He was sailing along the coast where the ocean met the jungle when he was about to exert some skillful maneuvering to make the balloon level off, catch the winds at the different altitudes, and ride it back to the *Black Moon*. Most of the time he landed squarely on the platform, but then there had been days . . .

The young captain was just reaching up for the valve line when the spine-tingling sounds of drumbeat filled the air. "What the devil . . . !"

He had spotted the girl. She was running in a crazy zigzag pattern toward the pale turquoise waters. He had a bird's-eye view into the jungle and could make out the dark figures taking the same jagged path the girl took. Spears poked from the foliage and shields were held close to the lean, glistening-black bodies. Drumbeats grew louder as the captain pulled the valve line, gas escaping as the balloon started down. Down, down, down, Benjamin dropped ballast discreetly in order to slow the Dragon's descent. He cast an eye to his instruments which showed the altitude and rate of his descent.

Easy . . . easy. Maneuver. Valve. "Level . . . Jesus, we don't want to land right on the scary black devils. Watch out for the girl!"

They were naked but for the raggedy cloths clinging to rawboned hips, and possessed broad flattened noses, wide thick lips. Bloodshot brown eyes stared up at the captain, eyes that carried expressions of stark terror and bemusement. Most of the natives wore red and yellow beads about their necks, wrists, and ankles. They jabbered in their native tongue, and then, seeming to come to a wise decision, all fifteen of the natives whirled about and dashed for the safety of their jungle. Captain Benjamin breathed a sigh of relief. If it had not been for the natives' terror of the air balloon, he'd have

18

been a pretty hunk of meat for the savages' stewpot this night!

Hunkering down beside the girl, the handsome young captain reached out both arms and gently turned her over. "Let's have a look at you and see if you've been hurt." He felt for her pulse. "Good, still alive." He was looking over his shoulder, wondering if he should go for some water and leave her alone, when she began to mumble disjointed sentences and reach out toward her forehead with a feeble gesture.

"Where am I?"

Opening her eyes, Stephanie winced, narrowing them against the spiky rays of sun. The man, white man, yes, tried speaking to her.

"They're brown as American mud, wouldn't you say." He did not really expect an answer; he was just trying to put her at ease and not frighten her.

"I—who?" Stephanie asked, wondering whom she was talking to that sounded as if he might be someone she could at last trust not to hurt her. "Are you an . . . angel then?"

A deep voice almost laughed its answer. "Hardly! But I won't hurt you, if that's what you are afraid of."

Painfully she tried shielding her eyes from the sun. She didn't have to; he did it for her with one of his own deeply tanned hands. "My name is Captain Benjamin. Are you all right, miss?"

Shivering from mild shock, she snapped defensively, "How do you know for sure I'm a 'miss'?"

"Well I—I guess I'm not all that sure." He frowned. "I asked you a question. Do I get an answer or do I leave you here with your African friends to consume at their evening meal?"

Captain Benjamin, looking around and then coming back to her, said, "Did I interrupt something? I have the strangest feeling I've come along at the wrong time." He came to his feet in one lithe, springy motion Then, stiffening his spine, he cried, "I think we better get out of here—and now!" as he unceremoniously pulled her along and hoisted her into the gondola, his big, powerful body following right behind.

Collectively then, they turned back toward the jungle and saw the sweat-slick Africans emerging, long spears in hand again. As the captain reached for the valve to add gas to the balloon, he spoke softly, "I think they have lost their fear." The balloon began to rise out over the turquoise waters and he peered down, seeing the Africans now heaving their long dangerous spears. One struck its mark and the girl screamed as a spear entered the basket and lodged itself one inch into the captain's calf. He winced with pain, looking down and yanking the spear from his leg while the girl stared on with a ghostly pallor. Pulling the spear up and through the basket he heaved it down over the side, watching the blacks scatter as it dived into the sand and buried its tip. Then another thud came against the basket, but luckily nothing protruded this time. The young captain gazed down at the woman sitting stunned and shivering, even though the strength of the sun expanded, and he could not help but notice the swelling of her breasts over her bodice and the well-turned ankles. Then he took note of the long pink scar running from knee to ankle, realizing the reason he'd seen her limping.

"I—I really am sorry for being such a bother," she blurted, her hand extended in friendship. He took it and his fingers felt warm and strong in hers. "My name is Stephanie Marylebone, *the* Marylebones of Charleston, South Carolina."

"Oh," he said, "that explains everything." He grinned when she frowned first at him and then at the hot air balloon rising enormously above her head. "What do you mean?" She gripped the sides of the basket as he worked industriously to bring it into the soft carrying wind.

Captain Benjamin turned about to face the lovely but haughty brunette. "The way you introduced yourself, you made no bones about who you and your folks are." He nodded. "That's important, huh?"

She laughed, tearing a piece of her chemise to bind his wound, but he stepped back saying his first mate was his *nurse*, with a low chuckle. Stephanie nodded and answered, "Very. Do you know that more than half of the population of Charleston is related somehow?"

"No, I'm sorry." He laughed, his strange-colored eyes sparkling. "I have to tell you I've never visited the Carolinas. At least," he said in a low voice, "I have not searched there yet."

"I heard that," she said with a charming smile.

"So you did." He looked out over the aqua sea and she gulped, following his gaze only briefly.

"What are you searching for, sir?"

"Captain Benjamin."

She nodded. "Captain Benjamin it is. First tell me: You said you are heading for your ship. I'm a bit afraid of heights. Are you certain you can land this

21

thing? And what happens if we fall into the ocean?" Stephanie held a hand over her fast-beating heart. "Are there sharks in these waters?"

"Yes. Too bad. And . . . yes, there are."

"Ohh," she said with a shiver. "To escape the natives only to be eaten alive by sharks."

The captain laughed, showing his evenly spaced teeth. "Trust me. You won't be eaten alive."

"But you said 'too bad' on your second answer, Captain."

"Please, Miss Marylebone, do put your faith in my, ah, shall we say, ability to maneuver this thing. *Dragon Lady.*"

"What?" Stephanie flattened her back against the basket at the harsh sound of hot whooshing air. "Oh, the beast's name, of course. I've heard of hot air balloons before, but where did you get yours from?" She laughed nervously, to quiet her apprehension over being so high in the air.

"Paris. And this one is not a hot air balloon, but don't I wish that'd already been a way to fill a balloon, maybe someday. Oh, did I say Paris?"

She frowned. "Paris?"

"That's where I got this old windbag from."

"Oh. Interesting."

"If I am not up on my history, let me know. But the first hydrogen-filled balloon was released in Paris by a chap named Jac Charles, a french professor of physics."

"When was that?"

"Seventeen eighty-three. First the Montgolfier brothers tried it. Jacques Etienne and Joseph. Annonay near Lyons, France. I used to live there."

Laughing, Stephanie said, "You don't have to shout, Captain. I can hear you. Did you have family in France?"

Clouds of melancholy filled his deep-colored eyes as he said, "No, not really. I mean, well, yes, I guess you can say they were family."

Stephanie had caught the lonely sadness in the man's eyes. "No *real* family?"

"None that I know of."

"Oh." Stephanie thought of her family, all ten of her brothers and sisters. "You're an orphan, sort of."

"There's my ship," the captain said, directing her concerned gaze from his sad, handsome face to the beautiful four-master.

"What is your ship called?"

"Black Moon Sinking."

Gaping at him, Stephanie said, "What? That sounds like a doomed ship."

"She was, until I saved her. Was a pirate ship, she was. Got her to the West Indies and patched her up. She was a mess, believe me. Leave off *Sinking;* she's become just *Black Moon.*"

Stephanie felt somewhat more relaxed as she gazed down at the billowing shrouds of white canvas below. "I was kidnapped." She turned and smiled when his face fell. "It's all right. You would have asked me sooner or later, I forgive you."

"Stephanie Marylebone." He grinned roguishly. "I like you. We're going to be great friends."

She laughed. "Just keep it that way." Holding up her hand, she stuck out her ring finger. "Used to have a diamond here. The natives took it."

"You are engaged." He shook his dark head.

"Damn, and I thought we would get together on this long journey back to the Carolinas." He gave her low French bodice a sweeping perusal of disappointment; it had been too long for him now.

Giving a squeal, Stephanie threw herself against the captain. "You're taking me home! Oh! I love you, Captain Benjamin! I love you!"

As the *Dragon Lady* landed squarely on the circle marking the desired landing spot, on the raised platform, Captain Benjamin's crew stood gaping, dumbfounded while a gorgeous brunette wrapped her arms around their roguishly grinning captain's neck and spared not an inch of his face with her noisy kisses.

"So," Benjamin went on, "I am running out of funds in my search for my true identity. My inheritance, too, if I have one to speak of."

Stephanie twisted her wine glass, lounging in the one, plush red velvet chair gracing the captain's cabin. Masculine articles of furnishings were pushed up against the bulkhead, while a massive desk with all the trappings of a true sailing master occupied a goodly part of the room. On the high seas things could get quite rough, and so, many of the bulkier items had been secured with lengths of wild silk and raffia. The young woman chewed her lip thoughtfully for a time and then spoke.

"Where did you get the name Benjamin? Did this wonderful lady, Monica Hawke, give you that too?"

"Yes, she named me. A woman I can dimly remember—for I've tried to wipe the face from my memory totally— but I remember her, the mean one, as being dark-haired, green-eyed." He laughed. "Of course, by now, she must have quite a head of gray hairs. But Monica, she had hair the color of sunshine, morning, noon, and night. Sometimes it had sunbeams in it; then moonbeams; and red like a summer sunset. She was . . . is beautiful."

"This Monica, who took you into her home, did she have her own children?"

"She has only one, I believe."

Shrugging, Stephanie said, "You don't know for sure?"

"I was just a spitting reed when I took off from El Corazón. And if I remember, the child, a girl, she was around ten, maybe younger. They were very protective of the child. The Hawkes sent for a kindly woman, Tina I think her name was, anyway, she came to El Corazón to care for the child. Jessica, that was her name, she was surrounded by people who doted on her. There was hardly a parting in the crowd of guardians in order for me to get a good look at Jessica Hawke and besides, I was too busy dreaming of aeronautics and balloons after old Gus down at the factory filled my head with them."

Stephanie canted her head. "There can be danger in that. I mean the girl, not the aeronautics. Too many watching over her, there's bound to be a crack in the defense work somewhere. What's the worry anyhow? Is there a fear of the girl being kidnapped or something?"

"Yes, there was danger there at El Corazón."

"Ah—from the dark-haired woman. Can't you recall her name?"

"I'm not sure. The 'Duchess' is all that serves my memory." He shrugged. "I can't be certain, Stephanie. All I know is she was the reason the girl was guarded so closely. At first she was anyway, they might have grown more relaxed by now. Her mother, Monica, helped me escape from—from . . ."

"Can't you remember even that? What is the matter, Captain, do you have a bad memory?"

He banged his fist on the table. "Damnit, woman, I have just made your acquaintance and already you are acting like a *woman*."

"Well, for your information, Captain, I *am* just that." She began to rise from the table. "I shall take myself elsewhere, if you do not care for my company anymore."

Reaching out to pull her gently back to her seat, Benjamin said, "I am sorry, please." He stared up at her with his beautifully colored eyes. She smiled and sat back down, curiously studying the rare shade of his eyes.

"Which parent had the pretty eyes, Captain?"

"Damnit!" He shot to his feet, storming about the room like a trapped thundercloud. "I do not wish to discuss my parentage, Miss Marylebone." Making his hair stick out as he ran his long tan fingers throughout the thick strands, he said so low, "I don't *have* any parents."

"You didn't just pop out of a watermelon either!" Stephanie glared right back at him when he looked at her with his teeth set on edge. More serious now, she said, "Come on. Sit down over here. I want to talk some more, Captain. You know, you really are a mysterious man, and I hate unsolved mysteries.

Maybe I can help."

"I don't want help."

"Yes you do."

"I am very wealthy," she began again. "My parents and I were on a trek, ugh, a *stupid* trek through the jungle. How asinine! Mama's idea. I was kidnapped, and now that they shall be on their way home, we will just take our time and get to know each other, famously. What do you say?"

"Fine." With a pinched look on his face, he looked down into the candid brown eyes. "Your mother doesn't care if you were carted off by a passel of tall, very virile, natives?"

"No. Mama has other daughters." Stephanie shrugged limpidly. "Steph is not Mama's favorite girl. That would be Elizabeth. Mama would have apoplexy right now if her *baby* had disappeared in the African jungle." Giving the captain a playful nudge in the ribs, she screwed up her face, drawling, "Very virile natives? Really, Captain!"

He grinned. "They appeared to be capable, at least."

"Captain, I don't think we should be having this discussion. It is one that could very well excite me, and I wouldn't like to lose my purity to someone before my beloved and I consummate our marriage."

Benjamin shook his head, muttering, "I can't believe *I* am having this conversation—with a woman at that."

Peering up at him from beneath her spiky black lashes, Stephanie said, "Now I remember. I know who you are, Captain. There was talk, of a lad, seven years old, back in '42, who disappeared from a plantation north of Charleston. Some folks suspected foul play. I mean, he was abducted, so rumor had it. But Mama and Papa had talked of it often, it's the subject of many a drawing room still."

"What do *you* think?" He didn't believe she was being serious; she was playing games again.

"I have the 'sight,' Captain. It happens to me, oh, once or twice a year. The event has to be significant in order for me to read anything into it. I once found a lost child by concentrating very hard. I found that child and her parents have been beholden to me ever since."

"Jesus," the handsome captain said softly, wiping the perspiration off his brow. "Any more, Miss Crystal Ball?"

"Aha. You're getting back at me." She frowned. "But, Captain, I am very serious this time. I also know *other* things."

"Like what?"

"There is going to be a war soon."

"What sort of war, and where?"

"In America. Between the states."

"Oh Jesus . . ." he said on a long breath. Sitting straighter, he asked, just for fun, "What is the name of this plantation I was kidnapped from?"

"Not kidnapped, Captain. Your father had . . . no, not your real father." Stephanie pressed her fingertips to her temple. "He hated you, with every fiber of his being. He . . . he had you taken away. I—I am getting a name. Melantha, Black Flower. Does that mean anything to you?" She snapped out of her trance, blinking up at him.

"Oh . . . I suppose it does," he lied. He had to hear

more, nevertheless.

"The name of the plantation I can give you, that's easy. It is Tamarind. I don't have to stare into the mists to know that."

"Is it still standing?"

"Of course. Why shouldn't it be?"

"You said there was a war."

"Silly, not yet." Looking away from the captain and heaving a deep sigh, Stephanie said, "Your name is Gypsy Smith, sir."

The man stood so violently sudden that his chair toppled backwards. He rasped. *"How did you know that?"*

Timidly she stared up at his whitened face. "I've hit on it, haven't I?"

"I have a feeling . . ." He stared around the room, expecting ghosts from the past to pop from seams and leap from every dark corner and mock his fool's emotionalism. He relaxed then, saying as casually as he could, "The name rings a bell, that is all."

"It is a very *loud* bell, Captain, uh, Gypsy Smith."

"Nonsense."

"What?" She narrowed her big brown eyes.

"I said, I don't believe any of it, Miss Marylebone."

"Yes you do."

"No."

Stephanie stood then, sashaying about the cabin, looking like this year's impoverished princess in her Paris white lawn. She halted before the captain, gazing up while he towered over her, hands on slim male hips, daring her to try his intelligence one more time.

"Gypsy Smith is the name of the sailor who back in

'34 got a woman pregnant, a woman by the name of Angelica Turpin. Putting it crudely, Captain, he rode in on the tide, came, and went back out again.''

The man wasn't looking at Stephanie now. He was riding a swift-winged horse back in time. Angelica. Now that name tugged at his heartstrings, got him where he lived. Still . . .

"This is incredible. How can you stand there and actually link me with this character, Gypsy Smith?''

"He was one-quarter Cherokee.'' She reached out and ran a finger along his smooth-fleshed, olive tan forearm. "Indian skin,'' she said.

"Oh God,'' Gypsy groaned, feeling confused. He'd been mistaken several times in the past for being part Indian. Was he? Did he have some Indian blood? "How can you?'' he repeated more harshly than intended.

"The eyes, darling. No one in Charleston, coming or going, has or had dark wine eyes like yours, no one but the *first* Gypsy Smith!''

Chapter Two

*South Carolina, Upriver from Charleston,
   Springtime
Eight years later . . .*

Tamarind plantation spread placidly beside the
Ashley River. The big white mansion, with long
dark green shutters, had six slender columns supporting the roof of the porch, and atop the roof of the
house was the mansion tower surrounded by a
narrow balcony with a fence decorated in white
filigree.

Some claimed Tamarind was the biggest house
along the Ashley River. Some prided it as elegant,
especially those within. Some folks farther down the
river, gentle neighbors though they may have been,
said it was "bulky." But the majority said it was the
handsomest residence in the Carolinas. Or used to be.

The white house with its tall columns and wide
porches bore areas of neglect but only the keenest
observer would notice that some of the paint was

starting to peel. Different, too, was the usually beautiful stretch of green lawn between the house and the river. It was sadly neglected now in times of war. There were just too many other items needing attention at Tamarind. Robert Neil, one among the foremost of planter aristocracy, had too many other things to do besides worry about the lawn. Some of his blacks had become runaways. Overnight, things were changing. The only thing that hadn't changed were the lavish parties and balls still thrown in Charleston and at the still elegant but slightly empty homes of high-browed planters.

Long verandas caught the evening breeze on many a warm night, but this evening the occupants had been forced to remain indoors while the lightning zigzagged to the earth in furious daggers and the thunder rumbled and the dark rain roared.

Angela, quiet and graceful, entered the riverside parlor. She jumped when the lightning lit up the window in a sudden flash. She relaxed then, looking for Blossom Angelica, but for the moment, the parlor was empty of humans. Only the heavy furniture greeted her, solid pieces of dark oak and mahogany. The fireplace blazed a cheery orange-red too. Each of the ten rooms in the house had a fireplace with a wide, decorative mantel.

Angela was of medium height. She was slender as a reed, her eighteen-year-old countenance sweet and innocent, with the meekness of an angel. Thus the name Robert Neil had given her when he found her. She stared into the leaping flames, her gorgeous opalescent eyes wide open. The clear whites of Angela's eyes framed narrow pearl-blue irises rimming immense dark pupils. Sometimes her eyes could become smoky and mysterious. They were set beneath thick, wing-shaped eyebrows; and her intelligent forehead gave her delicate brow added height. The soft depressions in her cheeks added to the sweetness of expression. Gentlemen on the street would smile warmly in passing, then turn in a double take with a feeling of loss as she vanished inside the doors of a shop, a haughty mulatress guarding her charge at her heels.

Angela's thick, rich chestnut hair with a soft glint of gold in the strands was worn in the fashion of the day, heavy braids looped saucily above each pert ear. When brushed out and cascading free, Angela's hair could be measured out by Mum Zini to be three feet long—and growing.

Moisture pooled in Angela's immense eyes; they drifted to the wall, where a huge painting of a galleon in full sail had caught her attention. She loved ships; she didn't know why.

The young woman alone in the riverside parlor listened to the steady rapping of the rain. It was a lonely world in which Angela found herself. Her mind was empty of the past, of everything human she'd known, inhabited only by faceless shadows and the faint faraway voices she could hear murmuring inside her head.

Angela had no idea how she'd come to be lying against the great knees of the water oaks, more dead than alive, her head pounding with terrible agony each time she tried to lift it. She'd heard the lazy waters moving past her, tugging at her skirts for her to come join them in their flow to Charleston. She had felt the cold gray-green waters swirl about her legs. She'd been bruised, her temple streaming a thin trickle of blood, every bone in her body battered. All she had known in her confused and frightened mind at the time was a desperate courage which made her cling to each precious golden thread to life. She dragged herself from the sluggish, inviting waters. Then, once more, the mists of unconsciousness had crept into her tired brain.

Presences, auras, lurking about her invisibly, again and again. As she stared around her unfamiliar surroundings, though they'd become somewhat more familiar the past two weeks, Angela tensed again as if she would be surprised at any moment to find someone she knew standing there.

Angela was the only one in the room until Mum Zini came to take her gently by the arm and lead the young woman back to her room.

"Why do you always stare at de painting?" Mum Zini asked the young woman Robert Neil had found washed up on the riverbank. Angela, not the girl's name at all but one Mum Zini's master had given her. Jasmine Joe had said after helping his master make the young woman comfortable in the parlor, "She jes' blew in wit de wind." He'd said this of another, not more than eight years ago, Mum Zini recalled now with a soft reminiscent smile.

"I really do not . . . know," Angela answered. As she walked, she slid one hand along the mahogany banister. This house . . . she felt strange things here. It was as if some unseen presence reached out to her, someone who had walked these halls before. Long ago. And *again*. She had a strong impression this person was male, incredibly so. He'd been here not too long ago. Why did she feel these strange emotions? What did it all mean to her? She was not even a part of these folks here.

Mum Zini and Angela reached the upstairs and turned down the long, wide hall. "Perhaps it reminds the mamzelle of someone?"

"I wish I knew," Angela softly returned.

Mum Zini opened the door to a spacious chamber. Again, that feeling. Angela always experienced it when she entered this room. Why mostly in this room? she wondered.

It was a comfortable room. But the others were quite fine, one of which was Master Robert's own. All the rooms in the house were large and airy, even this one which was for certain reasons Mum Zini's favorite. When the "black sheep" of the family came home, his visits usually brief, he stayed in this room. The Bastard, Blossom Angelica called him. Now a Yankee bastard. He had returned eight years ago to claim his part of the inheritance. Now the halls were lonely with the gentleman-rogue absent, Mum Zini thought to herself. Speculating to herself, she'd often looked toward Angela, wondering when the two would meet.

Mum Zini watched the mesmerized young woman walk suddenly to the long window that faced the Ashley River. "Pow'ful ribber," as Jasmine Joe described it. "Lak mighty fine jewels under de full moon."

Melantha, Black Flower, Mum Zini's mother, had stopped chanting blood-thrilling words about the "windswept angel" it would bring someday. Her

35

wrinkled lips had stilled. Melantha had also chanted before the "man with the black-orchid eyes" had arrived at Tamarind, "swooping down on dem like some big black bat a-knockin' at de do'," Jasmine Joe had said.

Mum Zini had to smile as she crossed the room to turn down the covers. Gypsy Smith. This was his own room. Her eyes drifted across the room to the silent girl still lingering at the window. Where was she going to put her when the real master of Tamarind returned? He was the real master here, or he would be. Jasmine Joe said, "Po' Robber Nell, he be teched in de head."

Softly Mum Zini came to stand beside the girl christened Angela, christened indeed by the waters of the Ashley. "Do you see som'ting out there, mamzelle?"

"Blossom."

"Blossom?" Mum Zini's finely arched brow raised in the air as she frowned at the girl, then looked back to see the stunning reflection of Blossom Angelica Fortune. Angelica, named after her dear deceased *maman*.

She had halted in the center of the room. Blossom Angelica was a tall, deliciously curvaceous young woman of eighteen, the same age as Angela, so they'd all guessed. She couldn't be much older, or younger, than Blossom. With luxurious hair which bounced in gay ringlets around her heart-shaped face. Blossom's gown this evening was a dark-blue-and-white-striped material with delicate lace adorning the bodice and sleeves. Darker blue piping ran from a V midriff to her tiny, sucked-in waist, falling with

36

belled out fullness to her daintily shod feet.

"You are de fortunate one to be able to stay here, mamzelle," Mum Zini had told the new girl, a serious expression on her *café au lait*-complected face. She'd said this the day before. "Mamzelle Blossom would have thrown you out long ago. She must like you, or else she has some mischief planned for your stay. Blossom Angelica has become quite thee airy one since she has come back from Paris." Mum Zini noticed that the girl started at the mention of the colorful French capital. "Ah . . . you know Paris?" All she'd received was a painful, searching expression for her efforts in trying to find out more about the lovely young Angela.

Mum Zini herself had the French-Creole blood that ran in her father's veins. But Mclantha, she was all black, *beautiful* black once upon a time. Now age had given her the look of grayed parchment. Melantha had already been ancient when she'd given birth to her only daughter.

"I tink you have pleased our Mamzelle Blossom. She has need of a friend. She has not taken a mate to marry with yet"—she sighed—"for all the money the master has spent to see her gone from Tamarind."

Mum Zini had seen that Angela was baffled by those words. Angela had spoken with soft caution. "Why should the master spend money to be rid of his only sister? I—I think—" Angela shook her head slowly. "It is really none of my business."

"Indeed," Mum Zini had said. "You do not dare question Master Robert. He is lord of de plantation when his half brother is absent. Dee man has thee Indian blood."

37

"Mon Dieu!" Angela had surprised herself with the foreign words spilling from her violet pink lips. "I—I am sorry."

"Ah . . . de mamzelle *is* French. I taught so."

After a moment's musing, she continued, "Thee men in this family are slow to have de childrens. Melantha, who has been with thee Fortunes forever, has told me dis. Thee first late mistress, Jeannette, had married for love, but Robert Neil de first was only a little in love with Mistress Jeannette. Her death had saddened him. But she bore him no childrens. Then thee Lady Angelica came as Robert's bride to Tamarind. Robert Neil de second, the one who saved you, is her second child. Angelica had brought with her dee bastard child."

Mum Zini had watched Angela flinch at the crude word. "If you stay, mamzelle, you may very well meet Gypsy Smith soon. He is quite dee man."

Coming back to the present, Mum Zini watched Blossom now turn her attention to the lovely young woman her brother had named Angela. She'd protested, however, that Robert Neil had named her so near to her mother's and her own name. Of course, it was only her second name, and Mama *was* gone now.

"Mum Zini says you can read and write."

Mum Zini's odd-colored eyes rolled as she corrected, "De mamzelle she writes dee French, not dee Engleesh."

"Oh, fiddle! What does it matter," Blossom said with an impish smile. "I want to write *something* and I don't much care what language I do it in."

"But Mamzelle Blossom has gone to thee finest

38

schools in Bos-ton.''

"Oh la! I did not learn well, Mum Zini, you know this!"

The *café au lait* of Mum Zini's complexion pinkened and her pale eyebrows rose as if this was the first she'd heard of Mamzelle Blossom's lessons having gone awry. She never liked it when Blossom Angelica's chin tilted at that haughtily defiant angle and her dark eyes snapped at Mum Zini from under hooded lids; she'd spike a lovely camellia shoulder up at the same time, glancing over it provocatively.

"I know that reading and writing are supposed to come first and are the most important." Black eyes twinkled mischievously. "But I had much better things to do at that time. At four o'clock precisely school was out. Us girls usually met with 'gentlemen' on Saturdays." Mum Zini knew exactly what "sort" of gentlemen Blossom saw.

"Oh la! I knew I should have been gorging myself on reading, writing, geography, ho-hum, history— oh, I did so like reading the poetry." A giggle rose in the air. "So . . . romantic."

Pearl blue eyes watched Blossom's dramatic motions. Blossom was so very beautiful. Her hands were like soft white doves. Angela, looking forlornly down at her own hands, wondered when her cracked nails would fully mend. If only she could remember more, she sighed inwardly.

Mum Zini was folding her thin arms over her waist. "You can read dee words but not write them?"

"Oh Mum Zini . . . you know this is so!"

Blossom sashayed about the room, sniffing disdainfully at the many articles of manliness left carelessly behind. It wasn't that she disliked manly items, on the contrary, but it was *whom* these particular possessions belonged to.

Coming to a halt before Angela, Blossom purred, "Oh, but I'd much rather gorge myself on something else than my studies." She softly taunted Mum Zini, knowing she could hear as she said, "On *other* sweetmeats."

"Mamzelle! Your behavior is most unbecoming!" Mum Zini chided. "It is true perhaps thee young lady does not have knowledge of thee gentlemans like Mamzelle Blossom does."

"The young lady is a married woman."

Three pairs of astonished eyes turned to watch Robert Neil move into the room. Blossom slanted her eyes toward Angela, smelling mischief in the wind. She quickly went to loop her arms into the crook of Robert Neil's. Defiantly she challenged Mum Zini to say otherwise as she began to speak.

"Of course. And you are her husband, darling, true?"

A dark frown appeared on Mum Zini's brow. These two were up to no good again. Only difference was, Blossom knew exactly what she was doing; Robert Neil II had a little softening of the brain now and then.

"Why . . . yes," Robert Neil almost shouted. Still, he was not all that intellectually unbalanced, at least not all the time. He smiled at his sister's impish look. "Angela dear, don't you remember, we were married not long after you returned. You had only been away for a time. We are so fortunate to have you back, sweet. Don't you remember, dear, we were joined

40

together in Holy matrimony at the Episcopal Church of St. Paul on Ann Street in Charleston.'' Feeling a tug on his arm, Robert Neil glanced down to see the delicious smile on his beautiful sister's face; Blossom's cheeks were sucked in and her magnificent black eyes were wild with deviltry. "What is it, Blos?" he asked, his eyes going back to Angela, his Windswept Angel.

To his mother's intense delight, Robert Neil had grown up disarmingly handsome. He was always clean-shaven. But Mama had known something was heartbreakingly different about her son. Shortly after Robert Neil I's death, she'd made up a codicil in her will, deeding over the strength of the plantation to Gypsy Smith, in the event he should ever return to Tamarind. No one knew this, of course, no one but the overseer and bailiff of the plantation.

"Oh la!" Blossom chirped. "Now you and Angela must go on your *honeymoon*."

Angela, looking to Mum Zini for help, but only seeing the woman frowning thoughtfully at the sister and brother, blurted out, "B-but, why haven't I heard this before?"

"But darling," Blossom crooned, going over to loop her arm in Angela's this time, "you were too ill. Now you are well, and you and Robert must have your honeymoon."

"No," Mum Zini said, under her breath.

"Oh la, Mum Zini, I know exactly what you're thinking." Blossom widened her dark eyes. "It will be all right, and good for Robert and Angela to get out. Charleston, we won't go any further than that."

"But why?" Mum Zini spread thin arms. "It is bad

that you play your games at this time. This is wartime in Charleston."

"How dare you say we are playing *games*, Mum Zini! This is wartime everywhere in the South. Soldiers are all over, hmmm, so many of them a girl can't decide." Blossom let go of Angela's arm then. "Shoo!" she told Mum Zini, flapping a white arm as if chasing naughty children from the room. "You too, Robert. Angela and I have a few things to throw into our bags. You go get ready too, Robert, and we'll meet you downstairs bright and early in the morning. I just know the rain is going to come to a halt. Mum Zini!" she called the mulatress back. "Have Jasmine Joe meet us at the dock and ready the *Lizzy-Mae*. Oh la, this is going to be such fun, and we shall keep busy paying a constant round of calls." She slapped a hand over her mouth, not seeing Mum Zini pausing in the door after Robert had gone to his own room. She giggled through her words, "We'll tell everyone that you and Robert Neil are man and wife."

With a sick feeling in the pit of her stomach, and finally getting a word in edgewise, Angela said, "I—I don't remember any of this, Blossom."

"Oh, darling, but you will." Blossom flipped her head airily. "We shall help you."

Chapter Three

Charleston, South Carolina

Angela's white gown blossomed among the pale pinks and soft blues of other young ladies' gowns in the sparkling room. She wore a narrow black velvet ribbon about her neck, hung with a single pearl teardrop. All this borrowed from Blossom. Angela's thick chestnut hair, swept back into one heavy loop, had taken on a golden sheen in the glow of the myriad chandelier lights.

Beside Angela, Blossom stood laughing and chatting with the uniformed lads, first one and then another. Her black eyes occasionally swept each one with a single provocative glance. Many handsome faces turned Angela's way and Blossom was beginning to boil. She would have to remedy the situation.

Across the room, a young woman with a face of gay freckles and a head of stunning red hair, stood beside a sweet-faced blonde. Both these young ladies knew that by the next morning, all over Charleston, it would be bandied about that Blossom Fortune had scored yet another "hit."

"She is the most unprincipled flirt!" Annabelle told her distant neighbor who'd come to stay the weekend and then it was back to Persimmon Wood. "Who are all those uniforms, anyway?"

"I'm not sure I recognize all of them." Daisy Dawn Fortune had eyes for only one. She could not see him just now, for Rider was hidden from view by several uniforms.

"How could you even talk to her?" Annabelle said, not realizing how foolish her question sounded.

Daisy Dawn's laugh was soft. "My cousin? Anna, how can I avoid my own relative?" She sighed. "I do wish sometimes she'd behave herself though. But Blossom is so bubbly and alive, she can't help it. Sometimes I wish—" she let the words drift away.

"Fiddle," Annabelle Huntington said, watching Daisy Dawn flush for a moment. She knew Daisy wished she could be more like her cousin—then maybe she could latch on to Rider. But Rider never seemed to be far from Blossom's side and it was inevitable the two would marry. Perhaps when this infernal war ended. Annabelle felt sorry for poor Daisy though; the girl wore her heart in her eyes at times and it wouldn't be long before Rider noticed this. Then again, Rider had known Daisy since she was a baby and he was a devilish eight-year-old. Would he ever catch what was in Daisy Dawn's eyes?

Tearing her eyes from Blossom for a moment, Annabelle perused the beautiful eighteenth-century drawing room of the Tradd house. Her gray eyes came to rest upon the delicate blonde beside her.

Daisy Dawn was sweet, always radiant. Her fine skin seemed as white as the linen in the dining room, where a variety of tempting delectables awaited the guests. With the deep blue velvet of Daisy's eyes, her skin was a dramatic contrast. The only attribute Daisy Dawn and Blossom Angelica held in common was a magnolia-fair complexion; otherwise the cousins were different as night and day. Different, too, in personality.

"Who is that lovely young lady with Blossom?" Daisy Dawn wanted to know. "I should like to make her acquaintance."

"You have not been to Tamarind in some while?"

"No. I am afraid Cousin Robert is put out with me."

"Why is that?" Annabelle could not imagine Robert Neil as having enough sense to be objecting over anything. "What did you do?"

"It is what I did *not* do that has Robert put out."

"I know, you needn't tell me." She was not surprised at all. "Robert Neil is trying to get you hitched up too. He has been forking out all that money to get Blossom out of the house. I wonder how many suitors he has paid and still been disappointed to find he still has a sister in the house. Why is he trying to get everyone married off? Just how daft is your Cousin Robert?"

"Annabelle, please. Let's not discuss it now. I would like to meet Blossom's new friend."

"Come on then." She chuckled. "Maybe Robert Neil has married this one himself!"

"Annabelle, that's preposterous. Robert Neil can never get married."

"Ah, so you said it yourself, Daisy. Now I don't wonder why Robert tries to marry everyone else off. He's so afraid that everyone else in the family will turn out just like him, unable to do anything with the functional parts God gave them."

"*Annabelle.*"

"Well, it's true. Now I know it for a fact. Robert Neil is daft and impotent."

"Shh—hh."

Annabelle touched Daisy's arm lightly. "Let's see if we can find a break in the crowd so we can get close to Blossom and *whom*ever. She is very pretty. Oh, the closer we get, the more I want to scratch her eyes out. Look, Daisy, she is just too beautiful for words, and how Blossom must be fuming, sorry she brought her gorgeous friend along. Just look," Annabelle whispered, "Tony Brewster is giving her the eye. He has two of the best horses in the Carolinas, my brother has the other three. That makes five. The biggest thing in Rider's life had been the races, before the war of course. Rider had such high hopes for Shoo Fly. But now the war has cut off those hopes. My brother is splendid in his uniform, no?"

"Yes."

And so he was. Daisy Dawn had never, in fact, seen such a fine male specimen. Ridpath Ewing Huntington. But all his friends and family called him Rider, for short. He came from a family that breeded thoroughbreds and his grandfather was a shipbuilder. Lately Rider had enlisted in the South Carolina legion of cavalry. Daisy had loved Rider all her life. But he didn't even know she was alive, it seemed.

46

Annabelle was wrong about the races being the biggest thing in Rider's life. It seemed only Blossom Fortune could hold that lofty position.

Suddenly Annabelle's mouth went agape and she clutched Daisy's arm as if she meant to rip it from its socket. "Lordy . . . who is *that?*"

"I don't see—" But then Daisy did see. The gentleman that had just entered the doors, the farthest set in the room, was the most thoroughly male animal she'd ever seen. That is, besides Ridpath Huntington. This man's whole body seemed to dare everyone mentally and physically to come challenge him in whatever they had in mind. He was just in the process of greeting a few of the ladies on their way to the powder room, his features bearing an overlay of fashionable smiling languor. "Oh!" Daisy Dawn began to laugh then. "I know him. He is my shirttail cousin."

Annabelle drew her friend out of the lane of traffic, pausing at the fringe of lady gossips. "What do you mean?" Annabelle asked, a little breathless as she watched the lithe, muscular body in the tight-fitting clothes move into the room. He was the most dangerously beautiful man she'd ever seen. He didn't look like anyone to tangle with.

"It is Gypsy Smith," Daisy began, "Cousin Robert's half brother."

"Lawsy, where's he been hiding?"

"In the war. Robert doesn't like him."

"Whyever not?" Annabelle kept her eyes glued to the pantherish male and felt her heart beat madly.

"For one thing, Anna, Gypsy came back to claim

47

his inheritance, and secondly, Captain Smith is a Yankee."

"Oh! God save us!" Annabelle clamped a hand over her breast. "Yankees in our midst. Why do they seem to be everywhere at one time? It isn't enough that the Yankee guns lie in wait for one of our ships to run the blockade and we have such a hard time getting food and clothes to our soldiers?"

"There is really nothing to worry about, Anna. This war will be over one day too. After a few years the scars of war will fade."

"Yes, dear Daisy, keep talking, we Charlestonians need every reassurance we can muster. Some of Charleston is already being overrun by Yankees!"

"Please, Anna, let's do try to have a good time."

"You are right. The air of festivity is as strong as ever." She giggled. "Perhaps even stronger. It is so important to keep up our spirits."

Across the room, Robert Neil's brown eyes flashed wickedly beside his sister's black ones. "Gather 'round," he called to everyone, "come, come. This Fortune has an announcement to make."

"Oh Robert," Blossom whispered in his ear, "this is going to be such fun. Imagine the shocked faces, it will help us forget this silly war," she said with a pretty pout to her red lips. Her eyes widened then, and her insides plummeted. La! Was that Gypsy Smith or were her eyes playing tricks on her? He just couldn't be here! He would spoil *everything*, with his calm, questioning ways. Contrarily, he possessed such a quick, hot temper too and he always ruined her fun. Her practical jokes unfailingly backfired on her whenever Gypsy Smith was around. La! He could be such a bore just when one wanted to have a good time!

All of a sudden, Blossom's eyes became frisky. If they could pull this marriage thing off . . . only if . . . then the joke would be on Gypsy Smith!

Captain Smith, wisely out of uniform, began to mingle with the guests. He walked easily, listening raptly to the animated conversation flowing about him. His eyes, more blackish tonight than the mahogany, seemed to have partaken of the color of his trousers and waistcoat, and had a smoky, sensuous look. He wore a plain white blouse, unruffled, and the stock at his throat was simple, a dark shade also. The shiny black boots that he usually wore with his uniform, the telltale sign of an officer, were sufficiently concealed by all the whirling skirts and candle-flickering shadows playing across the floor.

Gypsy B. Smith thought it odd that not one of the Marylebones of Charleston was present, and he had so desired to see Stephanie and her husband, Paul Browden. He would call on their house later, he decided.

For a long moment, while he stared into the gold-framed mirror hanging on the wall across from him, Gypsy Smith found himself surprised that the young woman with Robert and Blossom held such a fascination for him. Gypsy felt a warm stirring movement in his loins, and as he continued to watch, taking in her natural grace as she moved, noting the beauty of her features as she looked out over the chatting guests, he knew a strange enchantment. The moment caught him up and Gypsy knew he would never be satisfied just to gaze upon her loveliness from afar. He must come to know her. Every breath from this day counted on it.

Chapter Four

Angela excused herself abruptly after Robert Neil Fortune had introduced her as his bride. Although Blossom and Robert could chuckle over the moment all the astonished eyes turned their way, Angela did not think it was funny at all. Her shoulders drooped and she posed a dejected little figure in the garden, where she walked slowly up and down the paths, pausing finally beside a fountain which was flanked with many-colored azaleas. Sadly she sniffed, and sat down on a stone bench.

"If only I could remember more," she said. Her sigh, coming from deep within, was long and ragged. "They say they found me in the river, more dead than alive." With her chin in her hand, she continued. "What am I to believe? I seem to be surrounded by those who find joy in playing games with my emotions. Mum Zini is kind, or so she tries to be. Jasmine Joe is the same. The housemaids, ah well, they do not know anything, but perhaps they are ordered to seal their lips when speaking to me on certain matters. Robert Neil seems to favor the idea that his sister would be better off wedded and away. Blossom means well, doesn't she?"

Angela looked up at the moon, which was steadily arching itself across the studded night sky, and breathed another ragged sigh. "Who am I really? Could Robert Neil really be my husband? I think not." She shrugged. "But can I be certain of this? They said I had been away for a time. Who said this, was it Blossom?" Lord, she could not even remember that.

Why can't I seem to even remember from one day to the next? she wondered, her thoughts silent now. There didn't seem to be any sense in talking to the shrubs, and the moon, and the sleepy flowers, she told herself looking down at the molten water.

The soft scrape of a booted heel along the path caused Angela to start. She was about to rise when the deep male voice coming at her said, "Stay. You look so very lovely sitting there, and I would not like to be the one to bear the guilt on my conscience." His body then appeared and Angela heard herself draw in a sharp breath.

Angela could not help asking, "What guilt is that, monsieur?" There, again, she was uttering that foreign tongue.

"The one to disrupt such a charming picture, of course." He straightened, clicked his heels, then bent over to take the dainty hand in his own. Laying a soft kiss there, he peered into her eyes, introducing himself. "My name is, ah, Gypsy Smith." He had almost made the mistake of saying "Captain," and he could not be sure where her loyalties lay, North or

South. To lie to this young woman was not the way he wanted to start their acquaintance. Indeed he would like there to be more to it than "mere acquaintance." She gave a start and he let her hand go. "I see my reputation has already preceded me. Too bad." She stared at him with questioning eyes and he answered, "You see, I saw you standing in the drawing room with my, ah, relatives and I must be truthful in saying that I could hardly wait to meet you." He cleared his throat. "Would you stand up, please? I would like to greet you properly; you see, I've waited a long time for you."

Whether it was on command or shock, Angela found herself rising from the bench like someone's hypnotized subject. Discovering that he was beginning to frighten her, Angela started to step around him, but he instantly stepped forward, blocking her path.

"Please, don't go," he begged in a soft voice. He should not have frightened her like that, and decided to go a little easier on her. "I—" he began, trying to calm her, "I only want to hold your hand." Once more, he lifted that dainty member. He planted still another kiss in her palm, closing his eyes and savoring the taste and smell of this little lady that did strange things to his insides, somewhere in the region of his heart.

Angela pulled her hand from his, saying, "I think I should go back inside now. . . . They will miss me."

"If you go," Gypsy Smith murmured, "I will miss you too."

Do you know what it is that you do to me? his mind asked hers as he continued to stare. He could tell she was just as confused as he; maybe she was more so.

"I haven't asked you what your name is." He smiled, his rugged complexion softening, his eyes candid points of light. "Please." He was about to take her hand again, but she must have determined his move for she clasped her hands together in a maidenly gesture. Gypsy's face fell but he tried to conceal his disappointment by being agreeable. "I'll walk you to the doors."

"If you wish," was all she said to that. To his earlier question, she supplied, "My name is Angela . . . Angela Fortune."

Gypsy stared into fast-blinking eyes. "It can't be that you have married Robert Neil."

"And why not, monsieur?" She could feel a ghost of her real self slipping into place, what her real personality must be like. This arrogant male was assuming more than he should, and she just knew she'd not allow this if she had her whole wits about her.

Gypsy Smith was speaking to her again, before she had a chance to continue. "I've a strange feeling you are defending Robert Neil for reasons you don't even perceive yourself. How long have you been married?"

Angela didn't want to say the wrong thing. He'd said he was a relative to the Fortunes. Hadn't he? Or was it Mum Zini who'd told her? Still. Even if a wedding had never taken place between her and Robert, Angela decided to play it to the hilt that she was Robert's wedded mate. This man seemed to presume she could be his for the taking, and she didn't want to appear free for his possession. Not in any way. She did not like this man. There was something about him that set her on edge. Being with him was like treading on dangerously thin ice.

"We have only just become man and wife, *monsieur!*"

With that, Angela swept between the French doors, leaving Gypsy Smith staring after her. He watched as she paused only a moment inside the room, and then went directly to Robert Neil's side. As he bent his brown-haired head, Angela whispered something and then he nodded. Gypsy watched her walk to that black-haired witch, Blossom Angelica, and ask her something, too. But Blossom did not acquiesce as easily as Robert Neil; she only patted Angela's hand, then tucked her to one side and continued chatting brightly with the uniforms.

In those lacking times of war there was no orchestra playing at the Tradd's party that night, but from the hall came the haunting strains of a single violin and the voice of an angel accompanying the melody. Gypsy Smith continued to watch the young woman. He stared and ached.

"La! Rumor has it that Gypsy Smith is in Charleston . . ." Blossom shrewdly let it hang; she'd know for certain now. All she had to do is wait for Mum Zini to speak.

"It is no rumor."

"Oh . . . Mum Zini, you know Gypsy Smith is not due back yet!"

Blossom kept her back turned against the mulatress. But Mum Zini knew the girl was dying to know if the Yankee captain was nearby. That way, so Mum Zini thought, Blossom Angelica could prime her weapons and ready her defenses for what was to come.

"It is him," Mum Zini said, her tone casual and quick. "Jasmine Joe has seen Gypsy Smith himself." She chuckled. "He say, 'Gypsy Smith jes' blew in wit de wind.'" These words were becoming Jasmine Joe's favorite of late, relating to different subjects now and then.

"Well, for all I care," Blossom began, tossing her black hair, "he can just *blow* right out again."

"Why you say like that? You do not like our Gypsy Smith?" Mum Zini asked, folding a star-and-rose-patterned quilt across the foot of Blossom's elegant four-poster.

"You know I don't," Blossom said with haughty demeanor. She stood looking out her window, pushing aside the cream dimity curtains so she could see all the way down the oak-shaded lane. "Gypsy Smith!"

Mum Zini shook her head as if to clear it from the shrill shriek. "You do not have to shout, Mamzelle Blossom, I can hear you even if you speak in de soft tone."

"It's that damn Yankee!" Blossom snipped, snatching her skirts aside as she brushed by Mum Zini. At the door, she paused to look back at the housekeeper. "Don't look so dumbfounded, Mum Zini—why don't you just go down and greet him. Oh la!" Blossom grew angry and leaned forward in a huff. "He's here, Mum Zini, he's here, your favorite black sheep!!"

With a sneaky grin breaking out over her *café au lait* face, Mum Zini muttered to herself, "I know, child," she said, laughing, "I know." That girl sure gets herself ruffled up just like Quackser Henny in her royal residence—the chicken coop!

"Here now, what yo' doing gatherin' those eggs, li'l honey?" Jasmine Joe had come upon Angela backing from the chicken coop. She turned around, and making a secure nest in her apron, Angela smiled brightly at the black man. "I doan know how's Kapa Lu's goin' to take this, seein' as this here's her job, to gather the eggs and see after the feedin' of the li'l animals." Jasmine Joe smacked his big lips together and hummed his doubtfulness.

"I've done this before, Mister Jasmine, and"—she smiled a pretty smile—"I'll be sure to be very careful. As for Kapa Lu, she said to go ahead because she's very busy in the kitchen with Pandasala."

Pandasala was a huge black woman who hummed deeply in her throat all day at her task, in *Pandasala's kitchen,* and the poignant Southern tunes drew Angela to that part of the house, where she paused just inside the door with her head resting against the jamb. Pandasala's very pretty face would turn Angela's way and Pandasala seemed to be humming the melodies for only the lovely young woman's ears as she paused there. All the black folks at Tamarind had taken an instant liking to the Windswept Angel. Pandasala, in her nearly perfect English, called her Tamarind's Angel, her own choice for the wisp of a sweet angel. Only they knew that Angela had not become Robert Neil's bride. How could she have without their knowing? To keep secrets at Tamarind

57

was a difficult task, to say the least.

"Kapa Lu is wrong," Jasmine Joe said. "A gentl'womans doan dirty her hands with chickens 'n such. Angelica was a real fine lady. She was Master Robber Nell's mama. Never dirtied her hands, no sir, but she wasn't always the fine lady. Never shoutin' at us lak that Blossom Angelica, her youngest one. Miz Angelica was a real angel too, jes lak you, Miz Angela."

"You said she wasn't always the fine lady," Angela said to halt his rambling. "What was she before coming to Tamarind? If I might ask."

"Oh sho', you can aks me any time, Miz Angela. The lady was a sharecropper's only daughter. The first Robber Nell was named after his gran'pappy and then there was one who came afore. I wasn't here then. I only come when Robber Nell bought me."

Angela blinked in confusion again. "I've heard this before, Mr. Jasmine."

"When?" he said, curious as the rest of them were to know where she had originated from. They were all waiting for the day when she would remember where she came from, who her folks were, and how she'd come to be here, washed up on the banks of the Ashley.

"Oh," she said, laughing, "just lately. Tell me, why do whites buy blacks?" She sat on the wooden bench and Jasmine Joe took a seat beside her, asking first if she didn't mind him sitting beside her. "I really don't understand. . . . It's kind of sad."

"Oh no, Miz Angela. It ain't sad a'tall, not if the master is kind. Robber Nell ain't ever lifted a finger . . . but . . ." How could he say Blossom

58

Angelica had often lifted her hand to a cowering black girl and slapped her soundly? Called her "nigger" too.

"But what?" she asked Jasmine Joe. She sighed. Again, as usual, there seemed to be a lot of secrets upon Tamarind's soil.

"I really can't say, Miz Angela, it ain't my place to say whose . . . whose . . . I can't say." He flinched in surprise when the young woman placed a warm hand over his forearm, while securing her precious brown objects with the other twisted in the big white apron.

To keep from further embarrassing the black man, Angela took her hand away; besides she really needed both to secure the precious eggs. "I heard Blossom talking this morning," she began, "and I don't understand what this war is all about, Jasmine Joe. She said people are beginning to steal to stay alive and families, friends, are breaking up. Raiders roam the countryside. They loot. They steal. They terrorize. And Mum Zini said loyalty doesn't mean very much anymore." She paused, looked down and then up at Jasmine Joe, asking him, "What is this war all about?"

Jasmine watched her settle herself, making a nest in her lap for the eggs, and he only hoped Quackser Henny didn't come around the corner from her jaunt along the river because she would be mighty mad to see this stranger with all those eggs; Quackser Henny allowed only one person to take eggs from the chicken coop and that was Kapa Lu. Jasmine could see Kapa Lu just smiling to herself. Kapa Lu was all right, but she was a practical joker just like her mistress, Blossom Angelica, for the both had grown up together and shared the same sugar tit; there it ended.

Sighing, Jasmine Joe leaned back against the warming wall of the chicken coop. "Far back as I can recollect, North n' South been movin' to some battle meetin'. De South been watchin' de North makin' all that money, its cities growin' so fast. 'An de South, bein' unable to go without sales, out of de country, 'specially to that place faraway called England, for its crop o' cotton, them Northerners thinks they was seein' a lazy South crumblin' and spoilin' like rotten watermelons in de field, with our peoples, our 'whites' havin' to be propped up like a baby by de blacks who doan want to serve de whites an' make it easy for de white folks while freedom's bein' held back to dem."

"Everything *might* have been all right, you're saying?" Angela could see the knowledgeable black man nod; finding the conversation enlightening, she went on. "What else did the Northerners think about slavery?"

"They doan think blacks be their equals, but doan give a care if we was freed or not. I doan care to be freed, I like it here at Tamarind jes' fine. There be some blacks who already done run away, though, an' if'n they be found I doan know what Robber Nell goin' to do 'bout it." Looking at Miz Angela meaningfully, he said, "Most likely he won't do nothin', but now Miz Blossom, she be a different—" Jasmine Joe halted, and repressing what he'd been about to say, he continued sheepishly, "An' the

Northerners was fearin' slavery would spread West to de new Territories."

"Were the Southerners afraid of something, too?"

"Somethin' fierce. They was afeared that if those West Territories came into de Union bein' free States that it would be leadin' to the outlawin' of slavery all over de land. Then when Abraham Lincoln become President, the South really afeared, the whites I mean. Even before Abe got into Washington, seben States of de South had . . . withdrawn."

"You mean they seceded."

"Yeah, se-cede. Then comes the Confederate States of America. South Carolina was de first to se-cede. That was just before Jeff Dabis and Abe Lincoln was running for President 'gainst each other. It was right in our own Charleston harbor, Fort Sumter, when de Confederates fired on de Union."

"Yankees?"

"Yeah, that be dem." Jasmine Joe chuckled low, thinking of Gypsy Smith, who'd arrived a short while ago, and Tamarind was all in a dither, especially Blossom Angelica. The only one who didn't seem to care—or maybe it was to just not acknowledge the goings on and look the other way— was Jàl Stephan, the white overseer and bailiff of Tamarind. He didn't want to get involved, and no one knew where Stephan's sympathies lay concerning the war. At the moment Stephan and Smith were having their yearly "business" discussion in the study.

Looking in the direction of the house, the study in particular, Angela had the strongest impression

61

someone was staring out at her from that window. Gooseflesh rose on her arms and she shivered involuntarily. "I would like to continue this conversation, Jasmine, but," she said with a laugh, looking up at the flare of morning sun then down at the soft brown objects in her lap, "I think these eggs are going to cook right where they are and Kapa Lu will really have something to be fretting over!"

"Yeah." Jasmine laughed. Then he became serious, catching her off guard by asking, "Where you from, Miz Angela?" He knew that wasn't her real name.

Just then a huge white duck made a timely entrance, waddling around the corner of the henhouse, and flapping her enormous wings angrily at the young woman with the apronful of precious eggs, she flew at Angela, her webbed feet barely touching the pebbly ground.

"Shoo!" Jasmine Joe flapped his big black hands at the attacking duck. "Shoo! You git on now, Quackser Henny, you git, girl!"

"*Oh!*" Angela cried, half laughing and half alarmed. "What's wrong with—*her?*" She stepped back, looking down at one precious egg that had slipped and splattered all over the ground at her feet.

Angela, fighting to save the remaining seven eggs, rolling them all carefully to the center, did not see what Jasmine Joe saw, or who, striding across the yard. Receiving a dismissing gesture from the tall, muscled man in open blouse and tight breeches, Jasmine Joe gathered Quackser Henny and took her off for another stroll beside the river, despite the duck's enraged quacks and furious flappings and pumping webbed feet.

Facing the chicken coop after she'd finally gotten the eggs settled, Angela saw not hide nor feather of Jasmine Joe or the duck. Angela turned to carry her apronful back to the house. Before she took three steps, Angela found herself coming smack against a tall hard frame. This time her precious nest was saved by a long-fingered hand that shot out, followed by another, both very tan, very masculine in structure and proportion.

Angela snapped her head up, finding her eyes locked with mahogany ones. Her breath was snatched up and away. Her heart picked up a bruising beat in her chest.

"I—thank you," she stammered, trying not to stare into the eyes of this compelling stranger.

Cupping her hands beneath the apronful of eggs, he said, "I see you don't remember me."

She hadn't recognized him, but when he spoke, it brought the night in the garden two days ago flooding back in full force. If she'd thought his presence forceful then, it was now coming at her with the same power of a raging tumult.

Angela could only stare. Inside herself something wild and too exciting to bear was beginning to stir.

He spoke then. "I just wanted to tell you to get ready."

She calmed herself down enough to ask, "Ready? Monsieur, for what?"

"Get ready, mademoiselle, because I'm coming into your life."

With that Gypsy Smith turned and walked away from her. Standing stunned, Angela did not even notice when all seven of the eggs slipped to the ground and smashed. She was not even aware when Jasmine Joe came to her side, gaping first at her hypnotic state and finally, at the slimy yellow bubbles and cracked shells surrounding her feet which seemed affixed to the whole mess.

Chapter Five

Gypsy Smith's mahogany eyes made a slow scanning over Jal Stephan's almost sad face. Nonchalantly Gypsy said, "You mean to tell me she just appeared at Tamarind like some . . . some river waif?"

"That's right, suh."

"I know the horrors of war are upon us, with miserable folks roaming the countryside, all without purpose, most without a direction in which they're headed. Being an officer, I—" He paused to look directly into Stephan's eyes. "You do know I'm an officer by now, right Jal?"

"Oh yes, suh! And I don't care which side you're fighting for, suh, it's your own business. I just wish the war would get over, suh."

Gypsy Smith nodded. "Nice way to feel, Jal. As I was saying, I've seen wanderers, deserters, and the suffering faces of war . . . but a lovely young woman like Miss Angela out there on her own . . . it's hard to believe." His shrug was laconic. "How in God's name did she come to be floating down the Ashl like so much flotsam? Who would dare let such a—a little lady out of their sight?"

"I don't know, suh. We did scour the area where she came to be up on the bank, and we found she did have a lifeline: a big trunk she'd been floating on that came to rest in a small cove where other limbs and branches had come up the Ashley and gathered."

"The Cove, of sorts, yes, I know it," Gypsy Smith said.

"That's about all we found out, suh."

Jal Stephan watched the man turn brooding and thoughtful. He had known Gypsy Smith for several years, now, but he still wasn't sure where the man's sympathies lay. He had a strong feeling Smith was a spy for the Union. What did Smith hope to find here at Tamarind? Could it be he was only home for a short visit?

Gypsy Smith allowed no one into his personal belongings, not even the saddlebags of his thoroughbred, Big Red. Jal had been in search of a business paper he needed, thinking the gone-fishin' Gypsy Smith would have been carrying it with him, but he'd made a mistake when he had gone out to the stable to try and see into them. Jasmine Joe had guarded the worn leather pouches as if he were guarding his very own life, and that of his loved ones. Big Red, too, had put up much of a fuss over the safety of the saddlebags thrown over the edge of his stall.

Some___ Jal Stephan thought the black folks ___sy Smith too much, favoring him over ___irst holder to Tamarind Plantation. ___was not completely without feeling, though. When he wanted some maintenance at Wild Oaks, his own rundown, weed-crowded plantation and they didn't have the time, or couldn't be spared from Tamarind, Gypsy would go and do most of the tidying up himself. All the blacks that had been there formerly—before Gypsy Smith ever came to take Wild Oaks over—had run off. Robert Neil had allowed Wild Oaks to fall into disrepair. Why should he care, anyway, Robert had thought, when his mother had left Wild Oaks solely to Robert's half brother. Wild Oaks bordered with Persimmon Wood, Daisy Dawn's own plantation, up the river six or more miles as the crow flies.

Smith was still wondering about Miss Angela, or Mrs. Fortune, he didn't know which she was for sure. Did anyone, with all the practical jokers running around Tamarind?

"No one knows where the young lady came from," Gypsy Smith said ruminatively, echoing Jal Stephan's earlier statement.

"No, suh."

"No one knows her real name." He sighed wearily.

"No, suh. Robert Neil give her the name Angela because she looked like a lost angel, and because that was the name of his mama, and yours," he corrected. "Well, Angelica is almost the same."

"Could she be a spy, do you think?" Gypsy Smith asked quickly before Jal could breathe twice.

Jal Stephan chuckled, asking, "For which side, suh?"

Gypsy Smith returned the chuckle with a smile. "It is rather funny when you think about it . . . but she could be carrying information and got lost in—" He shook his head. "No, somehow I can't see her carrying any information that would endanger many lives."

"Are you looking for someone, suh?" And then he said, "I'm sorry, suh, I shouldn't have asked that question."

"Could be." Gypsy Smith smiled. He left the very mussed desk and went to the window. He recalled many a night gazing out on the moon-touched grounds of Tamarind, waiting for something, but never knowing just what it could be that tugged at his heart.

Gypsy Smith spun around from the study window. "Is she really Angela Fortune . . . I mean did Robert Neil really make her his bride?"

"Oh Lord, suh, I don't rightly know." His face fell. "I really do wish I could help you but Robert Neil"— he shrugged helplessly—"he's a difficult one to read. I'm sorry to say this, suh, and not meaning any disrespect, but, well, Mister Robert he's, ah, he's different from most folks."

"You needn't blush, Jal. We've been over this before."

"I know you like Mr. Robert, suh, very much. Not only because he's your half brother, but I do think you have a kind heart hidden in that, pardon me, suh, in that rogue's face and body."

"Whew!" Gypsy Smith laughed, "Rogue, is it?"

Chuckling warmly, Gypsy walked over to Jal Stephan and clamped a big hand on his shoulder. "I like you, Jal—and when are you going to stop calling me 'suh'?"

"Soon, Gypsy B. Smith, soon."

"Only you and I know what the *B* stands for Jal. That makes us pretty close friends, huh?"

"Yes suh, Gypsy Smith, yes suh!"

Both laughing, they left the study together, the slight, balding Southerner with stooped shoulders, and the tall handsome Yankee captain.

"There be no eggs today, Mistah Smith," Pandasala had announced when he had gone into *her* kitchen to visit her. Of course he didn't have to wonder why there weren't any eggs. It had been his fault the lovely young woman had dropped them all from her apron in the first place.

Gypsy had walked about the kitchen, and lingering a while to visit Pandasala, he had crossed his arms below his chest and listened to her happy humming. Then, when he'd begun to look over her shoulder at the jar of berries she'd opened, she shooed him out with her fattest wooden spoon. She'd heard Gypsy Smith's deep laughter as he'd gone back to the study.

Pandasala looked about her kitchen. She loved every inch of it; she'd never run away as some of the other blacks had. As far as she saw it, she was free, black, and old enough to do anything she wanted to, like slip out to "see" Jasmine Joe in the hayloft.

This room, huge and airy, was completely separate from the main body of the house, being entered only through a single door opening in the brick pavement that ran along the wing to the kitchen. But day in and day out, Pandasala's humming and pot banging could be heard all over the immediate grounds.

Gypsy smiled as he entered the study and closed the door. He wanted to be alone. Time to reflect, he thought, walking over to his favorite window, which gave a clear view of the Ashley River and anyone walking to or from the docks. The window was open, the birds were in song, and who would ever believe there was a war going on. . . . He shook himself from the transfixed moment.

He had cleaned his Navy Colts, done some paper work, both military and otherwise. He walked over to sit in an easy chair this time, a black one that still smelled of freshly tanned leather. He stared at the fireplace for a time. His eyes lingered on the table, where tall candles in silver holders decorated a corner of the room. The heavy white lace curtains with their creamy yellow tiebacks stirred in the languid summer breeze. Soft beige walls surrounded him. Stirringly beautiful eyes the color of blue pearls stared back at him from the pale walls.

Gypsy surprised himself by laughing softly. Angela, the dainty, mysterious maid, was always staring at him through his mind's eye. Her fragrance was so sweet, like attar of roses. "I think I'm in love," he said aloud. "Jesus, I feel crazy, I must be in love." He ran his long fingers through sable waves, imagining what it would feel like to have Angela do this. With heart pounding and arms aching to hold her, he stood abruptly, meaning to change the path of his mind's wandering.

Back to the window. Different, safer thoughts. Much safer, he laughed to himself. He was nigh onto bursting. He was certainly ready for Angela. But was she ready for him? Did she really belong to Robert

Neil? Damn, he wished he knew for sure. She couldn't be. It was . . . inconceivable.

"Come on now, Smith," he told himself. "Look out the window and forget Angela for a time."

Tamarind. All this could be solely his. He could snatch Tamarind away from Robert Neil if he was inclined that way. Robert was terribly unfit to run Tamarind, true, but as long as Jal Stephan was overseer and bailiff, there was no dire need as yet for him to take over. Besides, who knew, the War Between the States could wrest it from them all and he was powerless to keep the Yankees from taking it, or torching it, if they wanted.

Gypsy faced the room, his hands deep in his trouser pockets. He held no dislike for his half brother, even though Robert Neil had no love for *him*. When he'd first seen his half brother, he'd been prepared to battle for his inheritance, and then, much to his guilt and shame, he'd found he pitied Robert Neil. How could he ever snatch away anything from the wretched young man? he had wondered. Besides, Robert Neil was first heir to Tamarind and its holdings, all but Wild Oaks.

Robert Neil had come upon Gypsy's dark blue uniform, spied his black boots he'd just shined up. "Smith, suh!" Robert had stressed the last word, "get this bluebelly slime out of my house!"

A year had passed since that time when he'd volunteered to carry an urgent message for his commanding officer. He'd done this just so he could pass through Charleston and check on things at Tamarind. He had even made it upriver to his sadly neglected Wild Oaks that week with a feeling that

71

he'd never get to live there and restore the place to its former beauty.

"I was just on my way out," Gypsy had informed his mottle-faced half brother, who'd been hitting the bottle again hard.

"See that you do!" Robert had turned red. "Do . . . go!"

Then, ironically, Robert Neil had smiled and waved him off down the magnolia-shaded lane.

Gypsy Smith was growing concerned, increasingly, over his half brother's bizarre antics. Robert Neil didn't seem to be getting any better; his condition seemed only to worsen. Whatever ailment it could be, Gypsy wasn't certain. The company doctor in McClellan's regiment said the condition he described sounded like mental retardation, not a case of simple forgetfulness and rougish misbehavior or drunkenness as Gypsy had charitably thought.

On his return to duty in '62, *Captain* Smith found several changes. One of them was his rank. Another was that General McClellan had returned. McClellan was Winfield Scott's successor. Organizer of the army of the Potomac, of which Smith had belonged, McClellan had served on and off. To reorganize the Union force Lincoln had called on General Mc-Clellan, conqueror of western Virginia. Despite his being a vainglorious little man, he was a good administrator. He was capable of infusing his men with loyalty, discipline, and determination. Rushing to Washington in the wake of the debacle, McClellan quickly ringed the city with forts. They were manned by the three-year volunteers (Gypsy Smith among them), who increasingly composed what had become known as the Army of the Potomac. By the year's end McClellan could boast a disciplined military force of 168,000 men. Men who were proud of their units and determined to win. Captain G. B. Smith thought it was not unusual that George Brinton McClellan had been, from 1848 to 1851, an instructor at West Point. While McClellan was in the Crimea, where he observed European methods of conducting warfare and gained valuable experience, he took the time to design a new type of saddle. In a short time it became known as the McClellan saddle, for the cavalry. Gypsy Smith could see why the man had established a reputation as being the "Young Napoleon of the West" because of the bombastic manifestos he issued to the soldiers under his command. His organizing abilities and logistical understanding brought order out of the chaos of defeat. He was brilliantly successful in whipping his armies into a fighting unit with high morale, an efficient staff and effective supporting services. He was well liked by the men who served under him, and Captain Smith had had to chuckle to himself when the general was referred to as "Little Mac." Captain Smith was with McClellan at Fort Monroe. The man had been relieved of his duties as general in chief. Smith had been with McClellan when he was held up before Yorktown for a month in the spring of '82. He was with him when McClellan established his headquarters at White House on the Pamunkey River. He had succeeded in bringing over a million men, organized into five corps, within striking distance of Richmond, and brought events up to the Battle of Fair Oaks. This was where the "eyes" of the Union army came in and served. Captain Smith gave valuable service along with Thaddeus Lowe of the Balloon Corps.

There was a regular balloon staff attached to McClellan's army, with a captain, an assistant captain, and about fifty noncommissioned officers and privates. The apparatus consisted of two generators, drawn by four horses each. There were two balloons, drawn by four horses each also, and an acid cart, drawn by two horses. The two balloons used contained about 13,000 and 26,000 feet of gas.

One of those "eyes" was Gypsy's own *Dragon Lady*.

The battle was also known, alternatively, as the Battle of Seven Pines, which took place on May 31, 1862, in Tenrico County, Virginia, near the Chickahominy River, six miles northeast of Richmond. The Union Army of the Potomac was under G. B. McClellan, and the Confederate army of Northern Virginia was commanded by General J. E. Johnston. Johnston was severely wounded on the first day. Gypsy Smith thought back to the day, May 31, when, with General McClellan and 104,000 other men, they'd crossed the Chickahominy and were met by approximately 75,000 men under General Johnston, who attacked McClellan's weak left wing. They were driven back toward the Chickahominy, and at nightfall the victory seemed to rest with the Confederacy. However, the following day, with Gypsy's *Dragon* brought into service, they spied on the enemy from above, and the Union troops found an opening to be reinforced. Still using the balloon, the battle continued at Seven Pines, about one mile east of Fair Oaks. The Confederates were repulsed. So far as the victory lay with either side, Gypsy was convinced it was with the Union army, for the Confederates failed to achieve their purpose of destroying the almost isolated left wing of McClellan's army, and after the battle they withdrew into the lines of Richmond with General Robert E. Lee in command of the Confederates. The Union losses were 5,031 killed, wounded, and missing; those of the Confederacy were 6,134. He felt he was no hero, though there were others who thought it a fact. Gypsy Smith hated war. It was hell.

Gypsy Smith moves restlessly on the daybed in the study; he knows he is dreaming.

The sun rises like a huge sunflower above the sea, and he is in the yellow air balloon with a woman. Her hair is brown and windswept, her eyes filling with joy and gratitude. Everything has a clarity and an importance that delight her, and everything interests her enormously. She helps him discover his true identity. She is his friend and he is grateful to her.

The dark-haired Gypsy finds himself standing at the end of a long dark tunnel; actually it is the long, leaf-dappled drive leading to Tamarind. He sees the white house at the center of that verdant spiral, smells the fragrant trees blossoming in the air about him. Finally, his feet begin to move, taking him closer and closer to the lovely antebellum home.

A beautiful girl, perhaps in her early teens, with jet black hair swinging free about her slim hips that already show promise of becoming deliciously curvy, and white camellia skin, comes dancing toward him.

His dream seems to be growing wilder—and the air grows full of excitement. He can already foresee what lies beyond, for this has been the way of many such dreams.

She shows first surprise, this raven-haired beauty, then a pout comes to her face, and finally, a disapproving scowl. She is still pretty, he thinks, even while angry. He learns this beauty's name is Blossom Angelica Fortune—his half sister. He loves her at once; she hates him with a passion.

Robert Neil's behavior is just as bizarre, although he halfheartedly welcomes his half brother, whereas his sister finds Gypsy Smith's moods hard to manipulate and this deepens her wrath. The daffy Robert Neil Fortune had not much to say over matters of importance, like the "inheritance letter" made out by Angelica herself, their deceased mother, when his sable-haired half brother moves right into their life—and literally into their house.

Then the winds of war blow across the North and the South, and Gypsy Smith ironically finds himself going over to the North when a few friends urge him to be different and come join them. He is very unlike a Southerner, they press. Also, he has come to know George McClellan and likes him despite the contrary gossip of his being egocentric and pigheaded.

Another scene begins to reel out behind Gypsy's closed lids. Now he dismounts and kneels beside a wounded soldier in the dirt and his face turns gray, set like stone. Why . . . it is only a boy!

The emaciated lad's face is badly broken and twisted, and there is blood crusting all over his head, in his blond hair, in his ears—and even on the crucifix he wears around his neck. But he still lives—barely.

The smoke of battle clears and he carries the young soldier. . . . His hands tear at the bloodied blankets, and his face is twisted in suffering, a reflection of the lad's. From his own shirt, he rips a piece, and from his own canteen of water wets the cloth. He bathes the boy's face. . . . He is so very young . . . what—seventeen? eighteen? Dear God! He's as frail as a girl!

Like a sudden crack of lightning then come the shots. Birds stir startled into the air, frightened yet again by the unholy machineries of man. The sounds of gunfire echo across the acrid-smelling country-side. Dust only just settles when it is in foment once again and there is no rest for man or beast.

Then all is silent and still once more. Even the shallow breathing of the wounded lad has quit. Slim fingers clutch his hand even now in death. A last-minute plea, heroic somehow, a longing to be immortal and be remembered forever by someone, one special someone there to witness the last breath.

Captain Smith, his throat choked, finds himself looking up while he grasps with pain and frustration his Navy Colts. . . . He sees the hurried gathering of carrion birds in the sunless sky over his camp. . . . *It is finished . . . finished . . .* then wings seem to beat out the awful words, and he shoots the horrendous creatures from the sky.

Moving from one place to another . . . gleams of white . . . streaks of black. The inception of a love rises like the blaze of the sun, but vague as the opaque dawn of passion!

He steps back, afraid to move forward too fast;

otherwise he might lose that which he hunts.

The Southern belles and Northern ice queens he had known during leave fade away, to be replaced by a lovely lost angel, more beautiful than sweet, fragrant roses, more elusive and mysterious than life itself. So painfully young, full of life, bloom, and wide-open blue eyes, delft blue, staring at fate. Her voice, soft, sweetly living in the winds.

Ah, the torment of his heart!

The Angel grows manifestly stronger in his mind. Now she is proud, sweet, aloof. First he feels a warm stirring movement within his loins, lust, but he also knows a strange enchantment. He must come to know her, even if he has been chasing a will-o'-the-wisp. Every breath counted on his coming to know her!

The moon bathes the Angel in a soft silvery light, brooding delft-blue eyes of trouble, of longing, of sadness, even of discontent. He steps into the moonbeams and says to the Angel, "I would like to greet you properly, you see I have waited a long time for you."

His eyes are bright with adoration. Like a leaf in a storm, she stands on the threshold of realizing the fulfillment of womanhood.

Oh, I can feel *myself with you* . . .

Get ready, mademoiselle, because I am coming into your life. He can hear it crying out from her soul. Make me a woman, stay, do not go!

In the dark stillness of the night, tossed by love's torment, it is revealed to him how the winds transport the lovers into the resplendent future. . . .

They rise into the heavens, in the yellow balloon,

with the sun setting on one side of the sea and the moon and stars rising on the other, as if the universe revolved about them.

So gay is the Angel's mood, so lilting her laugh. . . . The moment grows serious and the heat within their bodies rises with the balloon. His big hands cup her face gently; his breath is warm against her flushed cheeks; her arms creep up and twine his neck. The kiss begins slowly; they become like wild things. Children of the wind, captives of the wind. Overwhelmingly conscious of the passionate storm raging in each other's soul. Their clothing is tossed aside, until nothing remains but flesh against flesh. He rains affectionate kisses upon her face, her young breasts, his tongue following the gentle twin spires of her camellia-soft curves. The affection turns to a great need that rolls over them with a savage intensity; they are both stunned by their passion. His fingers slide across her silken, silver-edged body in an ecstasy of abandonment. His mouth suckles her sweet, tender flesh while his large hands rove gently over her curved buttocks; she arches to meet him, aiding his possession of her. Slowly he begins the bittersweet torment. A sweet, wild elation moves over him as he sheaths himself within the velvet core of her being, on and on into the roaring furnace of desire. . . .

"Angela!"

Gypsy Smith awoke suddenly, bathed in sweet, erotic sweat from head to foot. He peered around the bedroom illuminated by the soft whiteness of the moon, seeing the haunting stars outside his window, wondering if he had called her name out loud and if anyone in the house had heard him. He lay back down, feeling a vague regret.

In the bedroom upstairs (Gypsy's own), Angela stirred in her sleep, dreaming that a deep masculine voice called out her name from afar. His hair was dark as night . . . and he sat the midnight stallion like an Indian prince.

Chapter Six

Gypsy Smith felt like a man who had been blind all his life and was suddenly given sight. Angela had just entered the room. She wore her hair drawn gently back from a center part and caught up on each side of her face with the mass of chestnut curls in back which fell all the way to her waist and some below it.

He watched her come into the room and thought her the most beautiful woman he'd ever seen. Her eyes appeared blue-violet with the borrowed maroon dress she was wearing. All eyes were upon her as she entered and Robert Neil continued in his rattling-on voice once his charge had been seated. Blossom continued to hum beneath her breath and buff her long nails. Every so often she would look up at Gypsy Smith saucily and narrow her black eyes in challenge.

Blossom would never cast her lot with that of her Northern enemies, and she considered Gypsy Smith her enemy. She could never think of him as her half brother, even though he indeed was just that and seemed to think he could lord it over her.

"If you have something to say, Blossom, I wish you'd open your lovely pouting mouth and say it." Gypsy Smith startled Blossom when his deep, masculine voice came directly at her.

Haughtily she sniffed, "I don't speak to Northerners, *suh.*"

"Blossom," Robert Neil chided, "Captain Smith is your brother. Know your place, dear sister. We must be kind to our guests, isn't that so." He reached over and patted Angela's hand. "Smith"—he went on looking over to his half brother—"have you met Angela?"

"Not formally," Gypsy said, and stood. He walked over to her chair and lifted her other hand, feeling the strong currents of electricity and desire at their contact. "Hello, Angela."

"H-hello, Captain Smith." She at once let go of his hand but found he still held fast. "I"—she turned to Robert Neil, blurting out for want of something better to say—"we've met before in Charleston . . . in Tradd's garden."

Now Blossom sat up and took notice, purring, "Oh my . . ." She giggled and moved closer to where Robert and Angela sat side by side and Gypsy Smith still hovered over Angela's hand.

Angela's eyes lifted to his and Gypsy felt himself turn to butter inside. He stared; he couldn't help himself. Beauty, he thought. A lady, a real lady. Like a man lost and adrift at sea, he found himself drowning in Angela's eyes. They were large eyes, a little slanted, and were a most startling luminescent blue-gray. They were set beneath full, winged eyebrows, which, at the moment he returned from the clouds to earth, were drawn together in a slight confused frown.

"You are staring, monsieur."

He kissed her hand and felt the shiver pass from her flesh to his tingling lips. Ever since he'd first seen her, the same thought reverberated through his mind: *I have to make her mine.*

"Oh . . . the Yankees *are* coming!" Blossom taunted when she saw that Gypsy Smith could not remove his eyes from Angela's face nor from any other part of her for that matter.

"No!" Robert Neil said, on a long-winded note. He rushed to go and peek out the window. "They can't be, I don't see any. Blos-som Angel-ica," he said, shaking his finger as he turned to his sister, "you are playing games with me again. I shan't speak to you at supper if you don't stop! You have been nasty to me all day," he whined, while on his handsome face every expression appeared normal, as if his voice didn't quite match his countenance.

With her black lashes sweeping across the room, from one brother to the other, Blossom found she wasn't prepared for the concerned look on Gypsy Smith's face as he stared at Robert Neil.

"Oh, fiddle, Robby, come and sit next to me." When his eyes found her demure countenance, she smiled coquettishly and patted the cushion beside her. "Come on, love, the sofa's big enough for both of us." When he did as she asked, she pulled his handsome head against her shoulder and rested it there. "There, now, isn't that better?" Black eyes sought Gypsy's and dueled with the others, snapping at him, ordering him to not be so concerned. Blossom

Angelica would take care.

Swallowing hard, Angela's misted eyes lifted from Robert Neil's resting head to Gypsy Smith's pale features. When his half brother seemed to be asleep at Blossom's breast, Gypsy held out his hand for Angela. As if it was a lifeline, she grabbed on and felt him helping her rise from her chair.

At the doors leading to the gardens, Angela glanced back to see Blossom Angelica staring straight at her; the black eyes were shining with a silver light. And Angela didn't know if Blossom was crying or if there was a wicked gleam in her eyes.

Spring had leaped headstrong into summer and the sun was hot as a day in August. The overhanging branches of huge trees shaded the area that the man and young woman walked into. Her maroon-colored skirts and creamy petticoats brushed the grass that was taller here than in other places on the grounds of Tamarind.

Gypsy Smith halted suddenly, reaching up and catching hold of a thick, horizontal branch that ran outward like a cooling green canopy above their heads and hid them from view.

"This is far enough," he said, his eyes sparkling warmth. When she stopped and turned to look at him, Gypsy looked deeply into her stunning eyes. The haunted look was there again and he knew that some part of her wasn't with him, not here, not at Tamarind, but somewhere else. There was a ghost of something in her eyes. Somehow that ghost must be either brought out or destroyed, and he thought himself worthy of the task indeed.

"What do you mean, Captain."

His look was half serious as he said, "We don't have to go any farther."

"Really, Captain." She blushed. "I'm not sure I know what you mean."

"Are you flirting with me, Miss Angela? Or is it Mrs.?"

"I think I am."

He caught her hand, saying, "Don't."

"Don't, monsieur?"

Something was coming back to her; something she was very good at, she knew.

"Don't play games with me," he warned. Then he brought her hand to his lips and kissed her delicate, tapered fingers. "Are you flirting with me? Answer that one first. Then tell me if you are Robert Fortune's bride."

"I'm not sure I know how to flirt, *Monsieur le Capitaine.*" He watched the slow blue fire in her eyes. "I believe I am *not* Robert Neil's wife."

Pulling her closer, he breathed against her forehead, "Good." When she jerked back, he snatched her a hair's breadth away from his countenance. "If you are not my brother's wife then I would ask something of you."

"Yes?"

"A kiss. Just one simple little kiss, dear lady?"

Now she stepped back, losing contact with his disturbing flesh. "I'm afraid, monsieur, I do not kiss with strangers."

Gypsy Smith sighed a sad sound, reaching a finger out to brush her dewy cheek. "I know you are the woman I must love," he said, his heart in his eyes. "I know this as I stand here before you, sane and sound."

"No." She put her back to him, and he stared at the chestnut curls and the streams of glistening light the sun put into the long strands.

Vividly aware of the muscular strength of his big body and the sun-warmed male fragrance, Angela stood rigid and afraid he wouldn't touch her again. She desired so much for him to touch her. But she was afraid. Afraid of who she was. What it would mean for her to love him. For him to love her. He was standing so close she could feel the warmth coming from his powerful body.

Angela forced herself to face him calmly. "Captain Smith . . ."

Gypsy's eyes wandered over her as she began to speak and then faltered. He asked, "What is it, Angela?"

"You will forgive me," she murmured, "if I am confused and surprised at your interest in me." She spread her hands in a helpless gesture. He was staring at her curiously. "I don't know who I am, monsieur, or where I come from. For all I know there might be a husband somewhere . . . *truly*, Captain."

"You're sure you don't remember anything?" He waited for her answer, which was prompt, a small "no," and continued, "I find that very hard to believe, Miss Angela." Then he laughed and looked at her sheepishly. Pressing his long tanned fingertips to his forehead, he said, "God, how remiss of me. You see, Angela," he said softly, taking one of her hands in his, "I have gone through a sort of amnesia myself.

It was a . . . spell that a black woman cast on me so I would not remember who I was or where I came from. It's a long story, but to make it short . . . I was taken from Tamarind as a boy, I think seven years old, and brought to a land full of mystery—Africa. There I served a lovely woman and a very mean woman also. Many times I believed the mean one would kill me with her whip, one that fell on me more often than I ate food."

"H-how awful," Angela breathed, her pink lips trembling.

"Let me finish." He continued to stroke her hand gently and tenderly as he spoke. "The beautiful lady was taken from me. . . . She died."

"Oh . . ." There was a sad note in Angela's voice.

"Don't be sad for me. You see, her name was Victoria and her daughter came to be in the same place several years later. To me she was an angel come to save me from a life of hell. We rode away on a swift mount, a horse that seemed to have wings that night. Her name was Monica." He shrugged, "The last name unimportant for now."

"What was her age?" she asked Gypsy Smith, and felt strange inside all of a sudden.

He shrugged. "Perhaps in her early twenties, I can't be sure. I was only a skinny lad that looked as if he would drop to the ground anytime in a pile of bones." Angela laughed and Gypsy delighted in the sound as gentle as midnight wind. "I love it when you laugh, you look so happy." Bringing her soft hand to his cheek, he said, "I want to make you happy, and discover your past for you, Angela, because I lo—"

"Angela . . . Mamzelle . . ." called Mum Zini. "Where are you, child? I see you come out here a while ago . . . *Angela* . . ."

"Oh, I have to go." Angela pulled her trembling hand from Captain Smith's.

"*Angela.*" Passionately, Gypsy Smith pulled her into his arms, and cupping the back of Angela's head, he pressed his lips to hers, gently and then more insistently.

Angela's head swam. She clung to Gypsy so she wouldn't swoon. Before long she was kissing him back, not even knowing if she knew how to kiss a man.

But kiss him she did. Gypsy had never tasted such honey-sweet lips before, but if he didn't stop this ecstatic torture to his already aching body he was going to shame himself and her where they stood.

"Angela," he moaned, pulling away. He looked down at her up-turned face, her moist, parted lips, her blurred eyes, and wanted so very much to make her his here and now. "I want you, Angela, I *want* you," he whispered in desperation.

"Oh Gypsy!" She hugged him around the waist and then, to his profound disappointment, she whirled and ran from their blissful sanctuary.

Her absence slashed like a knife through every fiber of his being. Why was she afraid to love him back? He had felt her tentative yielding and the shy pressure of her soft thighs pressing back. She'd wanted him too. But she was afraid.

She couldn't be Robert Neil's wife! Impossible!

Tearing the sweat-stained shirt from his chest and carrying it loosely, he set off toward the creek at a trot and then a lope. Before long he was running like a swift-footed Indian. Like his Cherokee ancestors.

Gypsy's blood pounded wildly. A primitive throbbing began within his loins once again. She couldn't be . . . couldn't be Robert Neil's wife or anyone else's as she'd thought a possibility. Angela was a virgin. He'd bet everything he owned on it, even the *Dragon!*

Chapter Seven

"You look lak the cat with her li'l pink nose in the cream," Kapa Lu said, standing back while Blossom sailed down from the side veranda in a rush, her hoops bouncing as she gingerly flew from one step to the next.

Blossom came and stood before the little black maid, snapping softly, "Now don't you go and tell Robert Neil, you hear, Kapa Lu?"

"Uhmmm." Kapa Lu seemed to ponder this a moment while she picked at her thin cotton dress, then said, "Where you be goin' all gussied up, Missy Blossom?"

Blossom postured and swept her black-midnight lashes low, purring, "Wouldn't you just like to know, you li'l black tart." She wore a perky hat with gaily streaming ribands, and when she cast a worried glance over her shoulder, the ribands tickled Kapa Lu's face, so that when Blossom swung back she met the wrinkled black nose and thought the worst. "Don't you be making faces behind my back, Kapa

Lu!" She sashayed closer while Kapa Lu retreated, cowering low.

"Doan you be slappin' me again, Miss Blossom. I be tellin' Jasmine Joe and he gonna tell Cap'n Smith and you gonna get it."

"Oh fiddle!" Blossom backed the black girl up against a purple flowered bush. "Gypsy Smith is a Yankee, and all Yankees are bluebellied cowards. All they have done is yelp about how terrible we are with our slaves and our plantation money . . . and all the rest!"

"I think Mr. Lincoln be doin' what's right for the whole country, Miss Blossom," Kapa Lu said, knowing beforehand what was coming.

Whaack!

"Why you little nig—"

"Blossom Angelica!" Mum Zini caught the girl in time before she punished Kapa Lu with another hard slap. "That will be enough," Mum Zini said in her precise English.

Turning in a high-shouldered huff, Blossom looked up the stairs at the mulatress towering there. Black eyes dueled with Mum Zini's stern ones.

"All right, I'll leave her alone—for now. But you tell her to keep her mouth shut, Mum Zini, she doesn't know what she's talking about." Giving Kapa Lu another narrowed glare, she softly hissed. "Really . . . *Lincoln!*"

While Blossom walked away in a hip-twitching gait, Kapa Lu repeated the Biblical verse Jasmine Joe had told her that morning, one that Abe Lincoln had quoted: "If a house be divided again' itself, that house can not stand."

Hearing Kapa Lu's taunting voice, Blossom kept walking, tossing over her shoulder, "Your day is coming, Kapa Lu!"

Once inside the stables, Blossom stepped into a cleared area in the back. Hiking her skirts up to her waist, she loosened the hooked band about her waist and the tapered circles at once slipped to the floor. She stepped quickly from the hoops, reached down, and hid them in the pile of hay nearby. Then from her skirt's deep pocket, Blossom removed the "page," an elastic band. When she was finished, her skirts were draped over the band and had become considerably shorter.

"Mus' be a plain nuisance to be a lady," said Jasmine Joe, chuckling as he turned his kinky black head aside. "You finished, Miz Blossom?"

Black eyes narrowed, Blossom said nothing but went straight to her saddled mount, Jezebel. Leading the witch-black mare outside into the sunshine, she mounted from the block. Kicking the mare into a screaming lunge, Blossom held on tight while she flew across the greensward toward her clandestine meeting with the Confederate spy.

Jasmine Joe shook his head. "That gal sho' gonna come to harm one of these days ridin' lak there ain' no tomorrow on that black debil horse. Should be tellin' Robber Nell, Ah should, but Mum Zini say 'Let it be, I will take care.' Humph, well, let her take care then, it ain' gonna be on my sou'."

Blossom ducked beneath branches flying fast overhead. From early childhood she'd learned how to ride fast and hard. Not content to simply ride around a ring, she had walked her pony into the woods and then how they had let go! Raised her buttocks off the saddle and sailed, as she did now astride.

Corporal Harv Jackson searched the line of woods between the river and Tamarind plantation. Damn, where could she be? Blossom Fortune, his contact, again, was late as usual. He had an important coded message to pass on to her, and then he had to get on, posthaste.

Reluctantly Jackson realized there wouldn't be any time for him to dally with Miss Blossom, not this time, not if he wanted to get back to his mother's and spend some time with her before his leave was over. And he wanted to see the girl he was going to marry, too. June Rose, she was such a pretty, dainty, blond creature. Nothing like Blossom, but given time and lessons . . .

He stood up suddenly. Churning up loosened turf, coming at breakneck speed, Blossom had burst from the wood like a dark avenging angel with black hair swirling about her magnolia pale face. Hair that matched perfectly the huge black thoroughbred carrying his beautiful mistress.

It was the hour of steaming wood and slanting sun, earthy smells that the sun had been warming over all day. As Blossom drew nearer, whipping off her perky hat and tossing it aside, and as Harv Jackson observed those bounteous beauties rising and falling and bobbing inside her bodice, he knew he was lost. And so was his time with Mama.

"Do you have it?" she asked, breathless, sliding down from her mount and into his gallant waiting arms. He was about to reach inside his jacket lying on the ground, when Blossom jerked him back with a handful of his hair and kissed him hungrily and passionately full on the lips.

Sinking to the dew-laden earth, Blossom undressed the corporal. Harv Jackson did the same for Blossom. Their kisses were hot, passionate, demanding. She took and gave nothing in return. When the corporal began to shake from strain, Blossom took the commanding position. If she wanted this to continue, she'd have to give a little . . . but just this one time.

"Just lie back, Harv honey, little Blossom's going to take care of you." She dipped her head and after a while purred, "How did you like that, honey? Just wait, Blossom's got more, darlin'."

The corporal panted, his arms above his head, his body looking like a dead soldier's. "You just drain a man . . . I don't think I can . . . go on anymore, sugar."

"Sure you can."

"Blossom," he groaned, witnessing the slanting rays of sun through the woods, "it's really time for me to go. Oh! Stop that Blossom, that hurts, it really does, 'specially at a time like this. I need some rest, girl."

"Oh!" She sat on her haunches, naked and disheveled and beautiful. "Well," she purred, "I'll just let you rest for a little bit, Corporal."

"No!" He rolled to his side, pushing her hands away. "Didn't I ever tell you I got a pretty little gal waiting for me?" He watched her eyes flash black fire. "That's right, we're going to be married soon and June Rose is the prettiest, purest, li'l angel you ever—''

"Oh hush up!"

Hastily the corporal began to gather his scattered clothing: smallclothes; blue patched pants, tattered hat, scarred boots, copperas-dyed yellow brown jacket—and the coded message.

When both were finished dressing, Blossom stood with hand outstretched. "Well, Corporal, where is it? I have to hurry now, supper's on the table—gravy and beef, chicken—" As she saw him begin to salivate, she dug the spur deeper. "Black-eyed peas, dumplings, wild rice, sugared fruit—" She laughed. "I'll bet Mama and Juney Rose don't have nothing like that on their table."

"You're a real bitch, you know that?"

"Of course." She tossed her black mane of hair, clutching his fingers with the note held between them.

"Let go, Blossom."

"Why, Corporal, don't tell me a li'l gal like me can keep you."

"Damn you, Blossom." Harv Jackson rubbed his other hand up and down his thigh.

"Rested, Corporal?"

Tucking the folded slip of paper into her deep pocket, Blossom placed her fingertips on her tiny bodice buttons. Sashaying toward a mound of turf, Blossom tossed a comehither look over her shoulder. "We really don't have to peel down all the way, Corporal, in fact we don't have to remove hardly anything. Come here, sit down right here, and I'll show you, honey."

Blossom twinkled her eyes, wrinkled her pert nose, and Harv Jackson was lost again to her erotic witchery.

The quiet way was crisscrossed with early moonlight and tree shadow as Blossom made her way back to the stables. There, she dismounted, and as a light drizzle had begun to fall, she reached for her extra cloak and took it down from the peg. Hurrying across the yard to get out of the rain, Blossom took no note of the yellow beam of light spilling into the bushes outside the study window.

On the other side of the house another cloaked figure stepped from the veranda.

Gypsy Smith was readying everything for his departure. His leave was over. The Union was experiencing extreme difficulty raising new regiments of volunteers. They were establishing conscription. Draft law required all men to register. If a man's name was drawn, he could avoid the draft by paying three hundred dollars or could be permanently exempted by paying a substitute to serve in his place. These were provisions bitterly resented by the poor, who could ill afford to pay. Captain Smith had seen enough of this war in March and been about to pay twice that much to get out.

He was war-weary, feeling the frustration and nerves, and the sorrow in both the North and South. Each side was holding fast, determined to force its will on the other.

Then it had happened, the deciding factor. A Confederate spy had been the cause of Bobby McFain's demise. His friend had been carrying a message, too, but Bobby had been the unlucky one. He'd lost friends at Bull Run and the Seven Day's Battles. Fair Oaks. With all the bloodshed around him, he'd been ready to desert, take up blockade running, anything, to get away from his friends. Now . . . he didn't seem to have many of them left. They'd kidded him about living in the South and defending the North . . . laughed all in fun when he didn't speak with a Southern drawl. . . . It was best he did not!

A light drizzle had begun to fall. Standing at the window, Gypsy pressed his forehead against the windowpane, grateful for the coolness that soothed his frustrated nerves. He smiled, thinking of another friend, a female. Stephanie, her last name wasn't Marylebone anymore. He straightened. He hadn't seen her since Lincoln appointed McClellan commander of the Union forces around Washington and he'd obtained leave and gone to visit her. She had been extremely happy—and pregnant.

"What's this?"

Gripping the windowframe on both sides, Gypsy leaned forward to better view what was going on outside. That looked like—it was—a Confederate soldier. He could only watch. By the time he quit the study and ran outside, he knew the soldier would have vanished into the trees. As it was, the man, his tattered hat dripping, his yellowish brown jacket soaked, seemed to be on a secret mission of some sort as he stepped from the mount he'd left at the first tall trees and walked hastily to the cloaked figure crossing the yard.

Then, through the slanting gray mist he saw it! The

soldier handed a folded paper over to the cloaked figure. As the man whirled back and took off running, Gypsy saw the hesitation in the step of the dainty cloaked one, saw the pale face turn to glimpse the house, then tuck the note in the arm holes of the cloak and turn back in the direction she'd come.

He was right. A Confederate go-between here at Tamarind. A very busy one.

Into the blue gray mist Angela had stepped. Hugging the cloak about her as she had made her way to the river, intending to return again to the spot where she'd been found, she'd been surprised when a man in barely serviceable uniform had moved in front of her. He hadn't even looked down into her face, only thrust a piece of folded paper into her hands. Accepting it had been an involuntary action, automatic. He'd mumbled something that sounded like, "Here, take it!" and before she'd known what she was doing, her hand had been holding the paper. "Oh . . . *dictionary*," he'd added hastily.

"What?" she'd uttered, and found herself questioning the moist air, seeing nothing but a fleeing figure of man.

Utterly confused, Angela had turned to go back into the house. Little had she realized how damning the scene had appeared to a pair of watching mahogany eyes, as if she'd gone out purposely to meet the Confederate with every intention of receiving the coded message.

When Angela stepped into the riverside parlor, she turned to secure the glass doors behind her. She released the cowl on her hood. Her glorious bounty of shining chestnut curls fell free down her back. Then, facing the room once again, feeling mixed emotions over the note she'd received, she made to step across the room to return to her room. A deep, thrilling voice came from the shadow.

"Going somewhere, little Reb?"

Chapter Eight

In the pearl gray mist, Corporal Harv Jackson mounted his dappled bay. He kept off the river road and close to the curving Ashley. Jackson cursed Blossom Fortune. It would be after midnight when he arrived in Charleston and saw his mother, and there would be no time for June Rose.

Lord. He'd have to stay away from Blossom; she was like a fire in the blood, a dark fire. Wanting her so badly at first he could taste it. Afterward damning her for the slut she was, and for leaving him emptier than before they'd begun.

Harv Jackson moaned. Captain Ridpath Huntington was on his way to see Blossom. He might even pass the captain on this very same road. He'd forgotten that the captain had been boasting he was going to take a leave and make Blossom Fortune his bride. The captain had gone to Washington on private business. Jackson chuckled. Wouldn't it be a good one if Captain Huntington himself turned out to be the contact? Who could tell? He'd had to deliver

100

coded messages to the captain before, in person. Mysterious business, this. He'd like to get out of the whole damn war, that's what.

Having gone only one mile toward Charleston, his destination, Jackson found that he had to relieve himself. While he was doing this beneath a huge oak with spreading branches, he happened to dig into his pocket to make certain he hadn't lost the list for the medical supplies the second-in-command had told him to get. He was to go to a house uptown above Broad Street. Families had moved there to escape bombardment as Union forces moved cannon emplacements onto one island after another. The largest section of Charleston had been evacuated, and day and night the screaming of the new shells, with explosive centers, crashed into the deserted part of the city.

Checking his pocket for the list, Harv Jackson stared wide-eyed at the coded message he'd been carrying. The one he had been ordered to carry to the go-between! Doing up the front of his trousers, Jackson remounted and turned his dappled bay in the direction he'd just come from.

After he had gone the mile, Jackson spotted Blossom just stepping from the side of the house. He'd spot that cloak anywhere; she'd worn it a half-dozen times before when he'd met her clandestinely. Good. She had realized he had mistakenly given her the medical list and was coming out to see if he'd return. Good girl. He'd just hurry over, give her the paper, and the secret verbal message. . . . Damn, he'd even forgot to give Blossom that because she'd gotten him so nervous and frustrated. This was the last time he'd make contact with *her!*

Not far away from the Ashley, Ridpath Ewing Huntington, captain of a guerrilla band, a force of irregular troops, known as Mosby's Rangers, rode fast along the river road toward Tamarind. He had forty-eight hours and then he had to return to Charleston, where he would decode the message and return to Virginia to follow Mosby's orders.

At the last minute the captain had been told there was a change in plans. Corporal Harv Jackson was to bring a message to Tamarind plantation. He couldn't give it to Huntington because the captain had been in Washington. So they'd turned to Blossom Fortune, who'd accomplished a lot of spying activities for them in the past. Far safer for the woman to hold it until Rider came for it.

Captain Huntington chuckled, his deep blue eyes twinkling.

For all he knew, he could meet the corporal on the way. But that wouldn't help him any. Harv Jackson would have already handed the message over to their beautiful contact, Blossom Angelica. Besides, he wanted to see her. . . . He had something important to ask Blossom.

Captain "Rider" Huntington did not see the corporal going in the opposite direction past him through the trees. The sheer curtain of drizzle hid each man from view of the other.

*　　　*　　　*

Upstairs in her bedroom at Tamarind, Blossom pulled the piece of information from her deep pocket. She'd seen them before but could never understand what the numbers meant. Curious as usual, she unfolded the square, thinking this one looked different from the others she'd passed on. The first line said: "List of Medical Supplies."

Blossom had sat as she studied the paper. Now she shot back up out of the pink velvet chair.

"Medical supplies! There must be some mistake!" Wrinkling her beautiful face in an ugly scowl, she uttered, "Harv Jackson . . . you idiot!" Twelve months with the Partisan Rangers hadn't taught Harv Jackson anything. He was still a complete ass. Last time they'd made contact he had almost ridden away without giving her a list of names, visiting folks from Virginia Colonel Mosby wanted her to contact in Charleston and draw into private conversation. Yankee jackasses were always willing to shoot their mouths off to a pretty Southern belle . . . especially while her eyes mesmerized and promised a little dalliance away from their silly little wives later on!

In the parlor, Gypsy Smith's face hardened into planes of anger. Angela watched him back her up to the chair by the window and felt her knees quiver and her heart pick up an abnormal swiftness. "Little Reb," he drawled again, and it went clear through her.

"Who and what are you? Where did you really

come from?" he fired at her. "I want some answers and I want them now!"

"P-please don't shout so, monsieur."

"Stop the bull—you're no more French than my big toe!"

"I-I do not know what I really am, *mon* . . . Captain."

"Oh yes you do." He gripped her wrist when she tried to clutch the cloak closer against her softly heaving chest. "I've known there's something going on around this area for a long time. Whose house did you invade before you moved in with the Fortunes?"

Gypsy Smith hauled her up until her toes were touching his. "I'm going to put a halt to your activities, Angela." He said the name in a mocking tone. "And I thought you were a lady. A real pure sweet lady who'd slipped and lost her way in wartime."

"Monsieur"—Angela squeezed her eyes hard—"you are stepping on my toe. Your boot is very hard. Please."

"Please?" He stuck his face close to hers, until she could see the slightly warmer shade of amber in his eyes.

So intense was their encounter that neither realized they had an eavesdropper right outside the door, which was one quarter of the way open.

Gypsy Smith held eye contact until she was the first to drop her gaze.

"Thank you," she murmured.

"For *what?*"

"For getting off my foot."

"Damnit it!" Surprising her totally, he reached up to give her shoulders a shake. "Who are you? Who do you work for?"

"I am Angela."

"No, you are not Angela. If you are Angela, then what is your last name?"

"I—" How could she tell him, when she didn't know herself? "You know that I have forgotten."

"Give me the paper." He watched her expression carefully.

"Was it meant for you, monsieur?" she said, hoping he wouldn't get mad at her anymore.

"Hardly," he clipped. After scanning the numbered page, Gypsy looked up at her again, his eyes narrowing. He asked, "The word, what is it?"

"The *word?*"

"Of course, you know that I need a 'word' in order to decipher the coded message."

Angela glanced up at him in confusion, then back down again. "I don't know what you . . . mean, *mon* . . . sir."

With a dangerous watchfulness in his eyes, Gypsy took his time tucking the note away on his person, his eyes never leaving her face. "Now," he said, measuring each word, "we are going to go up to my room. Follow me."

"No."

Gypsy turned back to her, saying, "Did I hear you right? You said no, didn't you."

"Y-yes." Angela began to shiver again, but not from cold.

"Do you know what we do to spies who say 'no'?"

"Spies, monsieur?" She tripped over the word again.

In a flash he was breathing down on her face, his voice harsh. "Little Reb, I think I will enjoy punishing you myself." He hauled her to the door, while she bumped against furniture knowing she would have bruises later.

"No . . . please . . . don't." She tugged at his hand, but her strength was no match for his. "I did not do anything, Captain. Honest."

"Honest?" He sneered into her face out in the hall. "Dare you speak to me of honesty when you have done nothing but lie to everyone here at Tamarind? Even Blossom, who sympathizes not only with your emotions but your cause?"

"Oh!" Now Angela realized what he was accusing her of. She'd talked some to Jasmine Joe concerning this crazy war that divided a nation in half. As he was dragging her up the stairs, she tugged on his arm, but he pulled her up harder, two stairs at a time. "I am not a spy! I have nothing to do with this silly war! Please listen to me!"

"Oh, and next you'll be telling me you are from a foreign country." He snorted without humor. "Like France maybe?"

"France . . . yes!" Angela felt something light up in her when he said the name of the country. "I think I am from this place . . . France."

"Oh, Sweet Jesus."

Opening his door, Gypsy swung her into the room and then kicked the door shut with the heel of his boot. At the bottom of the staircase Blossom muffled a giggle with the palm of her hand, then whirled, hearing the angry shouting and happy it wasn't her. She was glad that Robert Neil had been drinking most of the day and was going to be sleeping it off until much later. Which would give her time to plan her next step. Her contact, what was she going to tell him? And who would he be this time? she thought, licking her lips with a curling tongue.

Chapter Nine

From the window Angela looked up through the starry dark and wished fervently to know who she really was. The misty rain had ceased to fall. The midnight blue sky held a moon that fought valiantly to shimmer through the veil of haze that still hung between the earth and the sky. The same moon she had looked at on countless nights since she'd been a child. Luck was with them now, Mum Zini declared. Here at this plantation they called her Tamarind's Angel, because no troops of Yankees had come along to camp on the doorstep since she'd been here, and this made food and everything else more plentiful than if they'd come.

To herself, to Angela, she was the Lost Angel.

Very lost, and very frightened at the moment as the tall captain continued to pass by her in his maddening pacing, stopping to interrogate her every few minutes.

"Angela"—he raked impatient fingers through his mussed hair—"if you're found out you know you are going to be hung, don't you?"

"Yes, you have already told me."

"Damnit," he shouted, "stop acting the sweet and innocent, will you? Just tell me what the 'word' is . . . and maybe I'll let you off easy."

"If he told me a word, monsieur, I am unable to remember it now with you shouting at me and squeezing my arms all the time." She watched his reflection in the window and knew he was still standing behind her and had halted his pacing, but he would resume it soon enough. "You make me nervous, monsieur."

"If you don't stop calling me 'monsieur' I am going to turn you over my knee. It's what you deserve anyway."

Angela gasped. "No one has ever struck me, *sir!*"

"Not even on the behind?"

Blanching, Angela murmured, "No . . . sir."

"There is a first time for everything." Which led to another thought. "You are leading me to believe you are also a lady of questionable virtue, which is not really a *lady* at all when you think of it in those terms."

Innocent eyes turned to Captain Smith. A low voice spoke. "Captain, sir, why would you think such a thing?"

"You are just too damn innocent, that's what, to be genuine!"

"You needn't shout. I can hear you."

He moved closer, saying smoothly, "Well, then, if you can hear me so well, Lady Angela," then mockingly, "why don't you cough up the information I want. I'll tuck you away somewhere so the authorities won't find you . . . and I'll visit you now and then to see that you are well taken care of.''

"Sir!" Angela stiffened. "You are speaking of making me your mistress!"

A grin lifted the long, side planes of his cheeks. "I see you understand that much. You can help me out, and I'll see you don't come to any harm. I know of a place where I can take you."

"Why, if you think I am this spy, would you hide me and go against your own?"

A long finger curled from the tip of her chin around to the delicate dip in the heart of her lips. "Because I like you, Angela, and I want to save you from yourself."

"But, sir, how can you save me from myself if I do not know who myself is in the first place?"

Heaving an exasperated breath, Gypsy said, "You do complicate matters, you know that?" He watched her shift uncomfortably before him. Moving over to the huge four-poster, he said, "Come here, Angela."

Her heart trembled in her breast as he lowered his body to sit on the edge of the bed, and then uncomprehendingly, she stared at him. "What do you want, monsieur?"

She was back to that "monsieur" business again, so let her, he thought. Bound and determined to use the word, that's what she was.

On legs she believed had turned to lead, Angela walked slowly toward the unrelenting man. Had he no compassion? No mercy? Was he planning to keep her here all night questioning her? And what did he have in mind for her next?

"You are ruthless, monsieur." Then she bit her lip,

afraid she had angered him again.

"This is war, Angela."

"You and I, we are not at war, monsieur."

"Don't you have a better word to call me?" He looked at her with those deep, mahogany eyes that seemed devoid of all feeling to Angela.

"Why are you trembling, Angela?" Reaching out, he brushed her pink pouting lower lip with the tip of his forefinger. "I'm not going to hurt you, I only want to ask you some questions, and it will be up to you to supply the answers for me." He shrugged. "If you don't, it could go bad for you."

"What will happen to me?"

"It could be much worse than being hanged by that pretty neck. Then, again, it could be very pleasant. It is all up to you, little lady."

"You mean you will let me go if I tell you what it is you wish to know?"

"Of course. But you will not be allowed to go far. You must promise me you will put a halt to your extracurricular activities. You will remain here at Tamarind until I give you further orders."

"I see." Her head lowered.

"So"—he sighed, thinking he was finally getting somewhere with her—"let's hear the secret word and then the little lady can go. You can go from this room, for now."

He smiled nicely.

"I'm sorry, monsieur, I do not remember the word."

"Damn, *damn!*" he exploded.

He was up in an instant, pacing the four walls of the room. When he stopped this time, Angela did not care for the new look of determination that had come into his deep dark mysterious eyes.

"Take your clothes off."

She gulped. Her eyes went dark blue and rounder. "Monsieur, I did not hear you right, I think."

"Oh, you heard me right."

"I shall not!" Angela crossed her arms over her pounding chest.

He sat to remove his tall boots. "You will, Angela, sweet lady, unless you want that silly brown merino skirt and patched petticoats torn from your dainty little body."

"I am outraged to hear such a thing, monsieur! You will let me out of this room . . . at once!"

Next, off came his shirt. It was a blue one, standard military issue. He wore no smallclothes beneath and Angela felt her heart stop for a moment at the sight of the glistening strength, the powerful ribcage, sucked-in stomach, smooth waist, each long muscle indentation outstanding, separate in their strength and beauty, and a wonderfully carved chest that just begged to be caressed by a woman's eager hands. Angela stumbled back a step and came up against a chair.

She wouldn't . . . He couldn't make her . . . No, he was only bluffing. I am not that thoroughly washed of memories that I do not know what takes place between a man and a woman, she thought in no little fear. I have never been in a man's naked arms, but I have knowledge of what goes on . . . pieces of conversation . . . from other young women . . . at tea. Oh, that's *all* she could remember!

Gypsy Smith was down to his trouser buttons now.

He'd even run his tan fingers through his hair so that it looked mussed . . . and a burnished wave fell over his wide forehead.

"Get undressed now," he said, "*now*, Angela, or you will be brought to the authorities naked as the day you were born."

"No," she gasped, "you can't mean that. You . . . you can't." Fearfully, she stepped back but found she could go no farther. She tripped backward and was almost forced to be seated.

"'Can't' isn't a word with me, Angela. Believe me when I say I can do anything I want."

He advanced on her.

Angela stepped around the chair and held on to the curved back as if it could shield her from Gypsy Smith.

"You can't," she almost whispered from behind the chair while he stood in front of it, "you, you can't do . . . do what you are thinking."

"Can't what, Angela?" he taunted. "Bed you? You are the enemy—be assured I can do anything with you I want. You are mine, as surely as if I were the hangman with the noose."

"You—you're mad!" she said on a strangled sob.

"No, not mad, Angela, this is war and you are my prisoner, Lady Reb."

Angela dashed quickly around the chair, but he was already one step ahead of her. His fingers were in her skirts, tugging, while she clawed the air for escape. Spinning about, she came face to face with Gypsy Smith. His mouth was close as he spoke and unwittingly Angela provided every bit of encouragement he needed for she did not step away from his vibrant body as he thought she might have.

"I would have taken you gently, Angela."

She felt like a bird with clipped wings, with no protective corner to fly to and hide in and her delft blue eyes now widened in alarm while she awaited his next move.

"You mean you will f-force me now, now that you think I am the enemy? You are evil, monsieur, and I shall never submit to you!"

"Hah! I think I will enjoy forcing your submission . . ." He bent to nuzzle her cheek, then nipped gently at her unyielding flesh. "Either way, sweet, I will have you."

A callused finger tipped her chin and Gypsy almost felt remorse over what must be done, for she looked so small, frightened, and forlorn as she spoke in a faraway voice while her brown lashes slanted downward demurely.

"Please . . . I have done nothing, monsieur. Please do not do this thing to me."

The vibrant melody of a lonely mockingbird seeking its mate called outside the window and she gave a soft moan as his lips came down and fitted over hers. At once Gypsy felt the same spiraling need for her he'd felt the last time he'd kissed her.

It was a deep kiss, full of longing and loneliness—at first.

Through his lips, through his body, Angela experienced that implacable strength radiating from every pore of him. His lips were soft and hard at the same time, hungry, relentless, demanding more and more, making her dizzy with overwhelming sensations she'd never felt before. He'd kissed her before but not as he was doing now and she began to grow weak at the knees, wondering if she would soon die from the pleasure of the kiss he was giving her.

Lifting her in his hard, ruggedly sinewed arms, Gypsy carried her over to the bed to lay her down gently in the middle of it and the moment his arms came away she flipped her body over and began to scoot to the edge. Surprise registered first on Gypsy's darkly handsome countenance and then he spoke coolly, so sure of himself.

"Oh no you don't."

Gypsy was after her in a flash. "Why are you fighting this?" he questioned when he caught her, flipping her onto her back all over again and holding her captive in his vigorous embrace with no means of escape whatsoever in sight for her.

Angela swallowed hard. "You are behaving very badly, monsieur. Treatment like this to my person shall get you nowhere."

"Nowhere?" His eyes became serious and intent. "Do you want to make a wager on that?"

"I am not a betting woman . . . and I do not wrestle with strangers either," she said, with easy defiance this time as her mind began ticking with her own little plans.

"The 'word,' Angela, and then you can get up." Pinning both arms above her head in one big hand, Gypsy began his torment.

Angela felt him kiss her eyes, her cheeks, first one then the other, her chin, her lips. He nuzzled her ear, and finally kissed the rosy tip of her nose. "Are you catching cold, lost little angel?"

"No . . . I do not think so." She tried not looking

into the mesmerizing eyes peering down into her own. "Why?"

"Your nose is pink."

His tone was odd, yet gentle.

"Oh . . . it has always gotten that way ever since I was a child, when I am ner . . . nervous."

"Ah!" He jerked her up to a sitting position. "So you do know where you came from, who you really are."

The tears started in her eyes, she murmured, "Oh no, monsieur, truly I do not know . . . truly . . . it only came to me . . . just now."

"Rubbish."

"What, monsieur?"

"It means that it's . . . You are not telling me the truth, are you, Angela?"

His accusing gaze riveted on her and would allow her own eyes no escape.

"Yes! Yes!" Heaving a mournful sigh, she asked him, "Why can you not just believe me, monsieur? I tell you I am speaking the very God's truth."

Earnest tears began to fall, diamond-studded teardrops that rolled one after the other, and Gypsy placed his fingertip beneath one crystal drop curiously feeling the moisture there. Looking down at her disheveled chestnut curls Gypsy could not help himself and pulled her into his arms, burying his face in the perfumed softness of her glossy hair.

"Angela, sweetheart, you know tears will get you nowhere, don't you." He rocked her, then pulled her into his lap, holding her close. "Sh-Shh, please, it breaks my heart to hear a woman cry."

"B-But you said tears will get me nowhere—so

116

how . . . can it break y-your heart, monsieur? You are very—contrary."

Angela peeked up through her fingers as she covered her face. She had him now, she thought shrewdly, for what man would want to ravish a sniffing, tearful woman? None—that she knew of.

But that smallest, secret part of her that she had only been aware of slightly in the past was swelling into vivid life. Her softness felt his hard maleness against her, right through her torn dress, and the warmth of him began to send expectant shivers through her. She realized his deft fingers were caressing her hair and smooth skin at her throat with a gentleness that at once surprised and unnerved her. Every part of her body was beginning to feel sensitive, and to make matters worse, she was filled with an odd inner excitement that she seemed to have no control whatsoever over.

To her horror, Angela noticed that her legs had slipped apart, her skirts had risen scandalously high. She tried to draw her legs back together but he would not allow it and with a timid question in her eyes, she sniffed and stared right into his boldly handsome face.

Gypsy Smith laughed, having guessed her game minutes beforehand. His body moved and she gasped. "Ohhh, monsieur!"

He embraced her passionately, laughing softly at her gentle deceit, pulling her closer yet to the element of his most fervent heat source. "Angela, you are like a dream . . . you desire me don't you." He could not keep the smile from his eyes and he made no attempt to hide the fact that he was studying her closely. He repeated, "Don't you."

No question but a statement. Perhaps, Angela thought, if she kissed him a little and let him stroke her hair, he would be satisifed with that and let her go. Little did she know of men—she would later think back on this night with vivid images in her mind.

A shiver of great apprehension crawled along her spine; she felt odd suddenly, and afraid of him.

Angela's lashes were cast downward in a flash of brown as she demurely looked aside.

"I think so, monsieur."

In his dark lean hands he cupped her face and tipped it upward. Wildly, she thought, Don't kiss me again . . . please!

"N-no," she stammered.

"Oh yes," he insisted.

He brushed his lips against hers, delving deeply into her pearl blue eyes with his heated mahogany ones, and he said in an oddly gently tone, "You make my blood run like hottest fire, Angela."

"I am not sure . . ." Her small voice drifted away. Why did she get the feeling he was taking her winning hand from her? Well . . . she'd thought she was winning anyhow.

"I'll take you to heaven and back, my darling."

Little did Gypsy Smith realize he, too, was being caught up and away by a force greater than he was to ever come up against in his entire life. Even the rigors and pains of war could not compete or compare with its power, he would soon come to realize. He was about to take his first step into a world of the most passionate breathtaking beauty he would ever know—

like a treasure of flaming rubies and royal sapphires, a slew of diamonds, and find gold, even worth more than this, passion, bright and shining, all governed by this one tiny enchanting slip of a woman. Little did Angela know this herself—at least not yet.

The delightful fragrance of the graceful, pink mimosa wafted on a rain-sweet air current and entered by the half-open window, and it washed over the two in the bedroom. Angela and Gypsy Smith looked up at the same time as the romantic scent reached its fragrant tendrils about them, as if drawing them closer and closer still. He was waiting for her to say something, for he had been the last one to speak.

"I am afraid I am quite inadequate as a lover, monsieur." Shyly her eyes dipped. "You see I have never made love with a man before."

"You don't know how happy that makes me, Angela. Tell me, how can you know if you have ever been with a man if you can't recall any details from your past?"

"I—I just know it. A woman knows these things naturally, monsieur."

"Kiss me, Angela, kiss me as you would dream of kissing a man."

Winding slim arms about his neck, Angela, wide-eyed, stared up at him as she gave him a swift peck on his mouth. He pointed at the offended part of him, saying, "Again, Angela, longer this time, please."

Taking a deep breath she scooted closer to his chest, drawing a painful moan from the man whose lap she perched upon. Hers were the kisses of gentle raindrops when he would much rather savage her mouth with passionate ones—all in good time. While she paused between kisses, he brushed his lips against her hair, desiring so badly to share the joys of lovemaking with this young woman, his beautiful enemy, the one he would someday possess completely and make his fully, forever and ever.

Taking the tiny span of her waist into his hands on either side, Gypsy lifted her off his pulsing loins and deposited her carefully in the middle of the bed.

Her eyes were big and bright, delft blue, dilated, as she gazed up at this rough-hewn man in wonder and some fear.

"I want to make love to you, Angela, and also want you to know that I fully intend on making you my wife one day."

Good, she thought. She had his mind off her being his enemy and now she had him where she wanted him. Or did *he* have her exactly where he wanted her?

Neither of them, in their woven web of sensuality, noticed the slim cloaked figure slip into the room, find the damaging message, and slip back out into the hall, closing the door ever so slowly and carefully.

"Will you let me love you, my darling?" Gypsy said hoarsely, moving over her while his fiery mouth touched at her ear. "I want you badly, but I can't promise you I won't hurt you when at last I take you. Are you really a maid untouched, Angela, I must know?"

"You will not hurt me much, will you, monsieur?"

"Trust me."

"Yes . . . I will."

Nothing had prepared Angela for what began to happen next. She'd never looked on a naked man before, and neither did she think he could disrobe so swiftly. His trousers and smallclothes were off in a flash but it was just as well she could not clearly see that most shadowy part of him, for if she had, she'd have been off the bed and dashing for the door, she just knew it.

With one knee on the bed, he bent over her and caught her lips with his. With kisses that thrilled and excited, he began to undo her bodice to expose the gentle curves of her lissome body. She prayed he could not feel her inner tremblings, even though her knees were knocking together with the force of an earthquake.

When her sweet up-tilted breasts were exposed, like two white pearls tipped with delicate pink rosebuds, she gasped at the same time he did, but each for a different reason. He for her perfection; she for the embarrassment of having a man see her chest exposed. Her heart was beating much too fast!

"My God you're beautiful—Angela. A sweet, seductive temptress." She took his breath away. "If this part of you is beautiful, then—"

As his hand lingered at the pile of brown merino skirt bunched at her waist, his fingers itching to go lower, Angela caught at his wrist, feeling his pulse race there, and her own heart began to hammer in her ears with a loudness that nearly deafened her.

"Is this not enough, monsieur?"

Puzzlingly he frowned at her. "Enough, Angela? I must see all of you, my dearest heart. Please relax, for I will not hurt you."

"Well . . . if you will only look but not do anything."

Gypsy shook his head in disbelief. "Are you really that innocent of men?" he asked, bringing a thumb up carefully over the ivory molding of one exquisite breast while his glowing eyes devoured her with an intense hunger.

She felt the electricity of his touch and she almost swooned from the desire growing tauter and tauter inside her. She was beginning to feel like a tightly wound spring that would pop at any moment. A gasp fell from her lips.

"What . . . are you doing?"

But Angela stretched as she said this, missing the raging expression of hot desire playing across Gypsy's mysterious dark features. His heated gaze stayed on her nipples, which had hardened reflexively into hard little peaks at his look. Gypsy's hands trembled slightly as he brushed the brown merino skirts down over her belly, a little farther while her eyes grew rounder and bigger by the second and he felt her tense once more. Flames ripped through his loins when his fingertips encountered the alabaster softness of her stomach. He groaned then, fastening his mouth on a tender bud as he leaned over her, feeling intoxicated with not wine but passion's nectar.

As his lips touched her nipple, Angela's hips automatically lifted, and it was at the same instant that Gypsy's hand contacted the tawny silk of that first tiny hill. Again she arched, this time bringing him inside her, and his lean fingers mimicked the art of love, swirling in and out. He moved over her quickly, while she groaned and tossed her head back, murmuring and begging over and over for what she didn't know.

"Angela, Angela, God only knows how I love you."

She implored him with her eyes and arched gracefully, finally yielding herself to the wild arousal. Though his manhood throbbed to thrust home, he knew he must take his time and not hurry his possession of her. He had to ready her thoroughly, but that time was coming soon, sooner than he'd thought.

His body moved a little and she sucked in her breath.

He did not desire to bring her into womanhood by much pain, for surely she was a maid untouched!

"Don't be afraid," he breathed against her forehead as he began to mount her.

"Gypsy . . . please don't stop," she begged as he again paused against her.

The silken length of his greatest male power took her then, and he made a quick clean thrust to be over and done with the burning pressure as swiftly as possible. As the forceful thrust of his hips finally took its toll on the delicate membrane, Angela arched as that final surge brought them together as man and woman.

Gusts of bittersweet ecstasy shook her and she gasped out loud, raking her nails across his back.

"The pain will pass," he whispered reassuringly. "I'm not going to hurt you anymore, love."

Oh, he wasn't hurting anymore. . . . Something from the depths of her was stirring, soon to burst to life. The world caught fire around them in a deep purple swirl of passion. His possession was a thing of beauty and rapture, and her heart swelled as he tried so hard to be gentle. But she could tell Gypsy was holding all the glorious power she knew he possessed in check.

"Oh Gypsy . . . Gypsy . . . Gypsy," she moaned, with love expanding in every pore of her being. Surely this was paradise, and she felt shamelessly as though she could do this with him again, and again, thousands of times and never grow weary of this rapt splendor of love.

Time and place had no meaning as the exotic heat began to grow, and she gave her tongue to him as he bent to her for a rapture-filled kiss.

With each and every thrust, his lips poured out his love for her, repeating her name in a tumultuous rush. His very soul joined hers and played the sensuous music she wanted to hear. Holding her narrow hips to his, his hands almost hurting, he instructed her how they could move together, then apart, and even though she had not learned the rhythm he perfectly orchestrated, he knew she would in the days and months and years to come.

In a vicious fever of longing, his lips came down to her throat, and he murmured, "I love you, Angela . . . will always want more of you, and shall never ever tire of you."

A whole new surge of strength began to fill her, as if he was pouring his life essence into her, urging her forward and up, always upward, joining him at the gates of ecstasy that had swung open. He went ahead of her then, stopped, waiting for her to catch up. Her fingernails clutching wildly, and she thought that surely the tension would kill her! She strove to reach him, but she was nervous and shy. This was all so new to her. She felt like hottest fire while, like an imminent explosion, shivers of sweetest delight began to pour through her veins.

"Relax, Angela, come, fly with me, sweet."

His hands went around and caressed her then, pulling her tightness up to meet him all the way and she went to him, as graceful as a dancer. Gypsy could not get enough of her. Knowing that exquisite sensations had begun to ripple through her body, he plunged as deeply as he could. Angela now cried out at the huge blossoming flower that grew inside her, that he was creating and nurturing. It was a flower of fire, with a red heart more incandescent than that of any torch's flame. In a soul-shattering kiss of lovers meeting at the pinnacle of ecstasy, Gypsy embraced Angela with one last final surge of consuming flame that brought her tumbling before him while he chased after and caught up. Breathlessly they clung at the peak of ecstasy's heaven, looking at each other with souls steeped in this blissful interlude, drawing from each other the depths of perfect, radiant rapture. So intense was Gypsy's pleasure that he cried out in passion's sweetest moment and opened his eyes to his beloved three breaths later.

The tension broke at last, wave over wave, and washed Angela down and down and down. . . .

When Gypsy moved to withdraw, he met a most amazing sight there beside him in the greatly mussed bed. Angela was sound asleep!

Tangled provocatively with Angela's slim sweet body, Gypsy soon felt weariness overtake him too. He never heard the sound as a single word escaped her softly parting lips: "Dictionary."

But someone else had, as she slipped back into the soft moon-bathed chamber, cautiously scouring the place, sifting, rummaging, turning pockets inside out.

When Blossom Angelica turned away with what she'd been seeking, she had that smile on her face as when Kapa Lu had said, *Looks lak a cat with her nose in the cream.*

Chapter Ten

The eyes gazing into the parlor fire were so deep a blue that they seemed purple. Ruggedly handsome, with shaggy, almost shoulder-length hair, tall and lean, Captain Huntington rose from the chair when Blossom Angelica silently entered.

Her provocative purring laugh was close when he turned. "You clever boy, how did you know I had stepped into the room?"

There was the hint of a Southern drawl in Rider's stimulating male voice. "My goodness, as I live and breathe . . . Angelica."

"Oh stop that." She slapped his arm as if she held a flirtatious fan between them. "I've only been gone for a quarter of an hour, silly."

"It seemed like ages." He gallantly lifted her lily-white hand to kiss it. "You do melt my heart, fair lady."

A tingle of desire went up Blossom's spine as Rider reached for her waist. "Do you have it?" he inquired.

She squinted her black eyes and purred while

running her hands up his strongly muscled chest. "Of course," she said flippantly. "I-I had just forgotten where I'd put it, that's all."

He peered at her strangely. "It was written down?"

"Goose." Blossom laughed low. "I wrote it down so I wouldn't forget it. . . . I just had to go up and refresh my memory."

"I'll have to have it right away, Blossom."

The soft slur in Rider's speech caused Blossom's senses to swim dizzily. Rider had changed. He was a big man, but he'd gotten bigger yet. She wanted him now, now before they became man and wife. It was inevitable as the course of the sun and moon that they would marry.

Rider's heart was beginning to pound. "Typical Southern spitfire, aren't you. You are going to make me beg you for the message?"

He wore his hair in the unshorn fashion of the time, and Blossom couldn't help herself—she pushed her fingers through the deep auburn waves and tugged.

Rider's loins began to pulse with the want of her, Blossom Angelica, the sweet belle he would soon make his bride. He said his frustrating thoughts out loud: "Blossom, I have to get that message back immediately."

"If you only knew . . ." she said with a taunt in her voice.

"I can't stay, darlin'." He stopped to look at her seriously then. "What do you mean?"

"There's a Yankee in this house, upstairs in bed with Angela."

"Who is Angela?" As soon as he'd said the words

he remembered. "Oh, that Angela. So, Gypsy Smith has gotten to her before anyone else could, huh?"

Her fingertips nipping at the rough gray material covering the wide expanse of his chest, Blossom said low, "Aren't you going to go up there and take care of the matter? You could do away with Captain Smith this very night . . . hmmm?"

"Blossom, I don't believe this is you saying these things. Darlin', I can't just tiptoe up the stairs and murder a Yankee in cold blood while he's . . . It's just not honorable."

"Hmmm—for you or him?"

"Ahh—for either of us."

"Fiddle!" She whirled away, facing the orange glow of the fire, knowing her face looked beautiful and desirous this way; she'd held a mirror before her while alone in the parlor many times and studied her face from every turn.

Rider went to her, placing warm, gentle hands on her shoulders to turn her about. "Blossom, before this war ever got started I use to ride and hunt with Gypsy Smith, remember?"

"La, of course, but now you two are sworn enemies. You must do away with the enemy, Captain Ridpath Huntington."

Determinedly he shook his auburn head, saying, "Not while he's abed, my dear."

"Kill him when he gets up then."

Shaking her, Rider hissed, "No . . . no, I won't. Not for you, not for anyone. If we meet on the battlefield, well, then, that's a different story. You have become a coldhearted Rebel, my dear, I think you should halt your 'activities' for a time, you are becoming too caught up in this thing."

"Rider—don't go!"

As he strode toward the door, Blossom ran after him, her heart pounding in fear should she lose him for this night. When she caught him, she averted her head at once.

"Rider"—she looked down as if shy—"don't go. Please. Stay with me . . . tonight? One night won't matter, will it?"

Dazed by her black and white beauty, by lust, by whatever charms Blossom had hooked him with, Rider obeyed.

Livid bruises and deep angry scratches marred the smooth muscled flesh of Rider's arms, shoulders, and back. Frowning a little, he gazed down at the silken black head nestled against his chest. Carefully he shrugged himself from her clutches, catering to the strain of pulled muscle and tendon. His powerful thighs disengaged themselves from Blossom's.

"Mm-mm-mm," she murmured in drugged sleep.

Rider moved cautiously so as not to awaken her and he would have chuckled if he didn't feel so dragged out by satiation. He found himself staring at a white plump buttocks, wondering why he'd never noticed the wealth of flesh in that area, but then, she was always hiding herself beneath all those frilly skirts and hoops. Which brought him to wonder how Blossom still seemed to have all her clothes intact while all the other women in the South were going about in patched dresses and unmentionables. Even at the parties and balls he'd attended he had noticed the ladies' studiously fine stitching in the velvet and lace they lovingly tended. In the past he would not have noticed, but he'd come to learn the intricate stitches himself; otherwise he would have been walking about with open tears in his standard military issues.

As Rider was gathering his clothes to begin dressing, stubbing his toe in his eagerness to be quiet, Blossom came awake and reached for the warm body next to her. When she clutched nothing but handfuls of patched sheets, her eyes flew open and she came instantly to her elbows.

"Rider," she called breathlessly in the dark as she heard him readying to depart her bedchamber, "do you have to go so soon? I want you back here, sugar."

"Blossom darlin', you got to be kiddin'. . . . I just passed myself up in all the greenhorn couplings I've had since I was a skinny boy of fifteen!"

She laughed deliciously.

"All in one night!" he added, unable to suppress a chuckle himself. He straightened then as he noticed the fuzzy light. "Look"—he threw his hand wide—"it's the crack of dawn and I should already have my rosy butt in Charleston!"

Somehow, some way he didn't understand fully yet, Rider felt he could speak this way to Blossom Angelica—she hadn't seemed to mind it a bit or stop him when he'd used some coarse language when he'd started to make love to her. Which made him wonder all over again about the woman he loved and was going to marry as soon as this war was over. In fact, this night had been the deciding factor—he'd wait until that time.

"Blossom," Rider said as he looked out to the smooth-flowing Ashley just turning pink as morning sun struck the trees, "I'll have to be going any minute now." He went to stand beside the bed, looking down at her.

A rising sun pierced the curtains and shed saffron light over Blossom, and Rider thought she'd never appeared so very beautiful—and deliciously wicked. Which brought him to his next topic of conversation.

"You weren't a virgin—"

Blossom went quite still, giving Rider a moment to wonder further about her virtue.

Recovering, Blossom posed a picture of affectation, of sorrow over her lost purity. "I was hoping you wouldn't notice." She hung her head dejectedly. "But then—I should have realized how observant you are of most things—it was an accident. I—" Tears came to her eyes. "I was much younger than I am now—I was riding Jezebel at a furious pace, and—"

"And?"

"And when I fell I struck my hip pretty hard—there was blood . . ."

"Enough!" Rider held up his hand. "I don't want to hear the rest, Blossom, it must have been quite painful—" Rider blushed from ear to handsome ear. What did men know of such things; so he had to take her story as true.

"Oh—" Blossom picked up his sunbrowned hand and rested her cheek alongside the long fingers. "Yes—yes it was. I only wish—" She looked up at Rider with dark sad eyes. "Wish it had been you, my darlin' who took my maidenhood and not my carelessness."

Swooping down like a big hawk with wings outspread, Rider took Blossom in his arms and hugged her tight. "Sweetheart, don't worry about anything when I'm gone—I'll be back and soon you will become Mrs. Ridpath Ewing Huntington and you will share everything that I own. Wait for me, love!"

Smiling shrewdly over Rider's big shoulder, Blossom purred, "Oh, I will, Rider, I will—I love *only* you!" Black lashes slanted.

"Now"—she pushed away from him to bound from the bed—"let's go down to breakfast before you take yourself far from Tamarind again!" Placing a finger over his lips, she said, "Uh-uh, I won't take no for an answer, you lovely man, you're staying for breakfast before I send you out there to battle those arrogant bluebellies!"

Angela's smile was evidence of her vast happiness. Opening her eyes to the bright sun pouring in, she blinked, sat up—and gasped in surprise.

"Gypsy—you gave me a fright sitting there!" Peering at him closer, she could see something was terribly amiss. "What is it? Did I d-do something wrong?"

"If you are referring to what we did in this bed last night—no. If it is what you did after I fell asleep—yes."

A soft whimper broke from Angela's lips as Gypsy's fingers clamped sharply on her wrist, then he dragged her close to his face. Looking at his sensuous mouth, Angela remembered the feel of

133

them taking hers tenderly, parting her lips while he explored the moist warmth of her mouth.

Deep luminous blue pools were the only color in Angela's otherwise pale face. She'd gone as white as a sheet. Something was *terribly* wrong. Everything had changed over night.

"What did I do—after you fell asleep?" she began, her hand automatically reaching for his. For any whit of comfort. But there was none.

He ignored her gesture, moving his hand along his long thigh instead, avoiding any contact with her silken flesh now. Getting up, he looked down at her contemptuously.

"Where is it?" he said. He waited, not looking at her.

"Where is—*it?*" Angela said in confusion.

Gypsy watched as Angela's slightly uptilted eyes turned curiously in the direction of the clothes strewn about the floor, then widened as they encountered the jumbled disorder, inside out pockets, drawers pulled out—all as if someone had been searching the room.

"Memory of your midnight ransacking returns?"

"What?!"

"Tsk, tsk, you look rather indignant and abused yourself, *Lady Angela.*" A dark frown changed his face. "Or should I say Madam, now that you have been bedded properly and can be of greater use to the Johnny Rebs by trading your lovely body for the secrets of war. You should thank me for initiating you into the profession of whoredom."

Angela was struck speechless. She was angry too. But she had to know.

"What are you accusing me of now—Yankee."

She blanched when he spun around to face her, his mahogany eyes showing a glint of furious red, his cheek working in high vexation. With clenched fists, Gypsy Smith checked the urge to beat the little Rebel wench senseless.

Why had she used that word? Angela asked herself over and over while he stared scorching holes into her face. What did she know of Yankees and Rebels and this bloody war—only what she'd heard passed around here at this—this awful place called Tamarind. She hated it here—hated everything that was happening to her!

"You're a regular Belle Boyd, aren't you?".

Her head snapped up. She looked confused again. "Who is she?"

"Come now, the famous Southern beauty who made her way under fire through Federal lines to deliver to General "Stonewall" Jackson data concerning the movements and strength of *three* Federal forces?"

"I have never heard of her." Angela was becoming angry and frustrated; she'd had enough of this!

"Don't you want to know the outcome?"

"No." Angela hugged her knees, tossed her wealth of long chestnut hair back of her shoulder and watched the rays of rising sun strike the carpeted floor.

"Sure?"

A pert nose in the air was her answer this time.

"I'll tell you anyway, to refresh your memory— Jackson quickly put Belle's information to good use and thereby defeated the three Federal forces. 'I thank you, for myself and for the Army, for the immense service that you have rendered your country today.'"

"What is that?" Angela wondered if he was addressing her.

"That, my little Rebel lady, is the letter Jackson personally addressed to Belle Boyd."

"Oh." She put her back to him. "I don't know this person."

"Get up!"

Realizing she was lounging on Gypsy Smith's bed, Angela scurried to her knees, slid down, hopped off the bed. Realizing, too, she was naked as a jay bird, she dove back under the covers coming up in the same place she had been sitting moments before.

Chestnut curls lay disheveled about her angelically sweet face, her delicate ivory throat, her shoulders; saucy curls wound over her stomach, hips, thighs— her glorious mane was everywhere.

"I believe you are made up of three-quarters hair, woman!" Gypsy couldn't help expressing his conjecture out loud. "It is beautiful hair, if you don't mind my saying so, and I'd like to run my fingers through the mass of ringlets again, but I have more pressing matters on my mind—for instance, where are the goods?"

"The 'goods'?"

Dragging the sheet from the bed, with her luscious young body wrapped in it, Angela faced him squarely and thought to herself triumphantly that she'd detected a flushing of his skin—like a blush!

"You know," he said in exasperation, "the piece of information, the message you retrieved from my pocket last night when we, I mean *I* was sleeping very soundly."

"*After* we made love, monsieur?"

"Angela," he said, reaching out to wrap a sinuous curl about his finger, "if you don't think I'll hand you over to the authorities to have your pretty little neck hung, you should think again. Military Intelligence is probably looking for you at this very moment, knowing how infamous your reputation must be in the Rebel spy network. I'm beginning to wonder if you are not related to Belle somehow—could your last name be Boyd?"

She laughed, saying, "Of course not—my last name is Ha . . . Ha . . . Ha—"

With his ruggedly handsome face twisted in painful confusion, Gypsy Smith stared at her, wondering if she was coming unhinged. "Ha Ha Ha?" He frowned, barking, "What kind of name is that?"

Angela stared back at him, fear racing through every pore of her being—or was it excitement? She was coming close to remembering her last name; she could feel it; it had been on the tip of her tongue! But where was it now? she wondered sadly.

"So you think it is funny, ha ha ha." Wiping perspiration from his brow, Gypsy Smith bent to gather up his clothes, snatching up articles while Angela kept her back to his bare bottom, which the sheet hardly covered when he turned around and bent over from the waist.

Gypsy Smith stood briskly then, walking over to take her wrist and whirl her about to face his wrathful countenance. "I'll just bet you're out to make a fool of me, right?" When she continued to blink unresponsively, he went on. "Do you know

137

who I *really* am? I mean, do you know what my line of work is? You are smiling again. You think it's funny—"

Trying to suppress an impish grin, Angela found it was impossible not to smile while he seemed so serious and grim. "I know, monsieur, you are a Yankee captain, and I do think it rather laughable that you think I am this female Rebel who is trying to pass information. Did you think perhaps I used to live in this Washington of yours, inviting officers and their wives to tea to get them to confide in me?" She shrugged his arm off. "Yes, I do think it is . . . *funny*, Captain Smith."

"A man called the Black Moth, do you know of him?"

Gypsy Smith watched very carefully for any slight flicker indicating she recognized the name of the Military Intelligence agent. She hadn't blinked a lash. Her expression remained unchanged.

There was a knock at the door just then, and giving Angela a last scouring look, he went to answer the summons. It was Mum Zini.

"Good morning, Gypsy Smith." She handed him a small folded note, a very familiar-looking piece of paper. "This was outside your door, I think perhaps it is yours?"

Chapter Eleven

Angela thought Gypsy Smith was staring at her peculiarly after he'd shut the door and turned back to the room. Maybe she imagined the look, she thought when, after several moments of careful scrutiny over the paper he was holding, he shoved it in the pocket of his blue trousers and smiled while shaking his head.

"Must of have been sleepwalking last night. I wouldn't doubt it—after I'd just been through the time of my life."

Angela could not think of anything to say to that, at least nothing that would be deemed proper. And how could she know if she'd had the time of *her* life? Life before Gypsy Smith stepped in had been indeed vague. For all she knew she could have been an orphan. Yet somehow, she didn't think so.

"Get dressed."

Suddenly her dreamy world tipped and plunged. He had his back to her while he finished dressing. When he paused at the door before going out, he looked back once at her as if trying to decide what to do with her—as if she'd become a nuisance and a bore to him—and then he stepped out without further ado.

Deep within her heart, Angela knew she was falling in love with Gypsy Smith. But she was afraid to acknowledge the fact just yet. The man was just too complicated—and dangerous.

Out in the hall, Blue faced Gray.

Contemptuously the two grown men stared each other down. Captain Smith, in his dark blue stovepipe trousers; Captain Huntington, in trim gray jacket decorated with bright gilt buttons.

Captain Smith was the first to speak: "How good you look in your uniform—Captain Huntington."

"And you, sir."

Captain Smith nodded. "Halfway in it you mean."

"Nice trousers. I heard they had some problem with the dye, but you seem to have gotten a nice shade of blue."

"Yes."

"Well—see you around."

"Yes—we might at that."

"Good day."

"Good day."

After Rider had gone out the front door, Gypsy stood there shaking his head at the oddities of life. Today, of all days, he had picked to don his blues.

Stepping out onto the wide veranda, he was just in time to watch the Rebel captain ride away. He began to wonder if he could put two and two together here: For instance, did Rider have anything to do with the message he had in his pocket, one that had strangely vanished and then appeared right outside his door this morning?

Then again, there might not be anything suspicious about Rider's visit at all, for the man had showed up here at Tamarind almost the same time he'd done so himself on several occasions in the past two years. A few times they'd had brief encounters, where he had ridden in and Captain Huntington had ridden out not five minutes before, or in reverse order of each other, the minutes varying only slightly.

A slamming of pots and pans came from the direction of the kitchen, and as his stomach was beginning to rumble, Gypsy Smith took the outside path, following the delicious odor of bacon and pancakes that was leading him by the nose.

From a window upstairs, Blossom watched the interesting scenes below. First Rider galloping away on his gleaming bay. Then Gypsy Smith pausing in what looked like deep reflective thought, and turning back in the direction of Pandasala's kitchen. Smiling smugly to herself, Blossom went to see if Robert Neil was up.

On her way down the hall, she thought how proud she was of herself for pulling it off. She'd sent Rider on his way with the message following his hastily eaten breakfast; and during that time she'd taken the copy of the message she'd made when Rider first fell asleep and hidden it. Upon awakening she'd gone and dropped the copy in front of Gypsy's door, knowing Mum Zini was coming along as she usually did that time of morning.

What Gypsy didn't know was that by the time he'd wolf down some breakfast and head back to

Charleston—the nasty deed would already have taken place.

Using the "dictionary," she had defied her superiors and deciphered the coded message to ease her curiosity. An officer of Confederate Intelligence, somewhat enamored of her in Charleston one evening had shown her the decipher code employing the dictionary. Now, it went like this:

Richmond. Rush. Plan to Raid nearby Union Outpost and Supply Lines. Then Disperse.

Now Blossom's eyes flashed vibrant sparks. Once again, the joke was on Gypsy Smith!

Captain Huntington was on his way to Charleston. His swift mount traveled the dusty road but his thoughts were back at Tamarind with Blossom Angelica Fortune. As for Captain Smith, he tried not to think of the Yankee at all!

As he rode, he felt the brisk passage of wind on his face and the morning sun warmed his head and shoulders. Blossom had been a surprise to him. He'd never imagined she'd be so passionate and loving. Then, why did he have the strange feeling all the while they'd made love that she was holding part of herself from him? Though it seemed insignificant, it was in essence important that the woman he loved and married hold nothing back from him.

Up ahead was a heavily wooded area and he had it in mind to stop there in the shade and rest his mount for a spell. It was then that Rider heard the woman's scream pierce the air where only moments before all he'd heard was the constant thudding of Tiger's hoofs and the gentle passage of wind by his ears.

It was off the road a bit where the sounds of distress were coming from. But Rider halted; he couldn't go any farther. Swamp. The buggy was mired in the swamp—and then he saw the woman inside the crazily tipped conveyance.

Her blue eyes were wild. Her hair hung disheveled about her pink, flushed cheeks and she seemed to be gasping from great fear until she saw him. *Rider!* He was coming for her; he was her champion as she'd always prayed he would be someday.

Balancing himself as he walked out on the water oak's bony "knee," Rider reached the buggy, which had been sucked down into the mire up to the edge of the window, murky green slime already finding the groping white arms of Daisy Dawn Fortune; the floating black arms made him grimace painfully.

"Rider!" Daisy cried. "Please, help Lucy first! She has been swallowing the—Rider? What's wrong?" As she reached out and clung to the arm snaking about her waist, Daisy Dawn looked back over her shoulder. "No! Rider! Help her—her head has gone under! Please!"

Swinging Daisy up onto her slippery knees, trying to keep her there with one hand, he reached into the sinking buggy—but it was too late. There was nothing he could do.

"Rider!"

As he began to slip into the slime himself, Daisy reached out frantically to keep him from falling all the way in. He ordered her to let him go at once. The edge of the window was slippery with the oozy green stuff and his footing was precarious. Doing an about-face leap, Rider pushed himself from the buggy and made it onto the tree leg clutching the knee in back of him, trying not to throw Daisy Dawn off balance at the same time in front.

Guiding her off the slimy limb and onto safer ground, Rider scooped Daisy into his arms when she began to slide to the spongy ground in exhaustion. The arms that wound about his neck were frail and Captain Huntington began to think she'd not been getting enough to eat and had been working herself to death at the hospital.

Laying her down upon a swath of emerald grass, Rider disengaged her arms from around his neck. He looked down at Daisy Dawn. She was thin, frail, but still beautiful.

Rider caught himself. Since when had he thought of Daisy Dawn Fortune as beautiful and desirous? He'd always thought of her as a skinny child—she was still thin—but not without womanly curves. He noticed them now in her wet, clinging dress of pink, patched muslin. She was like a porcelain doll. White and pink and breakable.

Daisy Dawn cracked her eyes. Ridpath Huntington. Rider. Her mind spun back, back, to the first day she'd seen him. His auburn hair burnished by the sun. His smiling eyes—always looking past her to Blossom Angelica. In her dreams, in her heart she'd always cried out, *"Rider, Rider, why don't you notice me. I am pretty too. Can't you see and feel how much I care?"* If only she could see love for her burning in his purple-blue eyes. *"Oh . . . Rider, I love you . . . so much it hurts."*

144

"Daisy. Daisy." He pressed his canteen to her lips but the water trickled from the corners. "Daisy, are you all right? Speak to me."

"Rider." She opened her misty blue eyes all the way. "Rider? What happened? Where is Blackstrap?"

Blackstrap had been Daisy Dawn's protector for as long as Rider could remember. Always one could see the huge black man in attendance whenever the delicate blonde made her frequent trips into Charleston to the hospital. He was never far from her, which brought him to echo her question.

"Daisy, where is Blackstrap?"

The details of the accident came flashing back to Daisy and she spoke, as if it pained her to. "Blackstrap—has never lost control—there was something—in the road and Juniper shied."

"Juniper," Rider murmured. He looked in the direction of the buggy bogged down in the mire, sinking, sinking ever slowly. No sign of the horse.

"He took Juniper."

Rider frowned, then he understood. "Blackstrap rode Juniper back to get help?"

"Yes—Tamarind." She would not leave her maid. The captain swore. "He couldn't get to you?"

"Are you angry? Rider, don't be angry—I'm sorry."

Caressing the pink-and-white velvet of Daisy's cheek, Rider softly said, "Oh Daisy, don't be. I'm not angry, not with you." How could anyone ever find fault with Daisy Dawn or speak a harsh word to her? "It's just that . . . there's a Yankee there and—Daisy, why didn't Blackstrap pass me by on the road?"

Weakly she laughed. "First: The Yankee you speak of must be Gypsy Smith. Second: Blackstrap headed

145

toward the old tangled river road—don't worry, he's gone through there often enough when he wants to get over to Tamarind to see Kapa Lu."

Rider was forced to chuckle at that. "You mean Blackstrap actually leaves you alone for a few minutes a day to go courting? I can't believe it."

Unconsciously Rider was enjoying himself and time seemed to have no meaning. His main concern was for Daisy and nothing else seemed to matter much. Not even the message he needed to dispatch with haste to Charleston was of great concern now.

"Daisy—" Rider placed a comforting hand on her grubby arm, unaware his hands, too, were dirty. "Lucy has—drowned in the swamp."

Pulling herself up by holding on to Rider's muscled arm, Daisy said, "I know." Tears came to Daisy's eyes. "Did you know Lucy? No. I suppose you wouldn't have. She was very young. Lucy was so frail—she couldn't stand much of anything. Even though, she went with me into the hospital and—oh Rider, she cried every time one of the soldiers died. She worked so hard, taking jobs home with her, making bandages, there—have been so many casualties."

A surge of protectiveness washed through Rider, and along with it, exquisite excitement coursed in his blood. He felt, almost wildly, that he must take Daisy Dawn in his arms. What was this grand emotion he was experiencing?

"Daisy—" Rider cupped her fine chin in one big hand. "You are so thin—are you feeling well? I know you've been working hard at the hospital. I see you now and then—" *I wish I would have looked harder and noticed how lovely you really are.* He wanted to say this, but this was not the time or the place. Then the image of his beautiful bride-to-be flashed into his mind. Was he insane? He was getting married as soon as this war was over; he shouldn't be sitting here staring at Daisy Dawn as if she were the only woman on earth.

Several pairs of hooves sounded on the road just then, and Rider's gaze reluctantly left Daisy to see the three riders approaching. Good, he thought, Gypsy Smith was not among them. But Blossom Angelica was, and Rider wondered why her black eyes were narrowing just now as she expertly reined up before him and Daisy Dawn. The black's sharp hooves came near and Rider pulled Daisy to her feet just in time. Looking up at Blossom, Rider frowned. Her hard expression softened at once, then the lovely lips moved.

"Jezebel, you naughty girl," she chided the big black, "you just behave now, you hear? You stop that prancing around—you're going to step right on the folks. Rider, what has happened? I hear that Daisy Dawn has had a most unfortunate accident." Black eyes flashed down over the dainty blonde. "Poor Daisy Dawn, you do seem to have the poorest luck, honey. Where's your maid? Are you all alone?"

Clenching his hand at his side, Rider spoke tersely. "Her maid is no more." With his gauntlet he directed her gaze to the shiny black top of the curricle. "She's there."

"Oh deah," Blossom said, lapsing into her Southern drawl, "the poor black girl. I am sorry, darlin' Daisy. Now, you must come along to Tamarind—I'll take real good care of you until you are well enough to go home."

Blackstrap stepped forward. "Ah takes good care of Daisy Dawn, Miz Blossom. You doan needs to. Ah take her home and see dat she goes straight to bed."

"Hmmm"—Blossom's eyes slanted wickedly—"I just bet you do take good care of Daisy Dawn." Her eyes roved over the huge black man with muscles rippling from kinky head to heavily shod feet. "You are so big and strong," she complimented, drawing out the word *strong*.

The third rider, Jasmine Joe, shot Blossom's profile a look of intense dislike before he reined his mount over to the tragic sight to examine the damage and what could be done in getting the curricle out.

"Where's Captain Smith?" Rider clipped, unaware he had taken Daisy's hand into his and had been rubbing it slowly, comfortingly with his large thumb.

The tender gesture was not lost on Blossom Angelica. Inwardly she seethed with jealousy, and her eyes rested on Daisy's angelic face and plans ticked in her devious mind.

"He rode out not long after you did, *darlin'*."

"I must be on my way," Rider said, patting Daisy's hand before looking sheepish and dropping it to her side. Daisy had not said a word since Blossom arrived and Rider wondered what she could be thinking of so deeply. He turned to her. "Daisy, are you sure you will be all right if Blackstrap takes you home?"

Her eyes tried not to worship his as she looked up into them. "I'll be fine, Rider."

"Ah takes her home, Cap'n Hunt'ton. Doan you worry none about Daisy Dawn."

Chapter Twelve

Gypsy Smith's secret military cipher was decoded at headquarters. The Union forces were waiting and the joke was turned back on Blossom Angelica, though she had not caught wind of it yet. However, the seemingly minor event to commence was to have far-reaching results.

Both Robert E. Lee and Joseph Hooker were eager to take the offensive. Lee had been considering with Jackson an invasion of Pennsylvania, but in the absence of Longstreet's, divisions had to resign the initiative to Hooker. Hooker aimed at forcing Lee out of his entrenchments by a wide turning movement over the upper fords of the Rappahannock above its junction with the Rapidan, and sent his newly organized cavalry corps to destroy the railways in Lee's rear and intercept his retreat. He thus deprived himself of the "eyes of his army," and to the absence of his cavalry, all except one brigade, was largely attributable the failure of the Chancellorville Campaign. One month later Captain Smith was with Hooker when he retreated across the Rappahannock and Lee's victory was dearly bought at the price of Jackson's life.

When Hooker was wounded by cannon shot, Captain Smith had also taken a wound to his leg. Gypsy Smith now walked with a slight limp but was with Hooker when he retreated to the north bank of the river via United States ford. The campaign cost 16,800 Union and 12,800 Confederate casualties.

Captain Huntington with Mosby and his Rangers raided other Union outposts and supply lines, then, as usual, dispersed. Mosby's men followed the practice of dividing among themselves the property they captured and were therefore looked upon as robbers by the Federal authorities. The Rangers made one of their most spectacular raids to go down in history when they slipped through the Federal lines at Fairfax Courthouse and captured Brigadier General D. H. Stoughton and some of his men. These exploits were making Mosby and his men heroes in the South and forced the Union armies to devote a great deal of effort to hunting them down. Thus, the Rangers had been declared outlaws by the Union Forces.

With a thick braid down her back, and wearing a blue dress with fitted sleeves and patched petticoats, Angela helped make comforters for the soldiers who were going without blankets. She wondered if she'd ever see Gypsy Smith alive again—he'd been gone for more than two months now.

When Daisy Dawn came by to ask Blossom if she

could come to the hospital to help, Blossom had been too busy with a few friends that were staying on at the house, as their own house in Charleston had been closed for a week for minor repairs.

Some had stayed to protect their homes from Yankees in any way they could find. One girl had already returned home, but Annabelle Huntington lingered on, always eager to hear and spread gossip.

The August heat was oppressive and the leaves on the vines and trees in the gardens hung limply. The heat was even worse in Charleston, but at Tamarind, one could find a little bit of comfort with the evening breeze being cooled by the Ashley.

Earlier that morning Angela had stood at her window—Gypsy's window actually, for she loved to come and stand in his room to *remember*—and she'd watched the wide, curved, slow-rolling river. The Ashley was a platinum-pink blur and she could barely see it through wispy-thin floating wraiths of pale gray morning mist. She'd slipped out in dressing gown and robe, going to the spot where she'd been found by Robert Neil. She went there often, to try and remember back, back, always trying to see back into what was before.

Old gray beards of Spanish moss draped, motionless, from heavy branches of live oaks, pulled down with moisture from the cool, raw morning air. Angela's entire soul cried out for her beloved ones from the past. She knew there existed people she loved dearly. Inside of her, deep, she knew that they searched for her. And someday, someday, she prayed, she would be reunited with them.

Angela knew she'd not been married, for the night

she'd been with Gypsy Smith bore testimony to the fact she was—or had been—a maid still.

Angela had made friends here too, like Daisy Dawn Fortune. Instantly they'd come to enjoy each other's company. Robert Neil had even joined them, always questioning Daisy on the possibility of their being a husband in the near future. His care and love seemed to go very deep for his charming little niece. That she was tiny was an understatement. Angela was small herself but Daisy was as Robert called her—a porcelain doll.

Robert Neil would sound as if he were whining as he said, "Daisy Dawn, you are so tiny and frail I fear that you shall break one of these days, with all the work you're doing at that hospital. Can't they find more robust figures for nurses? You'll be in no condition to become some handsome plantation lord's lovely wife. Just look at your nails, they're worn down to a frazzle, dear dear Daisy Dawn. You are my niece, you know, and I must watch out for you as there is only that big darkie Blackstrap looking out for you. Look at Angela here, she is my wife and takes good care of herself, even though she is always rolling bandages and making blankets—why they've even torn up some of the carpeting at Persimmon Wood—ah yes, that is your Plantation, isn't it, dear Daisy? Here, too, the carpet is going. Blossom Angelica is fit to be tied, she loved that carpeting in the hall, but alas, we needed it, didn't we, dears?" He looked at Daisy first and then the young woman he still thought of as his wife, even though he had seemed to lapse into forgetfulness of what a wife's wifely duties even entailed. He only kissed her forehead and called her his Angel, and warned Blossom not to harm her in any way or it would grieve him so very much.

Daisy Dawn only smiled at Robert Neil, and he adored her. She was the very picture of sweetness and purity, as was Angela—his Windswept Angel.

Long moments stretched by now as the young women sat in the drawing room doing whatever their busy little hands could do for the Confederates. Annabelle was the first to break the long-held silence in the room.

"Where has Blossom gone off to now? She strolls around the garden with a parasol and a new French creation while we sit and work our fingers to the bone in our patched skirts and pettis. Why did she even ask me to come here?" But she directed her gaze at Daisy Dawn, as if that petite nurse was the cause of their not having any fun.

"Now, now," Robert Neil chided while rolling a bandage, "we must be nice to Blossom Angelica. She's a Southern beauty and she must be presentable to the boys in uniform."

"She's nothing but a Narcissa. Vain, arrogant—"

"And beautiful," Robert Neil finished for Annabelle Huntington. "Now do behave. Where is your brother fighting now, my dear?"

"Whitney Mayfield told me her brother has said Rider has become one of Mosby's Rangers."

Annabelle, with her eyes on her work, missed the movement when Daisy's head jerked up and her hands became still. The blonde's eyes lowered once again as Annabelle went on. But the redhead was not so ignorant of where Daisy's thoughts were—they never strayed far from dreaming of Rider Huntington and becoming his bride someday. She might as well dream on, Annabelle thought, for Rider was as good as Blossom's husband already. And Annabelle could tell that Blossom had not waited to become "his" on their wedding night. They'd already shared their night of wedded bliss.

Rubbing her nose with its field of gay freckles, Annabelle went on, "All the daring raids seem to be blamed on Mosby's Rangers. They're being accused of every crime, even the seven deadly sins—and rape."

"R-rape?" Daisy's head shot up, her bandage spilling to the floor and unrolling. "How can you believe that of your own brother?"

Annabelle grinned impishly. "Never said I believed all that trash being spread by Union sympathizers."

"Well!" Blossom appeared in the doorway. "That explains it then, darlings." Sweeping into the room like a ray of sunshine itself, she declared, "Those who side with Bluebellies are nothing but trash—black or white."

Blossom's French lawn day dress was the color of new green leaves in springtime. Her slippers were worn but better than most other young ladies' in the South. Her jet black hair had been pulled back from her forehead, leaving only a few curls coiling saucily upon her brow, the mass of it in back bouncing to her waist in long, gleaming, sausage curls.

Robert Neil started humming "Yankee Doodle," causing Blossom to gasp, going over to tap him chidingly on the head. "Now don't you be singing that Yankee garbage in here, Robert Neil, you naughty boy." Then she bent to kiss him sweetly on the forehead. "I know you're trying to be funny, love, but no one here likes Yankees." She turned to face Angela, Annabelle, and Daisy Dawn. "Right, ladies?"

Angela looked up just then, saying, "Gypsy Smith is a Yankee."

"Oh—" Blossom sighed and shrugged one shoulder. "Don't we all know. Everybody knows Yankees are bluebellied cowards too. You'd better hum 'Dixie,' little brother."

"I'm bigger than you are, Blos." Robert Neil stood up to show her. He began humming "Dixie" while marching about the room, tooting an imaginary horn now and then. He stopped all of a sudden. "There. Did you like that?"

"Yes, Robert, I liked it very much. Now, darling boy, why don't you go upstairs for your nap, I wouldn't want you to be tired out later. After supper we'll go for a nice walk in the garden."

"Yes." Robert Neil grinned from ear to ear. "I'd like that—indeed I would." He walked out of the room, still humming "Dixie" and tooting his horn.

Annabelle set down her bandages. Suddenly she blurted, "Did you hear that Gypsy Smith has been wounded?"

Both Daisy and Angela gasped. Disappointedly they wondered why she had waited until Blossom's appearance to tell of it. During the past few nights Annabelle had seen a visitor in the gardens, a young Frenchman who'd only recently become enamored of her, so she'd forgotten to tell about Gypsy Smith and his unfortunate accident, of which the news was several weeks old by now.

"How—bad?" Angela found herself asking, not even feeling Daisy's hand touch her arm comfortingly. She'd spoken of Gypsy Smith often, confiding that she thought she was in love with the Yankee captain.

"One does hear much of the gossip when one lives in Charleston."

"Boastful and braggart Charleston." Blossom giggled impishly, adding, "I love it!"

"Blossom," Annabelle chided, "do listen for once. Or don't you care that your own brother has been wounded?"

"La! Gypsy Smith is no more my brother than the man in the moon." Sashaying about the room, she snatched up a neatly rolled bandage and then tossed it back into the crate they had been carefully packed in.

"That is not a very nice thing to say, Blossom," Angela put in, unable to hold her opinion back. "I'm sorry, Blossom, but he is your half brother, is he not?"

"Oh yes, but I have none of that wild Indian blood that flows in Gypsy Smith's veins."

"Indian?" Annabelle looked thoughtful. "Yes, I've heard this before. Thought it was only rumor. Isn't he Suquamish?"

"Cherokee." She changed quickly to a different subject, disliking having Gypsy Smith as the object of conversation—unless it could somehow do harm to him. "Word from the boys has come through the blockade that your section of town has not taken on any further damage, Annabelle, your house won't be *completely* destroyed, I hope. But then you and Rider

156

always have Tanglewood Plantation. I still say it was Yankees who burned down that barn causing your parents to perish in the blaze—La! it was almost as if they'd locked them in there."

Angela wished Annabelle would say how badly Gypsy Smith had been hurt but she didn't want to seem overly concerned. It was uncomfortable being the object of Blossom's displeasure. The fiery young woman had complete control when Gypsy Smith was not in residence. Still, she had to have her say in some matters, like their gentle neighbors for instance.

"Yankees didn't do it, Blossom," Angela cut in. "Blackstrap has said that Tanglewood's black folks concluded it was nothing but a common accident. Doors have been known to latch themselves when shut from the inside—and then there was the draft caused by the blaze. They were found by the door, overcome by smoke. The barn didn't burn down all the way, Blossom."

Blossom turned on Angela. "What would you know? You have lost your memory, Angela. And you have no say in this war between the states, you can't even recall whose side you are on. Have you taken sides after spending a night in Gypsy Smith's bed, Angela darling?"

"No." Angela looked toward the window. "I can't say that I have."

"It should not be all that hard to decide. Would you like the Yankees to chase you out of the only home you know?" She spread lily-white hands. "You are living with us under the act of my brother's charity. It would kill him if he found out you spent a night with Gypsy Smith; he thinks of you as his

157

angelic little wife. If it wasn't for Robert Neil, you would be out there with the rest of the wanderers who have no more homes left to call their own—all because of the damn Yankees!"

"Blossom—" Annabelle covered her ears. "Such language."

"Fiddle! It's only a little bitty word, Anna. Don't be such a goosefeather."

Resting her hand on Angela's arm, Daisy Dawn said, "You can always come to stay at Persimmon Wood with me and Blackstrap, Angela. We don't have much, but what we do have we'll share. We still have a few cows and chickens, plenty potatoes. The blacks are all gone, so there'd only be the three of us."

"Shut your mouth, Daisy Dawn!" Blossom went to loom above the diminutive blonde. "Angela is the only one besides myself who is keeping Robert Neil from going crazy." When the three women exchanged slow looks, Blossom went on as if they'd not frowned at her words. "As you know, Robert Neil believes Angela is his bride—if he lost his Angel, I don't know what he would do. This war has already taken its toll on the poor boy, and I'm going to make damn—*darn* sure that nobody steals anything from him. Especially not the—the Bluebellies!"

Staring down at her motionless hands, Daisy appeared whipped for the time. She only said, "This war is making us have a bad case of nerves, that's all." Slowly she lifted her head, looked straight into Blossom's black eyes. "I would never steal anything away from my uncle—nor from you."

Blossom turned her back on Daisy Dawn, tossing

over her shoulder, "La, there's nothing you *could* steal, Daisy. Angela can go to your house for a visit if she likes. But she can't stay too long." Brusquely she faced Angela, who was about to say what she, herself, could and couldn't do. "Otherwise," Blossom finished, dashing anything Angela would have said, "Robert darling will worry and his health can't afford that, now can it?"

No one said a word.

The next morning Angela was about to return to the drawing room after she'd had a meager breakfast of corn muffins with a few bits of salted pork. It was the last of the meat from the larder. No coffee or tea remained—only water. A thief, or thieves, had come onto Tamarind land and stolen the chickens, but even at that everyone on the plantation had shared a laugh or two, for no one had gotten close enough to Quackser Henny to carry her away too. And the queer duck had probably even pecked a few shins before the robbers got away!

Angela stepped up to the drawing room door, about to enter when the voices of Blossom and Annabelle froze her in her tracks. That what she was hearing was merely cruel gossip about Gypsy Smith's affairs she couldn't realize at this time.

"I think Angela is in love with Gypsy Smith, don't you?"

"Love—pooh! Women don't love, Anna." Blossom looked at the young woman with the stunning red hair down to her waist. "We only *use* men, honey, use them for our pleasure. That's all men are good for."

Seeing the stunned look cross the freckled face, Blossom hurried on. "'Course, there's Robert Neil and Rider darling, both considered quite manly to me. Robert darling is only a bit confused for the time, when this silly war is over he'll be back to normal."

"What do you mean, we only use men for our pleasure? How many men have you had, Blossom?"

"La! Anna darling, I've only had one." Her eyes twinkled. "And he was very good."

"How would you know, if you've only had one man?"

Blossom swallowed slowly and peered into Annabelle's eyes. "Seriously, darling, a woman naturally knows these things, if a man is good or if he isn't. Would I still want to marry Rider if I didn't think he was the greatest? He's gorgeous and a wild animal in bed!"

Unfortunately Daisy Dawn had just joined Angela outside the door. She'd at first wondered what was holding the lovely Angela in a trance, until she came closer to the door herself. Together, both eager to hear more of the men they loved, they put their heads closer, keeping out of sight. It was wrong, but this was love not war, their eyes seemed to be telling each other.

"Blossom!" Annabelle gasped, waiting to hear more just the same. "What do you think Gypsy Smith is like in bed?"

"Anna dear, whatever are you thinking? That Bluebelly probably doesn't even have a manhood—nothing to speak of anyway."

Out in the hall, Angela seethed. She'd never witnessed this side of Blossom's nature. Blossom was beginning to appear tarnished in her eyes.

"Well, I've heard wild stories about Gypsy Smith and women, and wondered if they could be true."

"Annabelle, who cares. Gypsy Smith is a Yankee half-breed. But I'll tell you this, I think he has dallied with Kapa Lu before."

Annabelle breathed, *"No."*

Blossom's eyes danced with wicked fire and Annabelle thought they were the biggest, deepest, darkest eyes she'd ever seen. They had fire and velvet in them. Damp velvet. Soiled. At that moment Annabelle knew that Blossom had lain with far more men than only Rider. Annabelle had it in her to warn Rider, but she decided her brother would have to be blind if he couldn't see it—or he'd have to catch her in the act with another man.

"Yes, yes, yes." Blossom tossed her head, hissing the lie low, "I saw them with my own eyes!"

"I think Gypsy Smith actually hates all women," Annabelle said, to keep Blossom talking about the man; she thought he was one fascinatingly dangerous male.

"He's a coward, I tell you. Gypsy Smith is afraid of being hurt."

"What do you mean?"

"Well," Blossom began, "he's a bastard to begin with. He has deep emotional scars, ones that will most likely never heal. Never all the way."

"Why did your mother keep one son and discard the other like so much trash? Didn't Angelica send Gypsy Smith away?"

"Melantha has said that my mother thought Gypsy Smith had turned evil and she had to keep him away from her new baby, Robert Neil."

"How old was Gypsy Smith at the time?"

"Oh—about seven, I think Melantha said."

"Melantha is the old black woman they call the Black Flower, isn't she? She must be dead by now."

Blossom giggled. "Almost."

"Mama pushed Gypsy Smith out into the world when he was only a boy, sent him to some godforsaken place across the sea. Melantha said she'd seen a vision and in it she thought Gypsy Smith was living with some witch in Africa. Imagine that, but I wouldn't doubt it, him being the beast that he is. A witch is the only kind of mother capable of raising a bastard like Gypsy Smith."

"Why do you hate him so much?" Annabelle wanted to know. "Has he done something to hurt you?"

Her keen eyes catching a flash of blue muslin peeping out at the lower framing of the door, Blossom pretended nothing was out of order and went on following a deep sigh.

"Yes he did, Anna. When he first came here he said he must teach me a lesson because I was being so unruly. Oh Anna, you know how he always tries to take command of everything—he's so—overpowering. I'm ashamed to say what he did, but I'll tell you anyway and I know you'll promise not to tell anyone. No? Good. He dragged me—into the broom closet—and said he was going to punish me for being such a bad girl. Anna, oh, he is such an animal—he pushed up my skirts and—and shoved me down." Blossom choked back a sob, peeping up between her hands to see Annabelle's big eyes and anticipating the man's next move. "He beat me with a belt, Anna, he beat me black and blue—couldn't even sit down without a pillow for a whole week—that's what a cruel beast Gypsy Smith is!"

Out in the hall, the two young women exchanged searching looks. Angela had always wondered why Blossom had seemed to bear such a grudge toward her half brother. Now she knew. Or did she really, she wondered painfully.

Seated deep in the huge tub, Angela scrubbed her body vigorously as she wanted to cleanse her body of any memory of Gypsy Smith's deft hands, burning kisses, tongue, thrusts—everything.

After overhearing Blossom's horrible story, she had come to the conclusion that Gypsy Smith was nothing, and everything evil—a reviler, womanizer, user, and perhaps ever murderer. He had beaten a poor defenseless woman; what more proof did she need that he was no good?

Chapter Thirteen

Charleston, South Carolina

"Yankees! The Yankees are shelling the city! Run for your life! Yankee shells! They got past the forts!"

People screamed. Scattered in all directions. They ran to and fro against the backdrop of pale, narrow, tall houses that shimmered in the haze of heat blanketing the old city of Charleston. Where only moments before the wide streets had been quiet and deserted with only the deep bell sounding four strokes—four of the clock—now pandemonium reigned after the searing, crashing sound rent the heavy air.

Like a bird of prey, the dull black cannonball rose over the city. Falling lazily, it crashed into the marsh and was swallowed instantly by the oozy black mud.

The bells of Saint Michael's were still ringing, sounding the alarm when Angela and Blossom rushed to the windows on the second floor; they had been unable to see anything of the commotion from below. Whitney Mayfield followed, her patched pink muslin soaked through under the arms and between her pointed breasts. Her heart was beating fast; she was wringing her hands together continually.

"Oh where are they?" she said of her parents.

"They should have been home by now," Blossom said. "You're right."

"Don't worry," Angela tried to calm the frightened girl, "they will be home soon."

"Oh damn. What are we doing here," Blossom snapped, peering out the window, "we should have stayed at Tamarind."

"You said you wanted some excitement, Blossom," Angela reminded her. "You wanted to be near the harbor, where the action is taking place."

"Well, it sure appears to be *some* action. Oh! Was that a bomb? Did you girls feel the floor shudder?"

"Not a bomb, Blossom, a cannonball," Angela instructed.

"Oh la, Angela, what would you know about such things?" Going on without giving Angela a chance to answer she squealed, "Let's go up to the captain's walk! We'll be able to see everything that's going on!"

Whitney backed up, drawing her arm across her perspiring forehead. "Not me. It's too hot up there, and anyway I'm going to stay down here and wait for Papa and Mama, they should be here soon, don't you think?"

"'Course," was all Blossom offered in the way of comfort.

"I will go up with Blossom," Angela said. "You stay down here." She patted Whitney's hand. "And

165

don't worry—"

Blossom wouldn't let Angela finish. "Don't *worry,* the house isn't falling down—yet!"

"Ohhh," Whitney muttered, almost swooning.

Angela and Blossom were able to see for miles and miles from the fourth floor level. Whitney was correct. The scorching sun had been beating on the captain's walk all day and it felt like they were being slowly roasted alive. Shading their eyes with their hands they looked out to sea.

"There." Angela pointed to the dark speck rising from James Island.

"It's getting bigger—coming this way!" Blossom screeched. She ducked down behind the fence for protection, which was no protection at all. "Angela—get down!"

"It won't make any difference, Blossom."

Angela stood straight, with her shoulders back, her breasts thrust softly forward, watching the cannon-ball. She could also see shutters opening and heads popping out all over the city. The shot fell on Meeting Street into one of the walled gardens splitting several magnolia trees. Wood exploded. Wilted leaves went spinning high into the air. Below, doors to houses opened. Ladies and men and servants spilled outside, looking dazed, holding their heads, peering up into the sky.

"Damn Yankees!" Blossom shouted, rising, shaking her white fist. "Damn, bluebellied Yankee slime!"

The alarm bell continued to peal as the firemen burst into Saint Michael's, the voices almost drowned in the sound of the bell as they tried to get the people to leave.

Another cannonball. The deep booming of ship's cannons. Crowds of people were half wild, half terrified. Horses screamed in terror as another cannonball made its mark a stable and carriage house on Church Street. Flames burst and running people were being injured by flying debris.

Angela looked down at the billowing clouds of smoke. A boy pressed his mount on, galloping from house to house, street to street, yelling, "Yankees!" as another cannonball plowed a furrow in the cobblestones. "Yankees are breakin' through!"

As the black ball was falling toward them, Angela had watched, hugging Blossom to her. Both had been too mesmerized by all that was happening to move one tiny step. The scene so overwhelmed Angela that she felt her throat close painfully. Some part of her mind understood that she'd never known the horrors of opposition. She knew her life had been relatively peaceful and serene before she was discovered half-alive on the banks of the Ashley.

Just then a loud terrible rumbling filled the heavy air. "What is it?" Blossom stammered, clutching Angela's shoulders wildly. "Oh—" she moaned, "I just knew we should have stayed at Tamarind, we would have been safe there." Looking down to the street, she gasped, "Angela, look, isn't that Gypsy Smith? In civilian clothes? Surely—it's him. But—a beard?"

"He—he is limping." Angela covered her mouth with one hand. "It's his wound but—what do you suppose he's doing—?"

Blossom was fast recovering from her fear as she

snipped, "Look at that, will you? He's with that whore Stephanie Browden—see, he's pulling her along with his arm tucked in hers." Blossom tipped her chin haughtily. "How shameless, going to find a little nest to tuck Stephanie into—no doubt."

Angela, too, momentarily forgot her fear. Then the sound of artillery blended with thunder. Fire pumpers raced down the street. The last Angela saw of Gypsy Smith he was pushing through those milling about, still wondering if they should go home or stay out and watch the agitation on the street.

"The Yankees aren't getting through!" someone shouted. "They only got the one Parrot rifle gun!"

A robust Negress tossed her arms into the air, shouting, "Praise de Lawd!"

"Stupid blacks," Blossom snorted, "They never know whose side they're on, Yankee or Reb!"

"I believe most of them are neutral, Blossom. Those that have been set free by their gentle plantation lords don't care to leave, while the others rebel."

"Hush up, Angela, what would you know about it, you sound just like one of Lincoln's underdogs. You sound so simple. Freeing slaves is ignorant, so let's hear no more about it."

Undercurrents of compassion ran deep in Angela, for the blacks, for Robert Neil, and even Blossom Angelica. She'd come to care deeply for them all. As for Gypsy Smith, he'd cut her to the quick, and her feelings for him were confused and troubled. And now futile. He was an unfeeling rogue. A womanizer. Liar, saying he'd loved her. She'd felt a sharp ache seeing him with another woman. Could she ever

168

forgive him for that? It was a painful stituation in which she found herself.

There was another loud crack of thunder. This time rain came blasting down out of the heavens in a tropical deluge. People, ironically, began to run for home to get out of the downpour although they had not been in any hurry to hide from cannon fire.

With long hair plastered down, Angela and Blossom made their way carefully back inside the house. Picking up her sodden skirts on either side, Angela gave one more glance back out the window they passed on the way down, muttering under her breath, *"Damn Yankees."*

The sound of rain upon the panes lulled Angela as she sat with Blossom, Whitney, and her parents, who had finally come home after the shelling. She stared into the fire of the Mayfield's hearth, wishing she'd never witnessed the scene of Gypsy Smith walking with the Browden woman. Angela's heart was breaking in two. She knew he'd been her first love ever—and last.

Vern Mayfield rose from the couch, going to retrieve his slouch hat and long gray overcoat. His wife got up and followed him out into the hall, having explained to the girls that her husband was going out to visit some friends of his, then she was going up to bed.

"Good night, girls. Don't worry. The officers have been here reassuring us and warning to be careful when stepping out because of fire and timbers that might be falling."

"Oh wonderful," Blossom gritted under her breath while smiling Mrs. Mayfield out the door. When the woman had gone out, closing the parlor door, Blossom shot up from the deep-cushioned chair. "Daily the Union is adding ships to the blockade and she says not to worry. Reassuring? Pooh!"

Rising from her slumped position over the arm chair, Whitney listlessly said, "Mama means well, Blos, really she does."

"'Course," Blossom drawled. "Mama didn't even care if Whitney darling was burning to death in one of the fires, or being trampled in the streets, all she and Papa could do was to stand out there in a daze watching the shells fall with the other nincompoops!"

In one stiff motion, Whitney shot to her feet. "Don't talk about my mama like that, Blossom Angelica Fortune! If I remember right, you were up there on the captain's walk gawking down at all the folks running about and the shells flying into the city."

Now Angela rose, but more slowly. "Please, please, don't argue, everyone's nerves are on edge but that is no reason to be at each other's throats. It is the Yankees we should be railing against."

"La!" Blossom came around to face Angela. "Bless your little heart, Angela dear, you're becoming a sweet little Southern gal just like the rest of us. I knew you'd see the light, sugar, humph, especially after seeing Gypsy Smith strolling down the street with Stephanie Browden on his arm. Why darling, you could be with child, and do you think the bastard would give a damn?"

"Please not so—" Angela grimaced at Blossom's harsh words. She hoped that Whitney had not caught the hasty statement that had tumbled out accidentally from Blossom.

But Charlestonian Whitney Mayfield felt her proper little ears burning. "Blossom Angelica, remember that you are a young lady of the proprieties! And certainly, Stephanie Browden is not a—" But for some unknown reason, Blossom didn't want Angela to know that Stephanie was a married woman, her reputation clean as a whistle. Whitney couldn't understand why Blossom wanted to make either Stephanie or Gypsy Smith look bad. Scandalized by Blossom's behavior, she turned away, realizing what a mistake it had been to invite the black-haired vixen here.

Blossom's reputation was preceding her, but Whitney hadn't believed she was the flippant tart all the soldiers said she was. They'd been boasting of their conquests with the young woman, passing it around that she was an easy mark. They said she was a Confederate spy, too. Whitney, however, had given Blossom Fortune the benefit of the doubt. The spy activities she didn't mind. All but for one thing. Now she could see that Blossom was living up to her bad reputation. And Angela—Robert's sweet little wife. Pregnant? With Gypsy Smith's child? Shocking! And why doesn't she stick up for herself instead of just sitting there smiling charitably at Blossom Angelica!

Clearing her throat, Whitney brought up a question. "Is Gypsy Smith a Yankee captain?" She wasn't all that sure.

"'Course, honey," Blossom purred. "Didn't you know that?"

"I thought so." Gazing sideways at Angela, she gave the chestnut-haired beauty a dirty look. "Anyone who would make love with a Yankee makes love with pigs."

Seeing what Whitney was up to, Blossom saw red. Only *she* could make snide remarks to folks from Tamarind—no one else. Especially not puny Whitney Mayfield.

"Whitney honey, who do you make love with?" She tapped her lips. "Hmm, Harv Jackson?"

"Why—that was only—" Whitney blustered for words but could find none.

Clutching her hands, Angela rose slowly, announcing, "I think I will go to bed now. It has been a long day. Excuse me."

When Angela was gone, Blossom sashayed over to loom above Whitney's chair. "You little hypocrite. I know Harv Jackson got his hands into your bodice, honey, and he said he squeezed your backside too."

"Blossom Fortune!"

"Hush up, you little slut." Blossom shoved her back down into her chair. "You sit there all night." She poked the girl's chest. "And don't you move a muscle, you naughty girl."

Eyes round with fear, Whitney watched Blossom roll her hips as she exited the room, her nasty laugh floating back to Whitney. Afraid to move, even a muscle, Whitney turned her mind to musing over what she'd heard of the "Fortune twins," as they were called. Robert Neil and Blossom Angelica, both bad but in different ways. Rumor had it that Robert Neil

172

was mad as a March hare. What was worse, they said Blossom was possessed with a devil. Whitney believed it.

Whitney finally did move, and when she moved, it was fast. Grabbing her cloak at midnight, she slipped out the back way keeping out of the dangerous streets. All sorts of riffraff were roaming the city. She crossed Meeting Street and hurried toward the Browden house on the Battery. Gypsy Smith was the Black Moth, top *agent provocateur* for Union Military Intelligence—she was sure of it. Whitney was terrified to be calling on him at this hour, and she wouldn't except she had perfect knowledge of Stephanie's sterling reputation. Stephanie was no more a whore than her own mother was.

Blossom Angelica had gone too far this time, scaring Whitney half to death. "Now I believe Blossom did steal Lizzy's handsome Johnny Reb away from her. How many others have lost their loves because of her whorish ways?"

Whitney spoke to herself softly, mainly to keep her fear in check. Never had she been out on the streets at this hour by herself. Excitement flooded her. Never before, either, had she been so daring—and foolish. She was being a traitor. But then, so had Annabelle, she'd learned. The South was losing anyway, so what did one more Rebel spy tossed in jail count. The Black Moth had been searching for this one for a long time. Whitney knew, for sure, she was handing over into his velvet clutches the infamous Angel Dixie, rumored to be Gypsy Smith's half sister!

What would he do with her?

After Whitney Mayfield had gone, Gypsy Smith sat brooding in the Browden's dining room. He'd been having a late-night snack. Stephanié had gone to sleep after tucking her little girl into bed. Her husband, Paul, was north in Washington.

Strange, how the courses of people's lives became altered. Paul Browden worked for the Secret Service Bureau himself. He'd been a Johnny Reb a year ago, but when those same Rebs captured and raped his Northern cousin, he went over to the Yankee side. Though she was still alive, it was barely. Sara had taken great risks. She'd pushed through to great success in ways impossible for simple males. When first caught, pretty little Sara had received threats, then a prison term, and then she'd known the freedom to try again. But it had been Sara's last time. Some said it was deserters that captured Sara; others said not. Whomever, it was rumored to be the Johnny Rebs.

Gypsy Smith sighed and propped his stockinged feet up on a green-and-blue striped upholstered chair, sipping hot tea, though he would have preferred brandy or black coffee.

Sometimes it seemed that everybody was spying on everybody else and talking volubly on the subject, in newspapers, parlors, and bars, and on street corners. Nevertheless, few officials did anything to halt the enemy's espionage.

He'd never suspected Blossom Angelica. Or maybe he'd just been blind to the fact because she was his own flesh and blood. Moodily he stared across the table and a lovely vision came to him. His body hardened with a pleasurable ache. Angela. Why had he been so quick to accuse her when right under his nose all the time it had been Blossom who'd been involved in "activities." Of course, Angel Dixie.

Spies ranged from shoe clerks to young plantation owners, lawyers to *grandes dames*, actresses to plump housewives. Why not the sister of a young plantation owner?

What few men dared try, the women did, and got away with it. They bought, cajoled, stole, and seduced for their cause. They worked cunningly, boldly, snagging military secrets, plans of strategy, and vital projects.

Gypsy Smith stared at nothing. But who was this Angela? Angela with no last name?

There was a twenty-four-hour respite, then the Swamp Angel began shelling again. It was early in the morning as Angela and Blossom were making their way to the hospital, to see if they could get a ride back home with Daisy Dawn later that day, when the two young women bumped into none other than Gypsy Smith.

The Swamp Angel was just firing its thirty-eighth round when it exploded. The Charlestonians cheered when hearing the loud explosion rolling across the waters to the city and the bright glare was seen by everyone who was outside at the time.

Looking up into the sky, Angela was suddenly aware that someone watched them intently from across the street. Her gaze lowered. Then she saw him. He was so handsome in blue jeans and a blousey shirt that she stared open-mouthed.

Angela shifted on her feet uncomfortably.

Her curiosity rising, Blossom prodded, "Who *are* you staring at, Angela?"

Shading her eyes against the searching rays of sun, Blossom glanced across the street. Just another civilian, she thought. Where were all the officers when you wanted to be escorted somewhere?

"It *is* him," Angela softly said, liking the dashing beard.

Blossom looked again. Something about the way he smiled under that shadowed chin caught her attention. Suddenly a harsh scowl distorted Blossom's beautiful face. Under her breath, she said, "Oh—it's only *him*." Then she said out loud, with a snicker, "The bearded rogue."

Part Two

Angel Dixie

Chapter Fourteen

Angela wore a carefully mended dress of mauve lawn trimmed with pale pink and green ribbon. Captain Smith thought she had never looked lovelier or more desirable. There was no time to stand and stare. Work needed to be done. He stepped out into the street and headed toward them, revitalized by the sight of Angela but wondering what she was doing here in Charleston at this dangerous time. Did he see her back away just now?

Taking a deep, steady breath, Angela said with some bitterness, "Blossom, let's not wait for him. Look, he's coming this way and I have nothing to say to him."

Angela had to get away, for she was determined not to reveal her joy at seeing Gypsy Smith again. Despite his simple attire he could never remain anonymous to her; she'd know him anywhere. Even with the short beard he sported. Her nostrils flared with fury. Besides, he had been with the Browden woman after he'd declared his love for her. He was insufferable!

"You are so right, Angela." Blossom sniffed disdainfully. "Let us find our own way home, we can do it. We got here with the Mayfields when they were visiting Persimmon Wood, didn't we?"

"What?" Angela faced Blossom squarely. "I thought you said we could get a ride back with Daisy Dawn today. Have you already forgotten that we were headed there just now?"

"I—I forgot." Glancing back over her shoulder and seeing Gypsy Smith not far behind, Blossom pulled Angela along.

"Forgot what?" Her steps slowed, dragging Blossom back with her. "Blossom, if you think that I am going to accept a ride from just anybody you have got to be out of your—"

"'Morning, ladies."

They both walked on silently. But Angela had seen him coming and now she walked slowly, her hips swaying, pretending not to be in any hurry to avoid him though that was her sole intent.

As they continued to keep their backs turned, Gypsy narrowed his deep brown eyes and walked forward, stopping right in front of them. Blossom plowed straight ahead, bumping right into his powerful, well-developed body. Catching her by the shoulders, he set her aside.

"Unhand me, Yankee!"

Captain Smith glared at her. "Trying to get me in trouble, minx? The Confederates are swarming this city, as well you must know." He felt the tight stretch of the recently purchased clothes he was wearing, perfect for his mission, and his anonymity was pleasing to him. He'd even grown a short beard.

180

Spotting a young man across the street, Captain Smith called to him. His voice was resonant and impressive, sending pleasurable thrills up and down Angela's body. She swallowed hard, trying not to reveal her anger but her breath burned in her throat every time she envisioned him with the Browden woman on his arm—and she wanted to simply scream . . . scream!

"Bickles," the captain said when the corporal made to salute him, "not here."

"Yessir!" Bickles visibly relaxed his stance. "Nossir!" Then Alan Bickles's eyes lit up when the black-haired beauty turned her face toward him and smiled. He swallowed hard and squared his shoulders. Embarrassment crept across Bickles's freckled features. "You wanted something of me, sir." He stared at Captain Smith with a growing grin that said, "If it has anything to do with these *lovely ladies,* give the order, man!"

As Blossom half listened to Gypsy Smith speaking to the handsome, compact, young man, knowing he had to be a Yankee to be taking orders from Gypsy, she slanted thick, black lashes and blazed ebony eyes up at the corporal. Blossom didn't miss the gleam of interest in Alan Bickles's eyes.

"Yes, I would like you to escort these ladies to a plantation upriver." Corporal Bickles laughed, realizing his foolish mistake. "I mean," he flushed, "*I* would like to. And will you be coming along later, sir?" His gray eyes gleamed with a playful wickedness.

"Wait just one minute!" Angela interrupted as Gypsy Smith took the man aside and spoke too low for them to overhear. She stepped up to them, and

Bickles glanced sideways in surprise. Ignoring the corporal, Angela forced herself to keep her confidence from shattering as a probing query entered Gypsy Smith's deep mahogany eyes.

"Yes?" His left eyebrow rose a little. "You wanted to ask me something, Angela?"

She hesitated in dismay, the misery of the night before spent in imagining Gypsy in the arms of the dark-haired woman with the fashionable yellow dress still haunting her. A look of tired sadness crossed her lovely features and then vanished—right before Gypsy Smith's eyes!

"Angela." Maneuvering her by the arm, he now took her aside while the corporal snatched his chance and went over to strike up a conversation with the raven-haired beauty. "Angela, look at me." He tilted her chin and she stared with longing up at him— there was no help for it. "I am not angry with you anymore. Forgive me, it was a stupid mistake thinking you were—someone you were not." For a split second his eyes flashed over Blossom Angelica.

"I forgive you, Gypsy Smith." She turned her head aside. "For *that*."

"I—" His gaze fell to the creamy expanse of her throat and neck. "Look, this is no place to hold a conversation." A sense of urgency drove him; all he could think of was making love to her. "I'd like to know what you mean by what you just said, but it will have to wait till later." His eyes caressed her, eyes that blazed and glowed. "Can you wait that long?"

"Yes." She looked downward swiftly, realizing her eyes were misty. He wanted to be with his mistress, she thought as she ached with an inner pain, and then he would come to her later at Tamarind.

Angela could feel his beautiful eyes boring into her back as she walked away with the corporal and Blossom Angelica.

The two brown mares had been taken back to Tamarind's stables and the dusty wagon that had brought them home sat out front looking sadly neglected and broken down without the horses pulling it and no people seated upon its weathered gray boards. Angela, with a gloomy chin in her hands, had been staring out the window at the dejected sight. How long she sat there she couldn't know.

Then she caught the flash of a lone rider galloping up the tree-shaded lane. Gypsy Smith!

The sight of him was the sweetest sight in the world to Angela, and her features at once became more animated as she bounced away from the window. Wild, wonderful feelings coursed through her as she imagined the coming night.

Then she caught herself, slowed, and stopped tearing through the borrowed wardrobe. Suddenly Blossom's old dresses looked older than gray mold on cheese to her.

She sighed dejectedly, clasped her slender hands together, and stared down at them. Her nails looked terrible. She'd just bet Stephanie Browden's nails were perfect, without a crack, and buffed. Most *ladies* of her kind had every hair in place, makeup flawless, and not a rip or tear in their dresses to fret about.

Now Gypsy Smith wouldn't even look at her. Sure, her mauve dress had been fresh in the morning, her favorite, not her own but nevertheless her favorite. Just what was she going to wear?

Wait a minute. . . . What was she sweating over? She was supposed to be angry with the man. After all, she'd caught him with another woman. . . . Or didn't it mean anything to Gypsy Smith whether he had one, two, or five hundred mistresses? Availability must be the order of the day to men like him, or whichever female suited his fancy at the time.

Angela didn't understand everything that was happening to her, but her whole being seemed to be filled with wanting when she thought about him. She craved his kisses, and even in remembrance, she felt the intimacy of them. His kisses left her weak and confused, aware of nothing but the magic of his exquisite touch.

Suddenly she was furious over her vulnerability to him, and flounced over to the door to lock it, then, discovering there was no lock to speak of on her door, she grunted and groaned as she shoved and pushed and pulled heavy furniture over against the door.

Finishing that, she stood back and dusted off her hands. Crossing her arms over her breasts, she backed into a chair to sit—and to wait.

Downstairs, in the bare, spare pantry, Gypsy Smith sang a lusty song as he scrubbed his back with the long-handled brush and lingered happily in the huge copper and wood bathtub. Keeping her eyes averted, giggling behind one hand, Kapa Lu poured steaming water into the tub, and when the bucket needed another hand to empty its contents, she squeezed her eyes tightly and lent assistance to her other hand, tipping the last splash free.

"Thank you, Kapa Lu," he said, a flash of humor crossing his face, free of the beard he'd just scraped off.

"Thas all right, Mr. Smith." She brought her hand up to stifle her giggles as she went out. "You is sho' welcome." His rich laughter followed her out the back door and she skipped on her way to visit with Melantha. In a tight closed fist she secured Mr. Smith's special gift—several pieces of saltwater taffy. It had been a long time since she'd had anything as good as this, and she meant to share her treat, too.

As Kapa Lu neared the slave quarters, her enormous coal black eyes twinkled merrily. Even from this distance Kapa Lu could hear Blossom Angelica's enraged ranting and raving breaking the stillness of late afternoon. Kapa Lu kicked a pebble aside and continued on her way, feeling smug over Blossom's imprisonment. The heated conversation between that boyishly handsome young corporal named Bickles and Gypsy Smith and Blossom herself returned to Kapa Lu, and she faced the orange rays of the setting sun, her cheeks beaming like polished May apples.

Blossom was in shock. There had been stains of scarlet on her pretty cheeks. Kapa Lu giggled remembering—they'd tied Miss Blossom Angelica's arms behind her back! When she tried kicking the corporal's shins, Gypsy Smith whisked the poor gal right off her feet and tied them up real good too. At the ankles. Then Blossom tried using her teeth to nip the young corporal. Gypsy Smith, annoyed and

185

impatient, sighed. He pulled a nice long kerchief from his pocket, and stuffing the thing in Blossom's cussing mouth, he tied the rest of it around her head. Blossom had looked just like a trussed-up turkey, a live one, with muffled squawks, her pretty beak a-pecking, and all.

The conversation, as best Kapa Lu could recall, when she went to visit Melantha, was retold in her own halting, animated, knee-slapping, black folks' vernacular. However, in her mind, as first it filtered into her head as she hid in the folds of curtains near the window, it went like this. . . .

"Corporal, bring her in here," Gypsy Smith said, looking around the half-dusted library, noticing it was vacant.

Spurred by fear, Blossom fought against the corporal's hold but she was surprised to find he had the iron strength of two men together. "Unhand me, you brute!" Blossom whirled on Gypsy Smith when the corporal strode over to secure the door against her escape. "What do you mean taking me for one of those dangerous spies everyone is talking about—why"—she spread her hands for the corporal—"can you imagine li'l ol' me being a spy?" She faced Alan Bickles, but he stared aside with shirt-sleeved arms shielding a muscle-swelled chest. Blossom's eyes lowered. "My . . . corporal," was all she purred, rolling her eyes provocatively.

One big black eyeball took it all in from the heavy curtains' folds. Kapa Lu had had a hard time of it not to break out in telltale giggles. But she'd seen where Blossom Angelica's eyes had gone to as the corporal moved closer to the old library table.

"Yankees do punish *female* spies despite what you might've heard, Miss Fortune," Bickles said, all business now. He'd been informed about her identity and he held no sympathy for the gorgeous woman. Angel Dixie, oh yes, she'd caused them much trouble. Some of Angel Dixie's informants were not entirely unconscious of the help they'd given her. There were young government employees in strategic positions whom she'd chosen for their Southern inclinations, their resentment against Union plans, or their simple appreciation of Angel Dixie's feminine appeal. Without scruple she'd led Federal men to provide information, which she at once communicated with pride and "pleasure" to her Confederate connections.

Inside the curtain Kapa Lu wondered what was going on inside the corporal's pretty head. He, and Gypsy Smith, seemed to be planning their next move, their heads nodding agreement.

"I'm sorry but there is no alternative, *sister*, we are going to have to lock you up until this war is over."

Blossom stared at Gypsy Smith as if he'd gone mad. "Lock me up?! I'll die in one of those hellholes you Yankees call *prison* and I will never see the light of day again." Blossom's eyes were black pits of poison directed at her half brother. "You bastard, you would do that to me—you've always hated me!"

"Not true, little sister. When I first laid eyes on you I adored your beauty and your Southern lady charms. I loved you, whether you know it or not, doesn't matter much anymore, does it? There came the time when I discovered what a little bitch you really are . . . kicking a small black child, a girl, when she could not contain her hunger for a sugared delicacy . . . whipping a black boy for a minor infraction . . . slapping a black woman for slipping out one moonlit night to meet her lover when she should have been at your beck and call all through the romantic summer night. And lately I've only discovered what a"—he paused, glanced at Bickles, then went on—"we'll let that one go unvoiced for now. Even though I thoroughly agree with the young men who were so casually discussing your *virtues* on the street corner."

"You are no better, Gypsy Smith," Blossom countered. Her eyes became nasty slits. "Angela saw you with that slut Stephanie Browden . . . on the day you Yanks were shelling the city . . . saw you leading her away to a cozy little nest somewhere—" her voice died away.

"Why you—" Gypsy stepped toward her, then pulled himself up. His voice grated harshly, "Stephanie Browden and her *husband* both happen to be very good friends of mine and I have even on occasion brought their child treats when obtainable. She is, by the way, expecting her second child—Paul Browden's child."

"Humph—" Blossom stuck her nose in the air. "You never brought your own sister a gift."

The long lashes of his liquid brown eyes lowered as he declared softly, "I have no sister." He turned to face the window, ordering Bickles, "Bind her hands, Corporal."

The corporal beamed as he said, "Yessir!"

"You know where to take her."

"Yessir!"

Just then a firm knock sounded on the door. "Come in, Jal."

Jal Stephan entered, not even glancing in Blossom's direction. "Jasmine Joe is coming, Mr. Smith."

"Thank you, Jal." He'd recently discovered the man's sympathies were without claim; he just wanted to see this damnable war over like the rest of them.

Blossom screeched, "What?! Is everyone on the damned plantation in on this? Where is my brother? I want to see Robert Neil!"

"He's upstairs," Gypsy informed her, "taking his nap. Drank himself to sleep again. I wonder who supplies all his liquor for him?"

"You'd better not cut him off . . . you . . . you bastard!" Blossom screamed. "He needs it, to help him sleep."

"Not anymore." Gypsy leaned his slim buttocks against the library table. He folded his arms across his wide chest. "You've been killing him with all that liquor. I am going to make him dry, and keep him dry."

"*No!*"

That's when Kapa Lu witnessed the rest of the unbelievable scene while the men trussed her up and the corporal and Jasmine Joe entered and carried the snarling tiglon away, brought her to the secluded pink cottage way out back in the woods. Locked away. Right where Miss Blossom Angelica belonged!

Chapter Fifteen

Tamarind Plantation

The earth proclaimed the slow sensuality owing to the late summer season with the heavily perfumed richness of overblooming gardens and down deep earthy smells pervading the wet, lowland countryside. Spikes of orange-red sun, squatting far beyond the other side of the Ashley, set Tamarind Mansion on fire, and upstairs, Angela sat glumly with her chin in hand, scratching softly with her fingertips the white silk stockings that made her legs itch and feel so hot.

She wished she could take them off. If she did, though, she'd only look more disheveled than she already was. Bare feet and legs were not very ladylike in the presence of . . . was she going to think the word "gentleman"? Oh, no doubt Gypsy Smith could fit the role of such, but she'd have to say "gentleman rogue"; otherwise she would be crediting him with a gentility she believed he'd never really cultivated. Wait a minute. Affected? Oh yes, she could say he was genteel, for she'd seen him at the Tradd party, hadn't she? She wanted to giggle. Refined? Oh no. She'd been correct the first time—he *could* be pretentiously polite.

Angela pouted then. What made her think he was going to come busting down that door just to see her?

Strongly felt then was a profusion of red that flushed from her throat all the way to her forehead. He knows I'm hiding from him, she thought, feeling a small tingling curl up along her spine. She could almost see the deep mahogany eyes, black with some indefinable emotion, score into her own.

Of course, you ninny, she told herself. He knows and he doesn't give a toot—why should he anyway?

Folding her arms across her small, firm breasts, she sat and prolonged her torture for yet another hour, playing for time, twiddling her thumbs until she thought she'd scream for the keenly felt frustration.

A hundred times she thought footsteps were nearing her door, and sounds in the hall she'd never heard before, repeatedly making her heart jerk and her nerves stand on edge.

By the time it had grown quite dark in the room, Angela was a ragged bundle of raw nerves, her thin fingers tensed in her lap. She swore—something in French—she'd done it before. Bits and pieces of her personality were flying at her every day with increasing speed. She was coming to know who she was—really was—wasn't she? A name—

"Hawk."

A bird really. What does it mean? She'd almost said

this out loud to Gypsy Smith the last time he'd questioned her. Ha-ha . . . he'd thought she'd been laughing at him. Actually she had been trying to roll out the word "Hawk." What bearing could this "bird" have on her family name? A crest? Was that it? A hawk signifies—could there be a bird, namely a hawk, emblazoned on their family crest? Also, this indicated her family had been—could *be*—wealthy.

Angela stood, feeling better now. "Yes, I've thought this to be so. There is wealth in the family I'm from—I just know it." She walked about the room, ignoring the heavy barricade she'd fashioned at the door to keep Gypsy Smith from getting to her. "They are searching for me—even now. I can feel it!" She inhaled and her heart sang with expectation; she felt aglow, happy, fully alive.

Then she gave a choked, desperate laugh, following with, "But how *will* they find me?" She slumped back into the chair, thinking she was probably thousands and thousands of miles away from home, and no one would even begin to think to look for her in the Carolinas. Her spirits plunged dismally. Even if her parents lived in France, or the French Quarter that Blossom had told her of, neither she nor anyone else at Tamarind had the funds to help her find her parents, if—as Blossom said—*if* they were still alive.

"Angela!" The door handle rattled.

Angela had been tenser than she'd thought, she realized as she jumped from the chair and stood to do battle if need be. Gypsy Smith wasn't going to use his rugged male charms on her, no, no, no, not after she'd witnessed him and the Browden woman strolling down the street to their love nest.

"Angela, why do you have some'ting against the door? I cannot come in, chile."

Mum Zini. Angela hadn't thought about her. But the tense lines on Angela's face relaxed and she rushed forward to peel away the layers of furniture she'd piled there, breathing heavily when she was done, mostly from excitement at what she'd learn on the other side.

"Mum Zini." Angela couldn't contain herself and rushed on, "Where is Gypsy Smith? Has he tried to see me? Where—?" She blinked as the mulatress looked concerned and puzzled over the girl's fired questions. "He's not even here—is he?"

"No, chile. Gypsy Smith rode out right after his bath, for it seems he has business that cannot wait." Mum Zini went on as Angela followed her out the door. "You do not know the man yet, I see, for if you did, chile, you would know he is here one minute and then"—she made a whooshing sound—"gone the next!" Over her shoulder she stared back into the room, asking, "Now what were you doing with all that furniture, chile?"

But Mum Zini's perceptive eyes and keen mind had already ascertained the exact value of Angela's very busy and then long afternoon cooling her heels. And what it had cost the young woman, too. There was going to be a long emotional journey for this lost angel, for Gypsy Smith did not want to need this young woman even though Mum Zini had seen it in his dark eyes that he did need her comfort and her love. No one had figured importantly in Gypsy Smith's life before—except one lady, long ago, when as a child the lad had been sent from her bosom. Mum

Zini had to say something to Angela, to warn her, as Mum Zini could foresee the storm clouds ahead for them.

"Angela," Mum Zini muttered, placing a halting hand on the girl's arm. "Before you go to visit Robert Neil in de drawing room, I have someting that I must tell you."

Angela sighed, "What is it, Mum Zini?" Slanting her head to one side, she waited, beginning to feel this was something important and she must listen hard.

"The trouble, it is beginning for you and Gypsy Smith. You will not like what he has done. You maybe even will hate him for it."

A short laugh fell from Angela's lips. "I do believe some of that has already been set into motion, Mum Zini." She would not say that she'd seen him with another woman after professing his love for her. Just how many women did the man profess his undying love to?

"Well," Angela said, squaring her shoulders. "What has the black knight done, gone riding off into the sunset to hold yet another luscious heroine in his aching arms?"

Mum Zini frowned a little at that, but answered truthfully, "He has had Blossom Angelica locked up."

"What?!" she said, blinking with bafflement.

"It is all over de plantation and will run to Persimmon Wood by nightfall. He has locked up Angel Dixie, did you not know?"

"Angel . . . Dixie?" For an instant Angela hummed, then said, "And she, I would venture to guess, is

194

Blossom Angelica." Her mood veered sharply to anger at Gypsy Smith. "So, as much as I gather about all these 'activities,' Blossom has been passing messages, and to guard against any fresh mischief he has taken it upon himself to lock her up?" She received a swift turbaned nod once. "How can he do such a thing? Blossom is his sister—"

"Half sister." She shrugged. "The blood of Angelica flows between them. His father he does not know. Gypsy Smith was his name, but that was only his father's first two names, folks have said. The man had a last name also. Some say that his father has the blood of the Cherokee and that he now lives on de sea and makes his living by trading . . . goods. Who knows what is de real God's truth? Perhaps always it shall be a mystery."

Angela rubbed two fingers at her temple. "The man is an enigma, Mum Zini." This passed over the mulatress's head, for she'd never heard this word before. "It is too much to take in all at once. First, tell me, where has Gypsy Smith taken Blossom? I must go to her, and help."

"Oh no, you must not do that, chile."

Angela looked down at the long fingers restraining her. "Why not?" She stiffened resolutely. "I will take Blossom's place as Angel Dixie."

"You are mad, chile. Gypsy Smith will be very angry and one cannot tell what that man will do when he is in that mood."

"He does not need to know, does he, Mum Zini?" Angela paused before placing her hand on the doorknob to the drawing room. "You know we need help, Mum Zini, and now you know what Blossom has been doing—and is it so bad?"

The woman just stood there, profound fear glazing her eyes as she heard but did not really hear Robert Neil's voice call out a greeting as the door shut on Mum Zini.

Clutching her hands at her apron tensely, Mum Zini hissed low as she walked back to the kitchen: "I should have kept my mouth shut, not to tell that Gypsy Smith has locked up his sister. She does not know where Blossom is being kept, but that chile will soon find out. Kapa Lu has by now told everyone but the ol' man in the moon."

Great apprehension was painfully concealed as Mum Zini stepped into the kitchen to see what was being done about meals for the next few days. What were they going to do without Blossom having supplies picked up from the blockade runners who stole the food into the carts in the backstreets of Charleston to be brought upriver to the smaller crafts waiting low in the waters? Were they all going to go with less like the few folks at Persimmon Wood had begun to after their cow had been stolen? They'd given what they could to Daisy Dawn, but now their supplies would run from low to nothing. She had only learned lately that it was Blossom who kept staples and sometimes meat on the table. But Blossom had been helping feed the Confederate Army, she had overheard the young corporal saying to Gypsy Smith. Between her and Gypsy Smith, one couldn't be sure who was providing the most. For the Union. For the Confederates. Tamarind folks. Now there would be nothing much . . . Gypsy was hardly ever there . . . food shortages were growing worse.

Many soldiers were even going without clothes, without shoes, just rags. It was going bad for the South.

Mum Zini looked up. She was afraid where her thoughts were leading. If there was going to be a new Angel Dixie . . .

"Where did this food come from?" Mum Zini asked Pandasala as she entered the kitchen smelling deliciously of pork and biscuits. Butter too.

"Why . . . from Gypsy Smith 'course." Pandasala rolled her black eyes. "We don't have to have rice over rice again." She grinned hugely. "Leas'ways not for a while."

"Perhaps not—" Mum Zini said as she turned her back on the heavy but pretty black woman.

"What you say?"

Mum Zini started from the kitchen, saying, "It is nothing."

The square of window in the pink cottage had been boarded up so that if a person needed to inhale a good whiff of fresh air or soak up a bit of sunshine, he would be able to get only his head through and that was it. Only the strongest man could pry those boards loose, and that man, in this instance, was Corporal Bickles himself. Riotous black hair framed the white face that appeared there suddenly. Her eyes, like jet sequins on fire, searched the grounds outside and saw nothing, and then Blossom gasped as a cowled figure appeared against the gray backdrop of sky along with a small wary face.

After glancing uneasily over her shoulder, Blossom

came back to Angela, her voice low in volume. "What are you doing here? How did you find out where they took me? Angela, say something, la, you look so mysterious!"

"Shh! Not so loud, Blossom, the corporal might hear."

"Oh him," she said, though her eyes glistened with an inner fire. "He's an odd goose, Angela, he's out hunting—" She giggled. "Says he can cook us a big fat rabbit for supper." Blossom purred, coiling a black curl around her finger ruminatively. "The corporal is such a man . . . if you know what I mean, honey."

Ignoring the slumberous expression entering Blossom's eyes, Angela spoke of her real reason for daring to come here. "Kapa Lu knew where they had taken you to and I overheard her speaking to Pandasala, otherwise I would not have known where to look. You are lucky Gypsy Smith has not had you sent to a Union prison somewhere . . . Blossom," she readied herself to come right to the point then inhaled, "I want to take your place as Angel Dixie."

The twirling of the black locks halted. Blossom stared with a mixture of curiosity and amazement at Angela, then a slow smile started until finally Blossom's whole face squinted in humor. Winking both eyes, she said, "You want Gypsy Smith to strangle you, darling?" She kept smiling. "It might work—if he doesn't kill you after your first try."

"I can be careful, Blossom. Just tell me what must be done."

"La! I can't teach you all that I know in a few visits, honey. Besides, the corporal might catch you and then he will lock you up in here too . . . and I don't think he wants the extra company just now, and"—her eyes sparkled—"neither do I, to tell the truth. I'm beginning to enjoy my incarceration . . . at least I think I can stand it for a *little* while longer."

"Blossom, I don't care what you and the corporal do, or for that matter what you do with all your other beaux, I—I just want to know what it takes to become Angel Dixie."

"Why?" Blossom canted her head.

"Because . . . I really *feel* like a Southern sympathizer."

Blossom changed her tune, but it was the same question, *"Why?"*

She took a deep breath, blurting, "The South needs help—and you did it, so what's wrong with my giving it a try? I know I can do it, all you have to do is help get me started."

"Why?" she pressed. "Really . . . why?"

"Do I have to tell you everything, Blossom?" Angela exhaled sharply.

"I know why, Angela." Blossom narrowed her eyes. "You want a war with Gypsy Smith. You want to best him. I know exactly how you feel, honey, that man makes a person, male or female, feel like warring with him."

"No, you are wrong."

The truth of the matter was, the thought of Gypsy Smith in another woman's arms filled her with fury, indescribably! Whether she knew this or not, the emotion showed on Angela's small face.

"You love him, don't you." Blossom tipped her shadowy head. A vaguely sensuous light crossed in

199

Angela's eyes, then left, but not before Blossom had witnessed it. Sighing, Blossom said, "You don't fool me, Angela, you do love Gypsy Smith." Her black eyes flashed. "Don't," she said.

"What?" Angela wondered if she'd heard Blossom right.

"Don't love him, Angela, it's dangerous, you will be a fool to love him. Don't you see, honey, he has a twisted mind—"

"No." Angela shook her head. "He has said he loves me, and I believed it—for a while, and I think he really does, but—"

"He lied." Reaching out to stroke the dewy cheek, Blossom said with much conviction in her voice, "I know that man, Angela honey, and he will hurt you, it's there in his dark wicked eyes, he means only to break your heart. Listen to me, Angela, Gypsy Smith can say the words, any man can, but he is a real charmer, let me tell you, our Gypsy Smith."

"You mean he only said he loved me to get me to—to—"

"Course, honey. Any man will do that—but Captain Smith is an expert, the best there is when it comes to fooling poor little darlings like yourself who buckle at the knees over him. Did he force you?"

"Force?" Angela had to think back. He'd told her to get undressed or he would take her to the authorities naked as the day she was born. He told her to believe him when he said he could do anything he wanted—anything. He had even said he'd enjoy forcing her submission!

What had he said? *"Either way, sweet, I will have you."*

How he had frightened her as she begged him not to do "this thing" to her. Then he had kissed her and kissed her, lifted her in his arms—he had tried to make light of their "bedroom encounter," then he swore at her. She'd begged him to believe she was innocent but he was having none of it. The cad! Then he said it broke his heart to see a woman crying. Oooh! His maleness had seduced her. He'd caressed her as if she had been a sweet babe. The vivid images returned to her with full mortifying force. Then as now, she thought, how little did she know of men!

"I'll take you to heaven and back, my darling . . ."

Frowning, Blossom asked the cowled figure with the glazed-over eyes, "What are you saying, Angela? Is that what Gypsy Smith told you, he'd take you to heaven and back? La! What a devil that man is!"

Angela frowned even darker. "What a fool . . . I told him I was quite inadequate as a lover. You see, I had never made love with a man before. He said, 'Kiss me, Angela, kiss me as you would dream of kissing a man.'"

As Stephanie Browden dreamed of kissing him?

The remainder of the love scene wavered and then took flight from Angela's imagination. "Trust me," he'd said. *Oooh!!*

"Angela?" Blossom smiled as her friend seemed to glow with a new understanding. "But . . . you see why you must not do this thing, Angela? Gypsy Smith is a dangerous man. He might even . . . kill you."

"And"—Angela looked Blossom straight in the eye—"it is why I am now more determined to become the *agent provocateur* than ever and—I might

201

even do some murdering myself!"

"Angela."

Blossom tried to see Angela, but she had already ducked out of sight and the words wavered back to her on a vagrant thread of sound:

"Tomorrow . . . I will return . . . we shall begin."

"Whoever in the world taught you all this?"

Angela peered down at the sheets of heavy paper in her hands, paper Blossom had wheedled out of Corporal Bickles—for a tiny price he'd told her—because she'd been bored and needed something to do, and he was going hunting this time for bigger game.

"My secret," Blossom answered.

"My feet are soaked," Angela groaned, stuffing the papers inside a deep pocket of one of Blossom's borrowed skirts.

"I know," Blossom said with a giggle. "This is the side of the house closest to the river and it's almost always damp. I should know," she purred, "I've come here often enough." Angela gave her another one of her ever more curious peeps. "I mean, when I want to be alone, of course."

Angela slowly nodded, halfheartedly agreeing, "Of . . . course." She was beginning to wonder more and more about Blossom and her many male friends, why, a half dozen or more had taught her all this espionage stuff. She'd read the secret into Blossom's impulsively spoken words. Blossom hadn't known what she'd been revealing back then. What had Blossom credited each of her tutors with in return?

Perhaps they had not extracted a price from her; after all, the South was in this together.

"Hurrah! Hurrah!" Angela sang softly and Blossom shook her head with a grin as her compatriot sprang from the window, her voice trailing sweet as a yellow honeysuckle vine—"Look away, look away, look away . . . Dixie land."

"La!" Blossom started and faced the door as the mock-stern, sweet-faced, strong-as-an-ox corporal came barging through the door. "Corporal—you gave, uh, me quite a fright." She'd almost blundered and said "us."

"You been singing 'Dixie'?" He peered around the cottage suspiciously, his young face perspiring from his labors to catch him and his pretty prisoner a grand supper she'd be proud to sit down at the table to with him.

"Course, Corporal honey." She sashayed up to him, kissing the air between them as she came. "Course . . . you big hunk of gorgeous man. Mm . . ." Lily white arms crisscrossed the corporal's sunburned neck while his enclosed her small waist.

Gypsy Smith continued to watch from the cover of a stand of saplings—holding his horse behind him with a hand stroking the velvety nose. Ten minutes later, he saw the cowled figure detach itself from below the window of the pink cottage.

Whipping himself astride his prancing mount, restraining flight, reining Big Red back to keep him from leaping from cover, he kept a close eye on the figure—a dainty figure, yes, as he'd first thought—

and waited until the mysterious wraith ran toward the Ashley, in the direction of Tamarind. Again, as he'd thought. As the figure moved ever swiftly, glancing back with an alarmed white face, Gypsy Smith nudged Big Red's big ribs and moved out.

Angela felt it. Someone was following her. She'd felt that eyes were watching her even as she stood at the cottage window. Fear knotted inside her, giving flight to her limbs, which had been clumsy inside the heavy folds of her skirt. Making a mad dash toward the Ashley, icy fear grabbed at her as she heard the sounds of horse's hooves, muffled in the spongy turf, not far behind her. She gave her whole heart to flight. Her body tingled and a new emotion claimed it and her fearful thoughts. This was not just any person after her. A strong woman's intuition told her that her tracker was Gypsy Smith.

Chapter Sixteen

Poised in attack position, Gypsy Smith's body tingled in anticipation of discovering his prey. The big horse felt his master's body leaving him and skidded to a fluid halt beside the bit of fleeing cloth, while Gypsy Smith swooped down and tackled his scurrying prize to the dewy earth. At the same time Angela swerved to her left and pulled away from her attacker, leaving him in a swirl of dark cloth as he tackled the cloak, not her. And she was free.

Angela ran for all she was worth.

Muffled curses filtered through the cloak. It was tossed this way, that way, and still the length of cloth held the man down as if he were a spitting panther snared in a huge inescapable net.

His prey continued to run, getting away.

Big Red's eyes rolled and he backed up and snorted at the struggling batlike hump on the ground before him. As the curses grew louder, sounding unlike anything Big Red had ever heard, the great horse skittered in a sideways dance, tall ears flickering like standards in a tumultuous wind. He stopped, snorted, then blinked huge liquid eyes as his master emerged, black hair sticking out every which way, eyes dark as thunderclouds searching out the fleeing object to let loose his torrent upon.

Sprawling on his rump, Gypsy Smith dug his booted heels deep into the spongy turf, and fought the cloak snarled about one arm, whipping it this way and that until he glowered at the thing, cursed it volubly, and flung it aside. From beneath his disheveled brow he shot Big Red a nasty glare.

"Bag of bones—what the devil are you looking at? Haven't you ever seen a man in fiercest combat with a bit of cloth before?" The horse only peered down at him in an unblinking sheepishness, as if the tall beast had been the main cause for his master's ill temper and needed to lick the poor man's wounds.

Then he seemed to remember that he had been bested by a fleeing wraith whose delicate tint of perfume still lingered in the air about him, and in the folds of the cloak he now snatched up warily to bring to his nose.

"Angela," he said softly, then chuckled nastily as he came to his feet with a one-handed stranglehold upon the lavender-scented cloak. Favoring his bad knee, he limped toward the wary horse, mumbling, "A man can't very well fight with a cracked knee, you know." Climbing laboriously to the high back, he went on trying to convince his gallant steed, "She's fleet of hoof, that little filly, and smarter than you'd think—but we'll get her."

Gypsy Smith nudged Big Red and flew swiftly back into the hunt for his quarry. He'd get her, he would, and when he did . . .

In a tattered gray uniform Gypsy Smith stepped up to the wide front porch supported by six slender columns, then he paused and leaned a shoulder laconically against one of the tall sentinels to Tamarind Mansion. His cold brown eyes took Angela in where she sat—seemed to sit contentedly—on the wood planking of the porch, her feet planted on the stone step and hidden beneath the voluminous mauve skirt and patched petticoats.

"Been sitting there long?" His eyes were flat, hard, passionless.

The day had cleared from gray to blue. Now the sunlight found her where she sat and in her pearl-blue eyes it coruscated like spindrifts of light and shadow. She had not been sitting there long. But he didn't know that! Or did he?

Angela had seen Gypsy Smith coming at a right angle to the house, not in any particular hurry, and in his one hand resting against his thigh as he rode was the cloak, Blossom's cloak. She'd only paused for a moment when he'd gone down in a vertigo of gray uniform and dark swirling cloak, then she had raced toward the river path.

"Not too long," she answered, "but long enough to be bored." She'd tried not to stare too hard when he'd limped up to the house, and now she wanted to ask if his leg hurt very badly, but she couldn't bring herself to be such a hypocrite. After all, she'd probably been the cause of making it hurt all over again.

"You don't look bored to me." He cleared his throat; his eyes were shades of mahogany and black. "In fact, you look like you were out of breath not too long ago."

His voice gnawed away at her confidence. It was as if he was holding a raw emotion in check and was prepared to pounce on her at any moment.

"I—I was cleaning house and came out here for a breath of fresh air," she said, "and to rest."

"Doesn't take long for you to become bored, Miss Angela."

Angela swallowed hard and squared her shoulders, looking him right in the eyes. Then down his tough, lean body. "Now you have decided to side with the Confederates?" She gestured toward the tattered gray uniform he wore. "I thought you were all Yankee, Captain."

"Ran out of fresh clothes to wear," was all he said of his disguise.

"You could be killed by one of your own kind. Then what?"

He stood there, not making a move to leave the tall column, devastatingly handsome despite his tattered clothes of an officer and hair that looked as if it had been raked over and over with a frustrated hand. She raised her eyes back up to find his staring at her.

"Then I'd be killed I guess."

Nervously, she bit her lip. "Would you like something to eat? Jasmine and Jal killed one of those wild boars that have been running around in the swamp."

"They have been there for years."

"What? Oh, the boars."

Leaning over, he snatched up her wrist, and his voice was soft but alarming. "Where have you really been in the last hour, sweet Angela, can you tell me the truth for once?"

Angela felt momentary panic as his hand manacled hers, then her quick mind leaped on to save the day for her. "Cooking boar. Would you like some?"—her eyes snapped—"or not?"

With the way Gypsy Smith was looking at her she felt as if a cold hand had closed about her throat. A warning voice whispered in her head, "Don't say anything more!" She would only have to wait for him to break the silence first.

She didn't have long to wait. Gypsy Smith was not one to give up so easily, and seeing that his interrogation was having no result, he said slyly, "Where is Mum Zini?"

Angela was becoming increasingly uneasy beneath his close scrutiny and now she looked up at him with an effort, saying, "The last time I saw her she was out hanging sheets to dry."

"When was that?"

A shadow of alarm touched her petite face. "This morning Mum Zini and I had tea toge—"

He said tightly, "This morning, my dear, has nothing to do with what we are discussing now." Her breath caught in her throat and Gypsy heard it, murmuring, "Ah . . ." He reached down and caught something in his hard fingers.

The shoes she'd put on earlier on stockingless feet were serviceable, but hardly the sort a young woman would want a man staring at—not in the light of day—especially not without stockings!

"There is an embarrassment here for you, Angela?"

Gypsy Smith was held spellbound for a moment in time by the flowing warmth that emanated from Angela. He had taken a seat on the porch beside her now and still held her by the ankle, watching as she colored fiercely.

"N-no," she stammered. "Let go of my foot, Gypsy. Please, let go."

"Not until you tell me where Mum Zini was an hour ago. Truthfully."

"I—I don't know, truthfully." She lowered her head. "I was in the kitchen."

"Truthfully?"

"What?" Her head snapped back up; her heart hammered in her ears. "What do you mean?"

"I thought you were intelligent, Angela. It's either that or you are lying. Which is it, Angela? Were you in the kitchen an hour ago or not?"

When she wouldn't speak, Gypsy said, "Angela, you were very good back there, the cloak business and all." Gesturing to the length of cloth caught in Big Red's saddle, he said in silken syllables, "I suppose you will lie and say that is not yours either."

She was barely able to keep the laughter from her voice as she said, "No, it is not my cloak, Captain Smith. Now, if you will excuse me—"

His eyes were serious as he put a hard grasp on her ankle when she would have risen and gone into the house. "Sit down! We are not finished here, damnit!"

Angela felt a shudder of humiliation as he bared her ankles, brushing her skirts to see the dark mud encrusted there. "Tsk, tsk, Angela, you are sorely in need of a bath." Releasing her leg, he stood quite fluidly for one with a wounded knee, pulling her up with him, his voice deep and coaxing, "Come, my dear, I'll help draw a bath for you."

She would have said "No!" in a choked voice, but for some reason she could not speak when his gaze slid downward, slowly and seductively.

"I would carry you, mademoiselle," he whispered into her hair as he guided her upstairs, "but, you see, I have a wound that throbs very much at the moment."

After Gypsy Smith had carried up the buckets of steaming water himself, he slipped out, allowing Mum Zini to help Angela with her bath. The young woman glared at the door he'd just closed and ignored Mum Zini as she poured the precious few drops of lavender toilet water into the tub. Soon the steamy scent filled the room, shaking Angela from her glowering musings. Still she did not make a move to undress, just stared at the inviting vapors coiling into the air.

"You will take your clothes off now, mamzelle?" Mum Zini gave a low chuckle, adding, "Thee water it will cool and then you will not want to bathe."

Finally Angela acknowledged the mulatress's presence, but her vexation was evident. "Bathe? I never wanted to in the first place, Mum Zini. It is too hot to take a warm bath—I would rather take a dip in the stream to cool off!"

"Your plans did not work out so well?" Mum Zini said, laying out a crisp towel smelling fresh as if it had just been taken from the line outside.

The shoes with the caked mud made a dull thud as they hit the floor. "No," followed after the noise on the floor. "I doubt if I shall ever get anything accomplished with Gypsy Smith popping up all the time. Why isn't he off fighting with the rest of them?" Tossing the last piece of clothing onto the floor, heedless of where it landed, Angela knelt by the tub to trail her finger in the water, thinking it was still too hot.

"A man cannot fight with a cracked knee, mam-zelle. He must heal before he can go back, otherwise he will be no good to his men, he will just hold them back."

Gingerly stepping into the tub, Angela missed seeing Mum Zini lay out a lovely powder blue gown with a wide flounce running along the deep bodice. It had an off-the-shoulder neckline and would show a creamy expanse of bosom and throat. Mum Zini hummed as she situated the satiny folds delicately upon the flowered bedspread and stood back to gaze adoringly at it.

Angela halted the pinning up of her hair in back, her eyes going over Mum Zini and the lovely gown she was primping at with her *café au lait* fingertips. A soft gasp escaped her. "Where did that come from? It wasn't there before."

Mum Zini pretended surprise. "You did not see it, mamzelle? It was here all de time."

"Where?" Angela swiveled her head to look around the room, wondering if any more surprises lurked in the corners. Sure enough, there at the foot of the bed sat a perfect pair of satin slippers with mock-diamond buckles. And over on the chair, silk

212

stockings, one blue pair, one white. There, white lace petticoats. On the bed, above the bodice of the dress, seemingly having appeared as if by a magic wand, a strand of pearls that would clasp at the throat with a diamond catch. Above this, pearl cluster earrings with a single dangling teardrop pearl. The jewelry was white, like the shoes. Angela shrugged to hide her confusion, muttering, "Mum Zini?"

"I will go now, chile."

With that she crossed to the door, indulging the wordlessly staring young woman in a gentle smile. "It is wonderful to be young and in love, *oui* mamzelle?"

"Mum Zini?" Angela twisted about in the tub, turning in time to see the door close behind the Mulatress. Facing the larger part of the room once again, Angela took in all the feminine pretties. And then she thought she knew. . . .

"Stephanie Browden." She gritted her teeth together. "He borrowed all these things from *that* woman to seduce me. Well, he'll not be getting under my skin again." Love? Hah! What that man wanted from her was physical, and only physical. Her eyes flashed crystal blue as her eyes skipped to the wardrobe and a plan of action came to her.

Ah . . . she would teach that womanizing Captain Smith a thing or two!

Sometime later, in the musty darkness of the attic, Angela found all the items she needed to set her deception into play. Supremely pleased with herself, she moved about the house like a wraith, noting with satisfaction that Gypsy Smith was having their candlelight dinner set up on the veranda. The rogue himself was nowhere to be seen.

Outside the bushes rustled and moved, then became still again. Darting a look about the grounds and the veranda, Angela moved casually toward the house again, stepping carefully around the brushwood. Silently she slid between the French doors off the side veranda, back into the house, and up to her room to begin her toilette.

She fixed her hair in long curls at either side of her face, with a neat part in front. A sense of urgency drove her now. She wished she could be there to see Gypsy Smith when he finally realized he'd been played for a fool!

Gypsy Smith halted for a moment before going out the French doors, his heart racing like thundering hooves as he looked out at Angela seated demurely on the paint-chipped white wicker. Taking in her gentle loveliness, he felt like a besotted lovesick fool. Love? He glowered at his own reflection superimposed over hers in the polished glass. What did he really know of love? He felt an instant response from his big body as his loins tightened. Mentally he could feel himself taking her, plunging into her body while Angela gasped in sweet agony. Was that the answer? He hungered after her as he'd hungered after no other, and he wanted to fill her with pleasure, feel her soft lips crushed beneath his. He wanted only to make Angela his . . . forever . . . but could he love her for just as long? He stared out at her cream and peaches face and a grim smile curved the generous contours of his mouth. For the love of God! Would he ever be able to trust a woman again after the way his mother had deceived him . . . cast him aside?

Like a moth drawn to flame, Gypsy walked out onto the veranda. Seeing the tall male frame out of her side vision, Angela drew her gaze from the overgrown gardens and sucked in a deep breath when her eyes met the tall, uniformed man. All in blue with the guinea yellow sash of a cavalry officer, the outlines of his shoulders straining against the blue fabric, he carried himself with the commanding air of obvious self-confidence. Unconsciously, she stared with longing at him. He scanned her critically and smiled his approval, but she was caught up like a breathless girl of fifteen.

His voice was quiet and seductive. "Angela." Coming around the table he lifted her hand and kissed the satin-soft tips of her fingers in a suave play of gallantry. "You are lovelier than the fairest rose."

Angela laughed and smiled up at him saucily, saying, "And you are a handsome sight for fair eyes, sir." She peeked up at him from beneath sooty lashes as he went to take the wicker chair across from her.

The scent of jessamine mingled with the exotic smoke from dewberry candles and Angela felt the magical evening was like something out of *Arabian Nights* as Kapa Lu served them in her freshly laundered brown cotton, grinning from ear to ear and proudly displaying a string of multicolored beads that she fingered around her neck from time to time. There was no doubt in Angela's mind who'd given Kapa Lu the gift, for the black eyes alighted on Gypsy Smith and shone with a glow of eternal beholdenness.

All the while they were eating, Gypsy thought of how it had felt to have their bodies joined, to immerse himself deeply within her, and he knew if he didn't stop thinking about it soon he was going to take her then and there.

And Angela, though she, too, was having feelings, mostly of a romantic nature, couldn't help picturing Gypsy's look of rage when she would tell him to make love to her, and she would ask him to meet her in the garden where they would make love—that should cause him to grow even more excited—and then she would exchange the clothes she was wearing for the pile she'd hidden in the garden, dress the dressmaker's form with jewelry and all, and then watch from the bushes while he took the phony Angela in his arms! She wished she could be standing close to him to see it, but she would have to move quickly if she were to get away before he discovered where she'd been hiding while watching him make a total fool of himself!

Then they were alone, the last of the meal cleared away. "How did you come by all these things, Gypsy?" She felt all quivery just saying his name. He seemed not to have heard her as he stared and stared into her eyes. "You must have caught the trout yourself, but where did the ham and the wine and the fruit come from?"

Lounging back in his wicker, he said, "I have connections."

Angela thought she knew then, but she kept her back from stiffening as she remembered Stephanie Browden, who'd not seemed to be lacking in beautiful clothes to wear nor any pleasures in life for that matter.

"The dress and jewelry were the result of a long overdue debt owed me by a very lovely woman by the name of Stephanie Browden. I just thought this was a good time to collect, though I had never asked for anything before. I saved her life and she helped me discover my lost past. She thought it was not enough, however, for saving her life, and told me to just ask if I should ever need anything else from her in the future."

"You saved her life?" she murmured. "How?"

"It's a long story, Angela. You'd laugh if I told you where we'd been at the time."

"Try me, sir."

"You want to know, really?"

"Yes. I want to know—really."

Gypsy Smith told of how she'd been fleeing from natives along the coast of Africa, how he had swooped down in his air balloon and gallantly carried Stephanie Browden away to safety.

Taking another sip of wine, Angela found herself giggling. "Really, Captain Smith, that is quite a tale. Do you expect me to believe this is the God's truth? Or that you are merely entertaining me with a fantastic love story?"

His gaze was like a feather-soft caress. "No love story, Angela."

"What then? You just don't swoop out of the air to rescue a fair damsel in distress and not make love to her when you carry her off to your love nest." *Just like in Charleston!*

Gypsy's gaze raked boldly from her low bodice back up to her flushed face again. "Not my love nest.

217

My ship, Angela."

Curiously her deepened blue eyes peered up at him from under slanted lashes. "You constantly amaze me, Captain Smith. A balloon, a ship, a Yankee. You are fantastic—" She held her breath, waiting for him to tell her more. She'd completely forgotten her plans to make a fool of him as the fantastic idea of what it would be like to make love in an air balloon, high above the earth, floating magically through moon-laced clouds, came to her, and quickly she banished the dangerously tantalizing thought.

"These are fantastic times, Angela. This war has produced submarines, ironclad warships, trenches, automatic guns, a military draft, aircraft—and the first organized espionage that the country has ever known!"

At that, Angela coughed on her next sip of wine. She felt the inebriant racing through her blood-stream going ahead of its ability to bring her to mild intoxication in a measured period of time.

Though she didn't feel very confident at the moment, she said firmly, "You still think I'm a spy, I can tell."

"Oh?" Deep brown eyebrows lifted. "What makes you think that? Are you feeling guilty tonight, Angela?"

She threw the words at him like daggers, "Why ever should I be feeling guilty, monsieur?"

"Back to that monsieur nonsense again, hmm?"

His chiding tone made her angry. Her eyes sparking with fury, Angela pushed the rose-pink liquid aside and tilted her fine chin up. Gypsy Smith's mouth thinned with displeasure.

"Is something wrong with the wine, mademoiselle?" He didn't give her a chance to answer. "Angela, I am ten steps ahead of you. My dear, you'll never take Blossom's place as Angel Dixie. You realize that by now, don't you? Not saying anything that might incriminate you? Angela . . ." He caught her hand as she made to remove it from the blue tablecloth and he peered at her intently, his voice like black silk. "Angela, you will have to put a halt to this dangerous game you are playing. My men and I can be a sinister force you would not like to reckon with. I can always turn you over to one of them." He felt the nerves tense in her hand immediately. "We capture deserters, hunt for spies, and guard points of entry for civilians bringing in contraband. I am entrusted generally with order beyond the capacities of the local police in a city dislocated by war where a motley cross section of humanity flows in."

Angela blinked fiercely, muttering, "What are you, Captain? *Who* are you?"

He stood, towering over her, wanting to intimidate her, scare her, anything to make her quit this nonsense and tell him who *she* really was. Looking up at him, Angela's throat ached with defeat. She'd so wanted to best him, as Blossom had said. To show him she could do as well as a man in this war-torn country.

"They call me Gypsy Moth, Angela, or Black Moth, whichever one prefers. I was born in the South but not reared in the South. I have ties and interests here. I have another plantation, but Wild Oaks is wholly my own. In conscience I favor the Union, hated secession and whatever went with it. In my secret service work, you see, I actually favor the North. True, I admit to having given data to some of the Confederates, in the past, which might possibly have assisted them once or twice. Now I pour into the President's ears everything I can learn about the Rebels."

"Why are you telling me all this?" Angela twisted her wrist from his grasp and he let her go for the time. "I could turn *you* in to the Confederates."

"Ah . . . but you will not have that chance, Angela." He turned his head to the right to call for someone. "Kapa Lu. You can come out of the garden now and show *us* what you have found."

A suffocating sensation choked her throat as Kapa Lu, somewhat sheepishly, stepped up onto the veranda with the dressmaker's form, with wooden head and all, all the items Angela had hidden away in the bushes for her little deception.

"What sort of *scenario* were you planning, my dear?" His laugh raked her harshly as his eyes darkened over her shivering form.

Angela couldn't take it any longer. No wonder Blossom despised this man with all her heart and soul! He was an unfeeling cad! And she meant to tell him so—now!

"You—you are a heartless bastard, sir." She hissed, her breath coming raggedly in red-hot anger. Oh . . . my God . . .

With a whisk of his hand, he ordered the round-eyed black woman, "Put it back where it belongs, Kapa Lu—up in the attic."

"Now." He turned to face Angela. He could almost feel her shudder of humiliation. "Everything has been readied. While we are on our way, you can tell me all about yourself, Angela . . . Angela—what else can I say, as it seems you don't own a last name."

"Wh—where are you taking me, monsieur?" She tried to keep up with his long strides as he pulled her along, through the house, and to the foyer, where two packed bags waited beside the front door.

"Where?" she blurted out, afraid to leave the only home she could say she'd really ever known. What was he doing?!

In his long pink nightdress, Robert Neil came to stand at the top of the stairs, demanding, "Yes, you Yankee bully, just where *are* you taking my wife? First my sister disappears, and now Angela is being abducted too! Just where, sir, are you taking her—I demand an explanation to all this asinine folly!"

Yanking the young woman who'd been staring wordlessly and helplessly up the staircase, Gypsy Smith shot over his shoulder in going out the door, "Wild Oaks—where else!"

Whirling about with a sniff, Robert Neil exclaimed in an old-maidish voice, "Heavens to Betsy, this place is a *madhouse!*"

Chapter Seventeen

Persimmon Wood Plantation

Angela still wore the powder blue dress. She had removed the pearl-and-diamond jewelry, although she kept the satin slippers with their mock-diamond buckles. She would need the shoes, especially where they were going, she was told.

Gypsy Smith worked the cypress dugout upstream against the current, and the boat went smoothly beneath the fluid movements of his powerful rippling muscles. Ducks waddled through the tangled grasses along the banks and then took to air upon their approach, the flapping of their wings leaving shadowy ripples where the waters were sedate. Mesmerized by the sun on water, Angela stared while sluggish memories burned around the edges of her mind. She wished she could remember more, but again, her mind was inhabited only by faceless shadows and the faint faraway voices she could hear murmuring inside her head. The marsh they were traveling through was vague with shadow, as vague as the memories she tried so hard to capture.

Silence surrounded them, and in the silence she heard only one word—*Hawk, Hawk.*

Gypsy Smith selfishly guarded his own thoughts as he labored against the current. He, too, reflected back, but his recollections were clear, though this had not always been the case. In Africa, as a lad, cast from the only parent's bosom he'd ever known, he had been uncertain as to where he truly belonged. The truth had not been established until Stephanie Browden—Marylebone back then before she'd wed—had helped him discover his roots. Going back farther in his reflections again, to the Atlantic coast of Africa, to where the ancient whitewashed brick or stone houses stood, he could still hear the insistent whispers of the sea as it rounded their walls. In the unnatural quiet, they'd seemed to be waiting, and away from the town of Dar el Beida, where the sea mists swirled close to shore, there stood one lonely house still intact. Haunted, that is what the rumor had been, haunted by a beautiful golden-haired siren of the sea. The lone house had stood on a small rise, like a sentinel watching over its fallen neighbors, beautiful and skillfully fashioned in the style of a Spanish villa. Cassandra, that is what the evil woman had named the place.

Gypsy continued to stare past Angela, his thoughts taking him back, back. The woman had been like a witch of the wind with her loose dark hair blowing back in a seaborne breeze, emerald eyes piercing and full of hatred. There had been a horse, Cascara, a sleek Arabian—he could remember the beast's name but not the evil woman who'd held him and the beautiful woman, Victoria, prisoner. Now he could remember the name of the donkey he'd loved, his pet, Cuddy, which he hoped was still alive at El Corazón. And Monica and Steven Hawke, his saviors, whom he would be going back to see as soon as he could. And their daughter Jessica, Victoria's granddaughter. She would be Angela's age now . . . and now his eyes were filled with a deep curious longing as she came into his vision again.

"Are you comfortable?" he asked Angela, still wondering about Jessica Hawke and her wonderful parents.

With her fingers trailing in waters that made the sun dance in her eyes, Angela felt at peace for once in a long while and inhaled, letting out her words on the exhale, "Yes." She smiled as he looked back at her. "Are you?" she asked, feeling playful and happy and good inside.

"I feel as if I've had a good workout," he said with a returned smile. "Look, we are here. Persimmon Wood."

Before Angela could answer, they were bumping against the boat landing and she felt a little disappointment over having to move her muscles and stand up again after becoming so relaxed and somewhat lazy. Bending to pick up the tapestry bag with all her things in it, Angela was surprised when Gypsy said, "Leave it. We won't be staying. Just long enough to leave Daisy Dawn some food and supplies and then we'll be on our way to Wild Oaks."

Angela tottered, then grabbed the arm extended to her, while she asked, "Is it much further?"

"Not much."

"May I ask why you are taking me there?" she said. His eyes darkened with some unknown emotion, at least until she recognized the same look he'd worn before he had made love to her the first time and it was overwhelmingly evident what he meant to do during their stay at Wild Oaks. "Oh," she said, feeling a warm glow flow through her, "that."

"My prisoner," Gypsy said passionately, and snaked an arm about her waist to squeeze her there and yank her closer. "For as long as I want." He kissed the tip of her nose and then let her go, saying, "You'll have plenty of work to do cleaning and helping to put the house and grounds in order. We'll trim shrubs, weed gardens, move brushwood an—"

Her eyes flashing, Angela whirled in front of Gypsy Smith. She splayed a hand against his chest and her face grew rosy with emotion, but he kept on sauntering while she walked backward. "Wait a minute, Monsieur Smith, I have never done this heavy work before that you speak of—" Angela caught herself, frowned into the deep shaded eyes, then took her place beside him and walked with him up the hill to the house she could see now peeping between many live oaks and cypress trees.

"What's wrong, Angela, did you remember suddenly who you are?" He looked down at the face whose expression had changed from merriment to wistfulness within a few short moments. "You certainly do have your moods," he remarked coolly.

Angela came out of her daze a few minutes later as Daisy Dawn herself seem to float enchantingly across the lawn toward them, delight bubbling in her laugh, and her fingers were warm and surprisingly strong as she grasped Angela's with two dainty hands.

"What a pleasant surprise." As she said this, Angela saw Daisy Dawn halt all movement, like a Dresden doll in a showcase, but this real one was posed poignantly against the backdrop of her rundown plantation. She was wearing a simple beige dress with a pink Victorian shirred bodice and a princess waistline. Angela could tell that the dress was old. But it was still lovely, and such a lovely young woman was wearing it. "Come inside," Daisy said, looping her other arm in Gypsy Smith's.

"Do you have something cool to drink?"

"Cooled herb tea," Daisy told Gypsy Smith. "How does that sound?"

"Great."

"What are you carrying there, Gypsy?" Daisy said. He told her and her dark blue eyes lit up like a summer sky at dawn. "How wonderful, you are so kind." She tried not to show that she noticed his limp was getting worse as they climbed the rise to the house. "Blackstrap can take that for you, Gypsy, here he comes. Please"—she held up her hand as the black man neared—"I won't take no for an answer. Besides," she laughed, "it is my gift, you said."

"Well, it was getting a bit heavy with this bad knee and all," the white man sheepishly told the black man taking the heavy burden out of his arms.

"Doan needs to say a thing, Cap'n Smith suh."

"Blackstrap, put that in the back hall, would you?" He nodded while heading straight for the house. Daisy called after him, "That's a dear."

226

Turning to her company, she said sighingly, "I don't know what I would do without Blackstrap. God must have sent him to me long ago meaning for him to be my guardian angel, because he is no less than that—and he is much much more.

Angela and Gypsy Smith could tell that this diminutive blonde loved the hulking black man very much. What would happen to her if Blackstrap should ever be hurt, or worse, they wondered. Daisy Dawn would have no one to watch over her, for Robert Neil's mental condition was worsening with rampant speed and he would eventually perish from it.

"You are walking with a limp." Daisy stated the obvious as Gypsy Smith took the stairs with somewhat weary steps. "Which battle was it?"

Gypsy Smith chuckled. "Can't remember, there's so many."

"The Yanks are going to lick us," Daisy Dawn murmured, not looking at Gypsy Smith. Through those confused, troubled, sorrowing times, bands still played "Dixie" throughout the South, and despite all the heavy hearts over loved ones lost and fears for survivors, people still fell in love. She looked at Gypsy Smith and Angela . . . and wished Ridpath Huntington loved her. Even if Rider had been a Yankee, Daisy Dawn would have felt no compunction about returning his love. The man was everything in this world to her, but Rider belonged to Blossom Angelica and nothing would ever change that, ever.

Angela stared around at the latticed lower gallery; there was one directly above their heads too. Some of the slats were in bad repair and she could tell that the roof leaked. For a moment Angela listened to the woodbird's song and thought that it sounded somewhat sad, like a lament to the war victims. She herself had become a victim, and the realization struck her like a hard slap. No matter who or what she'd been before coming to this place, this country, whatever was the case, she'd become a part of everything past, present, and future here in this war-torn country. And she hadn't realized that Gypsy Smith had become such a powerful opponent, one not of her own choosing, in war, and now, in love. Passionate chains held her. Would she ever escape and find her way back in time to those loved ones that still dwelled inside her heart?

Gypsy captured Angela's eyes with his. "Daisy Dawn is waiting, my dear." He took her by the tips of her fingers saying, "Should we go inside?" She answered yes. "Good," he said. "Otherwise I was afraid you'd disappear into the hole you were staring into the porch floor."

Daisy Dawn leaned toward Angela, saying in a soft tone, "The Yankees were here last week . . . they must have passed right by Tamarind. Didn't you see them?"

"There were a few that needed food and Pandasala is always generous. Wherever there is a hungry mouth to feed, Pandasala is filling it, Johnny Reb or Union Jack." Angela kept her eyes trained on the wide, open hall leading to the study, where Gypsy had gone when Daisy said he could find a cheroot in the smoke box and a bit of brandy in the sideboard. "Have the Yankees burned any of your buildings, Daisy? I heard they will burn just about anything of value: barns, houses, fields."

"They haven't done any burning along the Ashley—not that I know of. All Yankees aren't bad, Angela. Some of them are God-fearing men, just like some of our boys. Human beings all of them, brave and gallant and kind."

Which brought Angela to remembering a conversation they'd had before. "You love Rider Huntington, don't you?" Angela smiled gently at her tenderhearted friend and Daisy smiled back with a little nod that was no less telling than if she'd stood and shouted her love for Rider from a Charleston rooftop at the top of her lungs.

"What the hell are you doing here?!"

Wide-eyed, both Angela and Daisy Dawn exchanged looks, one in half anticipation, the other in half dread. "That's Gypsy shouting at someone," Daisy said. Her heart began to speed up. "There is only one person Gypsy Smith would greet in such a manner. Oh Lord, Angela, what will happen now— Rider is here!"

When Angela and Daisy stepped onto the porch, they weren't prepared for the sight that greeted them. The two captains from opposite sides were deep in polite conversation, one with a booted leg upon the railing, the other leaning an elbow against his dusty knee. As soon as Rider looked up and saw Daisy standing there with Angela, he struck a gallant pose and cleared his throat. His travel-stained uniform was nothing but a gray ghost of a former handsome arrangement of material. Gold buttons and braid were missing and Daisy thought he looked as if he'd been in a battle with two very fierce jungle cats. He stood as a perfect example of what the Confederacy had become—especially the guerrilla units, the Partisan Rangers.

"Ladies," Ridpath Huntington said.

Daisy swallowed, but could only nod in greeting. So many questions—where could she begin? And how, without seeming too eager?

Gypsy Smith saved the day, for them all.

"Yes, ladies, Captain Huntington is a deserter." He turned to the blonde. "Miss Fortune, will you take one of Mosby's former men into your home? I'm afraid he's been wounded."

"Wounded!" Daisy Dawn rushed forward, her answer quite clear to all of them.

Later, while Rider slept peacefully in a sparsely furnished bedchamber where old white lace curtains blew softly in the September breeze, Daisy joined Angela in the kitchen and Gypsy went out to see about helping Blackstrap mend whatever he could, for the black man worked from sunup to sundown taking care of all the chores singlehandedly, chores that normally took ten or twenty black men. But that was when times were normal and they were certainly not that now.

"I can feel the restless winds of winter," Daisy said, coming into the kitchen, where Angela was extracting sugar syrup from fruits since there was no other kind of sugar. "Soon the weather will be cooler and

230

the oaks will be losing their leaves." Daisy sighed, going on as if she talked to herself. "There are some experiences so strange and new that we can hardly imagine ourselves undergoing them—even when we are."

Angela thought about that and she was surprised at the sense of fulfillment she felt. "Daisy, I've been trying to think of those exact words and have struggled and struggled in vain. This life, this war, is all so new, so strange, and you took the words right out of my mouth—I can hardly imagine going through this, but I am." She stared at Daisy Dawn through her tears. "I really *am*."

Daisy looked at her friend hesitantly before saying, "It must be doubly hard for you, Angela, when you don't really know where you belong. Oh, lesser human beings would find themselves going crazy, I know I would. You see, I've had to pretend a lot."

"Pretend?" Angela didn't quite understand.

Walking slowly around the table, her gaze settled outside the window somewhere to a distant spot, she said, "After my parents died in the yellow fever epidemic I had been alone with no one to raise me, except of course Robert Neil. Then Blackstrap came along—he was always there but I didn't know he'd so easily take me under his wing. At a very young age I fell in love. Rider Huntington was in love with someone else though."

"Blossom?"

"Yes. It seems he's always loved her and I knew there'd never be a chance for me, not with beautiful, charming, witty Blossom around. I didn't even try to outshine Blossom because Rider hardly knew I was alive."

Angela said, "He knows you're alive now, Daisy, I saw the way he looked at you and his heart was in his eyes."

"Oh please, Angela, don't say that. If Blossom was here he wouldn't even look my way."

Mischievously Angela grinned, saying, "But Blossom is *not* here now, Daisy. She's locked up with a Yankee corporal holding the key, under Gypsy's orders."

"She's Angel Dixie, isn't she?"

"Was."

"What do you mean?"

"Gypsy means to keep Blossom locked up until this war is over." She reached over to pat Daisy's pale hand. "Now is your chance, Daisy."

"Oh, I couldn't do that to Blossom Angelica. Besides, if I'm to win a man I want him without any deception on my part whatsoever."

"Daisy, you are every bit as beautiful as Blossom Angelica, and you are sweet and pure, unlike Blossom. Don't you think there will come a day when Rider will discover what a—I hate to say it—loose woman Blossom is? Yes, even though she is my friend, Blossom is wild and has an insatiable appetite for many different men. Would it be fair to allow rider to become the husband of such a woman? Blossom does not really love Rider, she only wants to add him to her collection. Give him a chance to love you, as you love him, Daisy." She smiled. "It is only fair, to the both of you. And then, you won't have to pretend to be happy anymore. You will be."

"Angela." Daisy slowly went to Angela and

232

hugged her. "You truly are my friend and I'll never forget you, no matter what happens. We will always be together in spirit even though we might be far apart!"

After two days Rider was well enough to travel with Gypsy to Tanglewood Plantation. The men had decided to leave the women behind with Blackstrap. Angela would just have to go with him to Wild Oaks some other time. But when Gypsy and Rider stopped off at Wild Oaks, they found that the house was no longer. The Yankees had burned it to the ground. Gypsy and Rider both agreed this was a crazy war. Men who'd gone home to harvest a crop, cut wood for their families against the coming nights, and make shoes out of cowhide for their children's bare feet were less likely to return to the armies. Desertions were continuous. Captured, the deserters would leave again, some three and four times. This, too, was a big influence on those soldiers whose will to fight was lessening.

Rider found yet another disaster waiting for him at the shuttered and boarded up Tanglewood Plantation. The few black folks left there, faithfully staying on, reported that Annabelle had been found murdered in Charleston. She'd been strangled with a blue silk stocking. Rider mourned his sister's passing greatly.

The year was coming to a close. All of Tanglewood's black folks came to stay at Persimmon Wood, and Daisy welcomed them all as they joined forces, Blackstrap, Gypsy Smith, Rider, Angela, to help keep the plantation going. For Christmas shopping, it took ten dollars to buy a yard of calico, a pound of coffee, or a quart of applejack. Wood for the bitter-cold winter was twenty dollars a cord and coal cost even more. Seven hundred dollars would buy a man's suit and two hundred his boots.

At Persimmon Wood there was plenty of wood for the winter fires. But it had to be dried out first, and Blackstrap, Gypsy, and Rider labored with the blacks from sunup to sundown. They also traveled back and forth along the river, making life worthwhile for those at Tamarind and those at Persimmon Wood. The South was losing to the North. Gypsy Smith left for weeks at a time, and no one questioned where he had gone. They all knew that the emotional scars of being banished from Tamarind by his own mother were deeply ingrained. He needed to go off and be by himself, whether he merely went off in the woods to hunt or still engaged in activities as the Black Moth. Soon, Gypsy thought, he would remove Blossom from her prison and let her come to Persimmon Wood.

Everyone agreed. Even Daisy Dawn.

Part Three

Gypsy's Angel

Chapter Eighteen

A mild winter had settled upon the lowland. Heavy silence fell on the small group as they rode cautiously into the clearing, where ash-filled smoke still drifted sullenly from smouldering timbers.

The dead horse was what Gypsy Smith saw first.

Actually he did not want to look at what lay beyond: *The ruins of Tamarind.*

The black horse Blossom Angelica had been so proud of. Gypsy flinched. Already maggots were crawling in the animal's nostrils, but the stench told him Jezebel had been dead for quite some time now . . . and over there, the remains of proud Quackser Henny.

"Doan know what sort of human could do such a thing to a pretty horse lak that. Doan think he was human a'tall, no suh!" Blackstrap shook his huge, round head. "Dis sho' is a mighty sad woh."

"Deserters. Many of them," Rider automatically answered. "Look," he said, "over there."

Beneath a live oak the washtubs lay where they had

been overturned, and an iron kettle had been carried off aways and then dropped, as if the one who'd held it had been startled.

"They must have come by boat," Gypsy said. "If they'd come on foot, they wouldn't have left that horse."

Gypsy thought of his half brother. Robert Neil. Had they burned him alive in his bed? Gypsy groaned. Poor, simple Robert Neil, he would not have had a chance because the man slept so soundly once abed. Robert Neil had asked nothing of life except to be left alone in his own mad world.

Rage foamed in Gypsy like hot roiling grease. He could taste resentment on his tongue, glimpse red flashes before his eyes. And into those flashes came the form of Blossom Angelica, laboring as she hauled a huge arched trunk across the ash-strewn greensward. She looked up then, saw them, and screamed one name.

"Rider!"

This alerted the mounted man who had been scouting the area for signs of life, anything, to give a clue as to where the folks of Tamarind had been taken—if they'd been taken.

A nerve in the muscle of Rider's cheek jumped as he heard the anguished cry of a woman. He recognized that voice. He wondered how he should respond, if he even could respond. They had given Blossom Angelica up for dead when they found the petrified ashes of the pink cabin, long since burned to the ground, bits of colorful cloth sticking out of the burned rubble, the corporal nowhere in sight. At least he himself had given her up for dead in his heart, long before he'd seen the burned-out site. Daisy Dawn had become so much a part of his happiness; she was the joy of his life. The tiny blonde possessed a rare inner beauty, and there was fire in her too—he just hadn't fanned the shadowed flames. He had really sweat it out when he'd wanted to kiss her, but she always drew herself inward just when he had the thought to take her in his arms. His love for Daisy Dawn ran deep. But what was he going to do now that Blossom was back in their lives?

Angela and Daisy hugged their shawls closer as they stared down the lane where the naked oaks spread their skeletal arms in wintry welcome. But no sign of the men appeared there.

"We might as well go back inside," Daisy said, looking over her shoulder at the hazy ball of struggling sun. "It doesn't look like they will return today. What could be keeping them? They have been gone for four days." She turned to Angela, her velvet blue eyes wide. "I'm afraid, Angela, something has happened, I just know it."

Angela sucked in her breath, then cried, "Look!"

Daisy choked back a cry. "Oh . . . my God."

Clasping hands until their knuckles whitened, Angela and Daisy went out to meet the band of trudging black folks from Tamarind. They looked as if they'd been in a war themselves. Among them were Jasmine Joe, Kapa Lu, Pandasala, Mum Zini, and Melantha, the Black Flower. The latter, the old black woman, was being held up between Jasmine Joe and Pandasala. Her prune-black face sagged in weariness, like her humped back, and her raisinlike eyes had long ago lost their look of intense hunger. She seemed to have given up the thin shred of life she'd clung to for over five days. Jasmine Joe had not been able to hunt while they'd hidden out in the swamps. He had a rifle, but he couldn't shoot. Even if he had been able to find them a meal, they couldn't make a fire because the smoke would have alerted the fiends that had come noisily to ransack Tamarind during the night. Jasmine Joe had been lucky to get all the black folks out the back way before the fire began in earnest.

Mum Zini spoke for the group. "They was crazy men. I tink they take what they wanted from the downstairs before they put the house on fire. I hear them from upstairs . . . I got out . . . Robert Neil did not." Her eyes began to run as she looked at Angela. "I wish to have saved him . . . it is thee God's truth." She straightened then, becoming the proud mulatress once again. "Among these men one stood back to watch. He did not soil his hands. This man had thee evil look about him. Eyes that glowed like a red dragon's in thee light of the fire. This man, he was looking for something." She stared directly at Angela. "Or he was looking for *someone*. He did not come after us when he saw us leave, but we could not trust such a crazy man. Perhaps he had been afraid when he saw that Jasmine Joe carried a big gun."

Angela stepped forward, leaving Daisy to stare down the lane vacantly. "Please, Jasmine, take these people to the cabins out back. There is food and comfort there." As Mum Zini began to follow, Angela took another step and placed her hands on

240

the woman's drooping shoulders. "Mum Zini, have you seen Gypsy Smith . . . or anyone else?"

"We have seen no one else, mamzelle. It has only been us, in thee swamp, for many days hiding from those madmen."

"Were they Yankees?"

"I think not, mamzelle. They had thee look of deserters, but I tink these men were from another country."

"Foreigners, Mum Zini?" Angela's eyes searched the smudged *café au lait* face. "Why do you think that?"

"I recognized a word one of them said, a bad word, mamzelle."

"What language, Mum Zini, could you tell?"

"Oh yes, mamzelle." Mum Zini started to move away. "It was Spanish!"

Stealthful, mean, and wicked, François moved like a cat on eggs, his hard brown eyes carefully whipping this way and that. He could see the house from where he hunkered down beneath the beards of long gray moss beside a persimmon tree. Brusquely he ran long, lean fingers through a wiry crop of dark brown hair while parting the Spanish moss with his other hand.

Aha! There she is, he thought.

Jessica. His prey. Jessica Angèle Hawke.

The hard, cruel planes of François's face softened congruently. He came from a militarist family. His father had been one of Louis Napoleon's henchmen in control of the French army. Napoleon was now a victim of a painful disease and aging rapidly. He was failing ingloriously in his ambitions and fumbling disastrously. François did not mean to fail. Juliet's promise was every dream he'd ever wanted fulfilled.

He never should have trusted Saville to do the job. Saville, too, had fumbled disastrously, so much that he had gone to his watery grave by François's own blade to his throat.

François thought he had been rid of the young woman Jessica. Bah! She was still alive. No thanks to Saville. She had not drowned after all. Juliet would be furious with him. He might even lose her passion. Ah . . . Juliet was passion herself. She was the most talented courtesan he had ever been involved with . . . even though she was losing *some* of her ravishing looks.

Juliet would be furious if he did not get the job accomplished. Though Juliet French (the last name her alias) was almost twice his age, there was not another lover like her. Besides, she had promised François the map for buried treasure along with a lovely villa by the sea. Cassandra, it would be his someday. Juliet said she would even obtain his own harem, with the Frenchwoman herself tutoring the young virgins all they needed to know about passion and how best to please a man.

Watching Jessica Angèle where she stood beside the dainty blonde on the porch, François again dreamed. He had dreamed of nothing else ever since Juliet had made her promises to him, on one condition, however, that he made sure Jessica Hawke had breathed her last. He had forgotten to seize the proof of Jessica's demise, the hank of Jessica's

242

lustrous chestnut hair, like none other, to bring to Juliet on a platter. It would have been her head, had Juliet had her way. Such a naughty woman was his Juliet!

Now he had been forced to return. He had had to come and go, for he had placed his head in the lion's mouth in this war-torn country just to get some proof that Jessica had gone to her eternal rest. Ah, but she had not! Now he had found his lovely corpse among the living once again.

He stared across to her and his heart ached. Ah, but it is not to be. This little *beaux yeux* was forbidden fruit. True, he had lusted after her. There would be others, Juliet had promised François and he could wait a while longer—but not too long.

Again he watched her. More enchantingly lovely than ever, even dressed in little more than rags! François had shuddered to think that he might have had to search for her body after she had drowned, to have to touch it when he chopped off the needed hank of hair. Murder he could commit, but corpses were another matter altogether.

His teeth set on edge, he thought, Why had he not gotten rid of her while he had the chance, many occasions had presented themselves. He had gotten into this business of blockade-running; it had grown to enormous proportions. Nassau, in the Bahamas, was the center of operations, where he had his little villa. Too small. He wanted to get away. To the African coast, where Juliet promised him a fortune in jewels and women. Every kind of article needed by Dixie, from munitions and medicines to cosmetics and the Paris modes, was handled by swarms of adventurers like himself who could afford to lose two ships if one got through, and generally did much better than that. Four hundred separate vessels cleared from Nassau for the Confederate States and payment was often accepted in cotton, which he could sell in Europe for ten times its original knock-down price. Yet the volume of trade was far below the demand. The blockade would doom the Confederacy.

Sarge Sorrel crept up beside François. "My friend, we must leave now. Others are coming." His shifty eyes rolled.

François swore violently. "I must have her." He clenched his tan fingers into fists.

"You mean you must cut off her locks." Sorrel chuckled. "Why not creep up on her while she sleeps and *zip*, you will have what you need, my compeer."

"She must die, it is not enough that I take her hair."

Sorrel shook his reddish head. "You had the chance, François, so many times. Why did you not do it then?"

The villain's face softened as he muttered, "This one is so fair, Sorrel, I could not do the dastardly deed myself."

"Ah, the little angel has gotten to you, too?"

"*Non!* We will do what must be done. But first . . . we must find a way to get to her."

Sorrel shrugged nonchalantly. "You had the chance while the others were away."

"*Oui.* But now they are back again, as you can see."

"I will do it if you cannot . . ." His eyes gleamed evilly.

"We will take her. But we will not kill her here."

"Ah," Sorrel said. "We will wait till we are back at the island in the Bahamas."

"We will send a man in." François whirled to face the red-haired man. "You."

"Me?"

"*Oui*," François said. "You have the isle in the Bahamas."

"Ah, you must leave my little island Paraiso out of this, François."

"You will tell them about your house there—a little bit of paradise."

"But why?" Sorrel groaned as he saw François's temper was becoming violent again.

"We will take the girl to the island. This tall man with the dark looks will follow. I have seen them together and I think he cares for our Jessica very much, enough to follow her trail if she is taken away. I would not try to take what I want while so many are about."

Sorrel threw up his hands. "But we do not want him to follow!"

"Ah . . . but we do. You see, this man has something I want very much."

Sorrel nodded, saying, "Of course, the woman Jessica."

"No, my compeer. He has something on board his ship in hiding below Charleston harbor. This is why I have been taking so long, I have followed the tall, dark one there. I have seen his bearded friends guarding this *thing*. One day I happened to see them through my spyglass checking it over to see if it needed mending."

"Why did you not just take it?" Sorrel wondered greedily.

"It is too big, my compeer, and there are too many rough sailors of this dark-visaged man guarding the Black Moon, his splendid, rakish ship."

Exasperated, Sorrel threw up his hands. "I give up," he said. "What is this fantastic thing?"

Leaning over the shorter man, François murmured, "An aircraft balloon."

His eyes bulging, Sorrel snorted, "What will you do with such a thing?" He cursed in Spanish.

"Many things. First, I shall impress Juliet by making passionate love to her . . ."

Sorrel nodded, finishing for François, ". . . in the clouds. Just like I thought—you are crazy in the head."

"Now," François said, turning about to face his half-French, half-Spanish friend, "we will stop here, for we have gone far enough to actuate my plan." A maniacal gleam showed in his eyes, and his child-hood pox scars, which made up the uneven planes of his face, grew ruddy in his excitement. He pulled out a French revolver, saying, "You will go in there as a neutral, tell them you have been wounded and are badly in need of their help. . . . You will gain all the information you can, then come with Jessica, I do not care how you do it, but meet me here in a week's time, at this exact spot. We will go from there. Do not disappoint me, my friend, or you shall take more than a mere wound in the leg."

With disbelieving eyes Sorrel watched as François lifted the revolver from his side and pointed it at his leg. A thick cloth was held over the long barrel to muffle the shot's report. The red-haired man felt a tearing heat enter his leg seconds before he was knocked to the ground. It was not until François had gone that the pain began in earnest and he knew that hours would pass before he could make it to the doors of the plantation house.

Angela was dreaming. In her dream, warm vibrant hands roved her body. Moist lips were moving over her face, down her throat, enticing, stimulating. She moved a little in her sleep, the slow, drugging kisses continuing to explore her ivory flesh. She moaned as the warm hands moved over her breasts, then to the magical place between her thighs. Then the voice, flowing with silken syllables, invaded her dream.

"Angela, say you want me, love, want me as I want you."

The sound of a lovely melody surrounded her, along with the man's voice. Awakened, she moved in a forward motion and was in his arms. "Gypsy, is that you?" Eyes, dark as jet, stared into her own. She could see him now; the room was filled with wintry moonbeams. But she was suddenly warm, so warm, feeling secure.

His hand cupped her face and held it gently. "I am here . . . and I want you. I have ached for you such a long time, my dearest. Will you let me love you?"

"When . . . when did you get back?" she asked, rubbing sleep from her eyes, her heart beating with the pulse of the music he brought with him.

"Just now." A soft chuckle followed. "I came to you as soon as I could get away."

Feeling a ripple of excitement as he looked at her intently in the moonlight, Angela shyly lowered her eyes.

"Where are the others? Is Blossom . . . is she here?"

"She is. Rider has put her to bed."

Pulling away from him, she said, "Rider? Oh no . . ."

Frowning lightly, Gypsy said, "Why do you say it like that? It is not as if Rider and Blossom are strangers, they have had . . ."

"Don't say it. Please."

"Pardon me, mamzelle," he aped Mum Zini, "but I will say what I will say. They have made love, my dear Angela."

Angela was covering her ears. But she heard him all right. Glimpses of Gypsy's moon-silvered body made her heart beat more rapidly. He was naked!

"Gypsy . . . I want to tell you something," she said, trying to catch her breath, seeing his bare, muscular torso. "I do not want it to happen again . . . between us."

"Why?" he asked, one hand sliding over her taut stomach and onto her thigh. He could tell her flesh prickled at his touch. "*Why*, I ask again, my lady."

"You call me that again. Why?"

"I asked you first." He laughed, pressing a kiss in her palm. "Why don't you want me to make love to you again. . . . It has been . . . almost, let me see, six months since I made love to you last. Didn't you like it?" There was a thin smile on his lips. "Didn't I make you feel good, my lady?" His need was becoming urgent. He could feel it pounding through every nerve and muscle of his big body as he seductively looked her over in the worn cotton nightgown, making out the softly curved hips and thighs.

Angela frowned unhappily. "I don't know who I am . . . Gypsy."

"I know who you are. You are the—"

"No." She'd placed two fingers across his lips. "Don't say it. Don't say you love me, Gypsy Smith."

"I do love you, Angela. My lady." He smiled warmly, adding, "Gypsy's lady."

"No, no, you do not really mean that."

"Yes, yes, I really do"—he cleared his throat—"believe me."

"Gypsy . . ."

"Marry me."

"How? That is impossible and you know it."

"Yes," he sadly sighed, "I know it is. But I still want you, even if we can't find a preacher at this time of night. I would like to make it right between us, Angela."

"You are old-fashioned, Gypsy Smith?"

"When it comes to the woman I care for more than anything in this insane world—yes. I am old-fashioned for you, Angela, and I know you are this way too . . . living in sin is not for us."

"Oh Gypsy, you *are* too wonderful to be real!"

His laughter filled her senses, her very being, as it drifted up from the tunnel of his throat. There was a sensual murmur in his deep-timbred voice and a teasing glint in his dark eyes.

"You laugh. But I think it is serious, Gypsy Smith."

"Ah, serious, my God yes, and you have finally

found the courage to call me by my rightful name. When I make love to you tonight you will forget all else, my lady. I shall make you ache with desire first, then squirm with pleasure, then with passion's delight." His hands caressed the inner skin of her thigh. His moonlit gaze seared her as he added, "I shall make you fall in love with me, Angela"—his undeterred tone hardened—"forever."

Chapter Nineteen

"Marry me now then, Gypsy Smith, and make me yours forever." Angela entwined her silken arms around his neck and turning, she gave herself up to his magical caress.

"Angela, Angela, God knows how I love you!"

Her hair, a silken sheen, drifted over the pillows, and Gypsy delighted in the feel of its weight as his fingers caressed the heavy skein over the tautness of her ivory breasts. She felt his lips brush her brow as her nightgown was taken expertly from the curves of her vibrantly glowing body. Her whole self opened to Gypsy, to the man whose inner vibrations she had come to know in this war-torn world, a world set apart from the one she'd known before—and knew for sure was nothing like the world she was in now. No world, other than here and now, could be both miserable and wonderful.

He took her by surprise, displaying to her his expertise in making love, love as she'd never known was in him. With every fiber of her being she was aware of him. Not wanting to cry out, she bit her lip. She felt the hard-muscled length of him. She blossomed when at last he touched her there. His long fingers explored her thighs and she gasped in the sweetest agony. He must love her . . . he *must*. For their bodies were in perfect harmony with one another.

Then she welcomed him into her body and moved as passion and ecstasy willed her. It was wild rapture. Each arrow of ecstasy was tipped with honey, no beginning or end. He spoke a different language, one that she had never heard before, and she held his finely shaped head between her fingers, mating with him, rising to meet his manhood as her body arched toward him. Her long lashes swept up as a soft murmured sigh of his name trembled from her lips. They reached the summit together, rolling forward and back in ecstasy, and began all over again as the moon rose to its crest and bathed them in a blue-silver mist of light. His voice, rough and impassioned, wooed her as he carried her into yet another explosion of pure sensation where this time laughter bubbled through her veins and a rapturous conclusion was found. Gypsy actually laughed in triumphant joy aloud.

Tenderly Gypsy rained kisses over Angela's face as they lay spent together. "Who are you?" he softly questioned.

She answered just as softly, "I am yours, Gypsy, I am *your* lady . . . remember . . . always."

The house became visible under the moon, squares

of illuminated windows seeming to stare back at the man who paused to wipe the cold sweat from his brow. Wintry shreds of fog came off the river to entwine about his legs, the good one and the leg with a hole in it. He swore vituperatively in Spanish.

Sarge Sorrel set the makeshift branch he'd managed to fix with his knife under his arm again, putting the weight of his left side into it. With every step he took, Sorrel cursed François Ce'sar and this mad mission he'd been forced to attend. All Sorrel wanted to do was get back to Paraiso, the tiny island in the Bahamas he loved. He had all he wanted there. One could live off the bounties of the island: a hundred different varieties of fish and crustaceans, abundant luscious, colorful fruit, even certain kinds of exotic vegetables. And he could make much love with Llana. . . . He made juicy kissing noises in the air.

The man spat disgustedly. "Pah! I spit on François's mother's grave too." He grimaced as he stubbed his toe on a knobby tree root. "The man is loco. I will help *estupido* get these people out of here and then I will make a run back to Paraiso and never look on his stupid face again. *Pahh!*" He spat again. "*I* will kill *her*."

A huge black form loomed up before a gasping Sarge Sorrel.

"Doan you take one more step, man, or I blow your head from here to kingdom come."

Another huge black form came up between them. It was a double-barreled rifle. The biggest one Sarge Sorrel had ever gaped into and probably the last one, Sorrel thought.

Lapsing into island lingo, Sorrel said, "Hey boy, I ain't got no bone with you." He spread his hands as best he could under the painful circumstances.

"And doan you be calling me boy. I be nobody's nigger. Now"—he poked his rifle lower—"what you be doin' here, white trash?"

Sorrel saw where the rifle went and felt it brush his private parts. A tic came and went in the white man's face.

"Hey, wait a minute, ah, whatever your name is—"

The voice boomed ominously, "Blackstrap."

Another black man stepped forward, deeply stating, "And I be Jasmine Joe." He aimed his rifle a hair lower than Blackstrap's, and Sorrel's tic became continuous.

Sorrel gaped at the two hulking black figures and seemed to shrink into himself as he stuttered, "A-And I'm Midnight the Mouse who wishes to find a hole to crawl in." (But if he had his men to back him now, he'd do away with these two and burn the house just as he'd done the last plantation where he'd thought Jessica slept.)

In her bed, with a sleeping Gypsy Smith beside her, Angela stared up at the now dark ceiling. One of her hands still rested beneath Gypsy's own, a tenderly possessive claim he'd staked upon her as he fell asleep. She turned her head, brushing her chin against his shoulder, and a contented sound seemed to come from a long way off. It was Gypsy, as he moved a little in his sleep and then settled once again, entwining his long fingers in hers, their palms pressed together in an intimate union.

Angela looked over at him but he was only a dark, exotic blur of man. Gypsy Smith. She wondered about him, as he no doubt wondered about her. They both had their mysteries, their secrets. Angela smiled into the dark. Secrets? What were her secrets? The only one she was aware of was that she loved Gypsy Smith beyond understanding. She could not let him know how very much, not yet, for a part of her was still missing and she must have that in order to give him her unconditional love.

The square of window came into her line of vision. Where would they be now? Her family, what were they like? Was her father handsome? Her mother beautiful? The corners of her mouth lifted in a sad smile. Did they miss her? She indeed felt the loss of their presence. Now she could almost see them, two beloved figures as if she were looking at them through a slowly lifting mist. They stood close together, trying to see her through that mist as she tried to see them. But they wavered and faded just as she was about to reach for outstretched arms.

A tear squeezed from Angela's eye, a solitary tear, and then another quickly followed. Hawk. She closed her damp eyes. *Hawk*. What does it mean? she wondered and wondered and . . . sleep finally came.

Angela was awakened suddenly. It was morning and the sun was streaming through her bedchamber and bathing the buttercup yellow walls. She yawned widely and stretched up to the headboard. Then she opened her stunning blue eyes to see a sweet-faced woman bending over her. She wore a crisp blue apron over a rustling black uniform of some kind and her hair was impeccable and white.

The woman's hazel eyes stared at the chestnut-haired girl in the bed. "Lord, are you going to stay abed all day? Jessica Angèle, what are you gawking at?"

"You." The girl in the bed stared around, her eyes widening at the lavish white and gold appointments that graced the spacious bedchamber. Looking back at the silver-haired woman, she said, "What is your name?"

The maid chuckled, "Now, you know my name, child. Your mother is waiting for you—in the rose garden."

"What rose garden." Angela felt her heart begin to pound. "My mother—what is her name."

Her questions received no answers.

The silver-haired maid began to fade from the bedchamber and Angela reached out frantically, shouting, "Don't go—please don't go—I have to talk to her. Come back, come back . . ."

Strong hands were shaking her roughly. "Angela, wake up."

"Come back, please, come back and tell me my mother's name."

"Angela," Gypsy crooned, folding her against his chest. "Wake up, love, it's only a dream. Don't cry"— he kissed her wet cheek—"don't cry, Angela. I am here. Please don't cry."

The sun was just tipping the horizon and the first rays sparkled in Angela's tears and gilded them. Hugging Gypsy tightly, she moaned, "Oh Gypsy, I was dreaming about my home. . . . I just know it. It was so beautiful. The sun was big and yellow, just like the room I was in. And I was lying in a huge bed . . . with pretty frills all about me. There was a silver-haired woman bending over me with a worried look on her sweet face."

Gypsy smiled against her neck as he said, "Probably your mother."

"No." Angela's lashes tilted. "No. She was not my mother, Gypsy, she was . . . a maid I think."

"Possibly your grandmother."

"No," Angela blurted out, "my grandmother is dead—" She blinked as she pushed away from him. "My grandmother . . . *is* dead. How . . . how could I know this?" She sat in the bed, wanting to put all the pieces together but reality avoided her like a nervous wild bird.

Gypsy picked up her hand to hold it and said, "Talk about it, dear Angela. This is what Stephanie made me do when I was trying to find my roots and she helped me rediscover Tamarind."

"Stephanie?" Angela blinked out of her trance.

"Yes, my friend. Someday I will take you to meet her—her and her husband. They had made one child, and there is another in the oven." He smiled and chuckled pleasantly.

"The dream!"

Feeling alarm at Angela's horrified look, Gypsy picked up her other hand and brought them together in a prayerful position between their bodies, his hands covering hers. Deeply gazing into her eyes, he said, "You will have it again, darling, I promise. I know." He kissed the tip of her nose. "I used to dream about a chestnut-haired angel every night before she

257

stepped into my life. In my dream I made love to her so often that I thought I actually knew her. It didn't take me long to realize the woman in my dreams was you, Angela. You see, darling, before these loved ones come back into your life, for real, you will dream about them over and over—and you might even learn their names if you are persistent enough."

"The maid," Angela said unhappily, "she would not tell me her name. I know her, she has to be from my home. Oh Gypsy, I know her so well!"

"Well then." He gave her a devastating grin while behind him the burnishing sun haloed his dark head as it peeped in the window. "If you know her so well, what is her name? Think of it hard, Angela, what is her name?"

Searching Gypsy's dark eyes, Angela bit down on her lip for several minutes before she groaned and her face dropped. "I don't know—" She struck the pillow and Gypsy grabbed both arms from behind. "Oh Gypsy, I don't know . . ."

"That's all right." Holding her close, he murmured, "We'll find them, Angela. Together, we'll find them." Kissing the top of her head, he murmured, with a helpless resolve, "I promise, Angela, honest to God I promise."

When he had laid her gently down upon the bed, he covered her shivering body with his own while his hands tenderly made love to her, cupping the warm firmness of her beautiful breasts until they swelled in his hand, his fingers moving lower to the tangle of curls between her thighs, and when she was shivering with a different brand of emotion, he joined with her. Slowly, slowly, to bring her to a moist passion. Her soft cry of acceptance mingled with his deeper cry as his large body responded to her yielding warmth. They gave gifts of passion to each other. And it was beautiful, this marrying of two souls beating as one. It was a joy that made her cry. At once Gypsy noticed her tears, and with his hard body atop hers, he rolled until she assumed the commanding position. A low whimper of delightful pleasure tore from Angela while she gave herself up totally to Gypsy's erotic caresses. As her tears slipped to the corners of her lips and threatened to roll off, Gypsy lapped them up, still joined with her. When he kissed her, she opened her lips to him. She could taste him, smell him, feel him, and he was so much a man that he made her feel like a lovely white feminine flame. Her flesh was a silken glove that he fit into tautly, perfectly. Love flowed between them like warmed honey as they moved in a rhythm as old as the ages. The liquid fire spread to their hearts and together they witnessed the deep purple of passion and all the other colors in love's marvelous rainbow.

Reaching the ultimate fulfillment of joining, with liquid fire vibrating and slithering against one another inside, Angela felt the erotic bliss rising inside her like hottest fire, while Gypsy's breath came out in stretching moans. And then they shivered and shattered like a million glowing stars and suns colliding, sending sparks throughout both the male and the female network.

While his love flowed into her like hot honey, Angela fantasized she was in Gypsy's aircraft balloon with him while the earth careened on its axis and she knew while the tides of ecstasy receded that Gypsy would someday take her up and there would be a repeat performance of the love they'd so fantastically just shared.

After the gusts of release passed, Gypsy held Angela close to his side, kissing, softly nibbling, nuzzling, murmuring love words of forever and ever, stroking her satin shoulders.

Angela tilted her chin up. "Gypsy?"

"Uhmm," he chuckled, "yes?"

"Will you take me up in your air balloon someday, maybe when the war is over?"

"I thought I just took you to heaven and back."

"You did, and you know we shared paradise together. But I mean"—her eyes flashed—"really take me up. I want to see the world from up there—and maybe we can even find my loved ones."

"Angela," he said, cupping her shoulder with a big, warm hand, "you can't see 'home' any better from up there. But yes, I will take you up—someday."

"When?"

"After the war." He chuckled.

"When everyone is happy again?"

Gypsy kissed her cheek, murmuring, "You are such a child, little one. Come," he shouted, "let's get up and face the day." He went to the window, and throwing up the sash, he felt the nip in the air wash over his moist, passion-flushed body. Looking down, he did a double take. "What the hell is going on?!"

"What is it?" Angela asked, reaching for Daisy's old robe, watching Gypsy slam the window shut again. He flew about the room, jerking on clothes as fast as he could. "Well? Do I have to look for myself?" She began to cross the room to the window and his urgent tone reached her just as she bent to look outside.

"We've got company."

What Angela saw made her sparkling pearl-blue eyes widen. There in the yard sat a rugged red-haired man with a crudely bandaged leg, and on either side of him stood two dark sentinels with dangerous-looking rifles at the ready should the wary man try to escape.

Angela threw off the robe. She splashed her face with cold water, grabbed an unpressed indigo frock, and hurried down as fast as she could. She did not want to miss a thing or a word for she was certain she knew this red-haired stranger.

"Are you one of Sherman's bummers?"

Angela heard Gypsy Smith fiercely interrogating the man with the bandaged leg as she neared the spot where they held the stranger captive. As his cinnamon eyes caught and held hers, Angela felt a second jolt of recognition and something clicked familiarly in her brain. The image of another man, with crisp dark hair and hard brown eyes, danced tantalizingly before her mind's eye and then vanished. It took with it the reek of something evil, a darkness she'd known before, before she'd come to be aware of herself in a world set apart from the one where her beloved ones walked with her.

"Uh-uh," the man was answering.

"Let's have your name then," Gypsy snapped.

"His name be Midnight Mouse," Jasmine Joe said with a deep chuckle, relieving the tension circling the group.

Sarge Sorrel did not like the way the tall man with eyes the color of darkest wine was looking at him as a muscle clenched along his strong jawline and his full lips were set in a grim line.

"My name is Sarge Sorrel," the wounded man said, not being able to recall that François ordered him to say otherwise.

"One of Wheeler's men?" Gypsy shot at him.

"Uh-uh."

"Mosby's?"

"No," Rider put in, bending a knee while he stuffed a hand flatly in the backside of his jeans, "I would have known him. . . . Remember, I was one of Mosby's Rangers."

Standing off to the side of the group with Angela, Daisy Dawn tried not to flinch as Rider said these words. Mosby's Rangers were rumored to have been bad men who robbed, raped, and murdered. And she did not want to believe Rider capable of such heinous crimes. Guerrilla activities. Raiders. All words that frightened her as Rider was frightening her lately. This was the man she'd loved more than life itself all her childhood and teen years, right up until she turned nineteen. She was that now, and the way Rider looked at her scared her for he'd never looked at her so intensely, as he was doing now. Rider was bigger than life to her, and she wondered how she'd ever thought she could be capable of trying to win his love. With him living on the same plantation with her, Daisy had learned he possessed a ruggedness and air of self-command with a singleminded presence she found threatening and dangerous. Just why he seemed to pose a threat to her she could not say. He had never made her think this way before. To be sure, she'd never really known how compelling a man Rider was, and she was afraid he was too much a man for her. His hands were big, his fingers long and strong. Working outside in his shirtsleeves, Rider looked tough and lean. Pitting himself against nature, with his wonderfully proportioned body wielding the ax or pulling, straining, pushing, or even just walking, she found him breathtakingly handsome. If she fell any more in love with him than she already was, Daisy knew she'd begin to flush miserably every time he opened his mouth to utter one teeny word to her. Across the way, she now met his intent stare, his dark eyes, almost a purplish blue, watching her until she felt a strange quivering that left her trembling and she had to tear her eyes away from him or else turn as red as a tomato.

"Are you feeling all right?" Angela asked, turning to look at Daisy and seeing Blossom come into her range of vision. The black-haired vixen had been coming down the stairs and was heading in their direction at the moment.

"I will be fine, Angela," Daisy said. "I feel a little lightheaded, that's all."

Angela was concerned. "You do look slightly flushed. Have you eaten something?"

"Pandasala made us all a huge breakfast." Daisy smiled, continuing to watch Gypsy Smith interrogate the man who was probably just a deserter. She wasn't sure; she could not hear all they were saying for Gypsy Smith had moved closer to the man and walked about the stranger's chair while firing questions at the man's head.

"So, Pandasala made everyone a huge breakfast," Angela was saying, "but did you eat anything is what I really want to know."

Seeing Blossom out of the corner of her eye, Daisy felt irritated all of a sudden, totally out of nature for the little blonde to become heated over a few concerned words. She snapped, "Angela, please, you act as if you are my mother or something. I won't blow away, you know."

Directing a smirk at Daisy Dawn's frail figure, the vamp put in, "Of course she will, won't she, Angela?" Blossom smiled around the blonde, who was humiliatingly conscious of Rider's interest in their conversation. To Daisy she said, "You're much too skinny, darling, you need to put some meat on your bones. Otherwise"—she shot Rider a long-lashed scrutiny—"no man will want to look at you. Isn't that right, darling?" She tried to bring Rider into the conversation; he'd been so distant ever since they had found her sifting through the rubble at Tamarind. That looney corporal had left her alone and gone off chasing those silly deserters. She did not even know if Alan Bickles would return and she believed she didn't much care.

"A young woman," Gypsy Smith was saying to their prisoner, "by the name of Annabelle Huntington was murdered not long ago. The man—I would assume it was a man—he used a blue silk stocking. Would you know anything about that, Mr. Sorrel?"

"A—A blue silk stocking?" Sorrel stammered.

Then he shook his head vigorously. "No, no, I know nothing of this young woman and this stocking you speak of," he lied outright.

Swinging around to face the blanching prisoner, Gypsy said, "I think you do. And I also think you know—and possibly were involved with the burning of a plantation down the road. Tamarind is the name of the plantation, but that means nothing to you, I suppose."

"No"—Sorrel shook his head—"nothing. Nothing at all."

Sorrel's eyes shifted back and forth fast. This was not turning out at all as François had planned. The tall, dark-eyed man would kill him if he knew he'd started that fire. Blood was soaking the bandage a black woman had earlier fixed for him but he was bleeding like a stuck pig again and the fierce-visaged man questioning him could see this, too. Was there no mercy in him?

In the next moment Sarge Sorrel sagged in relief. The angel of mercy had stepped forward, placing her soft-looking hand on the interrogator's arm. Angela could feel the muscles of Gypsy's forearm tense suddenly under her touch and she looked up into his face questioningly.

"I am sorry, love," Gypsy said loud enough for everyone to hear. She flushed as he went on in a softer tone. "Your touch on my cool flesh was like a warm blanket." His voice dipped lower yet. "Always your nearness overwhelms me, my lady," he murmured into her hair as a rush of rose tint stained her cheeks. "Now, what can I help you with?" His smile was as intimate as a caress as he looked down into her face.

"I"—she turned her back on the curious-eyed prisoner—"I think I know this man, Gypsy."

Sarge Sorrel watched the tall man stiffen at the young woman's words—the young woman he knew only as Jessica Hawke. He wanted to hear what they called her here and his curiosity was rewarded in the next instant as the dark-haired man spoke.

"Angela . . . are you certain?"

Out of the corners of her eyes Angela glanced at the prisoner once again. A light frown appeared between her eyebrows.

The prisoner suppressed a flinch as her serious scrutiny washed him from head to foot, then came to rest above the bridge of his nose. No! She could not recognize him. He'd always worn a bandit's scarf over his face . . . with the upper half visible! She could *not* be certain!

Angela touched her forehead absently as she turned from the red-haired man. His eyes had such utter fright in them. What was she to do? If she said the wrong thing an innocent man might come to harm. She wasn't sure just what Gypsy would do, but she had an idea that it would not go easy for the man.

"Angela?"

Gypsy was waiting.

"I—I am not sure." With all eyes trained on her every word, Angela repeated, "I just cannot be sure."

Tears pooled in her eyes, tears that Gypsy wiped away with his fingertips. "Daisy . . . take Angela inside for me, please?"

Sincerely sorry for being so short with Angela, Daisy stepped forward. But the black-haired vixen shot in at an angle, and wrapping her arm about

Angela's shoulders, Blossom walked haughtily to the house with Angela.

Rider watched Daisy standing there in the midst of the men, looking small and abused, while Gypsy, Blackstrap, and Jasmine Joe went back to harshly questioning the man.

All of a sudden a change came over Daisy and she whirled to face the two black men and Gypsy Smith. "Please, can't you see the man is wounded? He said he'd nothing to do with the fire. I think you've questioned him enough!"

With that, Daisy snatched her dusty-hemmed skirts up in a hand and walked in her graceful gait to the porch, where she looked back to see if they'd taken her advice. All of them had been so intently watching her move toward the house that not one of them had moved a muscle.

Now there was a great movement toward the man in the chair. All three helped the wounded man into the house while Rider kept right on staring at Daisy Dawn. With one hand stationed on a slim hip, he swept her a gallant bow and his dark amethyst eyes never left hers for an instant as he laughed across to her in a rich, deep tone.

Daisy Dawn smiled back. Then she vanished within her white-pillared house. Rider looked down at the ground while catching his full, lower lip between his teeth. That one tiny gesture from her . . . he was amazed at the thrill it gave him.

Angela had seen that brittleness that had crackled between Daisy and Blossom like a blade unsheathed, a look with a question in it and even a warning. If Blossom still wanted Rider, Angela suspected that she would use sly weapons in any conflict that might arise between her and Daisy. It might be very good, she thought, if one time in her life something Blossom coveted was denied her.

Chapter Twenty

With a soft lilac shawl across her shoulders, Daisy stepped outside and shut the door behind her. She looked up and took a deep breath of invigorating night air. A midnight sky strewn with numberless stars greeted her, and as she walked, the moon touched the path with a gentle blue wash of color.

Daisy had been unable to sleep. Every time she closed her eyes, Rider was smiling behind her lids. Then she would begin to fantasize about Rider again. The wild imaginings were always the same and she would begin to toss and turn in her mussed bed. She imagined what Rider's kiss would be like, imagined it just as she had the day he had saved her from a horrible death in the swamp. She had been wild with a temptation to wrap her slim arms around his neck, to run her fingers through his thick, burnished hair. She had always loved Rider.

Daisy was not watching where she was stepping, and before she could pull herself back, she found herself standing in the copse of moon-laced trees—

not ten feet away from the man of her dreams!

Rider hadn't caught sight of her yet; he was gazing out upon the moon-silvered waters. Fiery heat coursed through Daisy and her heart pounded turbulently. She could turn and run before he noticed her standing there.

Hurry! her mind cried frantically. Get away, or else he'll think you've followed him out here like a lovesick fool!

Daisy whirled, clutching at her skirts, ready to fly.

Rider turned just then. He recognized the moonlit wraith at once. Her pale blonde hair hung in delicate waves down her back, and her skirts, which he knew were worn without the devices Blossom employed, belled softly out from her delicate frame like the petals of a moonflower. She was moving away from him.

"Daisy please . . . wait."

Her eyes flew wide and her breath caught harshly in the tunnel of her throat. She rushed forward with such careless haste—needing only frantically to get away—that she stumbled over a fallen branch in her path.

In the next moment, warm strong fingers closed about the caps of Daisy's shoulders. The bone-softening warmth she'd experienced so often in her wild dreams of Rider now returned to her. She wanted to fly now, to escape. It was only another dream she was having, she told herself.

She could not know in her passionate bewilderment that she'd cried out when he had touched her.

Rider's grip on her tightened unconsciously. "Are you all right?" There was great concern, and something else in his voice.

"You're hurting me," she almost whimpered. In truth the slight pressure on her arms felt so good she was ready to swoon from the pleasure.

"Oh Lord, I'm sorry, Daisy, truly I am."

He at once released her, but his eyes held her as if he had in his possession a precious bird he couldn't allow to fly away.

That sweet Southern drawl . . . as always, just hearing Rider speak sent tremors of delicious torment through her breast. She looked up into Rider's eyes, which seemed to glow like moonstones in the night. Times without number, she'd wanted so desperately to see love for her reflected there but what she'd always seen was Blossom Angelica. The raven-haired vixen had stood forever between them, it seemed.

"I-I was just going inside," she said, trying not to look at the firm features, dark against the moonlight. Like an awakened river in springtime, delight flooded and coursed through her blood.

"Daisy, don't go yet."

She thought he spoke in a strange, yet gentle voice. What could Rider wish to speak to her about, out here, in the shadow-filled trees with the midnight sky sifting white moondust down all around them? Why out here, away from everyone . . . just the two of them?

"I really should go back," she said in a tone almost like a breath-held whisper.

"Why?" His voice was like dark velvet.

"Well . . . it is late"—she laughed softly—"and it is chilly."

"I'll stand closer," he murmured, "keep you warm."

"Oh, I don't know," she blurted out, scarcely recognizing the breathless voice as her own.

"What do you mean"—his mouth quirked with a smile—"you don't know?" He moved closer and looked down at her precious blonde head tenderly. "It won't frighten you if I put my arm around your shoulders, will it?"

"No." But when his arm brushed her shoulder and then settled about her, a brief shiver went through her limbs. Her body experienced pleasure, and wanted more and more.

"There." He spread his long fingers gently cupping her upper arm. "Isn't this much better?"

"Y-yes." Her voice broke, much to her dismay.

"Daisy, I'm a little confused. Tell me, why had you been avoiding me lately?"

"I was not aware that I was, Rider." The breath caught in her lungs. "There has been so much to do around here, and it has been a chore for us all just staying alive, trying to find enough for all of us to eat, afraid the Yankees will come and take what little we do have—"

"Daisy, you know that Gypsy Smith and I will never let them get to us." He chuckled softly. "We have a small arsenal here, an assortment of equipment carried by soldiers, several .56 caliber Colt Revolving rifles; .54 caliber Austrian rifles. Not to mention what the Negroes are guarding the place with."

"Yes." She smiled. "And the 'No Trespassing' signs you and Gypsy Smith have ringed about the property will mean nothing to those Yankees if they mean to take Persimmon Wood."

A faint tremor made Daisy's shoulders quiver and Rider pulled her closer. "Gypsy Smith knows these Yankees, and do you think he'll allow them to just step in here and take over Persimmon Wood?"

"He is a Yankee," she stressed, "and he still makes trips to God knows where."

"Daisy, we can trust him. He's one of us. He's wounded, remember."

"Has he deserted then?"

"Well . . . almost. Gypsy Smith, for one, doesn't want to be an instrument for the North when the guillotine comes down on the South. He looks around at his friends, his love Angela. He has a wound. He is no hero and he doesn't want to be. He would rather be a hero for a few dispirited folks than a hero of the North who wreaks vengeance on the whole failing South."

Gazing up at Rider's moon-silvered face, she asked, "Does Angela know all this?"

"Of course, darlin'."

A low gasp tore from Daisy, and Rider pretended he had not heard. Lord, but you are so tiny and beautiful, Rider was thinking. He became warm all over just imagining what the touch of her lips would be like. It made him feel good just being near her. How much more pleasurable to press her in his arms, he wondered with a passionate shiver.

"You are cold, too," she said. "We should—"

"Not cold, Daisy." Bending to brush a soft kiss on her forehead, he added, "I'm warm, darlin', very warm."

273

A tingling excitement flooded Daisy from head to foot and a flush of desire heated her face. And at the same time a wave of panic swept through her. *What if he were to kiss her . . . really kiss her?*

Her nerves tensed at once when he shifted and came to stand in front of her. Her heart began to leap in her chest then as his beloved face became a dark blur and she could feel his warm breath on her cheek. When his lips brushed her temple she experienced a shock and choked back a cry. She was frightened. She was hot. Dizzy.

"Daisy, don't be afraid, darlin'." Cupping the back of her head with both of his large hands, burying her face against his throat, he held her gently, with all the aching tenderness he felt inside for her. "I just want to hold you. . . . You don't know how long I been wanting to just hold you." His heart thundered almost painfully in his strong, wide chest. Still cupping her head, he moved her back so that he could look into her face. "I never really took a good look at you, Daisy, not until that day in the swamp when you became a woman in my eyes."

Her voice was shaky. "I have been a woman for quite a while now, Rider."

"Try to understand, darlin', I had always thought of you as the Fortune child, the . . . orphan." Feeling her stiffen, he hastened to say, "I'm sorry . . . I didn't mean it that way."

Trying to lower her face while he still held her, she said, "Yes you did, Rider." She spoke very softly. "I don't mind."

"What I meant to say was . . . everyone seemed to be overly protective toward you. Robert Neil.

Blackstrap. Even all your friends." He smiled warmly, but she could not see his eyes with the moon behind his head, to read if his words were spoken true. "Everyone seemed to"—he faltered—"to love you."

Like a heavy enveloping mist, silence loomed between them.

Rider stepped closer. Daisy's stomach clenched tight.

"No—" was all she could mutter. Her dainty hands came up to erect a fragile barrier between them.

Capturing her arms, Rider spread them back and away from her body, his head bending close to her ear. "Daisy—?"

Turning her head too quickly, Daisy's small frightened cry brushed against Rider's pulsating throat. That smallest touch of her sweet lips against his hot flesh was Rider's undoing. Without another warning, he swept her gentle curves against his chest while banding his arms around her back. He hugged her close, waiting for his wild heart to quieten a little.

Daisy had always dreamed of being crushed in Rider's embrace, but she had never imagined just how wonderful it could be. The feeling made her want to cry. She did not realize she was doing just that.

"Daisy," Rider said, cupping the side of her face in one warm big hand. "I didn't mean to make you cry. Please don't." Moisture sparkled in his own eyes. "You don't know how bad it makes me feel to see you cry. Daisy, everything will be all right, love, your life is in my hands and I will never let you be unhappy again."

Wrenching away from him, she cried, "But I will . . . I will! Don't you understand!" Whirling, she stepped out to hurry away from him, when Rider caught her by the shoulders and spun her back to face him.

A muscle leapt along the side of his lean cheekbone and angry desperation was in his voice. "Why do you constantly avoid me? Why do you go far out of your way to keep from coming too near me when others are near?" Shaking her, he ground out, "I want some answers, Daisy, now!"

"I-I'm cold . . . let me go, Rider."

"No. And you are not cold. You are as warm as I am, I can feel it, Daisy Dawn. You want me, Daisy, you want me as I want you."

"No." Her heart lurched as a betraying shiver of desire ran through her. "No. You belong to Blossom Angelica."

He swore softly. "I belong to no one." Again he stepped closer and felt the now familiar tightening in his loins. "Yet I would belong to one, only one."

"You and Blossom will wed, it is inevitable!"

"Nothing is inevitable." He cupped her face in hands that had tremors in them. "Nothing but you and I, Daisy Dawn."

Pulling her roughly to him, Rider lowered his head and captured her lips. Daisy all but swooned in Rider's arms as she drowned in the sweetness of his kiss. And her knees did begin to weaken as the kiss deepened. Deep, deep, and deeper still. When he stepped closer, and closer, with a knee going between hers, his tongue flicking in and out, Daisy felt the flame bursting to life, one that started in the center of her being and radiated outward.

When at last their lips parted, still moistly touching, brushing in a series of shivery feather-touches, Rider said the words she'd never in her wildest imaginings would have believed could come true.

"I love you, Daisy Dawn, I love you so much it hurts." His lips brushed an earlobe and the blood pounded madly in her veins. "Marry me, my love, right away."

"How?" Her voice emerged shivery. "There is no preacher for miles around."

"You love me, don't you?" Wildly his eyes searched her face in the shadowy moonlight. She nodded. "Say it, Daisy, say you love me please. I want to hear it spill from your lips like sweetest honey."

Dropping back her head, arching her neck while Rider pressed closer and buried his face there with a moan, she closed her eyes for several moments. When he could not stand the suspense any longer, Daisy fell forward into his arms, reaching up and pressing her lips against his ear. Her fingers circled his neck and he wrapped his arms about her waist.

"Oh Rider, Rider, I have always loved only you, my dearest, and I will love you forever and ever."

Sucking in his breath, Rider pushed her at arm's length, while he said in a harsh, raw voice, "How long have you been in love with me, Daisy?"

Her chin rose and her velvet blue eyes flashed wonderfully. "Since I was a child, Rider, I've loved you. It seems forever. No man has even kissed me, you are the first one I . . . I would have become a lonely old maid, you see."

Staring at her as if she'd suddenly become the rarest of gems, the purest of priceless, treasured gold, he swallowed hard, saying, "My god, I am going to find that preacher. All the horses in kingdom come couldn't prevent me."

Chapter Twenty-One

Daisy could not hear Reverend Jacoby because of the joyous bells that rang and were clanging in her ears. And Ridpath Huntington stood beside her, smiling, fine lines around his eyes fanning out as he momentarily recalled when he and Gypsy Smith had kidnapped the good reverend, snatching him from a peaceful slumber. The midnight raiders had promptly insisted the reverend bring along his Bible and the parish register from the Charleston church. Reverend Jacoby had demanded his abductors return him to the Mayfield house at once, shouting hellfire and damnation at their heads in his mightiest sermonizing voice. If Rider had thought their passage through the night in the swamp boat would never end, the reverend must have been especially of that frame of mind. The cleric had been ushered into a house, thinking, as he'd told them later, that he'd been mistakenly branded a spy and brought here to be hanged—wherever here was—and it was then that Gypsy Smith and Ridpath Huntington removed their rascally masks. Then the good reverend had smiled with great relief when the women, two utterly lovely women, appeared—first, Daisy Dawn Fortune, when he knew very well from her strict attendance and from his hundreds of visits to the hospital; and then Angela, the young lady he'd seen a few occasions in his church when she'd attended with the Fortunes.

Suddenly Blossom Angelica Fortune appeared in the door, wearing a bold red gown which fit snugly about her small waist. Carnelian rouge dotted her high-boned cheeks. The reverend suppressed an urge to frown disapprovingly. Blossom herself looked none too happy.

Was this some sort of practical joke, the reverend wondered at first. Then he looked Daisy Dawn over carefully and he suddenly realized the reason he'd been brought here.

Daisy smiled radiantly as she entered the drawing room. She had taken her dearly departed mother's wedding gown from the trunk where it had been carefully stored since her mother's own wedding. Jana had showed it to her daughter once and Daisy had stood in the tiny upper room with sun-captured dust motes floating about her, in that moment and from that moment on dreamily pictured herself wearing the lovely gown as she stood beside Ridpath Huntington and became his wife. As the years passed, however, Daisy had been saddened to think she'd never say her blessed vows alongside the man of her dreams, never, not as long as Blossom Fortune, her gorgeous cousin, was alive on this earth.

Daisy now gazed up at Rider, still unable to believe

this was happening. There were no dark shadows across her heart; his eyes were alight with tenderness and love and passion. His eyes were bright amethysts that took her loveliness in.

The gown she wore was of pale ivory silk brocade and trimmed with alençon lace with a deep pleated flounce around the hem that graced the bare wood floors. Her heavy blond hair was drawn back, soft waves framing her delicate face, and from the crown of her head a cascade of loose curls tumbled to her waist. Delicate pink rosettes crowned the sheer glory of her hair, with a veil of handmade lace floating in an ethereal image about her head and shoulders.

Smiling happily, Daisy looked over at Angela, stunning in a gown of pastel turquoise Swiss muslin; the lovely gown was one Jana's bridesmaid had worn. Angela's shining chestnut hair had been braided by Mum Zini's deft hands into a coronet atop her head with a headdress of misty azure Brussels lace, of a color like the sea at dawn. Her smile, like Daisy's, was radiant.

Blackstrap had been sent upriver to Tanglewood with Jasmine Joe and they'd loaded the boat with household items, among them Rider's many outfits of clothing and personal belongings, besides Annabelle's many frocks and gowns. Daisy had disagreed over the use of the latter; she felt it would not be right to take dear Annabelle's things. But Rider had gently argued they could be put to good use, even for the poor black women who were sorely in need of a change of clothes. With a practiced needle and thread the clothing could be made to fit most of the blacks. Pandasala was the only woman of wider girth, but she'd been wise to take along as many of her own dresses she could carry, among other items she'd discovered in the cabins when she had gone back to Tamarind with Jasmine Joe to sift through the scattered remnants earlier in the week.

Reverend Jacoby took his place with opened Bible, while the parish registry was set close at hand for the recording of the names of those gathered there in Holy Matrimony.

Gypsy Smith wore the dark blue of a Union officer. Rider Huntington wore the gold and gray of the Confederacy. At first the reverend's eyes had widened and then he had gone on without complaint. The only thing that bothered him as he began to speak was the cold-eyed stare of the young woman in heathenish red.

Angela had drawn in a quick breath as Gypsy Smith came to stand before the reverend stationed before the mantel in the drawing room. The sun was rising and a wan shaft of rose-gold struck the rigorously brushed waves of Gypsy's thick hair and it gleamed like black pearl. She had noticed a new contentment in his face. For the happy occasion, Gypsy had acquired a polished veneer, and Angela saw yet another side of Gypsy's many-faceted character. Truly he was a gem of a man.

Gypsy's fingers were cool, smooth, hard, soft, as they brushed hers. Angela knew one moment of fear, as if someone had walked over her grave, when she glanced at the witnesses and saw the somber cinnamon eyes of Sarge Sorrel staring at her from the corner of the room from where he sat under the guard of the hulking Blackstrap.

Angela had not been listening. Her mind was lost in the mists of the past. When it came time for her to speak, she followed automatically into the vows when Daisy and Rider had said theirs. She looked up into Gypsy's eyes and murmured tenderly, "I do."

Reverend Jacoby cleared his throat, seeing the double wedding before his tired eyes, and said importantly, "I now pronounce you man and wife . . . both of you . . . all four of you"—he coughed—"you may both kiss the . . . brides."

When it came time to sign their names, all were so happily engrossed and eager for the toast with Pandasala's berry wine that no one bothered to read the maiden name Angela had absentmindedly recorded there. She was the last one to sign, with the witnesses at her back also eager for the simple celebration to begin that they hastily put down their names beneath the wedded couples. One of the witnesses, gowned in garish red, was not in such haste as she drifted over to read the names recorded there. Looking down and then slyly up, across the room to where the couples stood toasting one another, Blossom let the name *Angela Hawke* burn into her brain like a fiery brand. Very slowly and cautiously she closed the register and pressed her palm upon it for several moments before moving away from the table. Snatching up a glass for herself from Pandasala's proffered tray, she sashayed over to the corner and joined the man named Sorrel, and asking him a question as he stood to his feet, she turned and gestured for Pandasala to bring their thirsty prisoner

283

a glass of the same.

After a few glasses of Pandasala's delicious wine the reverend—feeling quite relaxed now and thinking this was not such a wild idea for he was called upon at all hours to perform all manner of service anyway—was sorry to see the celebration come to an end. The boiled potatoes and smoked boar meat had been quite satisfying, too, not to mention the fine conversation with the gracious young lady Daisy Dawn . . . now Huntington.

"Ah—" Gypsy Smith smiled as he looked over at Rider. "I think we should change before we deliver the good reverend back to the Mayfields." He recalled how they had found out that Reverend Jacoby was staying with the Mayfields, and thanked God for a friend like Stephanie Browden; the woman seemed to know everything about everyone in Charleston and what they were up to. Just what the reverend had been doing at the Mayfields was not clear; perhaps it had something to do with repairing the cleric's quarters after the Union army had shelled the city. Shame on the Yankees, he thought with a click of his tongue.

"Yes, we should do that," Rider said, reluctant to leave his beloved bride so soon after the ceremony. They would be safe; they'd be leaving the black folks with the newly wedded brides. Rider chuckled before he went up to change, telling everyone, "I'll never forget when one officer was badly in need of some clothes. He donned gray pants and blue jacket and both sides shot at the poor fellow."

"Ah yes," Gypsy said, smiling at his happily flushed bride across the room, "I remember hearing

284

many such stories, all true, every one of them." His face pinkened. He'd not tell them he'd done the same and almost got himself killed just as the other poor fools who had not been as lucky to find themselves in one piece.

After the brides had been kissed and hugged once more, the mischievous grooms escorted the refreshed reverend to the waiting swamp boat, where they helped him get comfortable, his Bible and the parish register safely nestled in his thick-set lap.

Watching the boat from the upper gallery, the two lovely brides with their arms about each other's waist waved until they could no longer see *Lizzy-Mae*. Angela was the first to break the golden silence that had held them as they watched their beloved husbands leave the house and walk down to the boat landing.

Angela's teeth had been worrying her lower lip. "I wonder why I have this strange feeling . . . like . . . something bad is about to happen. Look, I am even trembling."

Daisy had been so ecstatic that she'd barely noticed anything but Rider. He was her whole world, and she shivered deliciously to think what would come later.

"Why—yes you are," Daisy finally said, feeling the tremors in Angela's body. "Maybe you are only excited?" she added.

Angela turned crimson. "That could be part of it." She had never let her friend know just how close Gypsy and she had been before this day. To her way of thinking, old-fashioned though it may seem to others, lovemaking was personal and not to be discussed openly or bragged about. Although most certainly, she could find much to boast about where Gypsy was concerned!

"What could go wrong?" Daisy said, frowning lightly now, her startling blue eyes riveted on the beaten path to the boat landing.

Following her gaze, Angela shrugged. "I guess nothing."

Turning to go back inside, however, both brides shivered as a chill wind swept past them into the house and molded their wedding gowns to their bodies.

Chapter Twenty-Two

Nassau, in the Bahamas, had become the center of operations in the business of blockade running, and every kind of article needed by Dixie, from munitions and medical supplies to cosmetics and the Paris modes, was being handled by swarms of adventurers. The operation had grown to enormous proportions. This was the main reason Julia French had moved from Nassau to the tiny island of Paraiso, privately owned by a man named Sarge Sorrel. She thought she had wanted to have some time alone, sunning herself on the white-sanded beach while she sipped sweet wine, walking alone at night under the big tropical moon and the glitter of huge stars while she made her plans . . . plans to be again with the man she had always lusted after—Esteban, Steven Hawke. Ah . . . such discoveries of the flesh she had destined for Steven. She even had a feeling that she might be in love with him.

Suddenly Julia felt very alone. She roamed the halls of the villa in search of something to do besides making plans of doing away with first Jessica Hawke and then Monica Hawke. Oh yes, one day she would succeed. She yawned, stretching her carmine red lips wide, and then pursed them in a dreamy pout. Ruminating, she recalled Steven's lazy seductive look right before they made love, and just the thought of him, even now after so many years apart, made her heart flutter. She would never forget the kisses that had left her knees feeling so weak that she had to lie down; otherwise she would have fainted in his arms. Hmm, she thought now, not so bad an idea. . . . It would make her seem young all over again once she had him in her clutches as before. Why had she not thought of it before?''

Now Julia wished she could be back on Nassau. She was bored to death. She needed a man. Where was that idiot François, she wondered. He had told her to wait for him here. She passed the mirror and gave her reflection another thorough scan. Then she moved back to the terrace doors.

At least she'd had more company back on Nassau and there had been more houses and humans than here on this lonely wild island. Nassau had its houses with wide verandas squatting on the low hill, shining like an open box of treasure in the hot shimmering sun. At night the yellow of moonlight etched the airy porches romantically. She would never forget the handsome blockade runner she had met there in the deserted lobby at the midnight hour. Raoul had been the only man to come along who most resembled Steven Hawke in appearance . . . and in other ways. Too bad he had been in love with a younger woman and had even called her name in the

288

height of passion. Ah, she had been so enraged that she had raked bloody trails down his tan, muscled back.

Julia gazed out the terrace doors to a distant spot. Here, too, were the graceful royal palms and dark green sea pines which waved exotically over white shimmering sands. Of course, Nassau had more movement, more excitement to fire the blood, more people, open landaus and carriages filled with women holding frilly parasols above their expertly coiffed heads, the red of British uniforms, and strong black men everywhere on the waterfront loading and unloading the vessels that had drawn up to the docks teeming with humanity. She had settled in the Royal Victoria Hotel there, for just any rooming house would not do for her—the Duchess of Fitz-James.

Juliette La Chappiere, alias Julia French. Some, like François, still dared to call her the shortened form, Juliet. Ah, she was bored and restless.

"Pah!" she spat, roaming through the West Indies–style house of rose-tinted plaster. She paused before the huge cheval mirror and studied her face and generous figure with a critical eye. Her red watered silk dressing gown showed off her generous curves to advantage—pah!—to disadvantage. She needed to lose a few pounds, that was all. "I am still the most beautiful duchess in all the world." She muttered a strong expletive. "I am . . . the most beautiful *woman* in all the world."

She would not think of him. She would not think of Steven Hawke. Her Esteban. She would think of him later. Why could she not get him out of her system? He was all she dreamed of, night and day, day and night.

She considered the color of her hair. Her gray-brown roots were showing again. Her hair needed to be dyed over, to vivify the strands of once gleaming brunette. Julia fastened her overbright green eyes on the reflection of the arched doorway behind her.

"Dimwitted slow native. She should have brought me my chilled wine long ago."

Just where was Llana? Perhaps she could send Llana's oafish brother Carolos to Nassau for some hair *cosmetique*. The French paste, that was the most excellent. Perhaps she should make the trip herself. . . .

Julia had thought it would truly be a pleasure to be alone and have some privacy. Her young lovers were always pawing at her, begging to make love. Some of them were even vain about their performance. Teaching them a thing or two might have been fun, and even though she had thought of it often, she had never given away all her trade secrets.

For all she knew, stuck on this tiny wild island, François and Sorrel could have deserted her. The mirror caught her reflection again as she moved into its view. Ah! She always ate too much of the rich food on Nassau. Perhaps she should stay here and lose a few more pounds. What could it hurt?

At least she received the American newspapers from Nassau when Carolos made his weekly trips there. She knew ultimate defeat stared the Confederacy in the face. The sole remaining hope was that the North, war-weary, might throw away the victory already won. Many of the war-hardened characters, with loyalty oaths to no one side, drifted into the position of bandits, riffraff that committed crimes against person as well as crimes against property. There was pillage and devastation. Horrors unthought of, no doubt.

Julia shuddered. She would hate to be in America now. If François did his evil deed well enough, who would question the death of one Jessica Angèle Hawke? Death was everywhere. It had been reported to her by a blockade runner of their acquaintance that a certain young lady with chestnut hair and a sweet countenance was still alive and well at a place he called Tamarind. But that was weeks ago. Julia smirked evilly. By now Jessica Hawke was no longer, if François had done his job well. And he had better have! Julia bared her claws. Or else!

Julia looked out from the spacious room, out across the white sands fringed with coconut palms grown forever leaning into the wind, stooped over, like old men, or, she thought with distaste, old women.

She grimaced, making her once beautiful face look ugly. Breadfruit. Bananas. Coconuts. Ugh! She'd had her fill of them. This was like a ghost haven, not unlike Porto Bello or Nombre de Dios. No better or more inhabited than Cassandra, her villa on the Atlantic coast of Africa. The wild province was abandoned for the most part, with the insistent whispers of the sea rounding the windswept stone walls.

Welcome to Cassandra, she had said to Monica Hawke and her mother before her. She had thought the only way to keep Victoria and her first husband apart was to take the woman to a place far away, to

Africa. She had lied and said Antoine had found himself another woman. With a dejected Victoria in tow, she had finally convinced her "friend" there was no other way than to go with her to Cassandra and begin a new life. She had hoped the brokenhearted woman would see to her own demise, but such had not been the case. The lovely Victoria had pined away but had not seen fit to take her own life. Cascara, the wild horse, had not killed Victoria as so many had been led to believe. Julia herself had fixed the English saddle with a broken cinch before Victoria had ridden out on that fateful day.

Poor Victoria. Jessica's lovely grandmother. The girl had never known her, thanks to Julia's scheming mind. . . . The woman in the mirror chuckled and there was a grisly sound to her voice.

Julia's face hardened into ugly lines. Then had come Victoria's daughter, Monica. It was bad enough that her cousin Antoine had fallen in love with the lovely Victoria. Then Victoria's equally beautiful daughter had taken away the only man she had ever loved and lusted after. Julia had had Monica in her clutches, but then that scrawny dark lad whom Monica had named Benjie had thwarted her plans and ridden away double in the moon-shadowed night on the wild horse Cascara. Her partner in crime had pursued Monica and the dark lad but everything had come to naught. Alex Bennington had found his death under the very hand of the man she wanted—Steven Hawke.

This time she would not fail. More important and consequential, François dared not founder. She would personally see to his death if he fumbled this one last time, for this would indeed be his last chance. She could trust *Sorrel!*

Bringing the duchess's chilled wine at last, Llana did not let the older woman see the dark hatred shining in her eyes as she smoothly exited the room as swiftly as she had entered it.

Going out onto the terrace, Julia took the chilled bottle and glass with her. She lounged in a chair, facing the sun-kissed sea, and gulped down a glass of wine in her thirst, and when she had satisfied it, she sat sipping a second glass of the fiery native drink. It was not long before she was beginning to feel the soothing effects the potent liquid always brought. No, she thought, she wouldn't be here much longer.

Julia thought she would have a chance with Steven Hawke once their only child was gone. With Jessica Angèle out of the way, Julia would have another chance for her Esteban, for the death of the child would drive him away from his beautiful Monica. She believed that the girl was the only reason they remained together; after all, Steven had been forced to wed the chit. He could not really love her.

She would have another chance. Yes, this she knew. They would not be able to stand each other's presence with the girl dead. Steven would blame Monica for allowing the girl so much freedom. Julia knew this was true; otherwise it would not have been such an easy task to steal the girl from El Corazón. And Monica would blame Steven for . . . whatever. It was perfect. Julia could step in and say she had tried to help. *How,* she did not know just yet. She had not gotten to that part of her plan but she would, she would. All she knew was that her revenge would be realized, someday soon, and François would give it to her. The stupid oaf. All Juliet had to do was have François eliminate the one person standing in her way. Jessica Hawke. Then all would be hers.

Lyons, France

The moon was white and heavy, hovering like an elegant Sèvres China saucer over El Corazón. Monica Hawke gazed out the window, wondering where her daughter was right now and what she was doing—if she was even alive.

Tears pooled in her jade-green eyes and Steven came to stand behind her, placing a gentle hand on her shoulder, pressing a tender kiss upon her throbbing temple, then laying his cheek beside hers.

"Darling, you are weeping again. Please don't. You know we have done all we can and it is up to God now if our beloved Jessica is returned to us or not."

Monica moaned, wrapping her slim arms about her husband's still slim waist. "But she has been gone for almost two years."

"Not quite, darling," he said, not letting her see the moisture forming in his eyes.

"H-How could she have just disappeared from the garden? Someone must know where she is, Steven."

"We have sent out search parties, love, you know that. Wherever Jessica is, I believe she is still alive," Steven said, closing his eyes prayerfully. Then adding, "Tina believes she is alive and well also."

"Tina?" Monica said, wondering what Jessica's

personal maid could know.

Tina Maller had been with Monica in California and had been with the Benningtons long before Monica had ever come along. The downstairs maid at Temloc, Tina had doted on Monica and her mother, Victoria, before her. Mother and daughter, near look-alikes, with their luxurious tawny hair and jade green eyes. Tina had never thought to see her beloved Monica again when the younger woman had been compelled to run away to Yerba Buena, a city in California now called San Francisco. Yes, Monica had run away. She had murdered her stepfather, Branville Bennington. *Murder* had been a word used by Alex Bennington, but Monica had only been defending her person against a horrible rape, an awful scene that had ended in Monica striking Branville over the head with a heavy pitcher. It would always be branded in Monica's mind, and only by a loving, understanding husband to guide her had she come to understand there had been no other way. Had her stepfather succeeded, she would have been an empty shell of a woman. Neither did Monica blame her stepfather any longer; he'd been imbibing quite freely and in fact had been imagining things when he'd stumbled into Monica's bedroom besotted like a drunken sailor. Tina remembered all this, and much, much more.

Temloc had burned to the ground, torched by Alex's own hand after he'd discovered Monica had done away with his father. Tina and the Indian girl, Maya, had fled. Tina had stayed at a nearby Indian village with Maya until the girl had wed her love, Chaka, and then she'd gone on to the Hawke house in Yerba Buena, where she had discovered Monica had again flown, this time to France with a woman by the name of Juliette La Chappiere. Bartholomew, the stolid butler at the Hawke residence, hired Tina on the spot, knowing his employer would not be pleased should Bartholomew lose this woman too, the only link to Monica should he return after going on a wild-goose chase after Monica, alias Mona Simmons.

"Tina?" Monica repeated, reaching up to touch her husband's cheek tenderly.

"Yes, love, Tina has had a dream of Jessica. In the dream Jessica was lying abed when Tina entered. Our beloved daughter was just waking in her bed. Tina heard Jessica ask her who she was and Tina, even disbelieving in her dream, chuckled and told her she knew her name. Then Tina told her you were waiting for her in the rose garden, the farthest arbor near the gazebo." Steven heard Monica gasp softly, for she and her daughter had stopped there often to rest their mounts or to get in the shade on a sunny day, and they'd never thought it an unsafe place for Jessica to go. But it was there, in the rose arbor, that their darling Jessica Angèle had disappeared, for her horse, Cascara's Pride, had been found standing there looking confused with her reins trailing in the thick green blades of grass. It was the same every time Steven mentioned the rose garden—Monica would begin to quake and in her eyes formed the shimmer of renewed tears.

"Wh-what did our daughter say in return to Tina . . . in her dream?" Monica was anxious to know as she tried not to let Steven see her furrowed brow.

"Jessica said 'What rose garden . . . my mother—what is her name.'" Steven paused to let this sink in before going on. "Tina said these were uttered unlike questions . . . more like statements." Should he go on, Steven wondered, but thought it was best not to hide anything from his wife. He had not held anything back since he had returned his wife to El Corazón after rescuing her from the madman, Alex Bennington, in Morocco.

"Oh Steven," Monica weeped, "she did not know my name."

"Hush, love," he said, brushing his lips over her forehead in featherlight kisses. "It is only a dream."

"Is that all?" Monica asked Steven, clasping his firmly muscled wrists while his hands rested protectively over the slight bulge of tummy, evidence of their love and the second child to come, one that was not made to replace the first, never that, for no child could ever take the place of their beautiful Jessica Angèle, named after Steven's deceased younger brother, the second name meaning she'd had the perfect face of an angel when she'd been born and had stayed that way until she had been kidnapped.

Steven was reluctant to go on; his voice was low as he continued. "Jessica begged Tina not to go. . . . She had to talk to *you*. But Tina had felt herself being removed from the dream and it was as if . . . Tina said she could almost feel the presence of a man . . . a very strong man taking Jessica into his care." This last he said in hopes that his daughter had indeed found a strong person to care for her, one who loved her dearly, and one who had not been among those taking her into captivity.

As Monica gazed up into Steven's utterly black eyes, shining with love for her and their daughter and the babe to come, Monica murmured, "Does this man really care for our Jessica, Steven? Really, really care as you care for me?"

Hugging Monica close, Steven whispered, "I hope so, my love, dear Lord I pray he does."

Part Four

Lady Hawke

Chapter Twenty-Three

Persimmon Wood Plantation, 1864

The delicate scent of potpourri roses trailed in Blossom Angelica's wake as she made her way to the backwoods cabin where their prisoner had been returned directly following the wedding ceremony. Black ringlets bounced at either side of her white velvet face and a neat part in the middle created one of the most favored styles as seen in *Godey's Lady Book.*

Blossom had an impish smile on her face. At first, when she'd read the name Angela had put down on the parish register, then turned her eyes upon the red-haired man, there'd been only the ghost of a revelation . . . and then it grew to monstrous proportions. Now Blossom could almost cheer herself out loud, and would have if she hadn't been nearing the cabin. She knew the blacks were having their own little party, but she still had to take caution and let no one see her. No one, that is, save Sarge Sorrel.

When the woodbird's song invaded Blossom's dark musings, she lifted her contemplative face, hissing, "Hush up your twittering, silly bird!" How she hated birds . . . such useless creatures which always seemed to be above one's head at the most inopportune moments, making nests in the dumbest places, and waking you when all you wanted to do was get a nice morning's sleep.

Blossom fingered the pearl eardrops she'd snatched back from Angela and pressed her damp palms along the red-and-white diagonal-striped skirt she wore, and stepped up to the window of the one-room cabin, her padded-heeled slippers making little noise.

"Mistuh Sorrel, suh," she called softly in her sultriest Southern drawl, "I'm here, honey. . . . Oh! You goose, why'd you go and scare me half to death?" She could see his ruddy face, mostly his great cinnamon eyes, through the cracks in the crisscrossed boards.

"It took you long enough, minx." A tingling of excitement raced through Sorrel as Blossom Fortune gave him one of her most provocative looks—like a promise of delicious things to come.

Sorrel was so excited. He'd never met a woman like this Southern belle that made his blood heave and boil to a feverish pitch. Not even his lovely Llana did to his desire what this one could do in the blink of a long jet eyelash or the merest brushing of her petal-soft fingertips.

"Come now," Sorrel almost begged, "you will take the double bolt off the door quickly? Did you make sure that the black men were drunk before coming here?"

"Sh-hh," Blossom said, placing a finger to her lips and blowing with the moist pink flesh parted. "'Course honey. I gave them several bottles of my brother's—God rest his soul—of Robert Neil's best firewater I'd hidden way out back of our house. 'Course it ain't a house any longer, just a pile of ashes that are taken up in the wind more and more every day, so pretty soon there won't be nothing left of Tamarind house. . . . My but you are in a hurry, aren't you? Such a big boy . . . I bet you really know how to please a lady," she purred, slanting her eyes down pointedly to that manly part of his anatomy she could not see for the boarded opening was in the way. "First things first, honey. I want you to tell me what you are really doing here . . . 'cause darlin', I don't really believe all that nonsense about you being neutral and losing your family. Goosefeathers! Something else brought you here . . . am I right?"

Almost drooling, Sorrel stared at Blossom through the cracks and saw her obsidian eyes narrow and flash at him. "Something . . . yes," he confessed, "I am here because my boss has sent me." Giving her a salacious grin, he ogled the raven-haired beauty's wonderfully shaped breasts, full and ripe, and her bottom he could tell when she walked with that sashay of hers was generous enough to fill his hands.

Blossom gathered her feminine wiles, and with a queer smile on her scarlet lips, she asked, "Why has he sent you?" Though Blossom asked this, she had a very good idea the "why" had to do with a "who."

"We are to—ah, no." Sorrel shook his head, thinking he saw her game perfectly. "You are seducing me into giving you information for your men, no? Do you think I am *estupido?*"

A sinister laugh broke from her. "*My* men? Hardly, Mistuh Sorrel. I'd like nothing better than to see those two dig their own graves, believe me. Darlin'," she breathed, moving her face as close to him as she could, "you can trust Blossom, cross my heart and hope to die. Gypsy Smith is my half brother, and I hate that man with a fierce passion." Here her face reddened with the thorough hatred she felt for Gypsy Smith, and Sorrel caught the intense emotion immediately. "He returned many years later to Tamarind after being banished by my own father . . ."

Sorrel cut in, "Was he not this Gypsy Smith's father too?"

"'Course not. Robert Neil, Gypsy Smith, and myself, we all are from the same mother, but Gypsy is the bastard that my father took in . . . until he could not stand the dark-countenanced lad any longer and sent him far across the seas."

"Who is the other man, the one the little blonde has made her husband?"

With a sneer, Blossom said, "Ridpath Huntington, Rider most call him. We were to be married, Rider and I, but that little slut Daisy Dawn snatched him from me." It was the first time in Blossom's life something she coveted had been denied her; it made her spitting angry too. "I have plans for them," she said, her voice soft and low and menacing.

"What would you like to see happen to them all?" Sorrel did not mention the young woman he knew as Jessica Hawke, for he wasn't sure just what Miss

Fortune had in mind for that one. For his silence, however, he was rewarded at once.

"You are here for Angela—hmmm . . . aren't you?" Blossom said point-blank, eyeing Sorrel carefully while he considered her question. She'd seen the name on the parish register. . . .

"Jessica Angèle Hawke," he said, then corrected. "Jessica Smith. She is now married to that one you call Gypsy Smith."

"What do you mean to do with her?"

Sorrel's cinnamon eyes suddenly squinted; he said, "Get down . . . one of them black men comes."

Moving into the shadows, Blossom ducked behind a rain barrel just as Jasmine Joe came swinging along, humming a poignant Negro song and livening it up now and then with a jauntier beat as he called to Sorrel, received his answer, then went strolling back to where the black folks' reveling songs was coming from, his long-nosed rifle leaning up against one muscle-padded shoulder.

After Jasmine Joe had gone, Blossom appeared again, this time going to remove the double bolt on the door. Before she could open her mouth, Blossom was yanked roughly inside and thrown upon the pallet where, after Sorrel had closed the door, he joined her. He was breathing hard when he came down and Blossom could feel the heat of his large body covering hers. Aroused at once, a great need crawled through Blossom. Sorrel's hardness set her on fire. She had been without a man for more than two weeks and thought that morning when she'd felt the flush of sexual desire she'd go crazy if she didn't have one soon.

305

"We can't stay here long," Blossom panted as Sorrel began to loosen first his clothing then hers.

"Once now . . ." he rasped. "More later."

As he moved between her thighs and swiftly entered where she was thoroughly moist, Blossom arched to receive his eager shaft, exclaiming, "Oh— you *are* plenty, suh!" Raking her nails through the thick mane of reddish hair, Blossom grabbed hold as he drove her to the height of carnal pleasures. She welcomed all of him, deeper and deeper, while all the men she'd known intimately danced around the edges of her brain as she imagined erotically them taking her one after the other, right at the same time Sorrel aided her as she reached an explosive conclusion.

When their swift and violent coupling came to its end, pulses slowing, breathing returning to normal, sexual flush cooling, Sorrel held Blossom close, as if she was a new possession he didn't want to toss aside from boredom just yet.

"How did you like that?" he growled into the curls of her damp hair.

"Mmm—" She raised black eyes and lowered them. "I liked it fine."

Sorrel closed his eyes and grunted. She did not have to look so bored, he was thinking.

Twirling a finger in the reddish mat of curls covering Sorrel's chest, Blossom repeated her question. "What do you mean to do with this, ah, this Jessica Angèle?"

"Do?" he chuckled nastily. "We mean to kill her, that is what."

Shoving him away and reaching for her carelessly

discarded pantaloons, Blossom sat prettily and began to pull them on, her voice husky as she asked, "What do you want me to do?"

Sorrel had been thinking, seriously for once. He had no intention of leaving this bit of talented fluff behind, and he'd been also considering the little blonde. She was lovely and would serve him and his friends, blockade runners and privateers, as well as Blossom here would. He clucked his tongue as he rose to pull on his stained breeches, grimacing once when his leg hurt him, then grinning as Blossom stood in the full moonlight streaming in and straightened her bodice, which had become askew from his pawing as he drove her to the peak.

"What do I want you to do?" Sorrel said, pulling away the hand that had been busy fussing with her hair. "My compeer, François, will be here soon. He means to arrive not long after the white men have left, and they have. François wants the young Lady Hawke and will stop at nothing to get her. We will meet the other men where they have the schooner *Delora* hid. Now, we must move fast and get the women together. See what you can do, and do it with haste."

As they made to exit the musty cabin, Blossom shrugged before preceding Sorrel with a haughty, queenly air out the door, and flippantly remarked, "I'm ready for anything—and everything!"

Sorrel turned to her for a moment, saying, "Even Lady Hawke?"

With a nasty laugh, Blossom answered, "Especially Lady Hawke . . . and her little blond companion. I happen to hate them both."

Keeping to the shadows, Blossom followed Sorrel, and when he paused behind a live oak, she asked, "Why do you call her Lady Hawke? Is our lost angel someone special?"

"She is." Sorrel crouched to keep down his height and pulled her along once again, making sure she stayed nearby in case she suddenly sprouted the wicked idea to leave him. For some reason he could not understand yet, Sorrel did not trust Blossom Fortune. "Very important. From a well-heeled family and François says her father is a dangerous man to come up against when he is crossed."

A soft chuckle welled from Blossom's throat. "La! and how he has been crossed." There was something else she had been curious about for a long time. She asked, "Is she from France?"

Squeezing her wrist in a viselike grip, Sorrel snapped, "Enough. You have asked too many questions. François will not like if it you know too much."

Nearing the house, which appeared deserted beneath the huge Carolina moon, Blossom put one more question to him, to her the most important one in this most dangerous episode of her life.

"Where are we going from here?" she whispered.

"No more questions after this?" He drew her up, searching her face for agreement. Quickly she nodded, just once. His earth-colored eyes reflected two moons as he said passionately, "To Paraiso, in the Bahamas."

"Oh." Blossom shrugged. Wherever that was.

Unable to get any sleep, Angela walked out onto

the gallery and found Daisy awake too, her blond hair waving down her back in silvery ripples as she leaned her elbow on the railing with her chin in her palm. Angela thought Daisy looked like a dreaming Rapunzel.

Going back inside, Angela returned minutes later holding a robe out to Daisy. "You will become chilled. Here, I brought you this."

Daisy took the proffered robe. As she pushed her arms into it with Angela's assistance, she asked, "Another one of Blossom's?"

"Of course." Angela laughed. "Who else? Yours and hers. I've none of my own wardrobe here."

Gazing up at the melancholy moon, Daisy softly said, "Anything new in your memory besides the one elusive dream you had a few weeks ago?"

Sighing, Angela turned her face to the moon. "Nothing . . . except . . ."

"Except?" Daisy was curious, noticing the change in Angela's face. Then she thought she knew. "You still have that creepy feeling like something is going to happen? Do you, Angela?"

"I—yes." Angela stirred uneasily, pushing the vision of a man with pox scars, crisp dark hair, and hard brown eyes out of her mind. "I am not sure I want to talk about it though. . . . There is something about someone that frightens me."

"I know what you mean." Daisy straightened, hugging the ruby-colored robe tighter about her. "It's that Sorrel, I can tell whenever he's around, you freeze and clam up, and I don't blame you, Angela, he makes me feel creepy too. What is he doing here anyway?"

"I am not sure . . . he looks familiar. Remember I

said that while Gypsy was interrogating him? Yes. He makes me think of someone else at the same time, another man, one with a cruel face."

"I know . . . you were kidnapped from your home." Daisy drew a dainty finger to her rosebud mouth while mulling this new revelation of hers over in her mind. "It has to be the way it was, Angela, and I think"—her eyes enlarged to blue saucers—"I think this Sorrel has something to do with abducting you from your home. He might have been Annabelle's murderer."

"Yes." Angela said this fiercely while pressing her fingertips to her temple, and an even more terrifying thought broke free and washed over her like a raging flood. "Daisy, we are alone! The men are gone . . . *that man* . . . this is the first time we have been alone since he arrived so mysteriously." Her eyes flew wide as she said in a frightening tone, "Daisy . . . have you seen Blossom since the wedding? She was sipping wine with that man and then disappeared. You haven't seen her either?"

"No." Daisy shook her head, feeling a shiver of panic as she stared at Angela. "What are you thinking? You look so strange . . . Angela!" A scream froze in the tunnel of her throat as she heard the footsteps coming across the bare wood floors inside the bedroom, many footsteps, too many to possibly be the bridegrooms. Besides, they would have announced their presence instead of creeping mutely through the house like robbers. Then, "Angela . . . what is happening . . . ?"

*   *   *

With a long cape and cowl concealing her identity, Blossom moved quickly about the room gathering clothing and other needed sundry items into a large bag that already bulged with some of Daisy's possessions. This she passed to the dark figure stationed at the door while Sorrel and his compeer François—who'd only just arrived—made quick work of binding the frightened women on the gallery and stuffing gags into the mouths. Now they were silent, resigned to their fate. No one knew, however, exactly what Daisy and Angela were thinking.

Smiling, pleased with herself, Blossom again scrutinized the rugged, French aristocrat and came up with a careless sketch of a dynamic and sinister figure of man. His face she had not seen all that clearly—he seemed to have scars or pock marks, dark hair and eyes, and he was as aggressive as a panther and just as dangerous. François was his name, their leader, and Blossom shivered deliciously to think what this powerful Frenchman would say or do when he finally looked upon her own striking face and figure. When François had first arrived, only a quarter of an hour before, he had sounded quite irritated to find that Sorrel had taken a woman into their confidence.

"But this woman is different," Blossom had heard him say of herself. Then this François had shot her cowled figure a black scour, and with a deep grunt he'd walked—no, run—up the stairs to hasten the abduction.

"Hurry!" Blossom hissed into the dark as the two of them prodded the women down the gallery stairs; Angela and Daisy, who seemed to be solidly frozen even as they walked, said not a word. "They will be coming soon." She hurried behind them and even brushed up against François's arm intentionally. The fiery shock raced along her arm and François seemed to be experiencing the same reaction, for he turned to flick his dark dancing eyes over her while a deep frown settled upon his forehead. Then he continued to move along, but his eyes returned every so often to the cowled figure walking swiftly beside him.

Because he did not know if he could trust this strange woman yet, François said nothing of the barrier of debris he'd had his men send down the river, and they'd even dragged fallen trees, dried out like so much floatsam, and tossed them into the river, taken concealed debris from so many ransackings . . . while all the time the night deepened.

François could not understand why the mere touch of the strange woman's hand had brought such a fire to his flesh. She must be a devil woman, just like his Juliet. Yes, there was no other explanation for the web of attraction that was growing between them. Pah! Crazy. He had not even seen her face yet. For all he knew she could be quite homely indeed, but for some odd reason he did not believe this was so.

The sound of revelry from the backwoods cabins was beginning to mellow and thin out even as they hastened along a recently beaten path through the woods. Angela was numb. She was ice cold and sick to her stomach, but the discomfort did not seem to matter. All that mattered was for her and Daisy Dawn to be rescued. Then the questions flew at her like rain pelting a windowpane. The tumult raged within her.

312

She had recognized Sarge Sorrel's deep voice. Seen his hair like a dusky rose beneath the rising moon. But who was the other man in charge . . . the one with crisp, dark hair . . . hard dark eyes . . . and scars? Had she been able to make out flaws in his rugged complexion? Yes. Daisy had been correct in saying these two had been part and parcel in abducting her from her home.

Now, the question was, where were they taking them this time? And why? Why Daisy too? And Blossom was in on this. How long had she been involved in this craziness? Was this part of an insane scheme to aid the North? No, she told herself, how could it be? Unless it had something to do with the Gypsy Moth . . . no, again. She did not believe Gypsy was involved in the war any longer, even though he made frequent trips to Charleston. He had only told her he had a ship and crew somewhere, not letting her in on their whereabouts. For a moment she felt sad. When would Gypsy learn to trust her? Hadn't he told her she was the part of him that had been missing? She had thought so. Perhaps she had only heard what she'd wanted to hear.

And where could Gypsy Smith and Rider Huntington be at the moment? What had detained them? Angela and Daisy continued to walk . . . walk . . . walk . . . until they reached a copse of densely populated oaks with thick beards of silvery moss hanging down everywhere. It was an ancient jungle of wood and nature's drapery, a part of the low country she had never been into. There they mounted horses and set off at a brisker pace and Angela did not even wonder that she could ride a horse. She rode . . .

and quite well. She might even be able to get Daisy to try breaking away from the group.

Where were they being taken to? How long before they reached their destination? Would she ever see Gypsy Smith again? If not, a part of him would always go with her, always remembering when she had first realized he was her everlasting love, in that wild interlude back at Tamarind between day and night . . . dusk . . . deep velvet . . . frantic heartbeats flinging night into dawn.

Gypsy, her mind cried out, *Gypsy . . . where are you?*

With the moon reflected in the waters off her bow, the plantation skiff moved with ease, silent and unseen like a dark swan in the night. It was late, and they were hungry and tired. The trip had taken longer than Gypsy and Rider had anticipated, and they were also eager to get back to their new brides.

Gypsy manned the skiff while Rider watched the waters dead ahead to look for any sign of danger and to keep a safe distance between them and the bank. The higher the moon rose, the harder it was to see where they were going. Soon they would not be able to see their hands in front of their faces. The fuel in the lantern had given out long ago.

"Damn, I knew we should have refilled the lantern," Rider said.

"It would have helped some," Gypsy returned, lifting his face to the ascending moon. "We'll have to go slower or else we might end up shipwrecked"—he smiled wryly—"and where is all this floating debris coming from?''

Rider frowned, wondering about the same thing himself. "Seems like someone is trying to slow us down, wouldn't you say, Captain?"

"Aye, I'd say so meself," Gypsy said with a wide grin, making light of the moments of frustration both were experiencing. That was not all. He had not been able to put out of his mind the cloud of worry that had darkened Angela's eyes just as he and Rider were leaving to take the reverend back to Charleston.

"If we don't get back to Persimmon Wood soon," Rider began, "I think our women will divorce us."

Rider's mouth twisted into a sad half smile. Before he had left, his lips had grazed hungrily over Daisy's and she had raised her velvet blue eyes in an unspoken question. A bittersweet memory. What had her beautiful eyes been asking him? Why did he think of it as a memory already? An aching hollowness filled him and for a heart-skipping moment he felt he'd lost Daisy. But that could not be possible. She was waiting for him back at Persimmon Wood.

They both heard a *thunk* just then and Rider gripped the gunwale, trying to see into the slurping waters. "I swear that was a half a tree that just hit the side. Where the hell is all this junk coming from?"

Gypsy stiffened just then, going very still. "Something is wrong, Rider, I can feel it."

"I can feel it too. . . . It just hit the side of the skiff."

"No—it's something else." Gypsy narrowed his eyes, seeing crates and other debris floating past when the moon left the cover of platinum clouds. "This isn't just the floating garbage of war. We're too

315

far from the city for that. There's something wrong here."

Rider sighed. "You already said that, my friend. So, we have enemies who are trying to keep us from returning posthaste to our breathlessly waiting wives?" He snorted. "Hardly. No one has the time to bother with frustrating our consummation. There's a war going on, Captain Smith." But Rider would not be of one mind with Gypsy Smith; that could only serve to double their fear.

"Angela is in trouble." The planes of his face grew taut with foreboding.

Laughing, Rider said, "What? Oh, I see. When you get there it's going to be an all-night thing, huh?" Clicking his tongue, he added, "Me too. As soon as I've rested up a bit, Daisy is going to be in my arms all night long, and if she's up to it, all morning too. I sure love that little woman and can hardly wait to prove to her just how much."

Rider caught himself up short. An inexplicable feeling was tearing at his gut, one that warned of a long wait before he and Daisy would share the great joy of fulfillment both anticipated with all their hearts.

When Gypsy held his silence, Rider repeated, "So, Angela is in trouble this night—"

"No . . . no . . . no!" Gypsy cut in, slicing the air with a clenched fist. "Angela is frightened. Something has happened. I can feel her hurt. Damnit, I can feel it."

Now the full force of Gypsy's premonition struck Rider.

"What?!" Rider stood and gripped the mast. "That

means Daisy is in trouble too." He glared at all the floating debris that Gypsy had to try and avoid by steering to the right or left and watching the bank at the same time. "Do you think the Yankees have taken over?"

With an elevated eyebrow, Gypsy peered at his friend and snarled, "Impossible. They are not in this area at the time."

"How would you know?"

"I—let's say I know for certain and leave it go at that."

Rider shook his head, saying, "You are still giving orders, right?"

Ignoring Rider's question, Gypsy asked some of his own. "Where was our prisoner when we left the house? Was he still quenching his insatiable thirst with Blossom on the porch and making jokes with Jasmine Joe and Blackstrap?"

Rider gritted his teeth and swore. "I knew there was something about that stranger. We shouldn't have left them alone. You are right . . . they are in trouble."

"How do you know?"

"I can feel it now too."

"Well then, let's get going!"

"What do you want me to do?"

"Grab that pole there and let's get this garbage out of the way."

"Watch it!" Rider yelled. "There's another tree heading our way. Off starboard."

Leaning his weight to the pole, giving fulcrum, Rider worked to keep the enormous branch out of their way with the sturdy prod.

"We're almost away from it," Gypsy called. "Keep it moving . . . or else it'll tear a hole in our side. Good, good, I'm swinging out of it. There!"

When the danger had passed and they were sailing in relatively safe waters once again, Rider turned to face Gypsy with an expression that was very grim. Almost defeatedly he said, "We are not up against only a few deserters trying to camp on our doorstep. This is something big. There's high stakes in this game."

"Yes," Gypsy Smith agreed, "and I think I know who the prize is going to be."

"Angela."

"Yes," he almost whispered, "Mrs. Smith."

"She must be someone special to receive all this undesirable attention."

Unreservedly Gypsy Smith agreed.

Chapter Twenty-Four

Somewhere Along the Ashley River

When the flare of the match blossomed to its greatest measure, François grabbed the hand that had lighted it and gave it a wrench. "Where did you get that? Matches are scarce." His voice was like a snarling dog in the hushed glade and everyone looked at him; Blossom was so surprised at the angry tone that she whipped her head around and in that instant her cowl fell back revealing her camellia face, liquid black eyes, and leonine mane of curling raven gypsy hair.

"Just going to light a butt," croaked Rusty, a little bit of a sailor with the stub of a cheroot barely clinging to his large lips. "D'ya mind?" He gulped, looking from the knifelike cut of François's eyes to the face of the woman in the olive-drab cowl. "Guess ya do." He looked from his boss to the woman who'd turned in their direction and the cheroot drooped lower as he saw her face.

In the few moments while the match flared and came to life, François found himself mesmerized, staring at the beauty across from him. Intoxicating warmth filled him, and for a brief passage of time, in the time it took the radiance of that precious light to exist until it was snuffed out, François had gazed into the eyes of love.

When it was over, however, François found a rare embarrassment greeting him. Everyone stared at him, but not for the same reason he thought. He could not know that it was only his nasty temper the women had glimpsed. The men were used to François's temper, but the women had reacted so violently that his men could only turn their eyes collectively upon what the women had given immediate attention to.

Now François was really confused. He was angry too. The young woman across from him had adjusted her cowl, lifting long white fingers he could barely make out the shape of, already knowing they would be beautiful to see, and to hold, and then she turned her back on him. François stiffened, feeling her aloofness.

"You," he said to the woman in the cowl, "pick up the bundle you have dropped. We must not leave a trail for them to follow."

With a haughty shoulder, Blossom turned, informing him, "My name is Blossom Angelica Fortune . . . and don't be calling me *you* again, *suh!*"

Before François could bite off a reply, Sorrel stepped up to remind him in a low voice, "You forget that you want them to follow. . . . They have something you want very much." Sorrel coughed, seeing where François's eyes lingered. "Remember? You wanted that *thing*?" A nudge in the ribs brought the dark eyes of François swinging around to the red-haired man who was bobbing his head.

"Keep to yourself, fool," François ground out. "Do not ever touch me again. Do you hear?" He received a nod. "Good. We will keep moving and remember"—he included all three women this time—"drop anything behind and I find out . . . the guilty one will feel the bite of this!" Making his meaning clear, François jabbed them one at a time in the back, and they did not have to wonder what it was he held in his hands.

Sorrel stood dumbfounded. Had he heard right when François told him he wanted to leave a trail for those men to follow? He'd even taken a shot in the leg to make their story sound authentic, but he'd never even gotten a chance to drop a hint about where they were going. Only the woman Blossom knew.

They mounted up again, and this time François gave two of his resourceful men charge of the two women, with a tether between each pair of horses. François then reached down and pulled the haughty Miss Fortune up with an arm crushing beneath her ribs and settled her in front of him on the prancing war horse he had swiped from a Confederate lieutenant. It had not mattered from which side they had stolen and murdered—the way François saw it, these brothers were all killing each other left and right anyway.

"Please, suh," Blossom protested, "you are digging your elbow into my hip."

"I did not notice." Though he said this, François

kept his arm exactly where he had placed it moments before.

Sarcastically Blossom said, "Would you be so kind and remove it? I bruise easily, suh!"

"Why did you not say so, madam."

François felt the pleasant shock of this young woman's nearness run through his body and he decided he did not like this feeling of losing control.

Wildly the pulse at Blossom's throat palpitated. This had never happened to her before. She had always been in control concerning men. This man was not for her . . . definitely not. At first she had thought to seduce him. But no more. The mere sound of his voice infuriated her. His touch repulsed her. Why then, she wondered, did she feel such a vulnerability toward him?

"Would you mind very much if I . . . walked?" Blossom finally got out.

"Something is wrong, madam?"

"Suh, I think it is *mademoiselle.*" Angela had taught her this much about French.

"Ah," François quipped arrogantly, "you are unwed."

"'Course I am unwed!" Blossom was breathless with rage. His voice, how she hated the sound of it! "Suh, let me down this instant."

Blossom shoved the hand aside that had been becoming familiar with the underside of her arm. She did not like this man touching her. . . . She did not even want to be near him!

"Now!" Blossom was on the verge of shouting.

"As you say, mademoiselle!"

Very unceremoniously Blossom was dumped onto

the earth, where it was wet and mushy from a recent rainfall, dumped without her cloak too. For it had come away, snagging on the saddle, so she wondered in a wide-eyed flash where her garment had gone.

"You!" Blossom glared up at the grinning Frenchman clutching a handful of the olive-drab cloak. She could see him now. One of the men had lighted a whale-oil lamp to see what the commotion was all about as the group of sailors had come to a halt. "You fumblin' . . . *oh!*"

Staring down at her pretty sapphire-and-scarlet dress with tiny rosettes sewn into the bodice, Blossom gritted her teeth. "Just look at what you've done to my dress. It's one of my favorites."

"Was . . ." François said with laconic sarcasm. "Too bad." He clucked his tongue. "Do you think there awaits a party especially for you where we are going?"

Where François could not see, Blossom was gathering balls of the sticky mud into her hands, preparing to blast him the moment he was caught off-guard. Rising most ungracefully to her feet, not missing the tiny grin lifting Daisy Dawn's mouth, Blossom stood erect with mud slides moving slowly down her back. Just as François's grin reached its widest spread, Blossom let fly with rapid succession both handfuls of Carolina mud.

"Mother of God!" François ejaculated.

The stuff met its mark, right on.

Only the whites of François's eyes showed. Mud slides moved slowly and bearded his chin with slimy icicles. His grin was not white now, but black.

Angela stared first in shock at the serious comedy,

323

then when she heard Daisy's soft "Oh Lord . . ." followed by a spurt of laughter, Angela could not contain the gentle laugh that rippled through her throat. Infectiously, the whole of them began to chuckle, and it wasn't long before François began to chuckle and then laugh full-heartedly.

In spite of herself, Blossom began to laugh. The merriment shone in her sparkling black eyes. François looked down and saw her. She was beautiful . . . beautiful!

François threw back his head and great peals of laughter sounded as light entered the eastern sky and slashed it with pink and lavender and up-shooting rays of amber.

Then François reached for his hanky. He looked at the vixen with a raised eyebrow. Blossom grew serious, brushing off her dress as best she could. Angela and Daisy exchanged looks of somber curiosity.

"It is time to move on," François said in a gruff voice.

Almost mechanically the group began to move upriver, led by a very confused but happy François. He could not understand why he felt this sense of well-being. . . . There was mud on his face and a wild vixen at his side. Once he was back with Juliet, all would be normal. He must not let down his guard again. There was a job needing completion and he meant to see that nothing or no one stood in his way. He would even kill if the need arose.

Angela and Daisy were still puzzled over the odd interaction between Blossom and their dangerous abductor.

All in all it was a crazy scene, one they would not soon forget.

It was misty black as the small three-masted vessel crept along the Carolina shoreline. François had waited the afternoon out after they had boarded under the cover of gray dawn with their human contraband, waiting for just the right moment to set sail. The time had come, well into evening.

Now the wind filled the *Delora*'s black sails while François softly barked orders right and left. Silently they slid past Fort Sumter and even more did they creep as they moved like a black sea wraith through the blockading fleet. Around the tip of Morris Island.

François wiped the sweat from his brow as they slipped through a narrow gap in the ominous ships patrolling the coastline. François smiled arrogantly to himself in the darkness. Mother of God, they had made it!

The *Delora* headed swiftly out to sea.

Chapter Twenty-Five

Persimmon Wood

"There must be something here." Walking around the small room in the cabin where the prisoner had been kept, Gypsy Smith sniffed the fetidness of the unemptied chamber pot. He was imagining the worst when a stricken Blackstrap stepped into the frame of the open door, his voice sounding heavy and grieved.

"My poh Daisy. Doan know where that debil could've taken her."

Gypsy whirled to face the towering black man. "Have you been to the house?"

"I been there. That man"—Blackstrap shook his head—"doan know how he could've taken all the wimmen."

Rider, stepping onto the porch behind Blackstrap, announced, "There was more than one man. We have been out looking and there are many tracks going upriver, and the three women are with them.

326

Mum Zini has just informed me that a lot of clothes were taken from their rooms."

Rider's hair was mussed from having raked his fingers through the deep auburn strands, and his face was perspiring from strain and frustration. He was ready to track them down, but he knew these men who'd abducted the women were no fools—they had planned this thing out well and had taken their time doing so. Now he anticipated the time he'd have Sorrel's neck between his fingers . . . and that time was coming soon.

"Damn that sneaking bastard!" Gypsy stormed, pacing the porch nervously. "I knew we couldn't trust that Sarge Sorrel. I even wonder if that was his real name."

"Could be." Rider shrugged. "We can't be certain. Are you ready to go out looking? I am damn good and ready to kill the bastards. I can hardly wait."

"We need some clues as to where they are going," Gypsy said, his eyes deepening the color of dark wine. His mouth was stretched into a grim line as he thoughtfully stared around.

From inside the cabin Blackstrap said, "Look at this here. That debil left somethin'."

"Let me see."

Gypsy took the piece of wrinkled paper from the black man. "There's a drawing here," he said. "Looks like—an island of some sort."

Looking over Gypsy's shoulder, Rider said, "Looks like a chain of islands."

"Yeah," Blackstrap put in, "sure do." Stuffing his big hands into his saggy pockets, he stared from one man to the other.

"One of the islands has an X by it." Gypsy turned it upside down. "By God—look! These here are the Yucatan and Florida peninsulas . . . and here are the Bahama Islands in the Atlantic Ocean . . . not far from the X."

"The Bahamas?" Rider's voice became tight and high-pitched. "Do you think this is where our women are going to be taken to?"

Gypsy Smith frowned at this question as he stared at the crudely drawn map. What if Sorrel had left the map in order to lead them on a merry goose chase? Worse, what if they had already raped . . . and murdered . . . them? Perish the thought. Angela had become a part of him and he couldn't live without her. He groaned softly. Had he told her how much he really loved her?

Suddenly Gypsy was unjustifiably angry. Angela had only said she loved him while they were making love. He had never heard her say it otherwise. Then he mentally kicked himself for a fool. She had married him, hadn't she? Or was that only because he had promised to help her find her loved ones? Had he really intended to help her find them, or was it always at the back of his mind that she could be from a well-to-do family and was promised to another in marriage? And when she did regain her memory—if she ever did—would she discover that her heart belonged to another and not him?

He had to find her; she had to be alive. There would not be a future for him with her not in it.

"C'mon," Rider yelled from the yard, "let's go and find them . . . before it's too late."

Gypsy Smith sighed heavily. Dear God, he prayed

it was not and they were alive and well. There was so much left unsaid and undone between them . . . and there were loved ones that needed to be discovered. A memory to be restored.

The Atlantic Coast

The moon had swung across the arc of the heavens and was hanging like a bright lamp in the west. The tattered black clouds had scattered and dispersed. Nothing impeded the flood of radiance that poured down upon the ship *Black Moon*, bathing the quarter-deck in silvery light. Amidships, however, on the port side, was a comfortable darkness, and here, were great square black patches cast by the sails and the mainmast.

Gypsy paced restlessly. Nothing stirred save the wind in the rigging and the fitful waves. Then the dying breeze pawed fitfully at the sails, now stretching them partly taut, now disappearing altogether so that they hung heavily from the yards. The rising sun, swimming out of the east from a mass of vapor, was like a molten ball, and it grew hotter as it ascended from the heavens. By afternoon the heat had become intense. It beat down upon the *Black Moon* from a brittle, cloudless sky. To add to their discomfort the ocean had reared itself into long, glassy swells that made the ship roll and pitch sickeningly.

They had gotten past the blockading fleet and slipped through the patrolling ships. The *Black Moon* had headed out to sea and then . . . not even a whisper of a breeze.

Gypsy fretted, with Rider beside him. All through the long, moon-ridden watches the *Black Moon* lurched from one crest to another and the rudder was useless. The ship groaned and retched laboriously, blocks banging, yards swaying, hull careening frenziedly until dawn. The second day was worse than the first. The swells broke off suddenly before daylight and now the sea was as flat and unruffled as a sheet of glass.

There was no motion.

The *Black Moon* might well have been impaled upon a rock. Now the sun bore down mercilessly, causing the pitch of the deck seams to blister and run; the air was stagnant and stifling.

"We can only pray and hope for the best," Gypsy said to Rider, as he wiped an arm across his brow.

"I am praying—believe me," Rider said. If only Daisy were all right, then he might begin to really have some hope, but as it stood, he didn't know if she were being mistreated or not. She was so frail . . . so lovely. He only wanted to protect her from any harm that might come her way. The thought that he might never see her alive again twisted in his gut.

All afternoon the ship lay on the sea like an inert thing, and the sun, reflected by the waveless sea, smote them blindingly. Yet in spite of the swelter, Captain Smith kept the crew at its work.

Gypsy stared out to sea. "There has been too much grumbling already," he said of the crew.

"You're right. They should not lounge around and be idle," Rider agreed, looking around the fast, topsail schooner. Was Daisy on a ship just like this one? Were they treating her badly, those that had abducted her and Angela . . . and Blossom. He swallowed down his fear, knowing if he didn't stop this he would be in no shape to fight for Daisy when they finally caught up to them . . . and catch up they would.

He had dreamed of Daisy the night before. His hands and mouth had caressed her ceaselessly as he brought her virgin body to unbearable throbbing hunger. He had promised her there was nothing to fear and guided her hand to himself, gently urging her hand back and forth. The dream had been so real he felt she was right there with him when at last he had opened his eyes. But she was not. His body had been spent, slick with the sweet wetness of the wonderfully erotic dream.

Rider sighed, feeling the heaviness return to his heart.

Everywhere about the vessel tension could be felt. It seemed to draw more and more taut as the fevered afternoon wore on. They wrapped themselves in a cocoon of anguish; it was like a physical pain.

Would they catch up in time to save the women?

When Gypsy heaved himself up the poop ladder and took his place beside Rider, he looked flushed, tired, and damp. "Any clouds making up?" he asked Huey, his red-rimmed eyes scanning the horizon.

"None, sir," Huey replied between dried lips. "Looks as if we're in for another windless night."

Now the sun was only a red smear in the west. Darkness was gathering fast. The sea was like a sheet of dull copper and the only sound was a faint murmur of water beneath the stern.

Then, through the tingling stillness came a new sound. It was far away and scarcely audible at first. Then it grew more distinct as it drew nearer. Like the sound of liquid music, running lightly, swiftly, toward them from astern.

Incredulously Gypsy Smith wheeled and ran to the rail, staring off across the water. A broad line of ripples creased the tawny surface, leaping and tumbling, and presently, they reached the ship, then came the sigh of a breeze.

Gypsy and Rider stared at each other.

It was only a vagrant breath at the start, but with every passing moment it grew stronger. Aloft the great sails stirred and shivered restlessly and then stretched themselves out taut.

Instantly the ship came to life, like a creature suddenly awakened and startled from slumber.

Eagerly the *Black Moon* began to move through the water, heeling ever so slightly.

"All hands!" Captain Smith shouted, leaping for the wheel and twirling the spokes.

"Lady Luck must be riding with us," Huey said, scratching under his cap while the other crew members stood around with big disbelieving eyes.

As Gypsy turned to Rider he shrugged, and that man did the same. They knew it was ridiculous, but something extraordinary, something glorious, seemed to be with them.

Part Five

Wild Paradise

Let those love now who never loved before.
—Parnell

Chapter Twenty-Six

The Islands of Paraiso, the Bahamas

The ship moved slowly across the sun as the Bahama Islands came into view. Angela and Daisy were standing alone at the rail of the *Delora* when Blossom joined them. At that moment they were all looking out to sea when the low-lying ranges—looking at first like nothing but gray clouds on the sea's horizon—rose from the sea, misty gray with distance.

As they stood there, the deep blue sea gradually took on a lighter tone, becoming the color of lapis lazuli and then merging at last into translucent aqua along the alabaster shoreline.

The wind ruffled Angela's burnished chestnut hair and sang in the sails. The sun was like a great golden disc hovering over the horizon's rim and it brilliantly lit the world as it climbed higher. And Angela lifted her face to its warm, invigorating rays.

The ocean breeze caressed Daisy's hair and made it

glow like spun gold. Her eyes seemed to have become larger. Though she had a look of fragility about her, Daisy's chin had a strong, stubborn tilt to it, and more than one of the scoundrels had discovered she could be a handful when she wanted her way or desired only to be alone with her thoughts.

Blossom had changed, in more ways than one. She had become wistful, almost quiet. She had an other worldly beauty about her now. Damp, gypsylike wisps curled close to her face. She had awakened in the middle of the night several times in the cabin she shared with Daisy and Angela, and was amazed to discover that the spot where her head had rested was wet with her tears.

They sailed past countless small islands in the chain, and then, from one that seemed a mere dot in the sea there arose a plantinum-rose mist that slowly drifted out over the water—as if in greeting. Swaying palms lined the cream-pink beaches. The sun-warmed scent of grass drifted out to them and the day was magnificent with only one cottony cloud to mar an otherwise flawless azure sky.

Now, with heart thumping, Angela looked from the island to Daisy, wondering what fate awaited them.

Daisy and Angela were both thinking the same thing: escape. They had tried to escape once before. Just as they had been about to board the *Delora* hidden below the Charleston harbor, Angela and Daisy had made a run for it. François and two others had been quick to catch them and bring them back. Angela had been in François's grip and her frightened eyes had met his. He had looked away, still holding on to her, but more gently. Daisy remembered it well and she had puzzled over François's almost regretful attitude. Something was driving François; it was almost as if he were possessed by a thing—or someone. This was not going to be easy, they were both thinking, almost ready to give up.

"We can always steal a boat," Daisy whispered.

"Where would we go?" Angela said just as low.

"What are you two whispering about?" Blossom asked, missing François's slow, mysterious smile, his tender glance as he studied her while she thought she was being unobserved.

"Nothing," Daisy said, looking straight ahead to the coral-white beaches and jade-green trees.

Angela nudged Daisy, warning her to say no more. François was watching them again, or, she wondered, was he really watching Blossom? She had caught him staring at Blossom several times, and once when there had been a storm on the way, he had seemed overly concerned for their safety—especially Blossom's.

"We are ready to go ashore."

Blossom turned with Angela and Daisy at the sound of François's deep voice. He looked very handsome. He wore a loose white shirt, open to the waist, and tight black britches with a wide silver-buckled belt that only barely concealed a pistol. His eyes had a mocking piercing quality, a look that inexplicably enraged and aroused Blossom, although she did not care to admit the latter even to herself.

"My men will bring your belongings ashore later," he said, looking at Blossom as if the other two were not even present.

"Thank you," Blossom said flippantly, hiding her face from François by turning it aside. No one knew that she was closing her eyes, holding in check a raw emotion she couldn't understand.

The boatswain helped Daisy and Angela into one of the landing boats. François gave Blossom a hand, but she ignored his comments on what a beautiful day it was. François took his place at the rudder while the crewmen were in front pulling strongly on the oars.

François's heavy lashes shadowed his lean cheekbones. He was studying Blossom thoughtfully, his intense brown eyes hooded.

Angela was puzzled. They were being treated not like prisoners . . . but almost as if they were royalty or something. Again, this honor seemed to go firsthand to Blossom.

Daisy felt the same. She studied François now without his knowing. He would never know she watched him. His eyes were always elsewhere. She looked quickly away, for to intrude upon his thoughts at this time would seem an intrusion of his privacy. What sort of villain was this man? At first she had feared him; now she doubted he could hurt a fly.

"Look!" Blossom exclaimed, her face lighting up like a child enchanted.

Angela and Daisy leaned over the side to see what Blossom was staring down into. The water was so clear. It was a breathtaking sight. In the jade-white twilight appeared fantastic lumps and mushrooms of coral, with huge dark holes and crevices in between. Giant sea fans, sponges, and all manner of odd plants waved and nodded in the currents that drifted back and forth. Angela thought it was like gazing down into a nightmarish forest inhabited by schools of brightly colored fish, grotesque eels, all sorts of mollusks, and globular jellyfish creatures which floated by, trailing long tentacles.

Daisy squeaked all of a sudden. But it wasn't something in the water that had caused her alarm. François had stood up, and as they watched, he peeled down to his britches, even removing his black leather boots.

The crewmen had ceased their rowing and sat watching their captain. In the second landing boat Sorrel and three other crewmen had also come to a standstill in the water.

François bent close to Blossom, speaking softly only for her ears. "You are so beautiful, Miss Fortune." His eyes caught and held hers and his look was as soft as a caress. "And because you are, I shall think of you every moment I am down there in the black depths."

Then he jumped overboard, falling cleanly, striking the water feet first. Blossom sat in shock as he sent up a great splash into the landing boat.

"Is he crazy?" Blossom turned to ask the crewmen. They just looked into the water and grinned. "Will he drown?" He had been acting awfully strange, staring at her all the time. "Why is he doing this?" Still no answer. "You all sit there grinning like—like idiots while your captain is down there drowning himself." Her lovely face wrinkled in worry. "La! Is there not one of you who will save him?"

"He be okay, miss," Rusty said with a grin, yet

another cheroot dangling from his large lips.

Blossom stared doubtfully at the stream of white bubbles that had risen to the surface where he'd disappeared.

Angela looked at Blossom. Her face had gone pale and she was staring down into the water as if she'd never stop. Then she turned bewildered eyes in Daisy's and Angela's direction. They said nothing. Neither did Blossom.

At length, only a few bubbles reached the surface and it seemed as if François had been swallowed up by the sea. Never to return. Blossom glanced at Rusty and then back at the water.

"Something has happened to him!" Blossom made to stand but Rusty kept her down. He was watching her closely. "The fool . . . maybe a shark has gotten him." She looked into Rusty's eyes. *"Are* there sharks in these waters?"

"Yep." Rusty nodded. "Barracuda too."

Blossom gulped. "B-Barracuda?"

"Yep."

Blossom sat rigidly, lips parted, black eyes wide with distress, and her white fingers clutched the sides of the landing boat.

"He's a diver," Rusty finally relented, "one of the best."

"What?"

Blossom had not heard what the boatswain had said, for at the same moment there was disturbance in the water. Suddenly François's head broke the surface. The sun touched his hair and turned its blackness to an iridescent blue. His face was livid.

340

"Oh!" Blossom became a flurry of activity going nowhere.

A thin trickle of blood showed at François's nostrils. Angela stared, clutching Daisy's hand. For an instant they thought he would sink again. François lay on his back gasping, paddling his arms feebly.

"Do something!" Blossom said to the crewmen, who still sat without moving a muscle to help the man.

Then with a visible effort, François swam to the boat. "He's crazy, for sure," Jackson said, "staying below for more than three minutes this time."

"Yeah," the other crewmen collectively agreed.

François hauled himself up and smiled roguishly when he felt Blossom's fingers on his arms, helping him. "For you," he raspingly said, and in his hand he held out a purple sea fan. It was the sort that grew on the ocean's floor in tropic waters. Paying no attention to the rest of them, he handed the sea fan to Blossom. "A gift from the depths," he panted.

Giving François a startled smile, she murmured shyly, "I feared you would . . . never come up."

"Did you?" The unspeakable villain gazed into her limpid black eyes as Rusty handed him an old blanket to dry himself off.

At once Blossom looked aside, her face flushed, her trembling fingers still holding the sea fan.

"A gift from the depths," Angela repeated to Daisy, who had not heard what François had said as he handed Blossom the purple sea fan. He had almost killed himself to get the most special one that grew only in the depths.

Daisy exchanged a look with Angela, then said, "A gift yes, from the depths of *his heart.*"

They reached the shore, and Rusty jumped in with three others to pull the boat through the water up onto the sand. Again, Angela was surprised when they were lifted from the boat so they wouldn't get their skirts wet.

François carried Blossom onto dry sand and set her down, then stood looking at her for a long moment. Daisy and Angela held their breath, wondering if François was going to kiss Blossom. It would not have surprised them that much more if he had. But he began to lead the way up the beach to a line of trees.

"I really can't understand what is going on," Daisy said in a low voice, staring down at the short, coarse grass sticking up here and there from the creamy sand as they walked. "We are kidnapped and then treated like . . . like friends or something by our captors. Now it seems that scoundrel is falling in love with Blossom. Can love change a man *that* quickly?" Daisy asked Angela, her eyes large and liquid blue. "He is not the same man who abducted us."

"You have noticed the difference too," Angela said thoughtfully, watching the tall rascal leading the way, with Blossom flanking him off to the side and keeping her face pointed to the edge of trees up ahead while François kept glancing over at her. "He cannot seem to keep his eyes off her."

"I only wish Rider were here. This would be the perfect place for our honeymoon," she said wistfully. "It is so beautiful." Daisy sighed. "What do you think they plan to do with us?"

"I am not sure. François does not give me the creeps as much as he did at first, but still, he had done a bad thing by taking us away like he did."

"He is the one who took you from your home the first time?" Daisy asked, seeing a house up ahead. "Do you think he is bringing you back home?" Daisy asked hopefully.

"Hardly," Angela said with a short laugh. "And I do not think François is the one who really wants to kill me—"

"Angela—what do you mean? Who would want to kill you?"

Stopping to pour the sand from her shoes, Angela said, "I only wish I knew, then I might be able to do something about it. All I know is there has been this feeling all along that someone wishes me dead. It is stronger than ever."

"I wonder who lives in the house," Daisy said, feeling Sorrel's eyes on her. She always knew when the red-haired man was close by; she got a premonition and then when she turned he was usually there. He was this time too.

Before they reached the house, François took Sorrel off to the side and had a private conversation with him. Angela could see François gesturing in their direction, and then to the house, to Blossom, and then back to Angela and Daisy once again. They seemed to be arguing about something. François looked frustrated, Sorrel angry.

Then François began walking in their direction, turned back, and shook his fist at Sorrel, shouting, "No! Do you hear me? No!"

"You have changed your mind," Sorrel shouted

back. "She will not like this."

Blossom joined Daisy and Angela then. The three of them looked back and forth between Sorrel and François, wondering what the heated argument was about.

"I do not care what she wants anymore," François ground out.

"You better care, my compeer. She will do away with all three of them otherwise."

François looked at Blossom, then back at Sorrel, thundering, "Never!"

"You dig your own grave," Sorrel said, washing his hands of the whole matter, so it seemed.

"No one digs François's grave. I will deal with Julia myself."

All Blossom had heard was the name Julia, but she knew that this was what Sorrel had been talking about. For some insane reason someone wanted to see Angela dead, and Angela was Jessica Hawke. Blossom finally put two and two together. This woman, Julia, she wanted Angela dead. Also, there was something between this woman Julia and François. She had a strong feeling that this Julia and François were lovers.

"Angela," Blossom began, walking closer to the other two, "I have something to tell—"

"Blossom," Sorrel said, directing her gaze to the West Indies–style house of rose-tinted plaster, with its terraces leading out into tropical gardens that led to the creamy beaches. "We are here. This is Paraiso."

Blossom could only stare. She hoped he could not tell what she was thinking. This was not what she wanted anymore. Revenge was unimportant now. Daisy and Rider's marriage did not matter. Most of all, Sorrel meant nothing to her, and she did not want François to find out she'd been intimate with Sorrel.

"What is the matter, Blossom?" François said, raising an eyebrow.

She was afraid he would begin to wonder why she had come along so willingly. Now, all that had changed.

"Oh—" She looked at Angela, the house, Sorrel with his warning eye. "Nothing." She shrugged. "Nothing at all."

"Sorrel, take them up to the house. If Julia is here—and I doubt she is or she would have come running out to meet us—but if she is, take the women to Llana and her relatives. They will be safer there."

"I understand," Sorrel said, clenching his teeth inside his mouth. He did not like the intimate looks François had been sending Blossom; it was fortunate she had not been receiving them, however. He considered Blossom his plaything—just as Llana was.

"See that you do."

With that, François strode back in the direction they'd come. On his way he directed several of his trusted crewmen to join Sorrel and the women, repeating his orders to the crewmen to make them stick. He trusted Sorrel about as far as he could throw that huge man.

"Who lives here?" Blossom asked Sorrel after François had gone.

"A woman by the name of Julia is staying here now." Sorrel stared possessively into Blossom's eyes and the creamy expanse of her neck and throat. "I own this island." He shrugged, adding, "Half of it anyway."

"Who owns the house?" she wanted to know.

Daisy and Angela hurried to get closer so they could hear what was being said.

"François and myself own it," he said gruffly, not wishing to tell her he'd become only half owner of Paraiso during a game of chance on the ship when he'd wagered it away. François had wanted to play for the whole island, but Sorrel had explained, even while he'd been half in the bag, that his native ancestors would never leave him in peace if he gambled the whole of it away. Llana would never speak to him again, and he did not want that to happen. Llana was like a tan flower. Blossom was like a white one. Both dark-haired women possessed the hearts of tigresses. Both were the best he'd ever had. If he were asked to make a choice, he'd rather plunge a knife into his own heart than have to choose between them. But then, he looked at Blossom and chose.

"Come," Sorrel said to the women. "Jackson has given the signal. There is no one at the house. There are many rooms, and"—he said with a smile— "many baths awaiting."

Angela chuckled, relieving the tension in the air, saying, "As long as there are three, that will be plenty."

"Good. Come along then."

It was not until later that François learned from Carolos that Julia had become bored and taken off to Nassau when the island-hopping steamer had stopped

346

by with some supplies for Llana and her relatives. He knew it was just as well Julia was not here. He needed some time to be alone and think. Also, he needed some time to be alone with Blossom—and he did not know why.

After they had taken their baths and eaten a supper of delicious fish, prepared by the beautiful native girl Llana, with her slant-eyed brother Carolos hanging around the whole while, Daisy and Blossom and Angela sat out on the terrace watching the mammoth cinnabar sun go down.

Blossom waited until the three of them were alone, then she turned to Angela, knowing she had to warn her before it was too late. Why she had to warn Angela she could not say. Angela had meant nothing to her before . . . yet all of a sudden everything seemed to have new meaning to her. The flowers were beautiful. Birds had lovely songs. She had hated birds before.

People were important. Kindness. Caring. These were words she had not given much thought to before . . . she caught herself. Before what?

"Jessica." Blossom found herself staring into startled pearl-blue eyes. "Jessica Hawke."

"That is me," Angela said, feeling faint.

Daisy took Angela's hand, knowing what Blossom said was unquestionable.

"Hawke," Angela murmured, her heart swelled to near bursting. The name: *Hawke.*

"Yes," Blossom said, squatting before Angela's chair. "You are Jessica Angèle Hawke. . . . I want to

347

help you because . . . someone is planning to kill you." Blossom shyly lowered her eyes. "And . . . I want to help because . . . I like you."

Tears gathered in Angela's eyes as she looked at Daisy and then Blossom's shiny black head of hair. Now she stared out to sea and the sun that was a huge orange ball above it. "I know, Blossom," she said with her heart turning over, "I know. And I like you too."

The very next day Blossom was her old self. Not toward the girls, but where men were concerned. Her wild sensuous nature was stirring again.

While she stared from the terrace out to sea, wearing a thin wrapper, she felt arousal stirring deep within. The sensations seemed harder to bear than usual and were much more intense for some reason.

All morning they had been allowed to explore the island, while François never seemed to be out of sight for long. His black hair gleamed thunderblue under the sun, and his long muscled body was like a Greek statue come to life when he strode with easy purposeful steps . . . and then from a distance she could see him strip and run out into the waters of the turquoise cove.

Dots of moisture had broken out on Blossom's forehead and upper lip by the time she and the others returned for lunch. And it was not solely from the exercise.

Blossom knew that something wild and elemental had come alive in her as she watched François swimming in the cove.

Suddenly Blossom was angry with herself, and with François. She recalled he had come upon her on many occasions while still on board. At those times she had been fighting off the advances of Sarge Sorrel. The man never gave up. And François had acted as if she had wanted Sorrel to paw her!

Blossom strolled along the beach. She was alone. The sun was low in the brilliant blue sky. She ached. She could almost feel his hands touching and caressing her, his lips kissing her, his tongue inside her flesh.

There had been times he had frightened her, for she didn't know what it was she really wanted from François. It was not just a quick roll, no, it was something she was afraid to think about. In fact, she had often tried to tell herself she did not want François that way at all. It hadn't bothered her, until today.

It was so humid and warm. Blossom wore little for clothes. She wandered to the secluded cove with a blanket under her arm just as the sun had reached its biggest form, blood-red and fiery, seeming to encompass the whole island right to its circumference. Like the rubescent eye of some monstrous sea dragon, Blossom thought as she chose a spot to spread out her blanket. She would wait for the stars to come out and the soft evening breezes to cool her passion-hot flesh.

As she lay down upon the sand, the full shape of her breasts became outlined in the skimpy bit of colorful material, a shift Llana called it, for the pretty native girl had shown her and Angela how to wrap and drape and wear the thing.

Her shapely legs and curvaceous behind were every man's dream. Even to the man whose dark shadow left the verdant cover and began walking toward her. The man was bare-chested, as most men were on the island, and his breeches stretched taut across legs and thighs that were strong and corded with muscle that resembled the boles of thick oaks.

Blossom did not become aware that someone stood watching her until he said her name. She sat up and whirled about and he repeated her name, as if he liked the way it felt on his tongue, even though he could not pronounce it quite right.

"Blos-zom."

"Oh . . . it's you. La! Carolos, you gave me such a fright." She looked up at the bear of a man. "D-Did you wish to speak with me?"

"No talk." Carolos shook his head, licking his lips as he looked her up and down.

"Well . . . what then?"

Blossom had met Carolos just that morning. She knew he was Llana's older brother. But what was he doing here when he should be out helping his relatives with their catches in the huge fishing nets as he usually did this time every day?

"No talk," he repeated, taking a seat beside her and Blossom could swear she felt the beach quake as he sat.

"Want to make love to pretty flower."

"What?!"

Blossom scuttled away from Carolos. He moved closer.

"Carolos been thinking about Blos-zom all day. I meet you today. I want you now."

350

"No! I am not yours just because you want me, Carolos!"

The bearlike man reached for her and caught her. Blossom tried squirming from his embrace, but all he did was put her in a tighter clinch.

From a distance, to one standing there, it appeared that Blossom was returning Carolos's embrace. Hard dark eyes glittered as François shoved away from the banana tree he'd been standing beneath for several minutes now, long enough to witness what was taking place upon the beach.

"Carolos," Blossom hissed into the young man's ear, "I don't want to!"

"You do, woman. I have see in your eyes you want Carolos."

He was so strong! Blossom felt as weak as a kitten in his clutches. She had never been raped; she had always gone to a man willingly, no matter who that man was. But now, for some reason she could not, or would not recognize, this man must not have her.

"Get up! The both of you!"

Carolos started.

"I repeat: *Get the hell up!*"

Blossom looked up. François stood there, his face an angry pinch of hatred and distaste. And something else she could not name.

Chapter Twenty-Seven

Carolos had been trying to maneuver Blossom onto her back in the cream-pink sand. Yet François's senses had become clouded by jealousy, and he saw only that Blossom was being caressed and compromised by another man.

"O-Oh François," Carolos stuttered as he rose swiftly to stand on not too steady feet, "I do not understand . . . she . . . the little lady—" He shrugged his arms and spread his big hands in a lame expression of apology.

"I think you both see only what you want to see," Blossom said, trying to keep from looking into François's dark dangerous eyes.

"Miss Fortune," François began mockingly, his eyes blazing down into hers.

"What?"

"Be still," he commanded. "I will have this out with Carolos and you keep your mouth shut."

Blossom controlled a shiver. "Why . . . you!"

Then she gathered up the blanket, making to rise

and quit this scene when François's voice cut across her path.

"Stay where you are, Miss Fortune, I would like to have a word with you." To Carolos he said, "Go now. Your sister is looking for you."

The sun was sinking fast as François's hard eyes became lazy and hooded; he turned back to Blossom. Her eyes were black snaps. François could not know that within Blossom's breast the heart that had never been given away was beating with an abandonment that shook her. Blossom could sense François's disquiet.

"What do you want, François?"

In her agitated state, Blossom was totally unaware that his name rolled from her tongue like a tender caress.

Wisely François chose to leave that question unanswered. Instead he asked, "What were you doing out here alone with Carolos?" His eyes narrowed suspiciously as he awaited her answer.

Choosing to ignore his question, Blossom finished dragging the blanket to her and stood shaking the sand from it. It was a bad choice.

The hard dark eyes followed Blossom as she began to walk toward the tall trees where heavy branches fell over a narrow path and hibiscus bloomed on either side in the thick grasses. Catching up, François grabbed her arm and twirled her to face him.

"Answer me!" he bit out, anger hardening his features.

"That is a stupid question! And besides—what I do is really none of your business!"

"I have made it mine," he said in a dangerously

soft tone.

"I see. You always seem to come along just when—"

Reaching a hand out he covered her mouth, warning, "Do not say it, Miss Fortune. I long ago realized what you and your *friends* are always about to do."

"I-I don't know what you mean."

Gripping her shoulders, François stared into Blossom's shocked face. "Are you a whore then?" he said.

Puffing up, Blossom hissed, "I am no man's whore!"

"Every man's." He snorted softly. "Women like you get paid well for what you give away so freely. Paid well, where I come from, Blossom Fortune."

"P-Paid?" she stammered. "Are you making personal reference?"

"Yes. Would you like to be paid in beautiful gowns, jewelry? I could even set you up in your own house by the sea."

"You?" She blinked at him, feeling a swell of excitement at the thought of François making love to her whenever he chose.

François nodded, feeling a hot flush cover his face as he awaited her answer.

"Would you also be my first customer?"

François caressed her hand and answered, "You could say that I would be your . . . only customer. Have you never heard of a mistress?"

"Oh—a paid whore," Blossom said defiantly.

Grasping her wrist, putting his face close to hers, he said crisply, "What do you think we are talking

354

about?" His voice grated on her nerves. "Of course. I prefer the gentler term—mistress."

"Are you married then?"

His eyes narrowed. "No." He'd thought to marry Julia on several occasions, even though she was twice his age he guessed. "A man does not have to be married to keep a mistress."

"No thank you, suh!"

Peeling his fingers from her arm, Blossom stepped back, feeling the tenseness in his body as she did so. His touch always unnerved her, made her feel hot and shivery all over. What could be wrong with her? No man had ever affected her as François did.

François trailed her into the grouping of banana palms. The last rays had vanished. Dusk had settled over the island. Inside the trees was like a high-ceilinged room, cozy and verdant and lush. Purple flowers fell at the feet of many tall trees, and the cream-pink sand showed here and there between the thick grasses.

"Blossom"—the voice followed her like a tenacious breeze—"where are you going?"

"Back to the house," Blossom called back, a warning voice within urging her to hurry.

Suddenly she was brought to a standstill. She looked down. Then turned to her right. She gazed into his face, sooty in the dusk, and thought she'd never seen a man look so ruggedly handsome. Her eyes fell again, then lifted over his body to his face. François had stepped onto a trailing corner of the blanket, and now, he barred her way along the path.

"What do you want?" she asked.

"More than you are willing to give."

Blossom stirred uneasily under his deeply intense regard and looked away from his shining eyes. She was experiencing feelings she'd never known existed. There was undefinable hatred. Fear. Despair. And a strange yearning she did not recognize.

"I have to go now."

"We are not through here yet," he said in a silky tone, staring at her hair, her face, her shoulders. . . .

"What do you mean? Not through with what, François?"

"Ah . . . discussing matters."

"What . . . matters?"

"Hmmm—" François only smiled.

"I have already told you the answer is no. I will be no man's—"

"Shh." With a finger to her lips he shook his head. "One thing, Blossom Fortune: You will stay away from my men—"

"La! I will do exactly as I wish—"

"My men—stay away from them. And Carolos. I give you fair warning."

"I told you! I will do—"

"—exactly as I command."

Closer and closer he came. "Ah . . . Blossom."

She heard him cluck his tongue and the sound infuriated her. "No. Keep your hands off me. I hate you . . . you are mean . . . you are despicable. François—you—"

"—I—am going to kiss you."

A cry of fear and some other emotion broke from her lips.

When his lips had merely brushed hers, Blossom cried out again and wrenched away. Shivering from head to toe, she stood away from him. While he kept on advancing on her. Backing her against the curved bole of a tall tree.

The blanket fell free of Blossom's grip.

Now he imprisoned her, with one arm on either side of the tree. He nudged her thighs apart with his knee and Blossom cried out even louder. While his eyes delved deeply into the black ones, he lowered his face, lower, lower, finally closing his eyes.

Blossom, too, closed her eyes. She waited. When his lips brushed again she was set aflame, her body spinning into a wild swirl and she could hear a moaning, soft panting, seeming to come from somewhere outside her body, not realizing she was making the sounds herself.

Kissing her slowly, not fully yet. Caressing, tenderly caressing. The kiss was so gently given then. He gave. No taking. Only giving.

The erotic ache began, unlike anything Blossom had never felt. He gave so much that it left her breathless. To return the kiss would be dangerous, she knew.

She struggled, in vain. All her struggles were useless, pitiful little poundings of her fists against the unmovable chest.

Wrenching her face aside, she cried, "François!" She pushed the hand that had slid up to her face aside. "I cannot do anything."

"I understand, Blossom," he said quietly. "I just want you to stand there and take my pleasure."

He caught her face between his hands, and at first he merely brushed his lips against hers. Pleasure radiated from the shadowed dark triangle between her softly downed thighs and spread outward, and he kissed her longer and longer, kissing the very breath from her. His kisses grew deeper and deeper, and he made a gift of each one.

François moved against her, and her body naturally arched toward that element of heat and the pleasure made her lightheaded. His breathing became increasingly urgent, as did hers. He kissed her until she became limp as a rag doll and she whimpered for him to leave her alone.

"Never!" he growled, parting from her moist lips, "never will I leave you alone."

"You are ugly!" she hissed, shoving him back.

He went awfully still.

She was so weak now that she knew she could not fight him. His teeth were a brief flash in the dusk and his teeth clenched as he held himself in check.

"What did you say?" he gritted out. Desire raked at his loins and he stepped back to get away from her; otherwise he was certain he would rape her here and now.

"I-I am sorry. I did not mean that."

Blossom was shaking inside so violently and mutely, she stared back at him. Her foolish heart thundered against her ribs. She had struck a weak spot in François. To her he was not ugly at all; he was the most compelling man she'd ever known. But he could not know what she was thinking. . . . He must not know how very much she desired him.

François felt confused for the first time in his life. No woman had ever dared say such a thing to him, much less make mention of his scarred countenance.

"You have wounded my pride, mademoiselle." He

358

executed a short bow. "Good night, Miss Fortune."

With that he walked away, leaving her standing there alone. She watched François until she could see him no longer. Looking around she found the blanket, then gathered it before her and slumped down onto its folds.

Suddenly Blossom was crying, heartbrokenly, bereftly, abjectly, crumpling the blanket and hugging it tight, her passion-cooled body shaking, her throat a cramped agony.

"Oh François . . . François."

She pretended the blanket was François's sleeve under her cheek, and she clutched it tight, letting her heart ache until she was weak with grief and at last she fell asleep under the canopy of moon and stars.

They had been on the island for two days. Angela, Daisy, and Blossom strolled the sun-blazed beaches during the day and at night Blossom ventured out alone, haunting the star-lit cove. They were free to roam, but always in the shade not far away lurked Sorrel or one of the other crew members. How could they escape? Where could they go? Carolos was set to guard the small fishing boats, and even if they could get to one, there was the question of how to man them. It took considerable strength to move one away from the island. And Blossom was confused. She wanted to stay and she wanted to escape. She tried to convince herself that François was homely. His face was scarred from the pox. His lips were slightly too large. Too soft . . . melting. His dark eyes never left her for an instant when he was about and his voice was distant when he spoke to her. Hour after hour, she grew more uncomfortable. The tingling sensation never ceased, not since he had kissed her with such giving, and she regretted she had been so harsh. She had not meant to be so cruel.

Seated beneath a grouping of sea grape trees that covered a small hill above where they sat and afforded them some shade, the three young women sipped an exotic drink Llana had whipped together for them. It was heady and intoxicating, and it was not long before Blossom's speech was slightly blurred. She'd drunk more than the others, stating that she was hot and nothing seemed to help her cool off. And Llana kept them coming, smiling in her shy manner while Carolos waited on them hand and foot. Carolos and Llana came originally from the Isle of Pines on the other side of Cuba; they spoke some English but it was halting.

"Carolos," Blossom said, flinging back her long raven tresses, "you can go now. No, please, we don't need any more fruit, we're stuffed as it is."

Grinning wolfishly, he set the pitcher containing the exotic drink on the table between them and backed away, his unbuttoned shirt blatantly displaying his strong, bronzed chest. When he was well out of sight, Blossom reached for the cooled pitcher and poured herself another drink, sipping slowly while Angela and Daisy exchanged concerned looks.

"Blossom," Angela began, glancing up at the sun, "you had better go easy on that or else you will have quite a headache later on." She frowned, adding, "I already have one and have had much less than you."

360

Daisy giggled. "I don't think I can see my way back to the house as it is now! What is in that stuff?" She gestured at the half-full pitcher resting on the small table, conveniently next to Blossom's elbow.

"Fire," Angela said, grimacing. She turned serious then, directing her next words to Blossom. "I do believe François is trying to get us intoxicated."

Blossom started. "Why do you say that?"

"Well . . . I happened to see him about an hour and a half ago, and he was talking to Llana."

"What does that have to do with anything?" Daisy wondered out loud, looking over her shoulder toward the house.

"He gave Llana something . . . it looked like a bottle of that fiery liquor I saw the men drinking on board."

"La! Why would François try to get us drunk?" Blossom said, tossing down the rest of her drink, and reaching for more. She was getting planked and she didn't care.

"He is after you," Angela said, studying Blossom carefully. "You don't care, do you?"

"No—why should I?" She laughed gaily. "I can handle François. He is a mere pup next to the other men I've known."

"Really?" Angela said. "I do not think that is true, Blossom. Tell me, what are they going to do to us, do you know? Who is it that wants me dead, Blossom?"

"I-I don't know," Blossom said, reaching for her glass.

Angela stayed Blossom's hand. "You do, Blossom. Or you have a pretty good idea. Tell me, who do you think is at the head of all this? Is it only a matter of time before François sees fit to kill me? And why?"

"How much do you remember?" Blossom asked, feeling sober all of a sudden. Angrily, she snapped, "Don't you remember *any*thing? You know your name now—why *don't* you know anything else?"

Staring off into the turquoise waters, Angela murmured, "It will come to me . . . in time."

Blossom became angry. "You haven't got time!"

Angela now felt a flash of heat behind her eyes and jumped to her feet, anger showing in her face. She lashed out, striking the pitcher and knocking it from Blossom's hand. "I have had enough of you!"

Blossom fell backward off her chair with a surprised look on her face as Angela whirled and started off at a run along the beach, weaving now as the hot sun and firewater began to affect her. She ran at an angle, with the other two women at her heels, where the sand met the trees. Blossom and Daisy came to a halt, ten feet from where Angela had tripped on a piece of driftwood in a field of the same, many of them now exposing their gray bodies in the creamy sand; she lay still.

Running to Angela's side, they gently rolled her over and Daisy gasped, "Blood! Oh . . . no!"

Blossom shouted, "Shut up! Tear a piece of your shift and run to the water and wet it for me," as she cradled Angela's head in her lap.

A blue welt rose on Angela's forehead, and her eyes fluttered weakly, then Angela looked up, saying "Where am I?"

Blossom answered, "You don't know?"

Angela's eyes looked over to Daisy running swiftly

362

toward them, now dropping to her knees beside them, with tears running down her face.

"Give me that!" Blossom snapped, and she yanked the wet cloth from Daisy's hand to place it on Angela's forehead.

Angela gazed up into Blossom's black eyes, saying, "Now I remember! Oh God, I remember *everything!*"

Chapter Twenty-Eight

All afternoon bits and pieces were returning to Angela's drowsy mind. She knew her name. But she preferred to be called by her middle name—Angèle—the twin to Angela.

France . . . her home was in France.

Her maid's name, the one in the dream . . . Tina.

Her mother's name . . . Monica!

Father . . . Steven!

El Corazón . . . home!

Even the name of the dark, handsome stable boy who'd been with them for years came to mind for some odd reason. Benjamin. Always he'd stayed outside with the horses, even though her parents had constantly invited him into the house. She had watched him ride the unruly stallion they had had shipped all the way from Louisiana. . . . Like an Indian prince, he rode.

On her back in the room alloted to her earlier in the day—for François had decided they each could have their own—Angela stared up into the ashes-of-roses canopy, the draping folds of special interest to her as she followed each train of thought back in time. Before she had returned to her room, she had wandered through the house. Mulling over thoughts as she walked silently alone. The big rooms had been lavishly furnished with massive walnut and mahogany tables, chairs, sofas, with large French mirrors in gilt frames between the windows and doors. Someone enjoyed studying her reflection in so many mirrors, she had thought. Brussels carpets with huge glaring patterns had been laid out without thought of matching the design, and a very expensive piano graced one corner of the drawing room. Again, as then, she reflected back. . . .

Benjamin. He'd had dark eyes, but she'd never gotten that close to the tall lad to pick out the exact shade of them. Benjamin. Benjamin *what?* No one had ever mentioned a last name. Benjamin had never paid much attention to her. She had asked Tina his age at one time, and the maid had only made a guess . . . perhaps ten years older than she had been at that time.

Why did the stable boy seem of special interest to her now? She rolled over to prop herself upon her elbow. Of course! The resemblance between Gypsy Smith and Benjamin, the stable boy, was . . . well, quite remarkable. And neither of them really had a last name; Gypsy had once told her that he did not have a last name. Smith was only his second name. But, really, was it?

The question arose in her brain. Could Gypsy Smith and Benjamin be related? Like brothers, or cousins?

Angela laughed at herself then. How could they be? It was preposterous to think they were related.

Just then Daisy peeped around the edge of the door, saying, "Can I come in? I would like to talk if you are rested."

"Of course, Daisy, do come in," Angela said graciously.

The blonde paused another moment, staring at Angela as if seeing her for the first time, and then entered the room. Daisy was wearing a plain blue dress this time, borrowed from Llana; the dusky girl seemed to have an inexhaustible supply of women's clothing. The afternoon sun was slanting into the window, bathing the whitewashed walls a delicate dusky rose. Soon the room would be a spectacular splash with the vermillion sunset coloring the whole island.

"I brought you something to drink," Daisy said, gesturing behind her. "It is out in the hall."

Angela held up her hand, begging, "No, please, nothing to drink!"

Daisy smiled her sweet smile, "There's no alcohol in it."

"Well then, bring it in." Angela adjusted her colorful print shift as she left the bed and padded across the floor to a chair. "How is Blossom?" she wondered out loud as Daisy entered with what looked like a lemon or lime drink, free of inebriants.

Setting the tray down, Daisy said, "She could be better. She's lying down in her room now. François has asked for her."

"What did you tell him?" Angela sipped the cool lime drink and stretched her legs out onto the

Egyptian-style ottoman.

With a giggle Daisy said, "I looked him right in the eye and told him he was a nasty man for trying to get us all inebriated!"

"Really? What did he say to that?"

"He laughed arrogantly and said, 'Not *all* of you, *cherie.'*"

"Only Blossom," Angela said, setting her drink on the table a little harder than usual.

In a soft voice, Daisy asked, "Have you remembered any more, Angela?" She laughed. "Or should I call you Jessica?"

"Yes, I have remembered more," Angela said with a smile. "And—no, please continue to call me Angela. I've gotten rather used to the name ... hmm ... I think it suits me better than Jessica and I wouldn't like everyone to get mixed up if I switched to another name all of a sudden. I could just see Gypsy Smith saying, 'Who in the world is Jessica Hawke?' He would never know it was me."

"You're different." Daisy tilted her blond head, her face pink with eagerness. "Tell me more, if you can. I'm interested, I'd like to know why we are here and where we are going." The golden mist of her hair fell across one eye as she leaned forward. "This all—everything here on this island seems ... too pleasant. I feel as if we are sitting on a powder keg."

"We are, I think." Angela sighed, then drew herself up as she turned serious, sitting straighter in the chair with her slender legs curled beneath her. For now, however, that terror-stricken day she had been abducted was washed as cleanly from her memory as if one had wiped a slate clean. "François has tried to kill me once, he will do so again. Only this time, I think he will not fail. As soon as Juliet, or Julia—I've heard her called both—when she returns I do believe the lid is going to blow off that powder keg you mentioned."

Daisy frowned, mulling over something before she spoke. "Don't you think François would have"— Daisy swallowed hard—"would have done away with you by now? He has hardly looked your way since he fell in love with Blossom. Or—do you think it is only that he, uhmm, he lusts after her?"

"Who can tell the man's mind, Daisy." She leaned back and closed her eyes for a moment. "He is dangerous, that is for certain."

"Blossom is used to danger, I think."

"This is a different sort of danger, Daisy. She has never come across his kind before."

"Will he—kill us all?"

"I am not sure. But no, I do not think so. Sorrel has something else in mind, I am sure."

"I had that feeling too." Daisy shivered. "The way he looks at me is so frightening, as if he is raping me with his eyes. Angela, we have to think of some way to get off this island."

"I know, Daisy. If only there were some way to contact my father."

"Where do they live? Is it far from here?"

Angela laughed, her blue eyes crinkling at Daisy. "Very far away, I think! Too far for us to safely get to. They live in France."

"France! That is halfway across the ocean again." Daisy groaned, then her perfect oval face brightened. "Maybe Gypsy Smith and Rider are on their way to save us—even now!"

"Hardly," Angela said, sounding depressed. "How would they know where to find us?"

"I don't think Rider would be one to give up trying, Angela. He would continue to search until some sort of clue was found."

"You are perfectly right. I do not believe Gypsy would give up, either. Hmm—" Angela tapped her chin. "I think a plan is forming in my newly invigorated brain."

Daisy laughed, saying, "Well, let's hear it!"

"First"—Angela shuddered—"I have to get Sorrel to like me." She stared into Daisy's uncomprehending eyes. "To *really* like me. Do you know what I mean?"

Daisy stared back into the eyes of determination, groaning, "Only too well!"

In another room down the hall from Angela's, Blossom was just coming awake. The bed sheets were tangled about her legs, and her long black hair falling to her waist was damp from perspiration, moist tendrils making tiny corkscrews at her flushed cheeks.

"I brought you something to eat," François said briskly as he entered, balancing a tray on one hand while closing the door with the other.

Blossom gasped. She was naked! Well, almost. She wore short pantalettes. That was it.

François acted as if it were the most natural thing in the world, to come upon a freshly awakened woman with her breasts bared to the world. He hardly glanced her way . . . at least he did not stare at her.

"I don't want to eat," Blossom snapped, reaching for the shift to cover herself.

"Do you have to do that?" François said, capturing her eyes with his.

Holding the lavender and mimosa pink shift against her chest, she blinked and asked, "Do what?"

"Cover yourself." François's eyes raked over her seductively.

After Blossom had left him feeling cold and angry the other night, he had walked away from her, telling himself resolutely, if he was denied today, he certainly would prevail another day. He wanted Blossom, badly, and he meant to have her. No woman had ever told him no.

"I wish you would not cover yourself, Blossom. I like to look at you."

She tossed long coils of blue-black hair, her head halting at a defiant tilt. "What you like and what you get are two different things, suh!" With that she squirmed into the shift, and had her pantalettes off lickety-split.

François's dark eyes glittered even darker. "You are used to making the quick change of clothes, Blossom. I know many whores that are not as swift as you, Blossom Fortune."

He was trying to bait her, but she was not going to let him do that to her.

"You are very beautiful, Blossom—a beautiful whore."

"What do you have there for me to eat?" she said, changing the subject quickly, as if he had not irked her at all. He was only calling her names because she had wounded his ego, she decided.

Lifting the lid, François displayed the delicious shrimp surrounded by curried vegetables sprinkled with exotic herbs, coriander, turmeric, and other spices.

"Ugh!" Blossom wrinkled her nose in distaste. "I'm downright sick of fish and stringy vegetables." She brushed her hand in the air, demanding, "Take it away. La! It smells awful."

"You have a hangover, that is why."

"No thanks to you, suh!"

Picking up the tray and unceremoniously tossing the contents at the wall, where the deliciously saucy vegetables ran down the whitewash, making ugly streaks along with pink smudges where the shrimp had struck, François demanded angrily, "What in hell do you mean, woman? I had nothing to do with you getting yourself sick!"

"You certainly did, suh!"

His dark eyebrows slashed into a frown as he said in a deceptively calm tone, "Explain yourself, Miss Fortune."

"Angela saw you!"

"What?"

"Jessica Angèle Hawke, you know, the one you plan to kill. Or your beautiful mistress plans to, I should say."

Dangerously François's jaw clenched and his eyes narrowed. "What do you know about that?"

They stared at each other across the bed.

"Everything!" Then sarcastically she added, "I know all about your precious Julia—your whore. I

371

just bet you can't wait until she gets here, that is why, suh, you are picking on me."

"There are plenty other women on this island, and you are not so unique, mademoiselle."

"First you call me a whore, then you call me by your pretty little French names. Can't you make up your mind, suh!"

"I am not 'suh'; I am François. And I said you are not so unique that I cannot find entertainment elsewhere."

"Why does your mistress want to kill Angela? Do you know? Do you even care?"

François clenched his long-fingered hands at his sides, grinding out, "I think that is none of your business!"

"It is! Angela is my friend! I don't want to see her killed!"

"Stop that shouting, or else I shall have to gag you."

"La! You might even kill me too, while you are at it."

That did it. François leaped across the bed like a striking cobra and grabbed her shoulders tightly. "Kill you? Are you crazy? Mother of God, never say that, or else I *shall* strangle you!"

"Go ahead then!"

"Blossom, you exasperate me!"

"If you or your woman do anything to Angela, the same will be done to me."

"What do you mean?" He shook her and Blossom looked up at him with a flicker of apprehension.

"I won't live, if Angela dies."

"You would take your own life?" He stared at her with a baffled look.

"Yes!"

"I see." François rose from the bed and stood staring down at her.

"Why are you so confused, François? It is simple. Angela dies, and I die. We are like sisters. In fact, she is married to my half brother."

"Who is he?" François said, already knowing she referred to the tall, dark man with the hawklike face and an air of authority. He *would* be related to Blossom; they both had a commanding look, almost aloof at times. "What is his name?" was what he really wanted to know. Was it really Gypsy Smith?

"Why?" She peered up at him, her breast tingling against the thin fabric of the shift. "Do you want to kill him *too?*"

"No, I do not want to kill him too. Blossom, I do not want to kill anyone."

François felt his face go pale. He was lying. Or *was* he?

"Why in God's name are we being held prisoners here then?! It doesn't make much sense. Why do you want to kill Angela? What has she, lovely little Angela with a heart made of gold, what has she ever done to you?"

"I have already told you it is none of your concern."

"Then see me dead too!"

Blossom rolled onto her stomach, not caring that she afforded François with a very lovely view of the tantalizing curve of her backsides. His gaze was riveted on it for a moment, then began to move slowly over the rest of her. He became aroused at once.

What would it be like to sink himself into Blossom's velvet sheath. He wanted to touch her; move his mouth against her lips; feel the roundness of her high, proud breasts; to enter the most intimate part of Blossom's body, to thrust deep, again and again, until she was sweet and tender from his lovemaking.

"Go away, François. I want to be alone."

François shook himself from the erotic imaginings. He turned and walked out of the room, making a mental note to have Julia's elusive maid come in and clean it up.

Blossom stared at the floor blankly. She was still so confused and couldn't understand why François and Julia would want to kill Angela.

When Blossom was feeling better that afternoon, much later, when the sun was going down again, she walked along the beach until she reached the cove. Choosing a different spot for her blanket than the one before, she sat gazing out at the *Delora* anchored out in the cove, black sails furled.

The waters were ever-changing. Sparkling in the sun. Mysterious in the twilight. Their moods changed from hour to hour. The surface waters moved with the tides and stirred to the breath of tropical winds.

The cream-pink sand still felt warm from the day's sun. She began to wonder about the man that owned the ship.

François was suddenly behind her. "You seem to like watching my ship. Are you planning to escape on her?"

"No." Does he never give up, she asked herself.

"Where did she get the name *Delora?*"

Blossom shivered when her eyes snagged on the ever-present pistol François wore at his side. He hunkered down in the sand, his face bathed in pink and lavender hues of dusk. Blossom hugged her knees to her, hoping he would answer her soon so that she would not have to repeat herself.

"It happened a long time ago, I do not think you'd care to hear about it. She was only a child, as I was myself."

"Have you . . . known so many women then?"

"Of course!" François laughed, the sound crawling up from his throat. "Women of all shapes and sizes, around the world!"

Preferring not to get into that, Blossom bluntly asked, "What are you doing here, François?" Her voice emerged so soft he'd barely heard it.

"Would you like to refresh our argument?" As he said this, he looked straight ahead to his ship and laid an arm across one knee.

Already the tropical stars were beginning to glow in the soft darkened turquoise and dusky rose of sky. They popped out, one by one, winking provocatively and beckoning a night of love.

"I want to know all about you and why you are here. Why does there have to be an argument, François?"

"You are baiting me, Blossom."

"Is that so bad?"

"Let me ask you a question. Are you prepared to pay the price for your foolishness?"

"Only," she said breathlessly, "if I get some answers, darlin'." Oh . . . she had not meant to use

375

one of her old endearments for her beaux on him.

"Darling?" His voice was soft and sensuous. "I like that. I will tell you . . . but there will be a price . . . as I said, *cherie.*"

"What does that mean"—she tried out the French accent—*"cherie?"*

"It is what you have just called me—*darling.*"

The shock of his terribly masculine voice ran through her body and her thoughts began to spin dizzily.

"What do you want to know?" His smile was open, intimate, his rugged olive skin taut over high cheekbones.

"What about the woman who lives here?"

"She is in Nassau."

"Already you are avoiding the issue, François."

"All right. Her name is Julia French and she is a duchess."

"Julia French?" Blossom laughed. "What is her *real* name?"

"Why do you think it is not her real name?"

"I have a strong feeling she is hiding something . . . like her identity for one."

"You are correct; she is."

"Why, François, won't you talk to me?"

He gave her a sidelong glance, and his voice was a velvet murmur. "What do you think we are doing, *cherie?*" He turned to face her suddenly and she felt as if her breath were cut off. "All right, I will tell you what you want to know. Julia wants Angela dead because of something in her past, revenge you might say, against Angela's father. It goes back even farther than that. Julia's cousin is Angela's grandfather. He, too, has hurt Julia in some way, so Julia has told me.''

"So, Angela and this Julia are related . . . in some way.''

"Very little, the blood is very thin between them.'' He sighed as if pained. "Yes, *cherie*, I had assigned one of my men the job of ending Jessica Angèle's life. His name was Saville, but he fumbled the job . . . with disastrous results.''

"What did you do to this Saville?'' Blossom asked, in a choppy voice.

"I sent him to his watery grave . . . after I set my blade to his throat.''

"So, you thought you had gotten rid of our Angela. You were angry when you discovered she still lived. You were afraid Juliet would be furious with you.''

"Do not say *Juliet*.''

"Why? Sorrel has called her this.''

"She . . . she does not like to be called Juliet. Just Julia.''

Ah! Blossom was beginning to see the light at the end of the tunnel. Juliet was much too close to the woman's actual name. Julia was . . . an alias to put her in concealment and cloak her real name.

"You thought you left Lady Hawke for dead,'' Blossom said, without thinking that Sorrel had used this name under wraps for Angela.

"Where did you hear that name?'' François gritted out, and cold fear twisted around Blossom's heart.

"Sorrel told me.'' She could not lie; he would become cognizant of it at once.

"So, you came here of your own free will, *cherie*. Why?''

"I don't have to tell you why, suh!" Blossom tossed her head flippantly, her cheeks like golden cherries as her face caught the last shooting rays of sun.

"If you want to know all, Blossom *cherie*, you will tell me."

Gazing into the hard, brown eyes, Blossom decided he was right. She had to tell him of her profound jealousy against Rider and Daisy Dawn. When she was finished, he sat very still and did not look at her, only watched the moon's ascent.

"Did he take you to his bed before this, ah, Daisy snatched him from beneath your nose?"

He was staring at her again, intense, waiting.

"She did not snatch Rider from me. We were to be married, as soon as the war was over."

"Ah, but this Rider fell in love with the lovely Daisy Dawn when he saw that her virtue was intact and a notch above the one he had promised to wed. *Did* he bed you, cherie?"

"It is none of your business, suh!"

François nodded, saying, "I have my answer."

The unspeakable villain looked out over the vermillion waters where the *Delora* lay anchored. What had happened to all his vile plans? He had vowed not to fail. Why did Julia's promise for every dream he'd wanted fulfilled suddenly go stale? He was a murderer. Cheat. Devil in human form, Julia had called him with that deep, throaty laugh of hers. That was why she loved him, she'd said. She had promised him when the job was complete, he would take possession of the map for buried treasure she held, along with the lovely villa Cassandra, by the sea. His own harem, too, with all the young virgins a

378

man could handle. All of it . . . so unimportant now. He did not believe a map even existed.

Blossom, too, was mulling over her sullied past. How could she change? At that moment, their eyes met and held.

"Have you ever . . . ?" he began, and coughed with embarrassment over something that had never crossed his mind before.

"Have I ever *what*, François?"

He rushed on, ". . . been in love?"

Something intense stormed her senses. Truthfully she said, "No."

"Like me, Blossom, you have only taken. Am I right?"

"Let's not discuss it, please, François."

"Blossom, I would like to make love to you," François said as velvet darkness settled over the island with only the moon and stars to see by.

Startled out of her wits, Blossom held her silence.

"Will you let me?"

A shaky "no" fell from her lips. A familiar shiver of arousal swept her from head to foot.

Reaching out a hand, François ran his fingers lightly up her arm. Her skin, like freshly skimmed cream, made him want to caress it. "I will beg if I must."

"I—I can't."

"Why not?" His voice was a mere whisper. *"Cherie,* I want to be inside you so bad that it hurts. I shall be a tender lover and make you swoon with passion. You will never be loved like I can . . . love you, Blossom."

His voice, deep with desire, warmed her whole

body. "N-No, François. Please—"

Carefully he laid her back onto the moonlit sands. Tenderly he caressed her face, cupping her cheek in one trembling hand, and his lips brushed her temple and his grip tightened on her. His scarred face moved above hers and then took possession of her lips. His kiss slanted, probed, and deepened, his mouth covering hers hungrily, with a savage intensity.

Blossom was set aflame inside while gently, tenderly he made love to her. She had never known such care a man could take. Magically her shift came off, and she was pressed against his hard male body, closing her eyes as the delicious reeling of dizziness overtook her. Soon, he was just as naked as she.

He worshipped each breast, cupping them while his mouth and tongue moved from one thrusting nipple to the other, leaving her body burning with fire. When his fingers finally touched her between her thighs, Blossom found release at once. While she was still quivering from it, he entered her. She cried out at the heavy fullness of him, never realizing a man could be so wonderfully endowed.

His body labored, seeking out the center of her being and she climbed into sharp ecstasy. They became one, losing all sense of consciousness and self. Blossom's hands spread wide and flat, digging into the still-warm sands of paradise. Along every inch of his massive length he felt her moist velvet surround and hold him, rippling sinuously as she rose against him again and again, taking him deeper and deeper into herself.

The chain of climactic explosions that rocked her were so intense that Blossom screamed and her biggest release mingled with the hot moistness of his.

The moon rose and began its descent. François and Blossom found joyous fulfillment over and over. They stayed within each other's embrace, wildly caressing at first, then their fondling became tender touches, gently stimulating, and François moved carefully now, still holding her, the flatness of his belly pressed tightly against hers.

All movement came to a sudden halt then. François had been kissing her face when he felt the wet saltiness there.

"Why do you weep, *cherie?*"

Blossom swallowed, murmuring, "I—I think I am happy, François, for the first time in my life."

"Oh *cherie*, I am so happy too!"

He kissed her forehead, her eyes, the tip of her nose, and finally, returned to her bruised lips. The sweetness of his kisses penetrated her deeply, reaching her soul.

"Blossom, do not cry anymore. You do not know what this moment means to me. I think I—"

"How very touching."

The lovers started and came apart at the sound of a sibilant voice close by, a woman's voice. Passion-sheened bodies were bared in the light of moon, and green feline eyes glittered hatefully over their beautiful nakedness.

"Just like a pair of wet Siamese twins," the woman taunted wickedly.

So shocked was Blossom that when she peered up to see the striking older woman standing there, she could not even move to cover herself. With the warmth gone, Blossom felt the relatively cooler air wash over her nude body, and the wetness covering her hips and thighs caused her to shiver uncontrollably, that and the embarrassing fact that she'd been caught in a clinch with François.

Blossom stared from the striking woman to her lover . . . but was he hers or did he belong to this woman she knew instinctively could be very possessive and domineering?

"I have just now returned, *mon cher,*" Julia said in a brusque manner that turned Blossom's stomach.

François stirred, but did not look back up at the woman again. "You always state the obvious, Julia."

So this was Juliet. Or Julia. Blossom's sense of loss was beyond measure. First time and last, she realized suddenly there would never come another night for her and François now that Julia had returned to wind her serpent arms about him.

"What? You do not call me by your pet name Juliet? François, for shame."

Julia glowered at the perfection of the young woman's naked body. As she unabashedly stared up and down the cream-gold length, the girl began to cover herself. Julia could see that the lily-white hands shook. Too bad, she thought.

"You could not wait, tsk, tsk, could you? Well"— Julia sighed in boredom—"I could not wait myself, *mon cher.*"

François helped Blossom to shield her lovely body from the older woman's malicious glare as he quipped, "I was beginning to wonder what took so long in Nassau." Julia did not miss the look of tenderness François gave the young beauty. "Was it a blond this time, Julia?"

"Call me *Juliet!*"

With an indifferent shrug, he said, "But you always preferred Julia."

"Nonsense! Come to the house, François."

"Sorry, Julia." He gazed at the dejected face beside him. "I am thoroughly fatigued—as you can see."

"I see nothing—pah! Nothing but a child making love with a man who could not wait to stick—"

"Shut up, Julia," François ordered, his tone calm but dangerous.

Julia watched her young lover rise brusquely to his feet. He stood for a long moment staring down upon the young woman still reclining silently on her elbow in the sand. He was finished with her, already bored, Julia could tell.

Blossom's arms felt cold, empty, but tingles of passion's remembrance rippled through her as François continued to gaze at her. Now his eyes were hooded like those of a hawk.

Reaching a hand to the flowered shift, she watched his eyes follow her movement, then return to lock with her eyes. The woman Julia had already begun to walk slowly up the beach.

What was wrong? Why did François look at her so strangely, almost as if he hated her for what they'd done? A heavy feeling centered in Blossom's chest. Confused, she lowered her face so he could not see her dejection.

François left her then. And Blossom stared after François as his shadowy form caught up with and blended into the other woman's. Had she only imagined it . . . or had she really seen the couple closing together for a kiss and an embrace?

Blossom hung her head, aware of the wetness on her flushed cheeks and also for the first time in her life of the futility of tears. It was the first time since Robert Neil's death that she had wept in genuine sorrow. In the past she had wept often in vexation, in anger when she found out Rider and Daisy Dawn would wed, in front of her beaux, and her tears had always accomplished their purpose or brought at least a measure of relief. But this time there was no such blessed respite and from this moment on, she realized, tears would prove useless.

Blood rushed and sounded in Blossom's ear like a tidal wave, but louder than before when François had first entered her heart. Her eyes filled with heart-breaking sadness. She was in love. For the first time in her wretched life.

Chapter Twenty-Nine

Against a low paradise moon, the silhouette of a lone figure hastened and ducked inside the canopy of low-hanging branches. She could not hurry fast enough. Ahead, the house could be seen, the pillared portico and shutters etched in silvery light.

Blossom stopped to catch a breath, her heart thumping hard in her chest. Resting for only a moment, she ran on toward the entrance that would lead her in the back way. Illumination came from only one room in the house—the room she knew housed François and Julia. She had no time to wonder what they were doing in there; she had to keep moving.

Hurrying inside, she felt her way along the dark halls until she climbed the stairs and entered the bedroom where Angela slept.

Angela came slowly awake, startled to see a dark figure hovering over her. Thinking she was having another bad dream, she gasped and clutched the sheets, her eyes wide with fright. This dream was too real, she was thinking—this woman looks almost alive!

"Angela," Blossom said into the fog of Angela's first startling. "Hurry, we have to get you and Daisy out of here. Julia is back!"

"Julia?" Angela blinked for a moment, then remembered that Julia was the one with the desire to see her dead. "But there is nowhere to run to, Blossom." Flinging her feet off the bed, she began to pull on a robe even before she was standing all the way. "Even if we could get out of the house before she or her men sight us, they would soon be looking for us, and as I said, there is nowhere to hide on this small island. She has too many men, Blossom. I've seen them lurking about watching our every move."

"Julia's men?"

"Yes, I spoke to Sorrel today." Angela smiled slyly in the dark moonlight. "I must have charmed him in some way because he was soon loosening his tongue and telling me a lot about the island. Oh—" Angela yawned. "I am having a hard time waking up all the way—"

"Angela!" Blossom threw some clothes at the sleepy young woman, ordering her around. "We haven't got time to stand around and chat, we have to get some things together, find Daisy—"

Pointing at the door and curving her finger as if around it, Angela yawningly said, "She is not far down the—"

"Angela! Stop procrastinating, we have to get you out of here before Julia finds you. She's awake, she's, ah, entertaining François and who knows what they are planning!"

"What?" Angela tied her clothes into a bundle as Blossom was indicating. "I thought François was on our side now."

"Come along, let's go get Daisy. Hurry—you don't need that!" Blossom groaned as Angela tucked the blue garter from her wedding into the bundle. "Come on, I'll tell you on the way to Llana's what happened about a half an hour ago when Julia appeared suddenly on the beach when François and I were—" She paused when Angela looked at her all of a sudden. "We were . . . talking." Well, that was the truth, after all.

"How do you know Llana will help us?" Angela whispered intensely as they stopped outside of Daisy's room.

"She has to, there is no one else. We will hide there—until . . . ."

"Yes? Until what? We can get our hands on a boat? Then what? I don't know the first thing about boats."

Just then a yellow head appeared as the door was slowly cracked. "What are you two doing out here, having tea?" she asked, noting the bundles of clothing they each carried.

"Yes," Blossom hissed sarcastically, "would you care to have some too?"

"Don't be funny," Daisy shot back, pulling Angela inside by one arm. "If you stand out there any longer clucking like two mother hens at tea there *is* going to be trouble. Now," she said, after she'd gotten them both safely behind the closed door, "what is going on? Something is, or else you two wouldn't stand outside my door making plans to . . . get away?"

"You could hear us through the door?" Blossom gaped at Daisy as the small blonde lit a slim taper and set it into its silver holder on the table. "You must have the ears of an elephant."

"Oh Blossom," Daisy chided, "just because elephants have big ears doesn't mean they can hear any better."

"You two are wasting time as usual arguing," Angela, bundling some clothes for Daisy, said over her shoulder, "Let's get out of here."

"Wait a minute." Daisy stood tapping her bare foot. "No one has told me what is going on yet! I am staying right here—" She folded her arms across her chest. "Until I get some answers. There're all kinds of spooky things out there in the woods at night and I just hate those creepy iguanas . . ."

Just then the door swung open and three pair of widened eyes gaped at the sight that greeted them.

"Well, what do you think, *mon cher?*"

In the ill-defined light of the bedroom, Julia had changed into a gown of soft emerald tulle. It brought out the deep green in her eyes, a green that could be seen to be faded if she happened to wear any other color. Aware of her nakedness beneath, François's dark gaze moved over Julia's body insultingly. François *knew* he could slide easily between her thighs, she was thinking. But he did not seem in any hurry toward that direction.

Hatboxes were strewn carelessly, on chairs, on the bed, everywhere. François moved about the room, as restless as a caged leopard. His lean grace never failed to excite the lounging woman in the green gown.

"You did not say if you like Juliet's dress."

"I like it fine, Julia."

Something *indeed* was wrong; otherwise François would call her by his pet name—the one she had just reminded him to use. But he'd preferred to call her by her alias.

Julia felt a light beading of perspiration on her upper lip as she reclined upon a couch of rosewood covered in scarlet brocatelle, her tanned arm resting upon a bolster of the same, sipping a mint julep, the bottle kept in a bucket of chilled water beside her elbow.

"Where did you get the expensive label?" He was speaking of the green wine bottle with the colorful label.

Looking up at him, her eyes wore a nasty gleam, and her painted red lips curled up almost in the makings of a feral snarl.

"Won't you have some?"

A crease appeared between François's eyes. She'd been to the dressmaker in Nassau again, he could see. The woman spent more money on clothes than the queen of France. Gowns. Liquor. Shoes. Even some hairpieces. And hats—he looked around. There were hatboxes everywhere!

"You need another head, Julia—several more of them."

Julia sipped her wine, murmuring over the rim, "What do you mean, François?"

François shrugged an indifferent shoulder, saying, "Never mind, Julia." He turned toward the terrace to gaze at the heavy tropical moon, imagining the sight of a beautiful young woman, her shining black hair streaked with silvery moonbeams, wearing only a bit of a shift, her long shapely legs kicking up sand as she ran along the beach where the sand met the turquoise waters. Alone. She was alone. . . .

François blinked and the wonderful image of Blossom by moonlight disappeared like a fleeting will-o'-the wisp.

"When did you make a 'run' last?"

"You are very greedy, Julia. I can only make runs during the dark of the moon for the cordon of Federal ships has tightened around Charleston and Wilmington."

". . . and Mobile and Savannah. You are not doing your homework very well, François. I know many who are making moonlit runs, yes, with ships using that new coal. Captained by most daring young men."

"I am sorry, Julia." François executed a short bow. "I do not have steam-driven ships that can do fourteen knots or better. What is the matter, Julia, is your supply of money dwindling?"

"Nassau harbor is close to being in a state of blockade itself and you—"

"Julia," François said, exasperated, "have you nothing new to tell me?"

"No. Not really. But you have something new to tell Juliet, do you not?" she asked, showing off the curves of her hip as she reclined in what she thought was a very provocative pose, when in fact all it did was display to full disadvantage the extra pounds she'd put on while cavorting in Nassau.

Hiding his expression while he pretended interest in the waning moon, François said with his back against her audacious scrutiny, "What do you mean?" He was giving Blossom time, although he

390

did not know why he was doing the three young women a favor. Why did he keep kidding himself? He knew full well the reason he was buying Blossom time to get away to Llana's, where he knew she'd go. Julia could become very dangerous if the situation warranted it, and he had a strong feeling Julia would not hesitate to send out her henchmen immediately to slay the three women on the spot.

"Who might I ask is the young woman with the shining black hair and tender thighs?" Julia snarled, and François stepped back. "The little bitch who seems to have stolen my lover right from under my nose?"

"Under your nose?" François snorted low. "Your nose was not here, Julia, it was off sunning itself on lover boy's—whoever he was this time—on his terrace."

"Your eyes are bloodshot, François, so impassioned. What have you been doing with that girl?"

"You have got to be making jokes, Julia. Making love to her! What else?"

She pretended not to notice his indifference. "Ah, you are like a cat on the prowl. François, look at you, pacing back and forth like a caged panther. Come, darling, give your Juliet a kiss and a hug." Simultaneously she rolled her hips with her eyes. "And perhaps a little more, *non?*"

"Not now, Julia." Seeing her eyes glare up at him with an insane light, François, afraid for the young woman, said, "Ah . . . perhaps tomorrow, Julia. Surely, you most of all, can understand my predicament?"

Giving him a thorough perusal, Julia indulged François in her best kindly smile. The smile did not reach her eyes. "What is she doing here, François? Did you pick her up at one of the small islands? What is she, a whore or something?"

"No, Julia," he sighed tiredly, "Blossom is not a whore—or something. She is just Blossom," he said caressingly, looking out the terrace doors again.

Julia's eyes saw red. "I will have her killed, François, I vow. Stay away from the slut!"

"Go to hell!"

Julia's shrill voice caught François at the door and held him there, sibilating, "We made a deal, my dear, or have you forgotten already?" Rising like a tarnished nymph from her pool, Julia followed him to the door. "No? That is good. Did you find her? Was our Lady Jessica Hawke dead or alive?"

Her arms wound about François's neck and at once he compared her to Blossom Fortune as her very womanly curves pressed close, her strong perfume invaded his senses—there was no comparison. Julia and Blossom were different as night and day. Good and evil. Blossom had changed for the better. Like a cunning leopard, Julia could never change her spots.

His eyes boring into hers, fingers unwinding her arms from about his neck, he said in a deep tone, "There was only one alive there that fit Lady Hawke's description."

"Chestnut-haired?"

"Yes."

"Lovely, with beautiful pale blue eyes?"

"Yes."

"That is her! She is alive. Why did you not kill her?"

"There was only one problem," he lied.

"So, François, what was that?"

"Her name is Angela Smith."

"Smith?! Are you certain she is not the same girl?"

"I am positive, Julia. This young woman is so different and she is married."

"Married?!"

"Very married—so I hear." François smiled. "We have brought her back here with us. . . . Her husband is missing. The war, you know." He shrugged and sighed; he wondered what Gypsy Smith would do to him hearing that lie. He could almost guess what kind of man he was after hearing Blossom describe him. As it was, the man must already be seeking his blood.

"Why did you bring her with you then? That is insane, François! So"—Julia eyed him closely— "how many women did you save from the grips of war? Do you plan to begin your own brothel?"

"That is not a bad idea. And Julia," he said in going out the door, "you shall be their *old madame.*"

When François heard Julia kick the door and slam home the bolt, he knew he'd done the right thing. How she despised the thought of growing old. *Gracefully* was a word the duchess couldn't fathom. Julia had been known to lock herself in her room for days—he'd witnessed this himself—pouting and fuming and pacing until someone went in to pet her and tame her down.

This time, however, François did not fret, and for all he cared, she could rot forever in her room!

Slowing walking along the hall, mulling and brooding, François came to a decision—pausing right before Daisy Dawn's door.

Voices came from within. Daisy. Angela. And of course, as he'd known, she'd become the heroine—Blossom was in there herding her pretty chicks together.

". . . in the woods at night and I just hate those creepy iguanas . . ."

Daisy's sentence was cut off abruptly as François swung himself boldly into the room and shut the door swiftly from any outside intrusion. The little blonde, her big blue eyes round and frightened, unused as she was to having a man enter her bedroom, wherever that bedroom may be, was even more scared by the wild look in the pantherish Frenchman's eyes.

"You've come to kill us," Daisy said, thinking she'd guessed right as he pulled all their belongings together into one huge ball, which he unceremoniously slung over his back. "I just knew it, this counterfeit paradise couldn't last much longer. How are you going to do it? Slit our throats from ear to ear? Sh-Shoot us? Wh-Why don't you say s-something? Is J-Julia waiting for the execution, watching from her bedroom window?"

The first paradise pink of dawn came creeping along the terrace, showing its infant-soft face in the opening as François pulled Blossom against his side, speaking not to her but to Daisy. "No one is going to kill you, little one, not you"—he looked at the chestnut-haired beauty—"not you, Lady Hawke"—and then he gazed down into the black eyes worshipfully studying him—"and not you, my love."

Part Six

Captives of the Wind

Chapter Thirty

As the evening sun began to set, the beautiful little island came into view. The shore line was irregular, rimmed in places with sunbleached, sandy beaches or pierced with bays and coves. From the crow's nest came a loud voice, "Land ho!" down to the captain that stood on the poop deck of the *Black Moon*. "Island in view!"

Gypsy Smith's voice boomed, "Take in all sails! We'll not anchor till the moon sets! Shake a leg now, lads!"

The crewmen scurried about the deck, taking down the sails and securing them fast. Gypsy Smith now turned to Rider. "We will not move in until the cover of darkness shrouds our movements."

"Aye, captain!" He grinned. "That's a smart move, if we don't pile our longboats up on a reef going in after the moon sets."

"I have a plan, let's go below to my cabin," Gypsy said, turning and going down the ladder with Rider close behind.

In the dimly lit cabin Gypsy laid out his plan, while Rider stood at his shoulder. Several other crew members were present also.

"Under cover of night we will sail the ship in close to shore and anchor. Just before dawn, you, Rider, and several of the men will take two longboats and head into shore, land, and set up a scouting party to try to find out where they are holed up. At the same time, I will launch the *Dragon Lady*"—he raised his head to look at them with a smile across his face—"and hope the wind is soft as a mother's breast in the morning."

The crew chuckled and beamed with excitement.

"As I raise the balloon above the island, I will direct you and you will attack as the men are sleeping. They won't be expecting us from land," he chuckled, "or from the air."

All through the hot evening they waited while the hills and the jungle still drowsed in the last rays of sun, unconcerned with the impatience of the men on board the *Black Moon*.

As dawn crept over the island, the longboats were lowered to the water and the air was as Gypsy Smith had predicted, soft, very soft. Rowing as quietly as possible, the crew pulled on the oars heading for shore, watching for any movement that might alert their prey. Hushed as a baby's breath, the *Dragon Lady* rose from the platform at the rear of the ship and moved silently above the masts and toward the island, gracefully moving over the men who rowed to shore, traveling at almost the same speed.

Landing the boats, the men looked up, waiting for some direction from their captain. Gypsy Smith looked down from the balloon, (his head directly below the small painting of a beautiful caricature of a lady in red silk), spotting the three huts and the larger house, approximately a thousand feet from the shore. Leaning over the edge of the balloon and sweeping his arm toward the right, he pointed down, directing his men to their prey.

Gypsy Smith watched now as his men crept silently, like tender-footed lions, around and through the trees and underbrush to where the huts and house stood. Surrounding them, his men stealthfully crept into the huts and he watched from above as they soon exited from them, giving him the sign that they had snared their prey. He saw his men bring out the captured men, bound with ropes, hoping that at any moment he would see his beloved Angela.

The sun rose above the horizon, and without warning, a strong wind began to move him across the island. This he had not anticipated. As he looked for a place to set down, he spotted an opening then, small at first, but growing larger as he moved across the heavens. Reaching to release the gas from the balloon, to ease himself into the clearing, he had now drifted off course about a mile from where his men were.

The balloon plunged and rolled, the gas pouring from both the upper and lower valves.

Dear God! What had gone wrong?

The balloon began to drop, toward the clearing, but something indeed was amiss—it was dropping too fast. He released the line attached to the discharge valve, but nothing happened.

He dropped . . .

Faster . . .

And faster . . .

Faster still . . .

He was experiencing a rush of euphoria suddenly. "My God, the release stuck." He smiled to himself grimly, thinking, I'll have to get that fixed before ever going up in this thing again. For he'd planned to spend his wedding night with Angela in the balloon . . . now he wondered if he ever *would*.

He could not control his descent any longer. Heading toward the trees, he knew he was going to crash for the first time in his life. He felt helpless. *So damn helpless.*

The trees seemed to loom larger as he crashed, the basket striking a huge palm, tipping it to the right and throwing him out into the air. He reached out to grab for anything to break his fall, and as a huge branch slammed him in the side, he could feel the air being knocked out of him. . . .

When finally he stirred, pain seemed to rack his body, and he tried to sit up but could not. He lay there, looking up, watching his balloon dangling from a tree. He heard voices, coming closer and closer, and darkness covered him.

Three feminine shapes led by one rakish male created of themselves indigo silhouettes as they crept across the fool's-gold face of the rising sun. Past the line of huts where Julia's henchmen still slept soundly—this was the impression they got, anyway. They heard some other noises but thought nothing of them. They were probably only snores. Now they were out of the woods, walking across the cream-pink sands toward the huts where Llana and her relatives lived.

Sounds of shouting could be heard behind them.

"It seems we have visitors," François said.

Suddenly Daisy looked up, seeing something descending . . . very rapidly. It was yellow. It was big.

"What . . . is . . . it?" Daisy said with bated breath.

"Oh, it couldn't be," Blossom said, then, "It must be *him.*"

"Mother of God," François breathed. "It is the balloon!"

"The balloon—*Gypsy!*" Angela shouted, running toward the line of trees where the thing seemed to be landing into. "No, Gypsy—to the right!"

"I don't think he can hear you!"

It was true. He was too far away to hear, and besides, in the rush of his descent all else but the air whooshing about him was blotted out. Now all Angela could think of was Gypsy Smith screaming in agony as he crashed into the trees and snapped every bone in his body.

Just then pandemonium broke out. The sands had barely begun to be warmed by the sun when the beach filled with men of all sizes and description. Some François's men. Julia's men. But mostly—and François stared around in awe—these were men he'd never seen before. Then again, of course! He had indeed spotted these same ones below Charleston harbor. Gypsy Smith's men.

The ship must be somewhere close by then.

Shielding his eyes from the fierce golden sun, François looked in the direction of Cay Lobos, and there . . . there it was. Gypsy Smith's *Black Moon*. Only the upper part of her masts were visible looking from this weak position toward the hilly section of the island. But she was here . . . and so was Gypsy Smith!

"Ah, so this is Gypsy Smith," said François as he stepped over to Blossom's side, eyeing cautiously over his shoulder the nasty-eyed men with long-nosed pistols trained at his back. "I've no argument with you fellows," he added.

Angela was kneeling at Gypsy Smith's side while two of his men swiftly and gently checked him over for injuries. Her eyes were squinting with concern over his body and didn't see his expression as he regained consciousness to see her bending over him.

"Lovely Angela," he said so very low, lifting a heavy hand to touch the thick strands of nut-brown hair curling down over her shoulders and breasts.

She looked down at him just as his eyes were in the process of closing her out again. Angela turned to Rider with wet, angry eyes. "How can you just stand there? Do something for him! He's dying!"

"He's not dying, Miss," Huey said, his eyes filled with concern for the little lady's near-shock.

With Daisy's hand tucked into his arm, Rider came forward. "The men have checked him, Angela, and he'll be all right, he's just bruised up a bit." Rider couldn't keep his eyes off Daisy and looked down into her misty blue eyes again.

With the pertinacious yellow-eyed sun peering down on the island, Llana and her relatives, native descendents of the Bahamas, grouped around to watch what was going on. Never had they seen such a commotion, or so many people from so many places. New Providence was the island with all the activity of blockade running from the Civil War taking place. Paraiso was relatively quiet. The chief institutions of the Bahamas were to be found in New Providence, its capital Nassau, the headquarters of lawless villainy.

"Where do all these people come from, Aunty?" Llana asked her one other English-speaking relative besides Carolos.

"Hell, I think," said Aunty, her leather-lined eyes squinting in the direction of the big house, where the most evil woman she'd ever known resided. "Mostly that one." She pointed up the wooded hill.

"Do you think she will come out?"

Aunty shook her head, chortling, "Naw, not that one, she is no brave woman I think."

"Look, Aunty, how the pretty girl with the shining nut-brown hair keeps close to the man who fell from the sky."

"Ah yea. The man who comes with the sun-colored ball that flies. That one might be sent from the gods." She chuckled, displaying rotten teeth in a fat, cheerful face. "He is very pretty."

"I like him too, Aunty," Llana said, her dark eyes trailing the makeshift stretcher bearing the man whom to her was no less the image of a perfect god. "We will take him to our dwelling, and we will go stay with our relatives."

"There will be more trouble." Aunty pointed to the hill. "From that one."

"Come relatives," Llana said, "we will return to our homes now."

Daisy, not far behind Llana and her relatives, turned to the man beside her, her beloved husband. "At last, you have come to save us, darling." She laid her soft cheek against his shoulder.

Rider chuckled, glancing over his shoulder to the tree filled with several of the crew, looking like so many monkeys, laboring to release the balloon from its waxy-leafed snare. "If it wasn't for the *Dragon Lady* scaring the pants off your abductors, we might not have been able to hold them all. Even now they are gaping awestruck at the aerostat."

"The *what?*" Daisy glanced back as the basket came untangled under the capable hands of the men who'd always in the past taken great care with Gypsy's balloon. "What did you call it?"

"Aerostat. Air balloon, same thing."

"I have never seen such a contraption, but then there have been so many new inventions coming to our attention nowadays." Daisy turned into Rider's arms just then, winding slim arms about his neck. "Kiss me, Rider, let me know how real you are."

"Mmm." Rider stepped closer yet, pressing against his lovely little wife's slender body. "I'd be happy to oblige you, Mrs. Huntington. You already know how much I love you, I've lavished you with the words often enough. More will come, more and more . . ." After they shared a sweet fiery kiss, Rider whispered into her ear as they neared the line of huts, "Tonight, love, come hell or high water!"

True to Rider's fervent vow, and much sooner than that night, the eager groom took his wife by the hand, and after leading her to the cove beneath a cathedral of banana palms, he pressed her into the secluded grasses and tenderly prepared her for his loving. A feeling of euphoria washed over Daisy as her husband swept her into ecstatic heights. He fondled her so gently that the little blonde wondered if he thought she was made of glass. He moved against her, urging her to draw her leg up to drape over his hip. Still lying on their sides, Rider entered her.

404

There was no pain, only pleasure as he pushed himself deeper into her. His patience was interminable. She soared and delighted in the strength of his powerful muscles as he moved with her. At the moment of greatest joy, when he brought her to her peak, Rider joined his wife and together they scaled rapture's heights. Daisy found paradise at long last in Rider Huntington's arms.

Wearing a red amber dressing gown that seemed to emit scarlet sparks, Julia watched the goings-on from her terrace and her lips twisted into an evil smirk when she saw where her men were being taken to and locked up.

"So," she snarled, whirling to face the room. "We have visitors. I do not like the looks of this—something is giving me a strange feeling, like a warning, and I believe it has to do with the man in that yellow balloon." Using both hands she forced the sliding tubes of her jointed telescope together. "Hmm, the Balloon Man looks familiar—where have I seen *that* one before?"

Tossing her spyglass aside, Julia changed clothes swiftly and donned something more suitable for what she had in mind. She would have to work fast to get Sorrel and her men free. As for that deceiving worm François, who she'd seen sticking close to the girl he'd called Blossom, for him she had other plans. When the time was right, she would take them all to Castle Island and throw away the key when she locked them up—all but the dark, handsome Balloon Man. For him and *Angela Smith* she had very special plans!

Chapter Thirty-One

A hush fell to the wind and a cock crowed in the roost out in back of the huts. Then suddenly the rain began to patter on the thatched roofs, and inside one of the cozy rooms Angela Smith moved around as quietly as she could, seeing to Gypsy's every need. But he hadn't asked for her yet, for he had been asleep several hours now. Hers would be the first face he saw when he awakened.

She smiled tenderly as she sat beside the bed on a little stool. Oh Gypsy, when are you going to wake up? I miss you so, dear one, I miss hearing your wonderful voice, seeing your beautiful mahogany eyes gazing with such amorousness into mine. You are my heart's blood, darling Gypsy. You once called me Gypsy's lady . . . am I still that, my love? How I wish you could hear me.

Suddenly she was hungry, remembering she hadn't eaten since . . . she couldn't remember. Beside the bed in a huge basket were her favorite fruits of the island. The basket was full, thanks to Llana and her compassionate relatives. There were tamarinds, oranges, pomegranates, pineapple, figs, sapodillas, melons, and bananas. Even more produce than this grew on the island, and the inhabitants derived their water supply from wells, the rainwater in which appears to have some connection with the sea, as the contents of the well rose and fell with the tide upon the neighboring shore.

"Oh!" Angela, peeling a banana, was startled for a moment as a green parrot came to land right outside the open window, shaking huge transluscent raindrops off its long feathers. The sun came out suddenly and aureately bathed Angela in its glow and she became like an angel with her sun-lightened chestnut hair falling in a delicate curtain around her shoulders with the shorter ends coiling about the gently pointed tips of her barely covered breasts.

Mahogany-brown eyes widened another fraction as the man in the bed came awake to the most glorious sight of womanhood he'd ever been witness to. She was beautiful, poised with a banana halfway to her mouth. His state of mind and body began to warm with longing. "What lovely native girl is this?" he said, and his voice was deep, making Angela jump off her stool and drop the banana she'd been eating. His gaze flicked down the length of her as she stood and then sat again next to his bed and he winked when he fully snagged her eye. "Your eyes are turning dark blue, girl, what ails you? Was it something you ate?" He glanced languidly at the dropped banana and then back up into her face, seeing the dusky rose of her healthy cheeks.

Cocking her head slightly, Angela stared at Gypsy

Smith as if he'd cracked his head during his fall and lost his mind for he seemed most strange indeed. And then she dropped her eyes before his steady gaze for there was a tingling in the pit of her stomach and she felt her body aching for his touch. She couldn't even open her mouth to speak his name, such was her discomfort, and her desire to be held close in Gypsy's arms was intensifying with each quivery breath she took. Soon she was going to take the initiative and haul him into *her* arms.

Fascinated, Gypsy had been studying the lean golden-tanned face and he was beginning to read her mood well. "Where am I?" he again pressed, feeling his face eager to split in a grin behind its coolly held facade. "Can you tell me your name, glorious goddess?" he said, reaching out a hand to caress the slim, tanned arm, and at once he was enslaved by her soft flesh.

Angela blinked, "Gypsy?" She finally spoke.

"Gypsy?" he said, his voice dark mysterious velvet as he gave her a languishing look that could have melted stone. "I don't think I am that, dear girl." A chuckle followed. "But you have not told me your name. What do they call you around here?" He smiled a devastating smile that reached all the way down to her bare toes. "And you haven't told me, where is 'here'?"

"You don't remember." Suddenly Angela was piqued. So, she could be that easily wiped from his memory from just a tiny bump on the head? And he thought she was a pretty native girl. And he was flirting outrageously, the cad!

"My, you are a winsome wench. Graceful. Divine."

He cleared his throat, asking her, "Are you love-worthy, sweeting?"

Angela stood in a huff, tossing her arms upon her hips akimbo. "My name, to your great curiosity, monsieur, is Angela Smith."

"Angela Smith?" He could barely contain his mirth. "That is a mighty strange name for a native girl."

Angela cocked her slim arm into a muscle and, bunching her fist, she said, "And this, monsieur, is a mighty strong arm! Would you like to see how it works on your lecherous face?"

With that, Angela twirled around and exited the tiny hut, the dust from her going almost visible to the rib-bandaged man in the bed. Gypsy Smith's laughter began to rumble the dry fronds of the hut and he laughed so hard that his head began to ache. Angela heard the resounding laughter and spun about to return to the room. Once inside, she kicked the door shut with her heel while she folded her slim arms across her bosom and began to tap her bare foot on the dusty floor.

"Come here, dove, I'd like to make love to you—"

"Oh! You . . . you—" Angela began to fly off the handle, prepared to spit out her fury. "You . . . squire of dames . . . blackguard . . . scourge of the human race!"

With a lusty leer stamped into his deeply tanned features, Gypsy narrowed his dusky eyes and softly snarled, "Come here, Mrs. Smith, and be quick about it!"

Her breasts rising and falling softly, Angela unclenched her hands and shook the dust off her feet

in a swift rush that took her to his side. And then into
Gypsy Smith's eagerly awaiting arms. He kissed her
soundly and when he lifted his handsome head, she
hissed in mock anger, "You wonderful rogue! Why
did you lead me to believe you had a lapse of
memory? Golden goddess indeed!"

Holding her oval face in his big, tanned hands, he
said, "I love you, Angela Smith. Have I ever told you
I am your devoted slave?"

With fingers enlaced, they smiled into each other's
eyes with a sensuous flame building between them.
She said, "I think you've said you love me once or
twice before." Her eyes caressed his and he found her
captivating, enchanting, and he was maddened with
desire.

"You've been badly missed, m'lady . . . I've had a
sickness—"

"What?"

Again he smiled with tender passion. "Lovesick-
ness, m'lady." Looking around the small hut, he
said, "Is this to be our nuptial chamber?"

"You, monsieur, have not even consummated our
wedding vows. I have been awaiting your coming."

Growling deep in his throat, he said against her
neck, "And I've been awaiting *yours,* dear lady."

"Mine?" She blinked. "How mine?"

Chuckling softly, Gypsy answered, "Never mind,
love, it is man talk and t'would burn a lady's gentle
ears."

Angela tickled him gently along his bearded chin
with her kisses, saying, "How do you know my ears
are gently bred?" She could hardly wait to tell him
her name! Now they could go to find her parents and

that should not be too great a task when she had their names and knew what to look for. All she needed was Gypsy's ship and his own valorous self to take her there. Her parents were wonderful people and they would be so happy to see her returned and married to a man who was much like her own papá. What joy awaited them and now they could leave this island, beautiful though it was!

"Your manner does not go with the simple cloth you are wearing, Angela." He held her back a way from him. "You have changed, and tell me, what is different about you? Do you seem more sophisticated, aristocratic, or what, hmm?"

"Well—"

"Your manner is such that you should be gowned in silks and velvets, with servants bustling all about you."

"And you, monsieur, look most like a dangerous pirate!"

He was still looking at her most strangely. She began again, "Well, you see—"

"And your hair, it is lighter, kissed by the sun." Deeply he said, "Would you like to be kissed by your very impassioned husband, my love?"

"Why—I—yes, Gypsy. Kiss me now—and I shall tell you later what I have discovered. . . ."

A short time later, when their lips were moist and clinging to each other's, breaths were hot and heavy, Gypsy whispered in Angela's ear as if there were others within listening distance hovering nearby, "Is the door secure?"

"As secure as we can make it," Angela said raggedly, her nails pressing into the hard muscles of

Gypsy's upper arms. "Gypsy, love me, please love me now. This is our wedding night."

"Night?" Gypsy chuckled. "Have you looked outside lately?" as he said this he kissed the golden column of her throat that was arched to receive his nibbling kisses.

"The sun is up?"

"Hmmm—it's been up for a long time," he murmured against her throat, sliding his hand beneath her shift and discovering the triangle of nut-brown curls nesting between her soft thighs. The salaciousness of his remark was lost on Angela in her present state. "You're soft as velvet here, you know that . . . can I kiss you?"

As if she'd been shot with an quick-acting aphrodisiac, Angela gracefully arched her hips, giving him her answer, for she was more than eager to discover every avenue of love's joys awaiting them now that they were truly wedded. He might have done this to her before, but now it was destined for blissful perfection; in fact every facet of their sexual love was going to be explored to its fullest erotic beauty, and this was inevitable as the rising sun each morning and the tide coming in and going out under the pull of the moon's spell.

It wasn't long before Angela's shift was lying on the floor of the hut next to her husband's buff breeches; all he had on now was a bandage wound around his chest. Angela was careful not to poke him in the ribs, but he seemed not so concerned with pain as he was with getting close to her vibrant body as he possibly could without bruising *her*. She was the one, however, to gently push him down upon the bed, then she followed him and rhythmically plied her body against his. Teasingly she kissed and nuzzled him, all the while her fingers adoring his muscle-bound frame and learning him as well as he'd learned her own shape in the few times they'd been together. Everything was different now; they were man and wife. With that, she thought, came the combined joy of new freedom and purity of expression that was sorely lacking in the clandestine meetings of the unmarried. Gypsy gave a languid sigh that reached all the way down to his hard chest, where Angela crushed her breasts flatly against him; his movements were slow, calculated to please her in the position she was in. All the while his hands did not remain still, but stroked and caressed her velvety flesh while his eyes devoured the blue of the half-lidded eyes that gazed into his own. Gypsy delighted in the ardent beauty of his wife, from her hauntingly beautiful face to the silken firmness of her breasts down to the glorious treasure of her womanhood. Angela, too, found her husband to be a perfect specimen of manhood. With a guttural sound in his throat, Gypsy clutched her hips, lifting her onto himself, and when he was satisfied with their position, he began to rock against her.

As she rose above him, her hair becoming a tawny curtain of loose curls and coils that wove sensuously between them, Gypsy bent to her breasts, a few strands of the silken stuff tickling his face as he employed his lips and tongue to their rosy peaks and creamy outlines. Inside her deeper now, Gypsy made each thrust and pull a repeated vow of his love and affection. Angela, too, made every second count, beckoning with her sultry eyes, luring with her satin-sheathed figure. When they could postpone the inevitable no longer, while each joining was still a moist kiss of ecstasy, her full young breasts now pink and hard in his mouth, each shivering, each climbing, Angela making soft pleading sounds. Only one more thrusting of his slim hips and they became one in body and soul. Muffled cries. Delirious kisses. Soft, adoring caresses. Then they became still, each locked in the embrace of the other.

When Gypsy woke a short time later, Angela had food and water waiting. They shared the flat cakes Llana had made and left for them outside the door wrapped in huge leaves of some kind, then Angela washed Gypsy all over with the cool spring water, and he did the same for her because he was able to sit up in the bed, swearing she'd made him all better, and tomorrow he would even be able to leave their honeymoon cottage. By the time their baths were completed, Angela was again eager for Gypsy's love. And he was more than delighted to comply with her wish. This time he was able to take the initiative, easing himself fully over her sweet young body as he strove to express the gentle love which filled his heart and soul. He was careful not to put his whole weight upon her and she was grace itself as she lifted and writhed in loving abandonment. He moved to possess her fully then and her whole being welcoming the smooth thrust caused Gypsy to moan in stirring triumph. The euphoria overwhelmed them then as together they were hurled heavenward where for a heartbeat they lingered in bliss-filled ecstasy, then finally slowed and now made the crawling descent back to earth.

They slept entwined as lovers are wont to do. When Gypsy awoke, he found Angela gazing into his eyes with tender adoration. Once again the honeymoon flame rose between the husband and wife. After washing her carefully and laying her back upon the lumpy bed, Gypsy's fingers pressing into her hips and breasts were gentle, his tongue a slow-moving exploratory whip of expressions and impressions that thrilled and delighted until she was quivering in fullblown desire for him to join with her. When he came to her with his hot, blood-pulsing eagerness, Angela was so ready for him that he slid effortlessly into her honeyed sheath.

With a throaty laugh, Angela said, "You might be sore tomorrow, love, and not even be able to walk. How is your bruised chest faring?"

Meeting her graceful rise, Gypsy answered in a passion-hoarse voice, "It is not my bruised ribs that concerns me." He moved ever so slowly now. "I am certain you, too, will reflect on the price of such lovely excesses and find a certain lingering soreness, ah, here and there."

Angela giggled softly, saying, "More *here* than there I'd say!"

Falling silent once again, they rocked together and every nerve in their bodies sang in tune with each other's vibrant melody, building up a throbbing crescendo, seducing each other as they fondled and kissed and caressed until they were both left breathless and ready to explode. Widening the spread of her legs, he went deeper, and only after he felt her womanly flesh throbbing about him did he allow his own culmination to explode inside her. Angela had sensed the whole of him, his body, his heart, his soul at that moment, and she knew that his precious seed had in all surety gone deep.

While the entwined honeymoon lovers slept and the island began to sink into a dusky rose hue and the tops of trees were bathed in soft antique rays, a full-figured woman wearing a lace mantilla which covered her entire face began her stealthy mischief for the evening, and she did not cease until all her prisoners had been rounded up and taken over to Castle Island.

And Julia laughed with unholy joy—this was only the beginning!

Chapter Thirty-Two

The wicker-work basket squatted on the ground with the webbing surrounding the yellow silk balloon stretched off to the left and seeming to go on forever. Upon the deck of the *Black Moon*, Gypsy Smith followed the same procedure to secure the mooring lines of the basket and to hang the bags of sand from the hooks on the sides of the gondola which would be his ballast. Stepping into the gondola, he moved to one of the large tanks kitty-cornered from each other in the large gondola. As soon as his men had secured the lines and added the ballast to the sides, he ordered, "Put out your cheroots if there are any of them lit and make sure there are no open flames!" At this point he opened one of the valves slowly, ever so slowly, as the gas rushed from the tank with a hiss and the bladder of the balloon seemed to breathe with life. It moved first with a rippling motion reproducing the undulating waves of the sea and then slowly lifted from the deck, ballooning higher and higher into the sky, as it finally filled and swayed from side to side. Even with the stillness of the air it moved gracefully as if the very fingers of God gently handled it back and forth. As Angela looked on with awestruck joy, her heart leaped into her throat and a flush came to her face. She could feel her body tingle with an ever-growing excitement. She now looked into the eyes of the man who would command this ship. The aeronaut looked at her with a sparkle in his eyes and pride written all over his devastatingly handsome face.

"Come aboard, my lady, come aboard. I will show you things you have never seen before."

"Am I the first lady to come aboard, Captain?" Angela asked in a throaty whisper, her voice as mischievous as the look that had entered his eyes.

"No," he said in truth, "Stephanie was the first, if you recall my telling you." He smiled at the gentle understanding in her pearl-blue eyes.

As she walked toward the gondola, her legs quivered and it was as if time slowed to nothing . . . then she was at his hand. He leaned over the edge of the gondola, lifting her effortlessly to him as he hoisted her gently over the side onto his airship. As she gazed around, now only a foot off the deck, her heart pounded and she knew not what lay in store for her, yet there seemed to be a sudden buoyancy in her mood. Gypsy Smith turned to his men.

"When I give the word," he commanded, "cast off all tether lines and play out the line slowly."

He now turned to Angela and gazed down at her. "Are you prepared for the honeymoon of your life, my love?"

She gazed up at him, with beloved fire in her eyes

and infinitesimal fear in her heart. "Yes," she said with breathless anticipation, "oh yes!"

Gypsy Smith now turned to his men, and with one each anchored on either side of the huge spool of rope, they began to play out the line. The air ship slowly moved from the deck of the ship higher ever higher as the captain yelled down, "Let it out all the way, men, and secure me fast!"

As the two rose into the air, the sun set on one side of the sea, and the moon and stars rose on the other, as if the universe revolved about them. Staring over the edge with a frightened look upon her face as if she would never touch the earth again, Angela clung to him, her round fullness pressing against his chest. She could not even think of the subject she should bring up, so gay was her mood, so lilting was her laugh. He put his arm about her waist as she clung to him and he pulled her even closer. The heat within their bodies rose, equally from the sun that was setting and the passion which grew within—one hundred feet, now two hundred feet the airship rose above the sea.

Angela gazed out and down, fear gripping her with deepening passion at the same time. She turned to him at once, saying, "It is beautiful, it takes my breath away! I could not ever imagine anything quite as lovely." The aspect of the clouds under formation before and during sunset was marvelous in the extreme, and baffled description. There could be sighted shining masses of cloud in mountainlike chains, rising, rising with summits of dazzling whiteness, and now in evening's arms forming breasts of pink on one side where the sun set and mauve and indigo on the other where the moon was beginning to show its curious face gazing down so close she thought she could reach out to touch the wondering grooves.

Gazing down rapturously into her lovely countenance, Gypsy Smith said, "I hope to make it even more beautiful," as he pulled her close and kissed her softly on her neck.

Angela shuddered, with passion and joy. "Hold me," she said, affectionately stroking his muscle-flexed arm. "Hold me close, Gypsy, and never *never* let me go!"

He gazed at her with perfect adoration in his mahogany eyes, murmuring, "Oh Lady, I will hold you, and more," as they both slowly sank to the thick downy quilt spread below them in the gondola.

As she gazed up at him and then beyond, into the darkening empurpled skies, with the moon rising, and the stars shining, she wrapped her arms about his waist and his neck. He looked down, nuzzling her ear. "This will be a shining night made for two in the Heavens above," he said.

As they lay side by side in the gondola, the cool air moved over their bodies, and the gentle rolling of the ship raised and lowered the balloon in slight shudders likened to their own bodies. Her slight form quivered and his shuddered with the insistent movement against each other as the moon rose even higher into the heavens. It crept over the edge of the gondola as the two lovers lay upon this heavenly bed enraptured and entwined in love that would last forevermore and beyond that even.

It was as if time flitted from one point to another

and their fevered bodies pressed and strained even more together. "Love me," she said, "love me always, Gypsy Smith!"

"You can rely on that, my dearest heart."

Gypsy's large hand cupped her face gently, his breath warm against her cheeks, which grew steadily more flushed as his lips captured hers. He began to kiss her slowly, his mouth sweet and searching, and the joy that rose in Angela almost made her cry, for his touch was almost unbearable in its tender affection. Gypsy's eyes glowed, his pulse throbbed madly as he gathered her in a moving, passionate embrace. She pressed her open lips closer to beckon him to taste fully of the sweet ecstasy only she could provide for him. Their needs escalated and Angela's desires were as great as his. She was hungry for him and she let him know in every way she could. They were like wild things, children of the wind overwhelmingly conscious of the passionate storm raging in each other. Hungrily now she responded to his eagerness to disrobe them both. First her garments were tossed aside and then his even more carelessly than he'd handled her bits of clothing. She did not object to his haste for she wanted him as much as he wanted her.

Now her breasts were free to his touch, his lips, and gently his fingertips began the movements of sweet torment, each touch insisting there must be more. He rained affectionate kisses on her face, her breasts, his tongue following the turn of her camellia soft curves. Then the affection turned once again to a great need that rolled over them with a savage intensity that stunned them both. Continuing his amorous assault on her senses, his fingers slid across her silken body in an ecstasy of abandonment. He took great pleasure in waking her love to a feverish pitch when her whole body would be aching to be taken, even at a time like this when his own was filled to the utmost and had been long ready for her. She opened herself to his kisses and tender caresses, pressing her slim body closer in order to receive all the sweet loving he was willing to gently inflict upon her moist, quivering flesh. A more tender lover she knew there could never be found and Angela knew at last what it meant to give oneself up totally to another. To love completely, unselfishly, offering their hearts to each other, for that was exactly what they were doing. She was wife, in every sense of the word. Would there ever, she wondered breathlessly, be another night like this?

His mouth suckled at her sweet, tender flesh while his large hands roved her gently curved buttocks and slowly, so slowly he began to move in and out until Angela cried out for him to again sheath himself within her velvet core, and both forgot everything else as the love-filled night went on and on and on into the roaring furnace of desire.

They were awakened the next morning by a slight bumping and her hair brushed his face, her slim arm wound about his neck as her eyelids began to flutter. Gypsy Smith gazed down at her as the warm sun filled the balloon, her countenance as beautiful as ever, a sleeping beauty that had lain at his side all night long. She now stirred and looked up as if she did not know where she was, pulling him closer to her and holding him tight.

Chuckling warmly, he spoke to her softly now.

"It's time, my sweet, we must get back to the business at hand." Then he rose reluctantly from the floor of the gondola, slipping on his breeches and she gazed at him, still in awe of his manhood.

"Dress quickly now, love." Then Gypsy called over the side to his men, "Pull us in as we let down!"

Angela hurriedly pulled on her chemise and her dress to be presentable when brought aboard the ship. Standing side by side, her hair blowing with abandonment and weaved with his, gazing down at the deck of the *Black Moon* she knew there would be many times like this yet to come, and they would again be likened to two lovebirds which sailed the rapturous skies together.

Angela blushed prettily when the skeleton crew on board gave her their warmest smiles and regards, and to her husband she saw they gave sly winks and even some healthy pats on the back.

A short time later when Angela and Gypsy had been rowed back to shore, the question arose as to where they would go from here and Angela frowned as they walked hand in hand back to the little place that had been their honeymoon cottage for the last few days while the men had been repairing the balloon and bringing it aboard the *Black Moon.*

The sun was climbing higher, bathing the island in a strawberry gold hue. There were many varieties of birds to be found in the woods and they could see them now in early morning as they hunted along the shore before returning to their wooded sanctuaries: flamingoes and the beautiful hummingbird, as well as wild geese, ducks, pigeons, hawks, green parrots, and doves. The waters were a-swarm with fish, and the turtle procured here was particularly fine.

"Gypsy," she began softly, "I realize you have many matters on your mind, like seeing to the minor repairs to your ship, for one, and I know we will leave the island someday, but *when*, do you have any idea?" Eager as she was to return to her parents and show them she had come to no harm, she too did not wish to rush Gypsy and have him believe their time alone together was not precious for it had indeed been glorious. She had to tell him all that she'd remembered. She could not put it off much longer.

"Soon, love," Gypsy turned to smile into her serene eyes and found they were not so peaceful as he'd thought a moment ago. As his pace slowed, he asked, "What is it, are you eager to leave this island paradise?"

"It is not that I am eager to end our honeymoon, Gypsy, but you well know that we, Daisy, Blossom and myself, were brought here as captives and it is still unsafe for us to be here. There are many lurking about who would wish to do us harm." Especially me, she did not add for reasons of her own.

Grinning, Gypsy told her, "Your lovely playmates are not even here, Angela, I was informed this morning by a lively old sailor that they had gone on to a nearby island"—he cleared his throat suggestively—"they, too, are on their honeymoon, as you well know. Most likely they wanted to go where it was not so crowded."

Staring around the surrounding island, Angela said, "Crowded! There are hardly more than two hundred people here now, the natives included. Tell

424

me then, where are your own men, if you are so wise?"

Pointing to his ship, he said, "Out there, and"—he shrugged—"the others have just gone on to find some entertainment a bit livelier than what they'd had on the ship."

"To another island?" she blasted into his face.

"Of course, what is so unusual about that?" His brow drew together in a furrow and his eyes squinted curiously. "Why be so concerned over their welfare when you are entirely safe now that I am here? Can't you just relax and enjoy? You must have had quite a harrowing experience being kidnapped and spirited away to this wild paradise. You did not look worse for wear when I opened my eyes and gazed upon your peaceful countenance, no my dear, you appeared to have been enjoying yourself quite nicely I believe!"

"Enjoying myself!" Angela stomped her foot. "When there were those here that would rather see me dead?! And just where is François? You should have taken him prisoner, he is the leader of this band of miscreants!"

"François Ce'sar?" Gypsy threw back his head to laugh. "I spoke to the man after my *little* accident falling from the sky. He came to see after my welfare while you were out gathering fruit for your supper. He was quite friendly and likable, besides being totally in love with Blossom Angelica."

Again Angela stomped her foot, but harder this time. "Why did you not tell me this?" she shrieked, and did not even bother to shield her eyes from the sun this time as she glared at him.

425

"Angela, you are behaving like a shrew. Darling, you are safe now and we shall soon be leaving this place." As he detected a frown of a different nature growing on her fine brow, he had another thought. "Perhaps François only wished to take Blossom captive and thought she needed her two lovely companions along, namely you and Daisy Dawn."

"That is absurd and you know it! His sole aim was to kidnap me, only me, and do not ask me how it was that Blossom and Daisy happened to be included in on the abduction, I haven't the answer to that question. I do believe it was Sarge Sorrel's idea. By the way, do you have the man locked up?"

Gypsy sighed with impatience, saying, "I have not had the time to ask each and every prisoner what his name could be. I haven't even gone to check on the prisoners, I've left that up to the men who were supposed to have been guarding those huts. It is all very peaceful here to me. And Sorrel will get his due."

Deceptively calm, Angela kept to herself.

"Have you met the woman up there on the hill?"

"No." He peered at her closely, wondering what she was up to now, for she had become almost a stranger since he'd come to rescue her. He didn't know this Angela at all.

"I am convinced we are safe for the time being at least," he said, then shrugged. "Why don't you put some trust in your husband, dear Angela, as I'd never allow you to come to any harm. Never."

"The woman up on the hill wishes to see me dead," she blurted out softly, and saw at once the ominous words had not moved Gypsy at all. He only

426

stared down at her strangely, his eyes beginning to fill with concern of a different nature than what she indicated was the case. "You do not even care, do you?" As he stood dumbstruck still, she pressed louder, "Why don't you say you could care less if she came at me now with a knife and stabbed me right in the heart? Admit it, damn you!"

"Angela, there is not need to swear, I can hear you. But you can't seem to comprehend that no one is going to kill you with me and my men surrounding you to keep you perfectly safe. If you say once more that I do not care, I'll take you over my knee and give you the sound spanking I think you deserve. For some reason you have become unduly concerned for you own safety, and that doesn't say much for your husband when you should trust him to hold you from harm, from any quarter."

A warning voice whispered in her head, something is wrong here, terribly wrong.

"I want you to take me to my home as soon as possible," Angela said without looking at him.

"Home?" Baffled now, he could only stare at Angela. But suddenly he was afraid she had indeed remembered where "home" was and he didn't want that, not yet. "Where is home, have you suddenly remembered or is this only a ploy to get me to carry you to safety when there is nothing to fear in the first place?"

"That was not a very nice question, it was quite unfair and one-sided." She tossed her head defiantly and would not look at him now.

"Angela—" Exasperated now, Gypsy could only stare down at her bent head, "What the hell is wrong with you? Did you come down with air sickness or something when I took you up in the balloon last night?"

"No!" Angela kicked the sand at his pant leg.

Shaking his head, smiling, Gypsy said, "I guess we are having our first quarrel as most couples do shortly after their wedding." Glancing up to the house on the hill, Gypsy frowned thoughtfully for a moment before advising Angela, "Go and lie down, love, I think you are overtired—" He grinned devilishly. "After last night what woman wouldn't be. I will set a guard at the door if you would like— maybe Carolos, that handsome native boy that can't seem to take his eyes from you whenever he's around."

"Carolos is fishing!" Angela said in a huff, determined not to converse with him anymore than she had to.

"Oh?" Gypsy came around to gaze down suspiciously into her defiant face. "How many other men on this island receive your constant surveillance since you landed here? Do they all get the equal attention of your many charms?"

"Of course!" she lied, angry with him now for not believing her fears were genuine.

As he continued to study her, Angela felt a sudden wave of apprehension wash over her. What did she really know about Gypsy Smith beyond the fact that he'd served as a Union officer in the War, was the black sheep of the Fortune family, and really could not call Smith his last name. He was a bastard, wasn't he? What did that make her, truly his wife or just his plaything, his mistress and nothing more.

"Angela," Gypsy broke into her insecure wanderings, "Go and lie down and I'll join you later as I have to see to the *Black Moon* and getting her repaired. Give me a kiss before I go?"

With her shoulder against him, she snapped, "What for?"

"Because you love me?" He moved closer. "Because I love you with all my heart and soul and would die for you if the need arose?"

"Would you, Gypsy?" she breathed as his lips brushed the upper heart of hers. "Do you really love me so much you would die for me like a gallant knight for his lady?"

Putting every ounce of energy that remained after a full night of love into this kiss was not so hard a task when the female involved was his heart's very blood. "I would, any time, dearest," he murmured when he at last lifted his mouth from her clinging one.

"Well then!" She shoved hard against his chest. "Put on your sturdiest suit of armor and find out what devious motive for planning my demise is on the mind of the woman on the hill—and I'll not rest until you do!"

With deep concern in his staring eyes that watched his wife go off to the hut displaying all the haughtiness she could muster, Gypsy began to seriously think there was something terribly wrong. It might only be the nerves of a newly wedded bride, he told himself as he went in search of a guard for the hut. He'd only been kidding when he had said Carolos could do the job, that one and his relatives were so peaceable they wouldn't fend off a fly if it were bothering Angela in her hut.

Now that he'd found Angela again he wasn't about to let her go, even though he had promised himself and God he'd search high and low for her relatives once he rescued her. Losing her once had been much too frightening an experience. He could not go through that again. Now she stated she knew where her home was, and if she knew that, then she'd know her real name, although she didn't seem to at all for he'd not heard her say it.

Gypsy Smith took himself down the beach, soothing his guilt with the fact that he was alone in the world. He did not have any relatives to speak of. Blossom, only half his blood. His love for Angela was all-consuming, and if he did not have anyone else in the world, why should Angela? Neither of them owned a last name other than Smith, which was not really one at all, but served their purpose well. They had each other; that was enough.

For his utter selfishness, Gypsy was to think later, he would suffer greatly. For now, this wild paradise was all the hiding place they needed, and later, after the war's end they would return to rebuild along the Ashley River. All he had to do now was convince Angela he was right. That, and the fact that no harm could possibly ever come to her as long as he was nearby.

Chapter Thirty-Three

Angela had to do no more than think of Gypsy's beautiful words to her and she would weep. . . . *Because I love you with all my heart and soul and would die for you if the need arose.*

In front of the hut, Angela stopped her pacing to stare across the sunswept sands. She could spot Llana and her Aunty strolling there to go and visit one of their relatives, and Angela waved to them. They had been more than generous, with Llana giving up her one-room hut to move in with her Aunty, and now Angela wished there was some way she could repay them. But sometimes she had to pause and wonder at the way Llana's exotic eyes slanted up from her labors to sweep across Gypsy as if she were considering the possibility of a night spent in his vibrant embrace.

Llana could look all she wanted, Angela thought, but she must not touch what belonged solely to this woman!

Going inside the hut to peel some delectable fruit

for her lunch, suddenly Angela became very still as a troubling notion occurred to her . . . *if the need arose?* Was the danger over, or did some of it yet linger? Why did she feel some danger from her own husband? Ridiculous! Yet the nagging suspicions in the back of her mind refused to be silenced.

There were just too many questions that sorely needed answering. For instance, where was Julia? The woman was here, she knew, so why had she not shown her face before now? Had she returned to Nassau? The island was like . . . like a tumultuous storm cloud waiting to burst into a million pieces. Where was Daisy? Blossom? François? Half of Gypsy's crew? All gone to another island, as Gypsy had stated? Absurd! He was keeping things from her—why? It just did not seem likely at a time like this that so many had up and vanished into thin air. Where was Sorrel, locked up? Just where the prisoners were being kept she had no idea, nor, she'd discovered, did Gypsy even seem concerned.

A sudden remembrance filled her with a deep dread. Another scene, another time, returned to her with stunning force just then. She'd thought she'd shoved it far back in her mind but it was still there and now she remembered it with frightening clarity, now that it had simmered in a corner of her brain for a time. Only several months before . . . Blossom's own words:

"I think he has dallied with Kapa Lu before. . . . yes, I saw them with my own eyes! . . . Gypsy Smith is afraid of being hurt. . . . He carries deep emotional scars, ones that will most likely never heal, never all the way. Mama pushed Gypsy Smith out into the

432

world when he was only a boy, sent him to some godforsaken place across the sea. ... Melantha said she thought Gypsy Smith was living with some witch in Africa ... wouldn't doubt it one bit, him being the beast he is. A witch is the only kind of mother capable of raising a bastard like Gypsy Smith. ... Oh Anna ... he dragged me into the broom closet and he was going to punish me ... an animal ... pushed my skirts up ... shoved me down. ... He even beat me with a belt—that's what a cruel beast Gypsy Smith is!''

Angela remembered she'd had to scrub herself vigorously afterward, after hearing Blossom relate those sordid tales to Annabelle, and she had wanted only to cleanse her body of any memory of Gypsy Smith's vile touch. Back then she'd come to the conclusion that Gypsy Smith was nothing but a reviler, womanizer, user, and perhaps even ... murderer!

And now. What was Gypsy Smith hiding from her? She had to ask Blossom how much of this gossip was true and if there was any truth in it at all; otherwise she wasn't going to be able to find rest at night—especially not in *Gypsy's embrace!*

Shaking her head to clear it, Angela stepped out into the sunshine and found she was standing face to face with a woman wearing a black lace mantilla, the thing concealing her features from the top of her head to her chest. Angela could only stare, although she saw nothing but shadows and vague features.

"Mademoiselle, I would like to speak with you if I might," the deep female voice purred, "privately." Sweeping her gloved hand, encased also in Spanish black lace, she indicated where it was she would like to have their private conversation held.

Angela's suddenly deep blue eyes lifted—to the rose-tinted house on the hill.

Startled, Angela thought, then this must be Julia, the witch, for now that she'd encountered the woman, Angela could think of no better way to describe her!

Part Seven

Gypsy's Lady

Chapter Thirty=Four

"Come into my parlor," said the spider to the fly, was all Angela could think of when Julia led the way into that rubescent room, her scarlet-and-black skirts creating rustle-and-swish sounds as she walked. No, Julia did not walk, Angela decided—she *slithered.* Like an intricately patterned snake. And red must certainly be the duchess's favorite color; to her it must be *de rigueur*, the fashion etiquette like a fine wine, Angela deduced, staring around the ruby, scarlet, crimson, purple, and blood-red furnishings.

Angela let loose a shiver, glad she'd not allowed her curiosity to govern her as she'd passed this room on several occasions when they—Daisy, Blossom, and herself—had been staying here. At night the room must take on the aspect of a tomb submerged in a sea of blood, she thought, and shivered worse this time.

"Cold, *cherie?*"

"Uh—no."

French? Angela, though well versed in that

437

tongue, decided it best to keep the secret to herself and not answer the woman in kind.

"I am fine—" She almost said *madame!* "It is just that I am not used to seeing so much red—all in one room. You certainly must favor the color."

"Oh yes, for one!" Julia laughed, peeling off her gloves with methodical slowness. "Also I love the color purple!" Swinging wide her wardrobe, still wearing the one glove, she added, "As you can see, *petite,* all my gowns are those vivid shades, all but for two or three other unexciting but still bright colors." Julia wrinkled her nose against the black lace.

"Yet," Angela interrupted, "I see a lovely green also."

"Ah . . . yes," Julia said, flashing her hidden emerald eyes, green yet paler than that of her younger days, "that color." Too bad green made her think of François—and other young lovers she'd had. Like Esteban, Steven Hawke, for one, ah, especially that one. Oh yes, she recognized through her spyglass at once that this was not any simple Angela Smith, but the delicate little lady beloved of the El Corazón household in France. Her little Lady Hawke.

How like your mother you are, Julia wanted to shout across the room to the lovely young woman while she stepped forward to scratch out her angelic blue eyes, as she'd so desired to scratch out Monica's and Victoria's before her. Beautiful, charming, slender, graceful, in fact *ravissante,* all three of them. Such glorious hair, too, and she would keep the hank of Jessica Angèle's lustrous hair for a prize—when the time came for her to take it . . . from the girl's corpse!

438

Julia snapped the wardrobe doors shut, and gritting her teeth beneath the veil to keep control over her murderous emotions, she crossed the room at an angle so she would not step too close to the young woman again—once had been enough. If she got that close again, she would be sorely tempted to strangle Steven's lovely daughter. She hated Jessica Angèle, for she was Monica's daughter!

Julia had sent word post haste to Steven Hawke by way of the infamous fleet schooner she'd hailed while on Castle Island. Captain G. S. Youngblood just happened to be on his way with plunder to trade in France for some very fine silks and agreed he'd send word to Lyons to a certain Esteban Hawke, sneak into his factory to save Captain Youngblood any unwanted *murders* to his men, and covertly leave the message there. For Julia, too, was certain that Steven would murder the mate on the spot—or torture him to screaming mercy for any further information he might be harboring concerning Jessica Angèle.

Certain she could pull this off now, Julia mulled it over quickly once again while the young woman seemed to be lost in her own thoughts. Julia would make it appear that the Balloon Man was the nasty villain who'd abducted Jessica Angèle from her happy home. Cunningly Julia would lure Steven to her. The message was clear, saying his precious daughter had been found and Julia herself would take all credit due then. Only one thing would be at variance to her former rules. Just before Steven arrived, Julia planned to see that Jessica Angèle suffered a, shall we say, very nasty bump on the head that put her into a coma and then, finally, the worst, death! Julia smirked. Blamed on that handsome devil, the Balloon Man, of *course*.

But first—Julia's mouth twisted in an even nastier smirk—first she was going to have a bit of entertainment, the main characters being the Balloon Man and little Lady Hawke.

"Now," Julia almost shrieked in her excitement but covered it up with a dainty cough as she turned abruptly to face her little victim, "would you care for some fine wine, my dear? I have a very expensive—"

"Please," Angela interrupted, lifting a slim-fingered hand, which held Julia's rapt attention for several seconds, "I do not care for *any* wine, Miss, ah, Julia, Duchess, or whatever they call you here. Oh— you needn't look so surprised I know your name, or *names*, for the man called Sorrel has told me you are a duchess, or he told Blossom, I cannot recall which; however, your secret is quite safe with me, I can assure you. I can only wonder why it is you wish to see me dead." Nervously she went on while the older woman stood agape, a beringed hand to her breast, "I am sure you must have a very good reason and it could very well be that you have me confused with someone else. You see, my real name, rather that is the last name has changed, but I am not really Angela, first of all my name is Je—"

"*Wait!*" Julia, holding her head as if it was madly spinning, moved quickly in front of the younger woman, not caring now if she could make out Julia's features or not. What did the girl really know of Juliette La Chappiere anyway? She was quite certain Steven and Monica had never described her to their daughter, let alone spoken one word about her; for all they had cared, she had already passed on at the Villa Cassandra and they wished only to wipe Juliette from their memory. Still, she must retain the disguise for certain other parties involved—

Angela could only blink and say the first thing coming to mind: "Why do you wear the lace mantilla covering your face?" Green eyes bore into her, and Angela swiftly added, "Oh, I am indeed sorry if it is that you've some disfiguring scar. You see, I thought perhaps you were mourning the death of a loved one or—or something like that?" She ended on a gulp.

"Indeed . . ." Julia drew out with sly undertones, turning away now. Her back to the other, she said, "I am. Or, I should say, I shall." Julia laughed inwardly at her cunning. "Now"—Julia sighed as if in boredom—"who has said I wish to see you dead? Was it François? Ah, I can see by your look that it is he—" It struck Julia then; she must have the name of the Balloon Man. François had said his name once, very unusual, one that is not easily recalled to mind. "Tell me, ah, the Balloon Man . . ."

"You mean Gypsy Smith?" Angela blurted without thinking. "What do you want to know about him? I cannot tell you much, for I do not know much about Gypsy myself. Only that I love him, and he is my husband," Angela ended softly.

"Oh, so you *love* him, do you?"

"Of course," Angela said, wishing she could see Julia's expression. What was the woman hiding? François had said nothing of her going around wearing a lace mantilla covering her face and shoulders . . . so what could be the woman's game?

441

Angela decided to tread very carefully and not say anything that would endanger her or Gypsy's life. "We were married not long ago," Angela said wistfully. "We've just had our honeymoon, and it was glorious."

"I saw the balloon go up," Julia said with a concealed smirk. "It must have been quite a honeymoon." Her eyes lit up with envy and she was glad the young woman could not see her intense hatred. "Now, you must trust me, *cherie*, I would do you no harm. But you see, there are others who do *not* wish your health as well as I. Sorrel is a very evil man, you see, and whether you know this or not, poor darling, ah, Gypsy Smith would sooner see you dead too."

Angela's long, brown lashes almost brushed her brows she was so shocked, and she could only stare at the older woman, whose features remained a hidden mystery.

"What are you saying?" Angela stammered, her worst nightmares coming to light. "A moment ago you did not even know his name, you called him the Balloon Man, and now you are telling me that he *wants me dead?* But why?" In her total misery of the moment, Angela flung herself into a fat-cushioned armchair and began to blurt things she'd not make known under normal conditions, but these were anything but. "Gypsy Smith is from Africa, at least that was where his mother banished him to and that is where he spent his days growing from lad to teen, I am not sure how old he really was when he left there. Once he told me of a donkey he'd owned—" She paused tearfully, then stopped talking altogether when Julia came to stand directly in front of her,

442

their knees nearly touching. She looked up, wondering why the woman had come to stand so close.

Angela swallowed tightly.

With a look of staggering disbelief, Julia stared back into the past, seeing herself while she took her whip and beat the little *Arab* boy senseless. "What is your name, lad?" she'd shouted at him when he would not even look up at her. "Faugh! You are full of lies, dirty stable boy. Simpleton! Fool!" she'd shouted at him while he looked up at her with wounded, soulful eyes. "You whip Cuddy. Him be sad, he run away!" the dark-skinned lad had dared, directing a dirty finger at the abominable quirt she'd always wielded. "Where is the girl who has fled on the jackass! Tell me! Speak!" Julia had warned him but the lad cried out, "Do not know! Do not know!" He would tell her nothing and then he'd escaped on daredevil horse Cascara with Monica—Julia stared down maliciously at the girl now—Monica, who was Jessica Angèle's own mother.

Now, as then, Julia narrowed her gem-hard eyes. *Simpleton.* The same child that had begged scraps of food in Dar el Beida before he came to work as stableboy at Villa Cassandra! Him! Gypsy Smith and Simpleton, one and the same!

"I *thought* I had seen the Balloon Man before." Though Julia said this out loud, her voice was not loud enough to seep into Angela's tormented musings.

"Did you say something?" Angela said, looking up in time to catch Julia sliding her hands from beneath the veil, as if she'd been running her fingers over her face. "Are you ill then?" Angela frowned, but she was relieved when the woman stepped back and seemed refreshed all of a sudden. It was as if she had gone into a deep trance she was just now coming out of.

"*Non,*" Julia said, her voice lighter by far this time, "I do not have scars that pain me, it is only that I wear this covering for mourning—you see, I *did* lose a loved one." *Meaning Steven Hawke, of course, you naive child!*

"I really must go now," Angela said, making to rise from the comfortable chair. "Gypsy will be waiting for me."

"Faugh!" Julia whirled on the younger woman, hissing, "Does it not trouble you at all that your husband is the one who wishes to see you dead!" Ahh, this was much better than earlier planned; now she had something to sink her greedy teeth into. "I will tell you who your Gypsy Smith really is. In fact, I believe he goes by many names."

With alarm Angela's eyes shot upward.

"What do you mean?"

"Benjamin, does that name mean anything to you?"

"B-Benjamin?" Angela stammered, then sucked in her breath in dismay. *Oh no . . .*

"Exactly. Benjamin." With a villainous laugh Julia threw her head back, the lace mantilla spreading like a dark fan about her upper half. "The *stableboy!*"

"S-Stableboy. He is not—he is not, oh please, say he is—"

"—is Gypsy Smith," came the muffled hiss.

"No!" Angela stood abruptly, clenching her hands into white-knuckled fists. *"No!!"*

"Disconcerting?" Julia said bluntly. "Yes. But it makes sense, does it not?"

Dismally Angela was conscious of her head beginning to ache. "Why did he wait so long to—to kill me? He could have done that many times. . . . He had so many chances!"

"Yes, Angela." Julia was being very careful not to call her Jessica; that would ruin everything with the swiftness of a blinking eye, for the girl had a sharp mind.

Unhappily Angela turned away. "What does he want?" Angela said in a quavering voice, not trusting her legs to stand and so she sat as if on eggs.

"How else would he have known where to find you, if not at El Corazón? He used to live right there with you."

"That does *not* make sense!" Angela shot back, still defending her husband, and she would until she made some sense of this craziness. He just could not be involved in this!

"Of course it does, *petite*, your dearest love was the stableboy at El Corazón, *non?*"

"Why did he capture your men and lock Sorrel up?" Angela tried a different angle to approach the duchess. "Does that sound like a man who has murder on his mind, a man who has just rescued his wife from the clutches of rapacious men and holds her against any further harm?" She spread her slender hands.

Now Julia frowned beneath the mantilla. She had to think of something fast. The girl had the advantage of being able to think faster than she could. She had to make Jessica Angèle believe that

445

Gypsy Smith really wanted her dead. Then she would let down her guard, and when the time came, it would be easy for Julia to swiftly speed her demise.

What could be Gypsy Smith's motive? Think. *Think!*

Julia spun about. *"He wants El Corazón!"*

"My . . . parents' home?" Angela's brow wrinkled disbelievingly.

Ah, good, the girl looks about to weep.

"Of course," Julia said smoothly, then turned her back on Angela once again. "He has always coveted El Corazón."

"How do you know this?" Angela said, narrowing her eyes over the woman's silk-clad back. Something was awry!

Countering the attack, Julia spun with questions of her own "What do you really know of Gypsy Smith?" Would the girl recall she'd said herself she did not know the man very well? Julia was spinning her web quite well, confusing her prey, just like a big black spider, weaving and crisscrossing until the girl would be left dizzy and more confused than ever in her life. "He comes from a long line of villains. Compare him with these rapacious pirates and blockade runners, why, you have a lion among lambs!"

"How do you know all this? You have not answered me!"

"I *do* know," Julia said in a sing-song voice.

"I cannot believe—how does he plan to get El Corazón for himself?"

You mean, How do *I* plan to get it for myself? Julia

446

could almost laugh in the lovely, pained face before her.

"I know none of that, Angela Smith. But I do believe he has sent for Monsieur Hawke by now."

"My father?"

"Why of course, who else? Is your father's name not Esteban Hawke?" Julia smiled coyly. "He is a very popular figure with the tradesmen of the great seas—and I hear with the ladies too."

Angela jumped to her feet, snapping, "I have heard enough of your tall tales and evil lies." She padded over to the door, her bare feet making no noise at all, her small derriere a-sway.

"Cherie!" Julia turned from the sideboard, where she'd been pouring herself two fingers of sherry. "Where are you going?" Julia almost laughed out loud at the girl's simple appearance. With her glorious hair cascading to the backs of her knees, her skin a golden tan, bare feet, freshly scrubbed face, she looked no less a native girl than Llana herself. "I warn you . . . you must not speak of this to Gypsy Smith." After taking a generous swallow of the sherry, Julia looked across the room and saw to her pleasure that the younger woman awaited further warning. "He will kill you . . . if you breathe one word!"

Angela spun on her heel, long golden brown hair the color of moonstruck wheat flung out behind like a banner in the wind.

Chapter Thirty-Five

Lyons, France

Monica Hawke sat on a padded Wedgewood window-seat in the drawing room oriel, gazing dismally out at the beautiful cobalt sky. She was totally convinced that nobody on God's green earth could be more miserably lonesome than she. Even her husband did not realize the agonizing depth of her despair, for she tried at every turn to keep him from seeing this.

Monica was posed rather dejectedly, the silken folds of her white jade gown delicately arranged over her crinolines when her husband entered the room. It seemed as if a breath of invigorating air had filled the glum confines.

"Good morning, my love!"

What is so good about it when our daughter is not here to share it with us? she wanted to blurt out like a shrew. But the sight of her husband as he approached, smiling with divine devilishness, his tight buff twill breeches displaying his muscular thighs and even his unquestionable manhood shamelessly, Monica felt a warm glow of affection flow into her. The thrilling current of desire had not moved in her for so many months now that she'd had to merely account it to her pregnancy. But everything else in that area went so smoothly. Of course it was the absence of their beautiful Jessica Angèle that robbed all the joy out of living for her and she knew it.

"You are most cheerful this morning, dear," Monica said, fluttering her dark lashes as if she tried fighting back the ever-present sorrow; she patted the windowseat for him to come and join her. Oh, how she needed this man with his gentle strength!

"And so I should be, my love. I've so many bits of good news to relate to you." His black eyes twinkled mysteriously and Monica lifted her chin a little, wondering at his lighthearted mood. "First, our new ships have just arrived, just like the ones the blockade runners use and they will do fourteen knots, or better at full speed." Tipping her fine chin, he said ever so softly, "We will need the ships, both of them, darling, because"—he paused, blinking his eyes with the moisture of intense emotion gathering in them— "because I have called together my crew for a very special mission. . . . We are going to the Bahamas."

Monica swallowed the tightness in her throat, trying, "The B-Bahamas? Whatever for, Steven? *Ohhh*"—she gave out a low wail—"Steven, Steven, darling, what have you h-heard?" She could see in his face it was something wonderful . . . *wonderful!* "You—you have found Jessica, you've had a message, tell me, darling, tell me! Please!"

"Now, heart of mine, do not get your hopes up."

Steven smoothed the silken strands covering a stunning knot at the back of her head while Monica clutched his shoulders and laid her cheek against the smooth front of his shirt, tears streaming down her cheeks unchecked and unashamedly. Softly, she asked, "Steven—is she all right?"

"Hush, Mona *ma cherie*. All the message revealed was that our daughter has been abducted from a plantation in . . . South Carolina, near Charleston." He waited, with the foresight of knowing what was coming.

"South Carolina!" Monica exclaimed softly. "Dear Lord, Steven, there's a war going on there. I have read in the *Paris Times* that that city has been under relentless siege from the very beginning, that they have suffered as great a damage as Atlanta and Savannah, its antebellum serenity as shattered as its buildings. The countryside has been plundered, the plantations in ruins, and the Carolina Low Country is a ravaged, haunted land now. Men, women, and children grub around in the garbage and slaves camp near the abandoned plantations—"

"Monica, Monica, I know all that, *we* know all about the devastating Civil War, but dearest, I said she is *not* there any longer. She is on a peaceful island in the Bahamas—"

"Is she married? Is our beautiful daughter happy, Steven?" Monica, terrified her daughter was not the same but some empty shell, clutched Steven's arms and stared into his handsome face with fearful intensity in her eyes.

"Stop this, Monica!" Steven ordered sternly, grasping his wife's shoulders to give her a good shake. "Stop it at once! She is not dead. Our daughter is alive. *She is alive!*" Overcome himself but with such a relief that was indescribable, Steven pulled her into his arms and buried his face against her pulsating throat. "Jessica Angèle is alive and I shall bring her back to you safe and sound and whole—so help me God!"

"Yes, Steven," Monica wept, holding on to him as if her very life and their daughter's depended on it, "I believe you . . . I believe you."

"Good. Dry your eyes now. I shall be leaving post haste."

"Tomorrow, Steven?"

"Tomorrow."

With that they embraced once more before Steven rose to go make last-minute preparations for his quest to the Bahamas, his hands steady, his handsome face resolute.

"She has been gone," Monica said, drying her eyes and staring up at a bird taking wing to the cobalt sky, "gone for such a long time."

Later that same day Steven Hawke let a tall, rakish man into his office at the factory and shook the long-fingered hand extended to him in friendship.

A twinkle in his deep, odd-hued brown eyes—eyes that Steven swore were a most unusual shade of that color—G. S. Youngblood said in a deep very masculine voice, "Everything has been readied, my friend. The *Crescent Moon* will set sail as soon as her captain returns to the Bay," meaning himself. "I apologize that I could not have been here sooner or

451

come at a more happy time."

Hawke, seated behind a massive, scarred oak desk, gave his silent partner a wry smile, saying, "Better late than not at all. It has not been a happy time with Jessica Angèle missing for so long."

"Almost two years, is it," Youngblood said thoughtfully, tugging on his short black beard.

"You say my daughter is safe on that island?" Steven wanted to get to the business of rescuing his daughter as soon as possible.

Spreading large, calloused hands, Youngblood confessed, "I did not see your daughter myself, Steven, but the duchess said she would be safe. Even though that is little guarantee that she indeed will stay safe, I thought it best to get to you posthaste and relay the message. You said not to do anything if word came about Jessica, so that is what I have done—come to you first."

"Does Juliette have any idea of our friendship?"

"None," said the other big man.

"I want to be very careful, you see the duchess has had a long-standing, ah, shall we say 'intimate feud' with myself and my wife. Juliette has never gotten over our marriage—Monica's and mine. She hated Monica's mother before her—and now"—he cleared his throat and went on—"she has no doubt planned her bittersweet revenge against Jessica Angèle. What she has in mind is what troubles me the most. In fact it makes me downright afraid for my daughter."

Moving his tall lean frame uncomfortably in the hard office chair, G. S. Youngblood said with some sadness, "I realize what you must be going through, Steven, for you see I lost my son"—he spread a big hand—"rather I deserted him, and his mother. He was not even born into this world yet. I was a big fool." He sighed as if in weariness, and said, "I returned for the lady but she had already gotten herself wedded to another, most likely to give the lad a name. I cannot say for sure what her motives were, love or what'er. Several years later when I asked of the child and learned it was a boy, and asked of my son's welfare, the man who'd married the lady sent me on my way with six black giants with their daggers prodding my back all the way to my ship."

"I never knew," Steven said quietly, wondering where the lad—or man by now—could be. If he was still alive.

"Hell!" G. S. Youngblood slapped his knee. "I've been a blasted fool! But that's behind me and there is nothing I can do about it now . . . perhaps someday, but let us settle this thing first. I want to see you get your daughter back more than anything in the world right now. That bitch Juliette can be a dangerous customer."

"Tell me again, my friend, you say Juliette wanted you to leave a message at my factory telling where my daughter was being held. Did she happen to mention any other names? Such as who'd abducted her in the first place. Did Juliette herself do the nasty deed, do you think?"

Hotly, the privateer said, "Of course she had the thing done herself, did not dirty her own hands naturally. At least now that I've spoken to you about it, I think she did put her men up to it." A frown crossed his rouguish face and he pulled on his short dark beard with a few gray hairs in it, "She calls herself Julia, but I knew her when she was Juliette, the Duchess of Fitz-James. She is very coy and cunning, a sly vixen, no matter if she's up standing or on her back—and she's on her back more'n her feet."

Steven coughed, saying, "I agree, I happen to know Juliette—or Julia, whichever—quite well myself. I just wonder what her motive is this time because I am sure she has one, she's a cunning witch, as you said. She will stop at nothing to gain her evil end."

"So," G. S. Youngblood said, rising to his full height of six-four, "time to be off and see to my men. They'll be restless as coons after foxes. As you said, Steven my friend, I shall get there one day ahead of you and your men and keep an eye on Jessica Angèle till you arrive—and Julia if need be."

The two big men shook hands again, Steven giving a last warning, "Take care, G. S.," he chuckled, "someday you will tell me what the G. S. stands for, when you are damn good and ready, I know. You have been a faithful friend for years. Watch out for yourself, I'd hate to lose you."

Chapter Thirty-Six

Paraiso Island

All morning long Angela had been cleaning the hut and washing her clothes and Gypsy's. Needing desperately to keep her mind off rampaging uncertainties, she kept her hands busy and therefore her mind also on her task. Her wash was flapping in the trade wind, almost dry where she'd hung it in the sun-dappled shade.

Down the beach Gypsy's men had been erecting several more huts for the small population of natives inhabiting the island, and a brand new one for Llana, who'd been more than kind and generous to her and Gypsy since they'd come to be there. They would be leaving soon, Angela thought, if she had anything to say about it!

Angela was truly beginning to worry and fret over the disappearance of Daisy and Blossom. Gypsy, too, had admitted just that morning he was concerned over the absence of Rider and the other half of his crew members so he had taken the *Black Moon* out to search for them but had returned with no word of them.

Gypsy had become silent around her, hardly approaching her after their glorious honeymoon and she knew he was refraining from taking her. What could be wrong? Did he sense she was harboring suspicions about his activities and what they were really doing here on this island? He did not seem to be in any haste to leave.

Just the day before, when she had gone to the house on the hill with the wraithlike Julia and returned, she found him standing there, obviously angered by her disappearance, for his brow was dark as a thundercloud and an impatient tick moved ominously in his cheek.

"Where have you been?" His expression remained cold as he had asked this.

"Walking," she said offhandedly.

"Doing what?"

"Nothing in particular," she said, and with a shrug she brushed by him into the little hut and began to see what she could toss together for their supper.

"Where did you walk to?" he pressed, hovering near her shoulder.

"Nowhere in particular."

"Angela," he growled, "be truthful!"

"All right," she said, tearing some lettuces into a wooden bowl, "I walked to the house on the hill."

"Perhaps someday you will tell me," he said in a sarcastic tone as he slammed the flimsy door in going out of the hut.

Striding down the beach, Gypsy's eyes grew darker and darker until they were like shards of obsidian. He wondered if he should go back and strangle Angela on the spot or give his temper a chance to cool. He definitely desired the first idea. He could still picture her profile becoming a flustered pink when he'd asked her where she'd tarried for such a long time.

For the first time in his life, Gypsy really wanted to strangle a woman—not just any woman, but Angela Smith.

Gypsy's heart gave a painful wrench. The mysterious woman in the black lace mantilla had come to him earlier that morning, and in a low, seductive voice, she'd informed him that his wife had been having an affair with a man whose name she'd rather not mention at the time but his identity would soon be revealed. Just who in the hell was she? he wondered now as he had then. Where, he also wondered, had he heard that low feline voice before? Who was this *lover* she spoke of, he desperately needed to know, because then as now he truly wished to end the man's life. The mysterious woman from the hill house, he'd wanted to strangle her too, for she had told him little else other than Angela had been his woman ever since he had taken her captive: Could she mean Sorrel? He'd checked and found the man was not among the prisoners, and come to think of it, the numbers of prisoners had suddenly seemed to dwindle. Why did he have a gut feeling that told him the woman in black was lying? And if a part of his mind found the widow guilty, why then had he as much as accused his wife of having a clandestine meeting with another man?

Gypsy Smith stomped along the beach, hoping to cool his hot blood. But it wasn't working; he could not stop seeing Angela wrapped in the arms of another man.

Angela was taking down her wash when a sudden blast of gunfire exploded in front of her. Her eyes wide, she peered between the stiff legs of Gypsy's pantaloons in time to see a man falling to the earth on the other side of the underbrush. Then her eyes moved slowly, carefully to the left to see Gypsy standing there, his long-nosed pistol still smoking. He walked right past her, without looking at her, and she followed him swiftly to the spot where the man had fallen. She gasped, spotting the dagger still clutched in the dead man's hand.

"Who is he?" Angela asked her husband, looking down at the pistol and then back up to his deeply tanned face.

"I might ask you the same thing," he said with an unusual crispness in his tone.

"What do you mean?"

"Another one of your lovers, Angela?" Gypsy drawled, shoving the pistol into the band of his pantaloons.

"Lovers?!" she spat. "How can you say such a thing when the man was trying to kill me?"

"Kill you, Angela?" He snorted through his long, aquiline nose. "Oh no, my dear, you were not his target—*I* was."

Angela grimaced. He might as well have slapped

her for all the stinging retort that had been in his words.

Unable to stomach so much blood while Gypsy began dragging the body away, Angela returned to her laundry. She looked over and visually followed the footprints in the sand. Gypsy was right. He'd been walking at an angle toward her, and the dagger could not have been meant for her. The rapacious sailor had tried to kill Gypsy. How many others were lurking in the underbrush just waiting for the right moment to pounce on him? Who, she wondered with an uncomfortable shiver, is trying to kill him? Wasn't there anybody on this island she could trust? How could she even trust her own beloved? There was evil here and it encompassed all, Angela decided.

That night when the moon hung heavy and white in the tropical sky, Angela found she could not sleep and slipped out of the hut to stand hugging herself beneath the rustling sea grape trees. There came another rustling and Angela, noticing at once the difference in sound, decided to hurry back to the hut. Biting her lower lip, she began to move a little faster. She had been insane to have come out here alone in the first place for the island was creeping with unseen dangers!

"Pssst!"

"What?" Angela halted, startled, and crouched her shoulders, saying, "Who is there?" She gulped, trying again, "T-Tell me who you are . . ."

"It's me!" the deep voice returned.

"Who—is—me?" Angela jerked out in a shaky voice. "Ohhh!" Suddenly a large hand clamped over her mouth and now Angela could hardly breathe.

"You better cooperate or else Gypsy Smith gets it!" the voice hissed into her ear.

"I—what do you want me to do?"

"It is easy, Lady Hawke. I just want you to get the dark-haired wench away from François."

Blossom? "Why?" Angela said, stalling for time, hoping that Gypsy would awaken and find her missing. Again, he'd refrained from making love to her and she wondered who had been telling him lies. Julia? "Dark-haired wench? You mean Blossom?" she asked her attacker.

"That is right—Blossom."

"I do not even know where they are, so I don't know how I can possibly help you—"

"Lady Hawke, I shall take you there. I'll take you away with Blossom aboard my blockade runner and I will see you get back with your parents."

"Did you have someone try to kill Gypsy Smith today?" Whoever you are, Angela thought, wishing she, too, had carried one of Gypsy's weapons on her person.

"I would not do that. Now you must come with me."

"If I do not?" Angela said in a muffled tone through his big fingers.

"Gypsy Smith gets it."

"I see."

"Come along, Lady Hawke, I would not like to drag such a fine girlie as yourself." He yanked her when she hadn't moved a muscle to comply. "Come on. Trust me."

About as far as I can throw you, Angela was thinking, which was not very far considering the size of this hulk.

"Angela!"

"Damn!" Angela's attacker swore, and yanked her behind him.

"Gypsy!" Angela was so elated she thought she would burst.

Before the villain could dive into the brush with Angela in tow, Gypsy was upon him, spinning the man about and driving his fist into the man's face over and over, not giving the man a chance to get even one punch in edgewise. But he finally let one fly, and Gypsy groaned as the ham-sized fist contacted with his jaw. Angela's long brown lashes swept her brow as she watched in horrible fascination as Gypsy beat the man to a pulp. When all was done, Angela stepped forward to see who her attacker had been. Gypsy was watching her face etched in silvery moonlight—studying her very closely for her reaction to his brutality to her lover.

"Sorrel!" Angela bent down, wondering if he was dead or not.

"You lover will live," Gypsy drawled, grasping her shoulder with a bloodied hand urging her none too gently to rise.

"What did you say?" Angela asked in a shaking voice. Her mind refused to accept his outright accusation. "Sorrel is not my lover!"

"No?" he sneered. "He is the one who captured you!"

"Let me go, Gypsy! I will not stand here and listen to you accuse me of something I am not—and never will be!"

His laugh was cruel and contemptuous. "Won't you?"

"No!"

With that Angela spun about and before he could react, she was racing off toward the beach and the midnight tide that was rolling in with ominous speed. A sudden wind came up and began to screech and howl, the tumultuous storm barreling toward the tiny island in the dark of night. Already, the moon had been swallowed up by the black granite sky.

By the time Gypsy reached Angela where she huddled beneath the cathedral of palms, some of the tiniest huts were rolling down the beach like windswept tumbleweeds.

Out of breath at last, Gypsy leaned against the wind, fighting to reach the huddled form of his wife. As he approached, Angela looked up and shot at him: "What do you want? Have you come to toss some more accusations at my head?" She was shouting; otherwise he would have been unable to hear her.

"So, my lady," Gypsy sneered, towering over her, his hair a black streak in the wind, his deep mahogany eyes sparkling dangerously. "To think you almost fooled me into believing you were a proper young lady and wife!"

"I am!" she screamed back up at him, the wind parting her hair at the back of her head and blowing it all around her face and shoulders.

"What?!"

"I am!!"

"Come now, surely you know what I am referring to. Is one man not enough for you?"

"What did you say?" Angela shouted above the wind.

Gypsy hunkered down, his white shirt billowing around him like the wild sails of a wind driven ship. He repeated himself, but still shouting.

"Oh! How *dare* you!"

Angela took a swing with her palm outstretched to make contact with his wind-slapped face, but he caught her hand just in time to save further assault to his person. The man named Sorrel had gotten one good punch in and it had equalled the might of several blows from a normal man. Sorrel was not normal. He was a hulk.

"Damn you, Gypsy Smith—why did you have to go and have me kidnapped?!"

Gypsy narrowed his eyes, muttering, "Kidnapped?" He threw back his dark head and laughed with a roar equalling the force of the driving wind. "You think I had you kidnapped? You are crazy, woman!"

"You seem to be such good friends with François—why not?!"

"François? I never met the man until a week ago—believe me!"

"No! I do not believe you!"

"And, Mrs. Smith, I do not believe you have not been dallying with Sorrel!"

"Why, you, how could you think such a thing!"

Shrugging against the wind, Gypsy nonchalantly shouted, "The proof was plain for any man to see, Angela, for when I came across you and Sorrel, you were holding hands like lovers and making haste to enter the underbrush when you heard someone coming."

"He was *dragging* me by the hand, you cabbage-faced dolt!!"

"Whatever." Gypsy shrugged again. "You were both dallying."

"You are crude, monsieur!"

"And so are you, m'lady. Sorrel is your beloved captor, no?"

"You—you insufferable—"

"Now, now." Catching the slim hand raised to inflict damage upon his person, Gypsy pushed her back upon the still-warm grass and sand. Spectral mists surrounded the couple inside the wooded sanctuary as the warm rains finally arrived, making loud patters above them. "I mean to have you, my wild, tempestuous lady!"

She fought him while the storm raged around them. Without preamble, his mouth lowered to cover hers, and before she could yank aside, he began kissing her methodically, with slow possessiveness. The kiss went deeper, hurting her with savage pressure. It was as if he were punishing her and for an act she did not even commit. Soon she could not take in a fresh breath and felt as if she might faint right there where she lay.

Gypsy had never kissed her in this fiery manner before, his mouth slanting unkindly. She was becoming lightheaded. Now his other hand grasped her tiny waist to pull her still nearer to him and she felt Gypsy's quickening maleness. Angela tried earnestly to wrench her head aside but his possessive lips and tongue were relentless in their provocative assault to her mouth, and the more she struggled, the more Gypsy seemed to want her.

Angela could not think, she was so confused. Gypsy had always treated her with nothing but tenderness and affection, and he'd never ever kissed her so *hard* before. Every kiss, every flick of his darting tongue seared her with sensations she'd never experienced nor even imagined. Slowly his hand had released hers and now began to travel leisurely over her flushed cheek, her hair, her throat, and then slid onto her breast and cupped the swelling mound ever so gently, his vibrant fingers teasing her nipple while his other hand began a slow exploration from her waist to her buttocks. He lifted her to him then, all the while his mouth possessing hers.

Dimly Angela became aware of her nightshirt being pushed aside, of his warm palm pressing into her most secret self. Erotic, loving images began to flash across her mind, and as some of the tensions began to leave her body, she relaxed beneath his passionate ardor.

"Gypsy—I love you!"

He chuckled, but it sounded strange to her hot, buzzing ears.

"Do you really think I am fool enough to believe you a second time around?"

"Yes!" Fierce tearing desire coursed through her as the storm raged not only around them but within their hearts as well.

"I love you, Angela!"

In the next instant he was deep within her. All thoughts of time and place fled their minds, and Gypsy was left with only one fervent wish—to prolong this exquisite pleasure, to bring them to a height of passion that equalled the one in the balloon. He wished to give pleasure as well as take it, sustain their passion until they were brought to mindless joy and soaring ecstasy. Angela wanted to laugh, to cry, to scream. And Gypsy did laugh out loud, and the sound was deep and warm and vibrant. After a time, they became lost in each other's desire and nothing else mattered but the burst of radiant rapture sealing their hearts and souls together for all time.

Gypsy closed his eyes, sighing as he thought to himself: *Forever . . . my lady.*

Chapter Thirty-Seven

A mirthless smile curved Sorrel's mouth as he let himself inside the back door of the rose-tinted house on the hill and walked directly to the red parlor, where he knew he would find Julia. When the duchess saw him, she rose angrily from her regal couch to protest his unannounced entry, but Sorrel spoke quickly, a snarl on his bruised lips.

"Mon Dieu!" she exclaimed. "What has happened to you?" She looked at his battered face, his broken nose, his split lips. Then she began to laugh, stopping only long enough to ask, "Did your lovely Llana do that to you for taking too many liberties on her person?"

"No," he growled, "it was your pretty Balloon Man what did this and he is going to pay!"

"Oh—Gypsy Smith." With a disinterested sigh, she began to fiddle with her black lace mantilla, almost talking to her self. "Hmm, I wonder if our stable boy has recognized me yet?"

Sorrel loosed a dumbfounded grunt. "Stable boy?"

"Oh, never mind," she said with a nonchalant wave of her beringed hand, "you would not understand. It is something from the past when our Balloon Man was a mere stable boy. But now he is a man, and quite a virile man I must say and almost as handsome as Steven Hawke. Who would have thought that dirty simpleton would turn out to be such a rakish figure. Faugh! It is too late for regret now. . . . Gypsy Smith has to be eliminated."

"I sent a man to kill this Gypsy Smith but his pistol was quicker than Garceau's dagger."

Julia's penciled-in eyebrows rose. "Gypsy Smith killed him?" Sorrel nodded and Julia said. "Too bad. I did not care for Garceau anyway, so what does one man matter, we have plenty more. Are you keeping our crew well hidden so that Gypsy Smith does not find them out? And yourself besides?" Again he nodded. "Good, we would not like him to thwart all our plans. Did you get to Angela and take her to Castle Island to join our other prisoners?"

With a heavy sigh, Sorrel answered somewhat sheepishly, "Gypsy Smith saw that I did not capture our little pigeon and take her away. It was dark, he did not, uh, see me."

"Ah," Julia said, enlightened. "Now I see where you have gotten the battered countenance, you poor darling. What else has happened that I should know about?"

Flinching from the mushy endearment, Sorrel snorted, "I have returned to Castle Island and the old lighthouse where we have our prisoners. Blossom Fortune will not come away with me. She swears she will do away with herself if I take her from her lover."

"Ah," Julia said with an ugly sneer. "François and his dark-eyed flower. So? Why do you not just take her from him? Is it François you are afraid of?"

"She was mine first. I had her first."

"So—was she that good that you must pine your heart away for one simple woman?" Julia looked closely at Sorrel and saw that indeed he thought Blossom was someone very special. "I asked you—why do you not just take her from him?"

Shuffling his overlarge feet, Sorrel mumbled, "She will not come with me, I have already told you. When I entered the chamber where they are being held, Blossom and François were snuggled together upon a pallet of his making and when she saw me standing there she wrapped her lovely arms about his neck and clung to the *bastardo* as if her very life depended on that one man." He could still see Blossom, her hair spread out in an inky fan across François's shoulder, the Frenchman's fingers entwined with hers. He would not add that François had told him to *get out*.

Envy shot through Julia, and the green of her eyes brightened to a shade matching that of her younger days. "It probably does," she said. Her red mouth quirked. "What about your pretty native girl Llana? You still have her—" Julia wanted to say, *you fool*.

Sorrel flushed, staring at the intricately carved sofa and said nothing. There was pain mixed with sore regret in his eyes.

"Ah," Julia murmured. "Llana has found another, I see. It must be that brawny young fisherman Carolos brought home from Elbow Cay, *non?*"

For his answer, Sorrel said nothing again, and Julia knew indeed that Llana had found herself another love. Why not? She would have done the same. It must have become perceivable to Llana that Sorrel had eyes for another. A native woman of the islands pledged to love only one man in her life, but if that man did not return her love, she found another immediately to take his place.

Everything was going much better than Julia had thought. Sorrel's mind was on the black-haired Blossom, and the little flower loved another. Revenge did strange things to a man. She would have little trouble now to get Sorrel to do what must be done, and all she needed to promise was the same things she'd promised to François, with one exception— Sorrel would get Blossom Fortune and sail away to the Villa Cassandra, or so he would be led to believe. No one but herself would possess the Villa—no one but Steven Hawke and herself, that is. For once Angela and Monica were put aside, she and Steven would together possess the Villa El Corazón and the Villa Cassandra, and they could live in both places throughout the year, naturally in different seasons.

"Now," Julia began, twirling her black lace mantilla that was draped over one hand, "I have made a change in plans having to do with our little Lady Hawke. You get Angela away from Gypsy Smith—I do not care how you do it, just see that you do. I shall do my part and get your precious flower away from François Ce'sar."

Blinking his eyes rapidly, Sorrel blurted, "But how will you do that? Blossom will have to be torn from François's arms to get her away from him."

"I do not think so, *mon cher*." Julia tapped her chin, tossing the mantilla aside with her other hand.

"There are ways . . . a woman's ways."

Satisfied with that for the time being, Sorrel said, "What do you want me to do with Lady Hawke once I have her? And did you not send Captain Youngblood to France with a message . . . uhm, to her parents telling them where they might find their daughter?"

"*Oui*, I did. But you see, as I have told you there is going to be a change in plans. I can see it now," she said as if speaking only to herself as she turned to face the terrace doors, "Steven Hawke will come sailing in here—or steaming, if he has purchased one of those new kinds of ships—and I shall greet him tearfully, sobbing that I tried to keep Gypsy Smith from spiriting Jessica away but he took her captive anyway and, I, being a mere woman, could not aid her in her distress. I shall fall to his feet, moaning my sore regret and wrap my arms about his long muscular legs"—Julia purred and licked her lips envisioning his tall, black-clad form—"and he shall tell me what a brave woman I am and how grateful he is that I tried to save his beautiful daughter from ravishment at the hands of that devil. He will be so grateful he will promise to return for me . . . and when he does I shall make the horrible announcement that his daughter has been killed, or"—she shrugged—"something like that."

"Hmm." Sorrel ran his fingers through his long, red beard. "You have forgotten one thing, Duchess— what about Gypsy Smith? Where will he be all this time? And who do you actually plan to have spirit our Lady Hawke away?"

"Why, monsieur Sorrel, *you* shall take Lady

Hawke away, along with Blossom Fortune, and you might as well take the cute little blonde at the same time. I will hold to the same profitable agreement we made. You will get everything that is coming to you," she said with a naked gleam in her eye.

"I asked you—what about Gypsy Smith? What do you plan to do with him?"

"I plan to put that one in chains in the deepest cell in the deserted lighthouse, along with François and that other handsome American with the nice, sandy hair. But it is Gypsy Smith who must not escape, for that one can do us much harm."

Sorrel blanched at the thought of even trying to capture that one, let alone even approach him in the dark.

"But who will be accused of ending Lady Hawke's life then if there is no one around to accuse of the evil deed?"

"You will take Lady Hawke away and simply dispose of her body in the depths of the sea—"

"Me?" Sorrel squawked. "Why me?"

"Oh, but darling, you will not be accused of the nasty deed—remember I told you, Gypsy Smith will be. Upon your return, all you must say is that you could not catch Smith but you saw whose body it was that he tossed into the sea."

"*Be Jaysus!*" Sorrel ran his thick fingers through his long red locks. "Is there no gentle bone in your body?" For her answer, Julia tossed her cosmetically enhanced hair over her shoulder and laughed a nasty laugh. "Is there anything else I must do? One murder of a woman is all I can stomach, so what else is there?"

472

"Oh yes, I forgot to mention one item: Be sure you get the hank of young Lady Hawke's lustrous hair, cut it off at the scalp and bring it back to me."

"*You want me to scalp the little lady?*"

"Not *scalp*, darling," Julia said with undiluted laughter. "Just bring me all four feet of her hair." She shrugged, adding, "That's all."

"You have beautiful hair, my love." Gypsy Smith complimented his wife as he drew the brush Llana had given her as a gift, drew it down through the glorious length of Angela's shining chestnut hair. "It crackles, and sparkles, and leaps as if with a will of its own. Don't ever cut it, please."

Angela stood and moved gracefully to nestle her back against Gypsy's powerful, well-built chest while his arms enfolded her waist, his chin resting on the top of her shining head. For long moments they just reveled in each other's presence, staring out to sea as the sunset colors of crimson and lavender streaked across the sky. The effulgence of the sun going down, a huge red-orange ball sinking into the sea, caressed their already glowing faces and to any passersby it could be noted how very much in love these two were.

"As soon as we repair the foremast that was damaged in the storm, we shall be leaving our little island paradise." He kissed the top of her head, adding, "I promise." What he wanted to tell her was that he planned to find her family, but he didn't wish to get her hopes up too high if the task should prove to be an impossible one. First he had to do some soul

473

searching, and he had to confess to himself, if not her, that he was afraid of what he would find out, if anything, about her loved ones, and the fear of discovering a man might be waiting in the wings for Angela. Even the thought of finding out her *real* name distressed him.

"Oh, Gypsy, you are my hope, my trust, my love, and apart from you I am nothing." How could she tell him she'd almost believed the outright lies Julia had told her? And to tell him she knew he was Benjamin, the stable boy, would eventually lead to the telling of those lies. She had to wait awhile, for she did not wish to shatter the beautiful love they had just discovered. Their quest for love had finally found perfection, so it seemed. But she had to start somewhere to resolve some of the things that still bothered her about him, so she began tentatively. "I have not been able to speak to Blossom about some *things* that have been troubling me. . . . They are about you, Gypsy."

"Well," he said with a chuckle, "you have the best source at hand. Why not ask the man concerned in this gossip—your husband."

Angela began with the time she and Daisy had been accidentally eavesdropping. She related the part about Kapa Lu, then repeated to him what Blossom had said about Gypsy's carrying deep emotional scars, and about his dragging her into the broom closet and beating her with a whip.

Gypsy was silent and somewhat brooding as she went on, "Then, after hearing those sordid tales, all I wanted was to cleanse my body of any memory of your vile touch. Back then I had come to the conclusion you were nothing but a reviler . . . womanizer . . . user . . . and—"

"Perhaps even a murderer?" Gypsy Smith finished for her. Tilting her chin up so she would be forced to look deeply into his eyes, he said, "And what do you think now, my love?"

Laying her cheek against his shoulder, she answered truthfully, "I know you are none of those, Gypsy, and especially not a murderer. You could never hurt anyone, for you are too kind . . . and loving."

"Well, I guess that answers all the troubling questions that have been plaguing your mind then, doesn't it. Angela, look at me." When she lifted her eyes, there was a look of remembered pain in his face. "I spoke to Melantha, you remember her, the old black woman at Tamarind they called the Black Flower? She told me all about my stepfather, Robert Neil I, who was the one that sent me away from Tamarind. Angelica, my mother, had just given birth to Robert Neil II. Since she had become pregnant with Robert's son, she had hardly time to miss or even think about her unruly seven-year-old. He was always in the stables with the animals anyway, and Melantha said the lad was always so hard to find just when someone wanted him for something or other. My stepfather had married Angelica to provide a home for her firstborn, who as you must have already guessed was myself. In turn she gave him what he wanted—a son from his own loins. How Robert Neil had hated Gypsy Smith, Melantha said. That should not have mattered to the lad, yet who was there to tell him that his stepfather was no good from the start? You see, Melantha told me a secret she'd kept for years and years, she said—that being Robert Neil had murdered his own brother to gain the Fortune inheritance.

"Melantha said Robert Neil's attitude had been 'one more drunk wiped from the face of the earth.' Robert had one other relative, a brother by the name of Harrison. Harrison Fortune was married to a lovely woman by the name of Jana, and Jana was Daisy Dawn's mother. . . . They perished in a barn fire at Persimmon Wood."

"Yes," Angela said finally, "I remember there being some talk about it and Blossom . . . she said some ugly things. Daisy had been hurt about it. But all that has changed now, now that Blossom has at last fallen in love, and François does truly seem to be a different person, almost likable."

Gypsy's voice echoed with his own remembrance. "Blossom used to bandy about lies and hurt so many in the telling, but now, as you said, she has changed. And Melantha, she never really chanted any words over my head to cast a spell that would keep me from remembering. . . . I know now it was something horrible that was inside me. I didn't want to remember. . . . It was too painful. I have something else to tell you, Angela dearest. I use to be a stable boy in Africa and then in France. The people there in Lyons were loving, kind, and helped me find myself. I loved them, Angela, and I still do. Someday I am going back to El Corazón and want to take you with me to meet them . . . if you would like to go?"

Perhaps, Gypsy was thinking, if he brought Angela to meet Steven and Monica, and their daughter, Jessica—he forgot what else they'd called

476

her—then she might not feel so lost and all alone in the world with sympathetic, wholesome friends like the Hawkes. . . .

"Gypsy!" Angela whirled in the circle of his arms, her face happily excited as she faced him. "Take me to them, please, I want to meet them as soon as possible."

Oh, how wonderful it was going to be when at last Gypsy took her to El Corazón and her parents would come running out to meet them—and she would turn to meet the surprised look on Gypsy's face. An impish smile appeared on her elfin face as she pictured Gypsy Smith, Benjamin, El Corazón's beloved stable boy, discovering her true identity . . . Jessica Angèle Hawke . . . no! Jessica Angèle *Smith*. She could hardly contain her excitement; she was almost jumping up and down!

"Are you sure?" Gypsy said, "that you want to go there first?"

"Of course!" Angela cried, hugging him about the waist fiercely. "I want to go there more than anyplace else in the world!"

If Gypsy had been surprised, he did not show it; he only seemed pleased at her eagerness.

"They are like family to me, you know." He chuckled and kissed her flushed cheek, so happy he'd found an answer—at least part of one.

Family was all Angela could think as she sailed through the remainder of the radiant day on a cloud of silver and gold. Nothing bad could happen now. They were on their way home!

*   *   *

Captain Smith kept very busy during the day, for he had decided to get the *Black Moon* in readiness to sail as soon as possible. Since most of his crew wanted to get back to their families, they were more than eager to put more effort into their workdays. At night Gypsy would often drift peacefully to sleep after making love to his wife, usually sleeping with Angela in his arms, but this night he had been so exhausted he'd climbed into bed right after their meal and was asleep before Angela completed braiding her long hair. Braiding hair that reached to the backs of her knees sometimes took Angela five minutes to finish.

About to climb into the dark bed after she'd blown out the lantern light, Angela paused in lifting the hem of her nightshirt over her head as a rustling sound came from outside the door and she turned just in time to see it burst open, flooding the room with moonbeams. Gypsy stirred but he did not awaken.

The moon wasn't the only thing that met Angela's startled gaze, but before she could cry out an alarm, two men rushed her. She was bound and gagged at once, and then her abductors wasted no time in leaving the island.

The guard that had been posted near the Smiths' cottage awoke with a huge lump on his head, but when he had finally recovered enough to alert the captain, the moon was on the other side of the heavens and the stars were going out one by one.

When Gypsy Smith could not find his wife the next day, though he and his crew searched high and low, he halted all his frantic activity and stared disgustedly out to sea. There! She was gone; the

Delora had set sail. When had she gone? How far was she out by now?

Running his fingers through his thick dark locks, he wondered if he'd have sufficient time to complete the *Black Moon*'s repairs before the others got too far out.

The woman in black was nowhere to be found. The wild island was almost deserted, but for the natives and his crew.

Ransacking the house on the hill, Gypsy grinned wryly when he discovered a neat supply of his favorite liquor, a fine brandy he used to imbibe in before he'd met Angela, and with bottle neck in limp wrist—his third one—he wandered the lonely moon-lit beaches and the starlit coves until he was thoroughly drunk.

Julia emerged from her web, her hiding place in the house, and saw the mess the handsome Gypsy Smith had made of her rooms before leaving with some of her most expensive spirits. With an evil smile on her face, she decided the time was ripe. Angela had been whisked away. . . . Now it was time to lock the inebriated Smith up in the lighthouse.

Little did Julia know that at that very moment Sorrel's men were sneaking back onto the island, acting under their captain's order to abduct the few men they sorely needed. Ah . . . there was one they did not even have to work at capturing—he was already three sheets to the wind!

Chapter Thirty-Eight

Castle Island, Leeward Lighthouse

It was well past midnight when Julia was rowed by one of Sorrel's men over to Castle Island. She had it all planned, what she was going to say to Blossom Fortune. Making her way up the beaten path to the lighthouse, she adjusted her black lace mantilla over her face, her passion for bright colors relinquished for the night; from head to toe she was draped in black. She might as well have been going to a funeral, she thought disgustedly, and besides, this visit was idiotic when all Sorrel had to do was drag the little wench from François's arms and be done with it.

When the guard recognized her voice, he let her pass and then summoned a man to go with her and unlock the chamber she wished to enter. Another man standing by held yet another torch for the lady in black to see by and stepped back when she approached.

François scraped to his feet at once and stood to

face the woman he knew could be none other than Juliette La Chapierre. Julia, the bitch. François would recognize her anywhere, and he smirked into her face—what he could see of it.

"Guard!" Julia snapped, seeing that François was in a challenging mood. Oh *Dieu*, the lion protecting his mate. It was sickening . . . but Julia remembered a time. . . . Ah well, that was behind her now. "Take this man outside and see that you guard his every movement well."

"What do you want, Julia?" François asked, steely eyes boring into hers while from his side vision he could see the guard's weapons trained on him. Two pistols. If only he could trick the man some way, but then he had no wish to put Blossom's life in further danger if his attack failed and he lost the woman his heart had always been awaiting.

"I have come to speak with Blossom. You need not fret for your love, François, just go and leave us alone for a time."

If Julia had so desired, she could have had Blossom taken from François by force, but that was not what Sorrel wanted. He wanted her to go willingly or else not at all. Sorrel was horribly unhappy, and unhappy men made miserable partners, Julia knew from past experience.

"All right," François conceded. "Just do not take too long." He had tried to make his own plans for escape, but as there were guards posted everywhere, he could not find an opening to get his love out with her friends, and he knew beforehand Blossom would never leave them behind.

François took one last look at Blossom before

going out, his eyes speaking of his loving affection for her. He would adore her to his last breath, he vowed this day here and now.

Blossom's eyes, like jet sequins, warily watched the woman in black step closer as the door closed them in the dank cell together and Blossom found herself trembling with nervous apprehension. The lace cowl came away and Julia's red lips parted in a smile that the younger woman could think of only as being a twist of mockery though the other thought she appeared quite amicable. All of Blossom's physical defense mechanisms fell into place and it cost her, for she had become weakened from her ordeal of being locked up for so long a time without exercise or fresh air. She had also found a lot of time in which to reflect back over all the bad things she'd done in her lifetime, recalling her cruelties to Tamarind's blacks, especially to Kapa Lu, and if God ever allowed her to return, she planned to make amends to each and every one she'd harmed or spoken a cruel word to. The men she'd lain and sinned with she could do nothing about, but she knew she had already paid dearly when François brought to her his most precious love and affection, giving of his heart so freely, gentling her anguish and guilt over past indiscretions, and knowing if she could she'd take back all those other times for just one oh so precious moment in François's loving embrace. François had told her she need never be afraid of anything, ever again. But now she was, so afraid of what this mean-spirited woman's visit here tonight meant.

"Blossom . . . ah, such a lovely name," Julia purred, moving closer to stroke the unruly coils of long midnight tresses. Julia sighed, as if pained, drawing her hand abruptly away and moving to pace slowly the confines of the dank, musty cell, the torches causing her movements to cast eerie shadows upon the moist walls. "You must be very eager to leave this hellish place. I know I would be, faugh, I suppose there are even rats here as big as dogs."

"Not quite," Blossom defiantly stated. "Almost."

"I would hate it here," Julia said again, looking around with a smirk of distaste.

A pert chin lifted toward the woman defiantly as Blossom snapped, "You are the one who has put us here. So why have you come? To gloat over our wretchedness? If you have something to say, Miss Julia, then say it and go away."

"My," Julia said with a click of her tongue. "Such a temper, child. That will get you nowhere, especially not with me."

"I do not wish to be *anywhere* with you. I only want to be with François! Send him back in here if you have nothing else to say!"

"Oh . . . but I do, child."

"Don't call me that. I am not a child! I happen to be nineteen . . . old enough to know that you will never ever get François away from me." Blossom could not see that the older woman seethed inwardly; all she knew was that this woman had once been François's mistress and that infuriated her, for she could not imagine him with another.

"Oh *Dieu*, I do not wish to take François away from you . . . quite the opposite."

Blossom looked up, startled, into the woman's fathomless green eyes. "What do you mean 'quite the opposite'?" she asked.

"I wish to take *you* away from François . . . simple, *cherie.*"

"Are you insane? I'll never leave François's side, never, ever! And he will never let me go!"

Oh, but he will, Julia was thinking to herself. For at that very moment, François was being taken to another "cell" far up into the lighthouse. In fact he was now at this very moment struggling in the observation chamber, his wrists and ankles bound, his mouth gagged while muffled curses fought to reach the ones who towered over him, giving him a swift kick in the behind every time he snarled up at them like a wolf gone mad. But Blossom was unaware of everything but the woman who stood before her, spinning webs of lies with merciless intensity, telling of the poor wife he'd left behind in France with three children under the age of ten, fatherless children that cried every night for their papa to come home and be with them. After that, Blossom could only follow helplessly as Julia led her out of the lighthouse and out of François's life forever. With tears streaming down her stricken face, Blossom never looked back as the small boat silently took her out to the larger vessel that waited in the moonswept waters.

It was the *Delora,* but Blossom never knew it, she was blinded by her sadness and grief.

Angela looked up as the door to the small cabin was unlocked and wrenched open. The color could not drain from her face, for there was no color left, yet

484

when she saw Blossom shoved into the room, followed by Daisy, both tired looking as she was feeling, Angela could not help but gasp aloud.

The three women looked at one another, thinking the same thing: they had been this way before, yet this time they sensed there was more danger in this abduction. Angela was about to say something, anything, when the door was again flung wide.

"You," the rough-looking sailor said, directing a stubby finger at Blossom, "come with me, girlie, the cap'n wants to see ya."

"La!" Blossom exclaimed, feeling anger begin to claim her emotions after the initial fear had subsided, "I have just gotten here and haven't even had a chance to sit down to *tea* with my friends."

"Don't be funny," snarled the big lad. "Just come along and keep yer trap shut, else I'll have ta shut it fer ya."

Thrusting out her bosom, Blossom said, "You just go ahead and try, *suh*, and I'll give you some of my *own* medicine! I've had enough of being shoved around these past few months and I've had it up to here!" Her hand leveled beneath her chin, showing the bold sailor the measure of this Southern belle's wrath. "I am tired of being sampled and cast aside." She began to break down then, tears pooling in her huge black eyes. "Tired of men who only need certain things f-from me . . ."

"Blossom," Angela began, fearing that something had gone awry when the girl had just started to really live. "Where is François? *He* did not have you taken away—"

"No! He has nothing to do with . . . yes, maybe

you are right, Angela," she said, trying to calm her devastating anguish. "He probably got back together with that *witchy* mistress of his . . . and there really is not a wife waiting . . . for him with three children . . . in France. There just couldn't be—ooooh!" She flung herself bodily at the nearest bulkhead and began to sob wretchedly, her cries breaking as she wept aloud.

Surprising both Angela and Daisy, Blossom turned to both of them, begging, "Can you ever forgive me for all the gossip . . . Angela? . . . Daisy?" She sniffled loud while the astonished sailor looked on, shuffling his big feet and wondering what to do next. "Please . . . *please* forgive me?"

Angela rushed into Blossom's arms, saying with tears in her own eyes, "Oh, Blossom, of course I forgive you. I know you did not mean all that you said, but I shall have to ask you to forgive me also, because I half believed it all and then when I came to know you after you . . . you fell in love with François, I knew you had changed. It was in you all the while, Blossom, the pure heart."

Daisy, too, put her arm about Blossom's shoulder and all three of the tearful women were too much for the mate; he turned to leave the cabin more swiftly than he had entered.

Angela and Daisy exchanged looks of commiseration for their friend who was weeping so heart-brokenly, but there was really nothing they could do for Blossom Angelica. Each of them wondered what part François had played in this or if indeed he had anything at all to do with this abduction, and each had their own gloomy forebodings on what the future held for the three of them.

Captain Sarge Sorrel waited for his lovely Blossom Angelica to be brought to him, and as he did this, he went over the events of the last several days. He had gotten the women on board, done everything as Julia had said to do with one exception. He was short of men. Most of the crew between him and François had gone over to the Frenchman's side, and Julia stated she needed some men to remain with her on Paraiso Island. He had waited until they were ready to sail, then had some of his crew members take more men from the island by force. Then he'd ordered them to return to the lighthouse for François and Rider; he planned to get rid of them at sea at the same time he tossed Angela and the little blonde overboard. He might as well get it all done in one fell swoop, then he could have Blossom Angelica all for himself. Angela would be easy to get rid of—she was small and dainty just like that Annabelle Huntington in Charleston he'd strangled when she'd stated she had eyes for the handsome Frenchman François Ce'sar, and all it had taken was a simple blue silk stocking. He had even started that plantation fire that killed Blossom's wretched brother, and an overseer who hung around there by the name of Jal Stephan, but François had no knowledge of the stretch of his villainous audacity. Now he even planned to get rid of Julia, once he'd gotten from her what was coming to him. After he found out how he could get to Villa Cassandra, he planned to go there and take it over. He and his pretty flower were going to be sitting well off and everyone else could go to Hades.

While he waited for his mate to bring him the delicious morsel he'd been long yearning for, his crew members unbound and ungagged in the hold the men they'd taken the night before. He had told them only to pick up François and the sandy-haired man they had imprisoned, and then return to the ship before Smith's crew spotted them, yet they had not heeded Sorrel's orders but picked up a few more on Paraiso. One of the men they had found wandering on the beach, potent liquor on his breath, his expression void of any emotion save inebriation, had been an easy catch, but now as one of the crew members looked down into the feral look in the man's mahogany eyes, he knew he'd made a drastic mistake.

"Tie that 'un up real good, Philo, it's Gypsy Smith, and don't let 'em go 'til the cap'n has done with his dirty work."

Little did the three women in the cabin know who had been brought aboard, other than there had been a lot of noise on the decks leading to the hold. All they could do was wait, while Blossom was unwillingly dragged off to entertain the captain, and they had begun to guess just who that man might be.

Chapter Thirty-Nine

The thick fringe of Angela's brown lashes cast shadows over the pale peach curve of her cheeks. A tiny contented sigh escaped her as she slept, dreaming she was home again surrounded by her loved ones. There was her horse, Cascara's Pride, and over there just dashing from the wooded copse was the lad who sat his horse like an Indian prince. He was so handsome. . . . Why had she not noticed this before?

Suddenly Angela was rudely awakened by a loud commotion, the shuffling of many feet and voices yelling as if sounding an alarm. Pulling her gaping shift closed over the circle of her breast and securing the cloth, Angela sat as best she could in the swaying hammock while she dragged her long hair over her shoulder and began braiding the ends that had come loose in her restless slumber. When that was done, she faced Daisy, who was trying her best to sit in the other hammock while rubbing sleep from her deep blue eyes.

"Where is Blossom?" Angela asked, looking

around and becoming alarmed at her disappearance. Blossom had been ordered to have supper with the captain the night before and then had returned to the cabin with the gloomiest expression Angela had ever seen Blossom wearing. "Do you suppose they unlocked the cabin door and took her away in the middle of the night? I think I know who that cut-throat captain is."

"Me too," said Daisy, shuddering inwardly at the thought of Sorrel holding them captive again; this time he would not be as lenient, she thought. What was going to happen to them?

"They're comin' straight for us, Captain."

"I think we are under attack," Daisy said with an impish smile this time. "I've been praying that we would be rescued."

"How do you know it is not just some more scoundrels attacking?" Blossom said with a yawn as the shiny black head popped up from nowhere.

"Blossom!" Angela and Daisy chorused together. "We thought they'd come for you in the night and brought you to that nasty captain," Daisy went on, "and I'll just bet Sorrel is his name!"

"He's a devil, that one," Blossom said, tossing her head in the manner of her old self. "I'm going to find a nice long dagger to plunge into that one's heart. He was very drunk last night, and the stuff loosened his nasty tongue. Ladies, Captain Sorrel is our villain— he not only set fire to Tamarind, murdered Robert Neil, who was inside, then he boasted he did away with Jal Stephan, who had been trying to put out the blaze by himself, with water from the well, the dear old man. Sorrel was looking for our Lady Hawke here," she said, glancing at Angela, "and thought she was inside burning with the house. Daisy—" Blossom hunkered down now upon the soft pile of blankets, avoiding the recalcitrant hammock. "Sorrel is also our blue stocking murderer."

"Annabelle!" Daisy said, sudden anger lighting her eyes.

"Devil indeed," echoed Angela.

"Listen," Blossom said. "I think we are under attack. I only hope the other ship is a friendly one." If only François would come for her with the others and say it was all a lie, that he had no family waiting for him in France . . . then she could continue to live again. As it was, she felt only half alive.

"Oh!" Daisy shuddered. "What was that?"

"Cannonfire," Angela said with a gulp as they heard the crack of timber and a loud crash, knowing that one of the masts had fallen.

There followed shortly a violent jarring and the women looked around wild-eyed, clinging to one another.

"The other ship is just bumping up against ours."

Just then they heard the sickening sounds of blades slashing and clashing, guns exploding, and the even more terrible sounds of men dying, some falling over the rail with a loud splash right outside the porthole where they were.

Some time passed while the three women huddled together and prayed that the attacking party would win and see them to safety—or that they were being rescued by their husbands. But of course Blossom could not say the same; she might never marry now that she and François were separated. She knew there would never be another man for her like her François.

When at last the sounds of battle had ceased and quiet fell, Angela stood up and went to peer outside the porthole. She gasped softly at the sight of sharks swimming about in pools of blood—human blood. At once she turned away, facing the door just as it burst open and a tall, rakish man filled the door frame. His eyes were blazing wild brown with victory, looking from her to Daisy to Blossom and then back to her again. Displaying a white grin, his eyes, so like another's in their hue, flashing over her, he said in a soft compelling voice, "Jessica Angèle Hawke, I would recognize your fair countenance even in a crowd." He executed a short bow, then straightened, gallantly introducing himself, "G. S. Youngblood—at your service!"

Chapter Forty

G. S. Youngblood had seen the chestnut-haired beauty through his spyglass and decided to take the ship *Delora* to get Jessica Angèle back; that had been the night before when the sun had been going down in a blaze of violent orange and soft pink hues. When the morning came, however, he was ready to attack and they hit the mast with a single cannon blast, fought the men, and took control of the *Delora* with the superlative strength of a man-of-war.

Deciding it best to torch the ship that was listing fast, he ordered his men to first check the hold. The men who'd been abducted were freed and brought aboard the *Crescent Moon*, six of them altogether. Youngblood beforehand had had the women brought to his cabin and made comfortable, then he ordered his men to release the unfortunates who'd been in the hold and be brought to him immediately as they set sail and the *Delora* was torched and sunk into the blazing sea.

"I must talk to them, separately," he said, "to

discover what this is all about and why the men were taken aboard the *Delora*, for from what I've seen these men were taken against their will and were being readied for reluctant service, and they themselves, though weakened from lack of food, were in turn readying to revolt."

Youngblood recalled the face of the one man who'd had the look of murder in his eyes . . . such strange eyes—where had he seen them before?

"Don't think they know any more than we do," said one of Youngblood's mates, scratching through his scruffy graying locks.

"Bring them to me anyway," he said, his look sinister and dangerous.

For some reason, call it circumstance or not, Gypsy Smith was the first man brought to face the ominous captain Youngblood. When Gypsy entered the cabin, his dark hair disheveled, his look murderous to say the least, Youngblood met this man's eyes head on and the two men stared across the space at each other, chills running down both their backs. It was as if this was someone the other had known all his life, but was just now coming face to face with.

As Gypsy stood before the dashing Youngblood, he was wholly aware of the power that emanated from the other man, who was perhaps twice his age.

G. S. Youngblood leaned to get a closer look at the younger man, and said compellingly, "What is your name?"

Standing proud and unafraid, Gypsy stated, "My name is Gypsy Smith, sir."

At once Youngblood leapt from his chair, facing

the man squarely, snapping, "Where did you get that name?" A menacing look in his eyes, he kicked the fallen chair aside.

Eyeing the other suspiciously, Gypsy said with much coolness, "That is my father's name . . . and mine also."

"Do you know who I am?" the tall, muscled captain drawled, looking the younger man over with some mistiness in his eyes that were so like the other's. In fact, the captain of the *Crescent Moon* looked quite stunned at what he was hearing and seeing.

"Hell no," Gypsy said. "I've no idea," he went on impertinently. "Who are you supposed to be?"

"My name is G. S. Youngblood!"

"So?" Gypsy Smith snarled. "What do you want me to do, bow down and kiss your—"

"Shut up, man!" Youngblood snarled back, smiling within at his good fortune. "Tell me, Gypsy Smith, who is your mother?"

Gypsy sighed as if in boredom, saying, "My mother is no more. She passed on. I am not sure when. I do not see what this has to do with—"

"Angelica."

Gypsy Smith had been staring down at his scarred boots, worrying about Angela and wondering where she could be and if he had any chance at all to rescue her now.

"What did you say?" Gypsy demanded quickly, looking up. "How do you know my mother's name?"

Youngblood cleared his throat, saying, "We have to have a long talk, son."

"Why is that?" Gypsy Smith inquired, beginning to feel the chills of recognition slide up and down his spine.

"Because, young man, my name also is Gypsy Smith."

Outside, the sun was like a great golden doubloon suspended above the horizon's rim when the furled topsails of the *Angèle* and the *Mona* first came into view, seen by Captain Youngblood's crewmen. Aboard the *Angèle*, Steven Hawke peered through his spyglass, making out the name of his friend's ship. He ordered his men to make ready to pull alongside the *Crescent Moon*, then they would board when they drew near, and make no mistake about it, he would be heartily welcomed!

Gypsy was still gaping at the man who'd just claimed to be his father when a commotion broke out above decks, and the two exchanged looks of surprise, realizing that another battle was in progress. Then they broke out in a run and made for the companionway.

Close on the heels of the older but no less vigorous man, Gypsy burst out upon the scene of fighting only one second behind G. S. Youngblood, and it took them by surprise to see that only eleven men or so were making all the noise of battle.

"How the hell did they all get loose?!" Youngblood bellowed as he watched the strange scene unfolding and the even stranger sight of his men standing back looking sheepish over something. "What happened? I thought these men were locked up," he said to his nearest mate.

"Don't ask me how they got 'emselves loose, cap'n. One minute we was mindin' our tasks and the next a big fight was cuttin' out. You didn't say to keep 'em out of the way, cap'n."

With a wry smile growing, Gypsy looked at Rider Huntington and knew who'd gotten the men loose. "Jesus, just so he could fight with them." He stepped forward to enter the melee, and Rider shouted him back with these words:

"This one is mine, Gypsy, stay away! He was boasting in the hold. He is the blue stocking murderer, Gypsy. He killed Annabelle! He was boasting about the fire . . . killed Robert Neil . . . Jal Stephan. . . . He's mine, Gypsy, keep back!"

Gypsy looked at the man who claimed to be his father and that one said, "I think your friend means what he says, my son. Listen, I believe he tries your friend's patience even further . . ."

Indeed Sorrel continued to boast, breathing heavily as he spat, rounding on the other to get in another blow, "Your little blonde wife is very charming . . . and very good in the bed. But you are *estupido* to think you can beat me!"

Rider's head was just snapping around from the force of Sorrel's blow when he heard those sickening words; though he knew they were not true, he began to wonder if Sorrel had been trying to get his hands on Daisy after the scoundrels had abducted the three women and taken them aboard the *Delora*.

"I've been anticipating the day I'd have your neck

497

between my fingers, Sorrel!"

With that Rider lunged and caught the man by the throat, then began to squeeze the life out of him. His face a grim mask of hatred, Rider pressed until the other began to show the color purple.

Then everything happened so fast. Sorrel disengaged himself from the death grip and leapt to his feet, spinning about with a pistol he'd gotten from nowhere it seemed and held it in a murderous grip.

A woman screamed.

Three other men were stabbed and tossed overboard by the men who'd been abducted by Sorrel's men; some of these were François's own, those who had been faithful to the Frenchman. Even when Sorrel had taken matters into his own hands and gathered his own crew—and Julia's—about him, the men had remained faithful to François. They liked the new man he had become.

Another woman screamed, and the two Gypsy Smiths turned at the same time to see three women gathered near a bulkhead, having just come out on their own from the captain's cabin to see what the commotion was all about.

"Angela," Gypsy said in a tone of sheer relief at seeing his young wife alive and, by the looks of her, unharmed.

The looks exchanged between Gypsy and Angela did not go unnoticed by the older G. S. Youngblood and he would have smiled his pleasure had the dangerous scene not been noticed out of the corner of his eye.

A woman screamed again. "Rider . . . no!"

Swiftly, borrowing Captain Youngblood's trusty

498

weapon, Gypsy Smith stepped forward to drive the yard and a half of shining blade deeply into Sorrel's chest just as the pistol reported and Rider was quick enough to step out of the bullet's path.

Reaching up to clutch the razor-sharp blade, Sorrel's whitened fingers let go of the pistol and it clattered to the deck; no other sound was heard but the sails flapping softly in the wind. Then one and all became still and looked on as the red-haired man began to choke on his own blood, blood that was coming to his lips in a red froth.

As Gypsy withdrew the sword, Sorrel fell back, bounced once on the railing, then his body went plunging into the sea that waited to speed him to his watery grave in the midnight blue depths.

With a sob clutching her throat painfully, Angela ran to Gypsy and he wound an arm about her waist, apologizing, "I am sorry, my lady, so sorry you had to see me do that."

Angela said nothing. She had witnessed the demise of another man by her husband's fleet hand, the one named Garceau, but this was by far the more gruesome death indeed.

Rider's arms tightened about Daisy's tiny waist, his manly strength a safe haven enclosing the dainty young woman. The sandy-haired man had been frowning at his friend, but that was before he realized Gypsy Smith's sole intention had been to save his life, and not to steal from him the pleasure of ending Sorrel's mean existence.

"I am just glad that it is over and the varlet is dead," Angela said, loud enough for everyone to hear. "Now we can all breathe normally again," she added, having forgotten that one female cur still lived and breathed.

"I am so happy to see you alive, my beautiful angel." As Gypsy said this, he lifted her off the deck and spun her in his vibrant embrace. He was so thrilled to see her, it escaped his mind just now to ask how she, too, had come to be aboard Youngblood's ship.

Watching his son—for he knew indeed this young man was his flesh and blood—G. S. Youngblood said with a deep chuckle, "What is this, the handsome rogue has found himself a beautiful angel?" The couple looked at him with beaming smiles, Angela's not without some curiosity. Where had she seen this captain before, she wondered, for her mind was still foggy after having suffered amnesia for such a long time.

"This is my wife!" Gypsy announced proudly to the tall, rakish Youngblood. "My beautiful lady, my Angela," he murmured, gazing into the eyes of his most radiant love. What would she think when he told her that Youngblood was his father, for he was certain as the other was that they were truly flesh and blood.

Stroking his bearded chin, Youngblood said under his breath, "This is going to be very interesting," and just then he spied the twin ships, the *Angèle* and *Mona* steaming toward them, and he repeated to himself, "*Very* interesting indeed."

A very curious remembrance occurred to Youngblood just then. *Indian prince...* he saw a tall willowy lad ride across his mind's eye, riding like a young Indian prince, always holding himself from others, a lonely sad boy. Tears gathered in the corners of Youngblood's eyes. . . .

For now he knew the name of the dark-eyed stable boy he'd seen riding on El Corazón property, always curious about him but never getting close enough to see the true color of the lad's eyes. Benjamin, his own son, Gypsy Smith . . . oh yes, he had a last name to give him. What would he think of calling himself by the name Gypsy Youngblood? Forget Smith, he'd always hated it, even when his beautiful mother, Hahlona, half Cherokee, had named him that. He'd always wondered, as no doubt his son countless times had, just *who in hell was Gypsy Smith?* Youngblood? Ah, well . . . that was another story.

With unhappy tears pooling in her eyes, Blossom watched the happy reunion from where she leaned in utter dejectedness against the bulkhead of Youngblood's beautiful ship. François, her heart cried, oh . . . *François!*

Chapter Forty-One

The *Crescent Moon* lay off anchor on the leeward side of Castle Island, the gentle rhythm of turquoise waters lapping against her sides softly. The moon was just making its majestic appearance in the evening sky. Huge stars were beginning to twinkle. There was laughter in the captain's cabin, as Rider and Daisy, Angela and Gypsy, the captain himself and his trusted mate John Kent shared a light meal of succulent fish and heady wine. They also shared stories and Angela felt a poignant tear at her eye as Gypsy Smith Youngblood and his son were reunited. Her heart sang for she knew that soon another reunion would be celebrated.

"We are going to meet another ship here," G. S. Youngblood said cryptically, a smile ruffling his well-shaped mouth.

"Another ship?" Gypsy said, feeling the effects of the potent brandy he and his father shared with the other men while the women sipped daintily at their light wine. He was in the lightest of moods for

Angela seemed happy and that was all that mattered. "What ship could that be?" he asked, hoisting his tumbler, a deep chuckle coming from his throat.

"You will see," Youngblood answered, saluting Angela with his own drink as he stared around the table with an utterly roguish grin.

"Captain," Youngblood's mate announced as he entered, "your company has arrived, they are just now boarding."

A wave of anticipation swept Angela, and Gypsy peered at her, wondering what could make his lovely bride experience such anticipatory excitement; as it was, he also felt that something throbbed and played in the wind. Who was it that could be boarding the ship?

Gypsy's eyes were glued to the door, as were Angela's. Daisy and Rider, too, exchanged glances of expectation.

No one even stopped to think that one was missing; and that raven-haired beauty was in her cabin all alone pining for the love she'd lost and could never retrieve. She was staring out at the huge, rising, jonquil moon, tears shining on her pale, heart-shaped face, apart from the others sharing in the gaiety of the occasion.

In the captain's cabin, Steven Hawke was just making a dramatic appearance, his huge frame filling the doorway. The heavy brown lashes that shadowed Angela's cheeks flew up, her wine spilled, as she rose instantly to her feet, consumed with bottomless joy.

"Oh . . . my God!" Angela cried, her laughter like a bubbling spring.

With a wild shriek she raced across the space and threw herself into her father's waiting embrace. Gypsy, going deathly still, looked on with surprise and anger. Who was this man that he could create such a wild response in his beloved that she would run to him and throw her arms about him so blatantly? With clenched teeth, he watched his wife hug the man in desperate abandon.

"My darling, my sweet one, I have missed you so!" Steven Hawke cried, hugging his daughter fiercely, tears misting his jet eyes.

Gypsy Smith sprang to his feet to do battle but found the firm hand of his father upon his arm, as he said, "Hold on, my son, do not jump to conclusions! Wait . . . and see."

With her arm still about Steven's neck, Angela turned to the man with defiant fire in his eyes. Love bloomed in her heart as she held her hand out to her husband, and he took it; she pulled him into the circle of her arms, while he looked warily at the other man, who'd won her affections so easily as he'd stepped into the room.

Gypsy's mouth dropped open as he recognized the other, and he exclaimed, *"Jesus,"* and the older man looked back in amazement.

"Benjamin!" Steven Hawke said, holding his hand out to the man that had joined their circle of embrace. "What . . . ?"

"Steven!" Gypsy cried; and then as recognition of so many things dawned on him, he said, *"Oh Lord, it can't be,"* as he stared down at his beautiful Angela. "Angela?" he said. "Jessica Hawke?"

Impishly she said, "Mmm-hmm, yes darling hero,

504

Jessica Angèle Hawke."

"How . . . ?" Steven Hawke asked, staring from one to the other; then it dawned on him too. "Your hero?" he said, staring down into his beloved daughter's joy-misted pearl-blue eyes.

"Yes, Papa. And," she said proudly, *"Gypsy Smith* is my husband!"

Steven Hawke smacked his forehead, saying to Gypsy, "I am even more pleased to see you . . . Gypsy Smith!" He looked between his friend G. S. Young-blood and again he exclaimed, "Damn . . . Gypsy Smith . . . ah *Dieu!"*

Angela, smiling happily, said, "Oh, Papa, the things we have to tell you!"

Later, as the moon rose high and spilled over the silvery decks of the *Crescent Moon* and most were abed, Angela and Gypsy strolled together hand in hand, the yellow of moonlight painting their countenances a palomino hue, the stars huge and bright in the tropical paradise. Angela's beloved husband said, "I never thought I'd be able to trust a woman again, but now I see that I can." He recalled the conversation he'd had with his father a short while ago.

"It's heartbreaking," Gypsy had said, "but people are always going to hurt other people. It took me a long time to realize this. Even sometimes without meaning to do it, they hurt each other. But the ones who are really cruel are those who choose to continually ignore someone, even if that person tries his darndest to get himself noticed. Some cry out to be recognized, to get others to notice, to get them to understand they are only human and are not all that

505

bad if people will really take a good look and see them for what they truly are, and give them a chance to forgive and start all over.''

"Do you think your mother was like that, Gypsy?''

His sigh was so deep that Angela almost could feel it in her own breast as he said, "I have forgiven her for neglecting me and not trying harder to see I was crying out for attention. She must have thought I did not need her. It was my stepfather—actually he never did give me his name—he hated me from the first and never gave me a chance to make him like me.''

"Perhaps it was not in him to love,'' she said with the gentle heart of a caring woman.

"He even sent my true father away, when he would have come for me and my mother.'' Gypsy shook his head, lowering his hand from stroking her hair to rest upon her shoulder.

"Robert Neil I was probably jealous, Gypsy, afraid your mother would lavish more attention on you than him.''

"My father says he was just one of those downright cruel, devious people only looking out for himself.'' He sighed again. "I don't know for sure as I never really got to know him.''

"I guess we have to forgive and forget those bad things people do to us, and start afresh.'' She hugged close to him, loving him near her. She'd missed him so and had been afraid of never seeing him again or feeling his love surround her. "We must start somewhere else and go on with life. Otherwise we will always be living in the past.''

"You are so wise, darling Angel. We shall live for the future now and not glance back even once to the bad moments, and God help us that you and I will always understand each other. No matter what storms we must weather, we'll look to the radiant future, love."

"Oh course, Gypsy."

He chuckled, saying, "And now we have a name to give to our children . . . Youngblood. What do you think?"

"Jessica Youngblood . . . hmmm . . . I like it."

"Mrs. Gypsy Youngblood. I must confess, my love, I was afraid I'd discover a man waiting in the wings for you . . ."

"Never!" she exclaimed. "You were the one, dearest, how could there ever be another." It was not a question she asked, but a statement of fact.

"I would like to make love to you."

"Now? Here?"

"Anywhere," he cried as his lips descended over hers with sweet intensity.

Love enveloped them, moving ponderously, majestically, and then they were lifted and carried along the avalanche of radiant rapture as he found easy access beneath the flimsy shift she wore, his movements speaking far more eloquently than words ever could, again and again.

In the wee hours of the morning, G. S. Youngblood takes the raven-haired beauty to the lighthouse, delving, knowing of her sadness and her plight. While the others rest securely on his ship, they go and find the woman who is to blame for all their troubles. With the cunning instinct of a wolf circumventing its prey, he discovers Julia in the yard overlooking the cliff. She is like a spider, yet spinning her evil black web.

She turns, seeing before her the old and new faces staring at her from the past and she puts her hand to her mouth to halt the sounds of horrendous terror. Her eyes are wide with fear. She knows her end has come.

Steven Hawke has followed. He says, "It has been your doing, from the beginning!"

François steps forward and he sees his love, says, "Blossom, stay away . . . I am doing this for you!"

"No!" Blossom cries, following him to the upper room of the lighthouse and to the edge of the towering gallery, "let her be!"

"I love you!" shouts François, so close behind the evil temptress. "I am doing this for you, Blossom, go back!"

"You cannot die with her!" Blossom shrieks, throwing herself from Youngblood. "No! You must not die together. François, tell me," she cries, the wind fighting her voice, "who is this woman that awaits you in France?"

"None, my beloved, the black witch has lied to you!"

The wind shouts even louder.

As Julia, the trouble of all, steps closer to the ruined clifflike edge of the lighthouse, and François pursues, ever closer, Julia turns, and in her impasse, her feet give way in the crumbling stone as François lunges forward to catch her, then, like a clawing witch, Julia goes screaming over the edge.

François catches Blossom in his loving embrace,

holding her close as she buries for a moment her wet face in his chest. And then they look upon each other, love a shining token in each other's eyes, a promise of never-ending love. She turns her face up and François dries her eyes with his fingertips.

Blossom sadly looks down at the broken and twisted body that lies upon the jagged rocks, and as a collective nod goes around, all gathered here realize the one who had caused them grief and tribulation has finally met her demise—her clawlike hands are empty, without the hank of chestnut hair she'd so desired to add to her collection of pretties. *She is finished.*

Epilogue

Home Sweet Home

'*Tis sweet to hear the watch-dog's honest
   bark
   Bay deep-mouth'd welcome as we draw
   near home;
'Tis sweet to know there is an eye will mark
   Our coming, and look brighter when we
   come.*

—*Byron*

It was a beautiful sight as the two ships set sail for France, the sun a fool's gold glimmer in the sea-swept sky. Gypsy's fast, topsail schooner was in the lead, with the *Angèle* and *Mona* not far behind.

They had stayed long enough to witness Blossom and François become man and wife with Llana's relative, a clergy of sorts, uniting them in holy matrimony; and as the War Between the States was over, Daisy and Rider would be returning on another ship to rebuild at Persimmon Wood along the Ashley River. The beautiful, sun-drenched ships separated there at Castle Island, enduring friends waving farewells, promising to see each other again someday in the future.

Angela had been informed of her mother's pregnancy and she was thrilled beyond words—a baby sister or brother! The son she and Gypsy would one day inevitably have, Angela and her husband had already agreed to name Gypsy Smith Youngblood III. He would have his sire's and his grandfather's wild gypsy hair and features, but the eyes, ah! Gypsy said laughingly, would be blue as Angela's own.

The paradisiacal wind took them all in their separate directions, destiny's paths, these children, captives of the wind, but the *Crescent Moon*, like a guardian angel, was not far behind the *Black Moon*.

As for Julia, Angela concluded as she stared out to the sapphire sea, holding the notion to herself: She must thank the deceased woman for one thing—if it weren't for her evil schemes, Angela would never have met Gypsy Smith Youngblood. . . . Out of the bad and evil sometimes good was born. And then she turned to her husband, and he smiled as he approached her from across the sun-swept decks with a lovely, knowing smile, as if he'd precisely read her mind.

Author's Note

In the American Civil War, balloons were used a good deal by both the Federal and Confederate armies. There was a regular balloon staff attached to McClellan's regiment, with a captain, an assistant-captain, and about 50 non-commissioned officers and privates. Their apparatus consisted of two generators, drawn by four horses each; two balloons, drawn by four horses each, or taking a crew of men to transport it to its destination. The two types of balloons used in the Civil War contained about 13,000 and 26,000 feet of gas each. Fair Oaks is noted as the site of one of the little-known battles of the American Civil War fought on May 31 and June 1, 1862, and alternatively known as the Battle of Seven Pines. I hope I have shed some light on the less popular events of the war in which observation balloons were used. They were not a part of popular history, but were still an important aspect of the four years of bloody encounter between the blue-clad Union armies and the gray-clad forces of the Confederacy.

Sonya Pelton
Stillwater, Minnesota